Praise For *Chronicles*
Pe

'A vivid and wild romp ... *Chronicles* is Soyinka's great~~~ ~~~ to be widely read' Ben Okri, *Observer*

'Is this a good place to confess my crush, an overly bashful crush, on this politically courageous literary stylist ... I look to Soyinka's life, not so much the choices he has made but the courage it took to make them, as a source of light' Chimamanda Ngozi Adichie, *Sunday Times*

'A lion of African literature ... A brutally satirical look at power and corruption in Nigeria, told in the form of a whodunnit' *Financial Times*

'A Nigerian icon ... A high-jinks state-of-the-nation novel' Chibundu Onuzo, *Guardian*

'*Chronicles* is many things at once: a caustic political satire, a murder mystery, a conspiracy story and a deeply felt lament for the spirit of a nation ... For all its sarcastic undertones, for all its puns and plays on names, *Chronicles From the Land of the Happiest People on Earth* is a pessimistic novel, the work of a man with no illusions' Juan Gabriel Vásquez, *New York Times*

'A black-humoured satire of contemporary Nigeria' *Telegraph*

'*Chronicles* is a good model for what the political novel should be: fearless, disdaining formal constraints, sparing no one ... A triumph' *Guardian*

'This is an extraordinary novel that is both in and of Nigeria. It contains elements of Yoruba culture and, in the middle of it all, is a gourd full of satire, humor and pathos. It is a chronicle of human folly among the happiest people on earth. The writing alone is a wonder and a fitting coda for the career of this great writer' *New York Journal of Books*

'Inspiring and original ... Soyinka's analysis of the 20th century problem of memory and forgiveness in the African world is both timely and important. Soyinka's analysis of the problem is an initial volley in what will surely become a 21st century debate' *New York Times Book Review*

'With caustic wit, Soyinka's carnivalesque depictions of venality ferret out hypocrisy from behind its elaborate guises and condemn crimes that challenge "the collective notion of soul"' *New Yorker*

'Soyinka employs characteristically flamboyant language in a devastatingly detailed examination of Nigerian society' *Times Literary Supplement*

'Wole Soyinka is a legendary writer … He has inspired generations of writers worldwide … Wole draws on his lifetime steeped in resistance for his new novel, *Chronicles From the Land of the Happiest People on Earth*. The title is ironic. It's a caustic, satirical takedown of corruption in a country not unlike his native Nigeria' Kirsty Wark, Newsnight

'Swaggering and scabrous, at once a verbal spree and a fierce assault on totalitarianism' *Observer*

'A whodunnit that turns into a searing indictment of modern Nigeria' *i paper*

'A caustic satire' *Daily Mail*

'A savagely witty whodunit, a scathing indictment of Nigeria's political elite and a provocative call to arms from one of the country's most relentless political activists and an international literary giant' *The Voice*

'Soyinka is the tour guide for the last sixty years of Nigerian history and there is so much to see … bursting with humour and irony' *Litro*

'Back with a roar … Kafkaesque … A shocking, scathing and gripping look at society and human behaviour all in one' *Shiny New Books*

'A juggernaut of a novel … Bold and chaotic, it is somehow of the moment … This is literature of the dynamic kind, fed not so much by carefully honed craft as by a profound, urgent energy: both cry for help and call to arms; a response, a lament, a reckoning' Lunate.co.uk

WOLE SOYINKA was born in Abeokuta, Nigeria, in 1934. He is an author, playwright, poet, and political activist, whose prolific body of work includes *The Interpreters*, his debut novel, which was published in 1965, and the play *Death and the King's Horseman*, which was first performed in 1976. Soyinka was twice jailed for his criticism of the Nigerian government, and he destroyed his green card in 2016 when Donald Trump was elected president of the United States.

BY THE SAME AUTHOR

Novels
Season of Anomy
The Interpreters

Memoirs
You Must Set Forth at Dawn
Ìsarà: A Voyage Around "Essay"
Ibadan: The Penkelemes Years:
A Memoir 1945–1965
Aké: The Years of Childhood
The Man Died: Prison Notes

Poetry Collections
Samarkand and Other Markets I Have Known
Early Poems
Ogun Abibiman
Mandela's Earth and Other Poems
A Shuttle in the Crypt
A Big Airplane Crashed into the Earth
(original title *Poems from Prison*)
Idanre and Other Poems

Plays
Alápatà Àpáta
King Baabu
Document of Identity (radio play)

The Beatification of Area Boy
A Scourge of Hyacinths (radio play)
The Detainee (radio play)
From Zia with Love
Childe Internationale
Play of Giants
Requiem for a Futurologist
Opera Wonyosi
Death and the King's Horseman
Jero's Metamorphosis
Camwood on the Leaves (radio play)
The Bacchae of Euripides
Madmen and Specialists
The Road
Kongi's Harvest
Before the Blackout
The Strong Breed
My Father's Burden (television play)
A Dance of the Forests
The Trials of Brother Jero
The Lion and the Jewel
The Swamp Dwellers
The Invention

Wole Soyinka

Chronicles From the Land of the Happiest People On Earth

BLOOMSBURY PUBLISHING

LONDON · OXFORD · NEW YORK · NEW DELHI · SYDNEY

BLOOMSBURY PUBLISHING
Bloomsbury Publishing Plc
50 Bedford Square, London, WC1B 3DP, UK
29 Earlsfort Terrace, Dublin 2, Ireland

BLOOMSBURY, BLOOMSBURY PUBLISHING and the Bloomsbury
Publishing logo are trademarks of Bloomsbury Publishing Plc

First published in 2021 in the United States by Pantheon Books,
a division of Penguin Random House LLC, New York
First published in Great Britain 2021
This paperback edition published 2022

Copyright © Wole Soyinka, 2021

Wole Soyinka has asserted his right under the Copyright, Designs and
Patents Act, 1988, to be identified as Author of this work

All rights reserved. No part of this publication may be reproduced
or transmitted in any form or by any means, electronic or mechanical, including photocopying, recording, or any information storage or
retrieval system, without prior permission in writing from the publishers

A catalogue record for this book is available from the British Library

ISBN: HB: 978-1-5266-3824-3; TPB: 978-1-5266-3823-6;
PB: 978-1-5266-3825-0; EBOOK: 978-1-5266-3822-9;
EPDF: 978-1-5266-3821-2

2 4 6 8 10 9 7 5 3 1

Printed and bound in Great Britain by CPI Group (UK) Ltd,
Croydon CR0 4YY

MIX
Paper from
responsible sources
FSC® C171272
www.fsc.org

To find out more about our authors and books
visit www.bloomsbury.com and sign up for our newsletters

*To the memory of DELE GIWA, investigative journalist,
and BOLA IGE, politician sans pareil,
both cut down by Nigerian assassins.*

*And to FEMI JOHNSON,
a thorough rounded human being
and rare species of the creative joie de vivre*

Part I

Part I

1.

Oke Konran-Imoran

Papa Davina, also known as Teribogo, preferred to craft his own words of wisdom. Such, for instance, was his famous "Perspective is all."

The early-morning Seeker, his first and only client on that day and a very special, indeed dedicated session, looked up and nodded agreement. Papa D. pointed: "Move to that window. Draw back the curtain and look through."

It was somewhat gloomy in the audience chamber, and it took a while for the Seeker to grope her way along the wide folds to find the middle parting. She took the heavy drapes between both hands and waited. Papa Davina signaled to her to complete the motion, continuing in his soothing, near-meditative tone: "When you step into these grounds, it is essential that you forget what you are, who you were. Think of yourself only as the Seeker. I shall be your guide. I do not belong to the vulgar traders in the prophetic mission. The days of the great prophets are gone. I am with you only as Prescience. Only the Almighty God, the Inscrutable Allah, is Presence Itself, and who dares come into the Presence of the One and Only? Impossible! But we can come into His Prescience, such as I. We are few. We are chosen. We labour to read his plans. You are the Seeker. I am the Guide. Our thoughts can only lead to revelation. Please—pull the curtain apart. Completely."

The Seeker moved along with the other half. Daylight flooded the room. Papa D.'s voice pursued her.

"Yes, look out and tell me what you see."

The Seeker had come up on the opposite incline, which was total, unrelieved squalor. On this face of the hill, however, what leapt instantly to her gaze was a far more eclectic jumble. Far down below were scattered ledges of iron sheets, clay tiles, and rusted corrugated tin rooftops, pocked here and there, however, with some isolated but neat rows of ultramodern high-rise buildings. Threading these zones of contrasts were snarling lines of motor vehicles of every manufacture. And the city was just getting into its morning stride, so there were pulsating beehives of humanity, workers on pillions of the motorcycle taxis meandering between puddles from the night rain and overflowing gutters. A sheet of the lagoon shimmered in the distance. The Seeker turned and described her findings to the apostle.

"Now I want you to bring your gaze closer up to the level at which we are in this room. Let your gaze rise upwards from that city where it festers, bringing it closer to our level. Between where you stand and that scene of frenzy, what else is there?"

The Seeker did not hesitate. "Garbage. Piles of waste. Just like the other route—it was an obstacle track, threading my way here. Just mounds of the city's waste deposit."

Davina seemed satisfied. "Yes, a dung heap. You did come through it. But now here you are, and would you say you are standing in a dung heap?"

The woman shook her head. "Not in the least, Papa D."

The apostle nodded, again seemingly satisfied. "Close back the curtains, please."

The Seeker obeyed. The room interior should have returned to its earlier gloom and she expected to half grope her way back, but no. Multicoloured arrows, rather like the emergency exit lights on the floor of an aircraft, directed her feet towards a different section of the chamber. She did not require the safety recital of an air hostess to inform her of their purpose—she followed the lights. They stopped at a stool, exquisitely carved. It reminded her of an Ashanti royal stool that she had seen in pictures.

"Sit on that stool. I have to take you on a journey, so make yourself comfortable."

Now it was the preacher who stood up. "There are many, including our fellow citizens, who describe this nation as one vast dung heap. But you see, those who do, they mean to be disparaging. I, by contrast, find happiness in that. If the world produces dung, the dung must pile up somewhere. So if our nation is indeed the dung heap of the world, it means we are performing a service to humanity. Now that is . . . perspective. Shall I point out yet another?"

The Seeker nodded. "I am listening intently, Papa D."

"Good. Even from the moment you spoke to me on the phone, I knew you were no ordinary seeker. Your voice reached out to me as belonging to someone eager to learn. I counsel all kinds. Every strand of humanity passes through those gates. You'd be surprised what contrasting souls have sat on that very stool, if I chose to tell you."

The Seeker smiled wryly, gestured away the offer. "Papa Davina, that is why I am here. Your reputation cuts across not just the nation, but the continent."

"Ah yes, perhaps."

"And even beyond."

"Oh? So tell me, what have you heard? Those who directed your feet here, what do they say of Papa Davina?"

"Where does one begin?" The woman sighed. "Well, let me take the most recent, the candidate from the Seychelles . . . You prayed over him, and the world knows the results."

Davina executed a self-deprecating gesture with his hands, turning them into limp vessels that ended with palms upturned, as one who gave the credit—and glory—somewhere else.

"For you, I have mounted a . . . special perspective."

As he spoke, Papa D. appeared to dissolve into the peripheral gloom, but the chamber, whose curtain opening she had barely been able to find moments before, became gradually suffused with light, as if in replacement of the daylight she had just effaced. It proved to be just the beginning. Under the Seeker's gaze, the drab consultation chamber was turning into a fairyland. The woman gasped. Her host, one arm outstretched, appeared to be spinning slowly. In his hand was a little silvery gadget that also moved with the widening arc. Clearly he was standing on a sunken turntable. Papa D. pointed his control to the ceiling, and there was light. Next, another nearly inaudible click, and a gurgle of water interrupted the silence, its source gradually revealed as a cleft in a rock that had risen magically, a spring whose glistening waters cascaded in a lulling caress, then snaked into a grotto and vanished forever. An undulating vista of hills and valleys, plains and plateaus, shimmered into distant horizons, while soft luminous tubes rose from the floor towards the ceiling, bathing the chamber in a psychedelic sheen. Gradually an alcove shimmered into view, then another directly opposite, then a third at ninety degrees, and finally a fourth to complete an emerging three-dimensional installation. The alcoves were evenly spaced, emblematic as housing for the four compass points. On the floor, made of polished wood tiles, a large embedded map of the zodiac embarked on its own progressive illumination. From the ribbon folds that served as capstone for the archway across each alcove, a spiral of smoke billowed downwards, then began to curl all over the signs of the zodiac. The Seeker was enveloped in a medley of incense.

She heard Papa Davina's voice: "I was speaking of other perspectives. You see, if you inhabit a dung heap, you can still ensure that you are sitting on top of it. That is the other perspective. It is what separates those who are called from the common herd. It sits at the heart of human desire."

The Seeker sighed. It had been a long journey to this moment, a journey of startling contrasts and revelations, both physical and mental. Tutored in the mandatory protocols of the prophesite, she had embarked on full compliance, even to the contents of the pink envelope she had brought with her and laid solemnly on a small altar-table that stood by the entrance to the building. What was at stake did not permit any deviation from redemption rites of passage, a number of which she would normally consider degrading to her social status. After all, it had taken a while, nearly a full year, to arrange this audience—it was not the moment to place salvation in jeopardy. On the way she had caught sight of scavengers glancing slyly at her, transferring their gaze from hillside foraging to Papa Davina's eyrie, as if to say, *Ah yes, one of these days we also shall qualify to mount those final paved steps and be admitted into the Prescience.* They had heard all about it, heard stories of the magic interior that spelt transformation, belying the exterior of chapped walls and cracked cement. News filtered through and touched lives of longing with intimations of a changed destiny. Some played the football pools religiously, others the annual National Lottery and more, but craved that final touch of the magic wand—Papa Davina's blessing. They dreamt of the day they themselves would climb the paved approach of twenty-one glistening steps and be ushered into his Prescience. Active or dreaming, they hoarded images of the splendour of the recluse, the magician known as Papa Davina.

The Seeker felt thankful that her sister had faithfully contributed her tithes to Papa Davina's ministry. One did not earn a private audience with Papa D. until after at least a year of attending the open services that he conducted below for all and sundry, and with an unbroken record of tithing. Her sister had even transferred her "redemption coupons" to her. There were, of course, exceptions for emergencies. To bypass any unplanned constraints, the seeker must first cover the year's arrears—among other charges—and at double tithing. Emergencies covered vicissitudes such as court trials, where divine intervention was needed to soften the judge's sadistic soul and pronounce a full acquittal, sometimes even citing the prosecution for abuse of process and contempt.

Her own predicament was not that drastic, and as some patients are prone on visiting the doctor, she was not without her self-prescription. Hers was simply a case of poor business choices, a spate of ill luck that had persisted for three years, leading to losses. Then there was the bane of customs levy on goods that barely survived the depredations of sea pirates now massively invested in the nation's eastern creeks. Nothing that could not be offset by the allocation of a single oil block. This was what mandated the recourse to Papa D.

And now, finally, she was face-to-face with Destiny, a pursuit whose fulfillment nested in the hands of the sole guardian of the prophesite. There the Gardener of Souls—another of Davina's titles—stood, arm outstretched as one who wielded the staff of Moses, his electronic gadget a wand that could make barren rock yield its most prized, procreative, life-sustaining secret. But that was a primitive era when

Moses could produce only water—the staff of modern-day Moses was tuned to oil gushers. The black gold, nestling beneath farmland and ancestral fishing ponds. Perspectives changed with modernity.

As if her thoughts were being read, the visual display was now augmented by the aural, as the sonorous and wheezing pipes of organ music began to dispense an uplifting composition. It transported her to lands yet undreamt of, to visions of the attainable. Papa D.'s voice gathered together the emotions that had sprung up in her troubled, frustrated mind and, at his chosen moment, brought them down to earth.

"There is a drawer attached to your stool—by the right side. Pull it out. You'll find a folder and a fountain pen. Old-fashioned fountain pen, not ballpoint. Open the folder and extract one sheet."

The Seeker obeyed. Her hand touched the folder, and she needed only that one touch to feel the luxury of the finest vellum. "I import it directly from Jerusalem," revealed Papa Davina reductively. The Seeker was already persuaded that this was papyrus on which the angels wrote the Book of Life.

"Write on it what it is you seek," he invited.

By the time she had completed the task and looked up, Papa Davina was standing beside her. In one hand he had a small, delicate flask filled with a clear liquid, in the other a midsized shallow dish. The Seeker offered her script to Papa Davina, but the Prescience nodded it away.

"No. I already know. You have no revelation to make to me. Place the vellum in this dish."

Davina poured the liquid over the writing, shook the dish lightly, and the Seeker's mind journeyed to her childhood, the early days of photography, when the image was captured on treated paper, then developed in just such a shallow tray. One placed the seemingly blank but image-impressed sheet in the tray of chemical fluid, shook it lightly, and gradually the image began to form, all wet like a newborn baby. Perspective was now reversed. The process began with the visible and ended with the invisible. The words wobbled, dissolved, returning the vellum to its pristine state. But the once-clear liquid was now streaky with ink.

"Drink," Papa D. ordered.

The Seeker hesitated only briefly, recollecting herself on the instant. To hesitate was to betray a lack of faith and jeopardize her mission. She smiled happily. She had come this far—she drank. She felt light-headed, buoyant. Papa Davina offered her a small perfumed cloth with which to dab her lips. A huge load floated upward from her shoulders. Suddenly the future opened out before her, a gleaming spreadsheet of infinite possibilities. Already she felt fulfilled. She stretched out the serviette to the apostle, but he waved it back.

"Keep it. Beginning from tonight, keep it under your pillow. For the next two weeks, let no one into your room."

The Seeker nodded rapidly, increasingly elated.

The voice cut into her euphoria. "This year's approaching festival, do you plan to attend?"

The woman hesitated. "I had not thought of it, Father Davina."

"It is a Festival of Joy—be part of it. It is promised that you shall receive news of interest at that event, and signs in your search for fulfillment."

"Of course, Father Davina. Once you command it."

Davina placed a hand on the Seeker's forehead. "Seek, and ye shall find. Be at peace. Across the archway to the coming Festival of Joy, I read your name writ large, in golden letters. Happiness is on the horizon."

The Seeker fell on her knees, praise-giving, her eyes shut in rapture. Tutored in the protocols of the Ekumenika audience, she did not prolong her prayers unduly. Lighted arrows—plain this time, not in Technicolour—pointed her way to the exit.

The Seeker had hardly passed through the gates of Ekumenika and stepped onto the peak known as Oke Konran-Imoran—the Hill of Knowledge and Enlightenment—when Papa Davina, known also as Teribogo, pulled out his mobile, dialed a number. The voice at the other end drawled, "Ye-e-es?"

Papa Davina responded, "She has just left. You can take it from here, Sir Goddie."

2.

The Gospel According to Happiness

That the nation known as the Giant of Africa was credited with harbouring the Happiest People in the World was no longer news. What remained confusing was how such recognition came to be earned and, by universal consent, deserved. Aspiring nations needed to be rescued from their state of envious aspiration, a malaise that induced doomed efforts to snatch the crown from their head. The wisdom of elders counsels that it is more dignifed to acknowledge a champion where indisputable, thereafter take one's place behind its leadership, than to carp and wriggle in frustration. As the Yoruba are wont to admonish, *Ti a ba ri erin igbo k'a gba wipe a ri ajanaku, ka ye so wipe a ri nka nto lo firi.* When we encounter an elephant, let us admit that we have seen the lord of the forest, not offhandedly remark that we saw something flash across our sight.

Not many nations, for instance, could boast a Ministry of Happiness. Yet this was an innovation that came from one of the most impoverished states within that federated nation. Its pioneer minister, known as commissioner, was the spouse of the imaginative governor, while other members of the family and relations filled the various positions generated by the unique cabinet installation. Lest that first family alone be credited with this feat of a unanimous jury decision across the world, however, it must be mentioned that, among other credentials, the love and liberal distribution of titles played their role.

Often overlooked was the fact that the celebration of a single title by the people was often sufficient to implement the annual budgetary plans of other nations. There were other, often overlooked, yet monumental credentials. Need one cite, for instance, the constant, exponential distensions of the line of traditional rulers at the stroke of the pens of state governors, across histories and cultures?

An ancient Yoruba city known as Ibadan, a formerly self-sufficing monarchical domain without any visible sign of pregnancy, was delivered of twenty-four new kingdoms one day in an era of rampaging democratic attestation. That feat did not remain uncontested. It was soon matched—or nearly thereafter—from the opposite end of the national axis by the parturition of fourteen emirates from another historic entity, known as Kano. The new kings/emirs were presented with their staffs of office and scrolls of royal enrollment by their presiding governors, generating colourful massed ceremonies amidst popular jubilation. Individual crowns/turbans, evidently tailored and fabricated to suit each royal skull, were set on/wound round the heads and jowls of the new monarchs—formerly mere village heads and petty chiefs. And so on and on; the professional nay-sayers of the world remained incapable of the imaginative feat of projecting the massive cross-country festivities that would naturally inundate such a liberal state of elevations, the guarantee of carnivals almost as a daily event, enabling the growth of tourism and a boom in the complementary industry of kidnapping for ransom.

Many, many salient contributory factors were often overlooked by competitive nations, largely owing to vested interest and an obsession to wrest the happiness crown from the head of the richly deserving. Unfortunately such partisan, self-interested attitudes merely sowed confusion over even the routine year-round festivals—religious, secular, memorialist, etc.—to which any sovereign nation, with the slightest modicum of traditional respect for the world of the living, the unborn, and the ancestors, was surely entitled.

Typical of such misunderstandings by fun-seeking tourists—and indeed some careless nationals themselves—was the tendency to confuse political carnivals with people's fiestas. This was a burden of mistaken identity that was borne most notably by the Festival of the People's Choice. Admittedly political and cultural fêtes shared a number of similarities. Most notable among these was a habit of occupying nearly the entire year round, year after year, despite being allotted specific dates, clearly delineated even on the national calendar. The two were, however, two distinct entities. Variously known as the Bash of the Year, People's Concordia, Night of Nights, etc., etc., the Festival of the People's Choice, a distinct people's fiesta, under strict compliance would be celebrated annually on the weekend that followed Independence Day. That last named was unambiguously a political event. This proximity created yet another source of confusion, but only a minor one, of no consequence, since hardly anyone still remembered what independence was all about. A military parade, a listless address to the nation, calls for patriotism, recital of an insipid National Honours List, and the nation quickly returned to business, awaiting the real event of the year—and its night of awards—by popular acclaim!

Some cynics and revisionists tended to insinuate that that festival was a creation of the *People on the Move* Party. That again was far from the truth. Of course that party also preened itself as a model of democratic practice, but there all associative notions ended. POMP—the obvious party acronym—claimed credit only for its liberalism, which enabled such a festive, all-embracing, nonpartisan celebration not only to take root and thrive but to steadily distend on both sides of its advertised dates until it filled out the rest of the year and sometimes spilled over into the next, its events stretching to catch up with the new beginning. No other festival in the world could boast such a constant backlog. It became not just a moving feast but a festivity constantly in event arrears, the residue carried over into subsequent editions.

What the People's Choice achieved went beyond burnishing the image of the government or the party in power; it vastly improved the battered profile of the nationals in the eyes of the world. The festival, veteran of numerous editions, proved that despite the contrary testimony of political elections, the citizenry, if only given a chance, could teach the world a thing or two in that political culture so wrongly attributed to the Athenians. If the government was guilty of any form of intervention, it was only that it formally decreed its climaxing Night of Nights Fiesta, with its maximum-intensity Yeomen of the Year Awards, a National Heritage. The government took the unprecedented step of forwarding the enabling resolution to UNESCO—with no less than twenty-five million signatures from across the nation, computer verified, a feat that had yet to be attained by three National Census editions. *If we had failed to do so, we would have failed in our duty, and of course stand accused of indifference to patriotism, art, and creativity. Now that we have done what we should, we are pilloried for furthering some sinister government agenda. There is simply no pleasing our people!*

The Festival was routinely timed for the weekend that followed Independence Day, that manifest expression of the triumph of a people's will, a historic day on which the former imperial masters were peacefully voted out of office without the shedding of a drop of blood—independence on a platter of gold, it was trumpeted by a foremost nationalist, later the nation's president. That the nation proceeded to more than make up for that lapse through a civil war that lasted more than two years could not be laid at the feet of POMP, which did not even exist at the time of independence, much less at the time of the war commonly known as the war of Biafran secession. What mattered for the people was the phoenix of splendour that rose from the ashes of colonization.

This festival was indeed unique. It ended in a plethora of awards, catapulted into public prominence a new class of citizens known as Yeomen of the Year—YoY—a people's recognition of public service over and above the call of duty, gain, or praise. And what a contrast it offered to the annual Independence Day Honours List, rather like alternative Oscars. The Independence Day list was administered by a secretive National Commission of Grace whose existence and composition were known to hardly anyone. It had no input from man, woman, or child beyond the behind-doors conspiracies of a secret cabal. YoY, by contrast, established its place as the one genuine, authenticated, open democratic balloting the nation had known since she embarked on her voyage of independence. YoY rose to become the barometer of the public pulse. It stamped the foreheads of its winners with that rare, indelible stigmata of primal humanity before the Fall, moved to paralyze all competition, and became known as the 21st-Century Reality Show. It vanquished even *Big Brother Africa* and other voyeuristic favourites of virtual audience participation.

For a music-loving people, whose loyalties oscillated largely between the polarities of soccer and song, even the Grammy Awards and Venice Biennale Global Song Contest were eclipsed by YoY. *Africa Can Dance* developed two lumpen left feet. The famous Cannes Film parade of fashion, glamour, and hopefuls lost its global rainbow spectrum with the disappearance of Nigerian contingents—known with stunning originality as Nollywood—that had once dominated the Mediterranean beachscape with textural exotica. YoY induced a massive haemorrhage and turned the famous film festival scene pale and anaemic. Betting houses alone survived, even proliferated—who would emerge in the various categories of YoY?, variously pronounced "Why oh Why" or simply "Yoy," as in a lisper's Joy—with which it was soon nearly totally conflated. Not one aspiring film or video starlet or hip-hop dance athlete could afford to miss the dominant national extravaganza—Yeomen of the Year. An attempt to pander to gender equality and establish a rival Yeowomen of the Year ended in predictable collapse—the women informed such proponents that YoY was gender-inclusive, demanded a straightforward contest on a level playing ground, not a token concession that only degraded the female sex even further. Such was the universality of its acceptance.

The buildup to the award gala began with calls for nominations at least four months before the Night of Nights. Online platforms changed authorship overnight. They were bought or rented under aliases within the umbrella transnational known as Be the First to Comment, an open-house platform of subscribers of marginalized—some preferred to call it marginal—humanity. Some of these subscribers became overnight semi-millionaires. Image-making companies on the verge of collapse became solvent; many took their profits and branched into allied consultancy operations, specializing mainly in a spinoff that grew in range and enterprise to become celebrated as Fake News. Opinion formulation became synthesized, distilled, and digested in a trice. YoY swallowed Gallup polls and other indicators of human trends and preferences. It was consulted before the opening of the foreign exchange markets, listed on the stock exchange, swapped data with at least two-thirds of the continent's ministries of finance, culture, and development. It spread its wings beyond the continent and extended its influence over quite a few members within the EU and Asian nations. Yet it all started as no more than a shrewd understanding of social values within just one nation, undoubtedly a unique piece of real estate widely celebrated as the Giant of Africa.

Originator, sponsor, sole organizer, and one-man jury (despite a formal thirteen-member panel which met, was wined and dined, and collected honorariums on the night of awards), Chief Modu Udensi Oromotaya, proprietor of *The National Inquest,* possessed an astute business mind which accurately assessed the market value of vanity and limelight, single-mindedly invested in them, and ensured their access to all citizens in average financial standing. His given name, Udensi, was adjusted to read Ubenzy, an ingestion of the *Benz* in *Mercedes Benz,* the status symbol after independence, before the motorcar was displaced by the private jet. This initiative of the private sector was consecrated in one ritualized but gargantuan event, the Yeomen of the Year Awards, a brilliantly elastic concept. It applied to any human activity, from exposing a paedophile ring to assisting an elderly woman across the road, simply ensuring that the event was captured on camera. Each year the Awards Jury received additional categories—at the latest count, this stood at thirty-seven. It all depended on what new entrant into the public arena had been sighted, targeted, and netted.

Chief Oromotaya was a man of inventive vision. When the public—the aspiring elite, that is—presumed that they had reached the ultimate in titular desire, he simply upped the ante, thus creating an ever-rising peak of aspiration—not unlike the National Independence Day Awards, another source of confusion! The discerning, however, easily recognized a crucial difference—the latter were set in stone. As for the rare confusion with traditional honorifics, even the most casual observer recognized that the latter were largely slapdash, localized, promiscuous, and horizontal. Chief Ubenzy's creations were vertical and autogenic. He thus instigated a competitive spirit which sometimes resulted even in returns to new starting blocks for the already honoured. The condition became a cultural feature captured so vividly in the title of a work by—naturally—a son of the soil, Nkem Nwankwo's *My Mercedes Is Bigger Than Yours.* It created a condition not too dissimilar to the emotions experienced in that state of rapture undergone by the religiously possessed. However, of the expanding award categories—each of which logically developed concentric circles of subsidiaries of its own—none ever came close to displacing the crème de la crème that rose by common consent—at least at the time of these chronicles—to its destined place as the ultimate crescendo of the annual ceremony: the People's Award for the Common Touch, PACT. (Predictably: *We make a Pact with the Common man—National Inquest.*) No one expected that climax to be reached till daylight was seen breaking through the silvered louvres of the main bowl of the events venue, but not one single seat in that packed arena remained vacant for long. The queue in the standing room section swiftly released a waiting occupant, already armed with a numbered tag. They stayed the course, excitation at palpable fever pitch as the moment approached for the ultimate prize. And there was a traditional and international breakfast spread that made the endurance worthwhile—another source of confusion with political carnivals, which ensured the feeding of thousands before, during, and after the electoral contests, after pledge, act, and proof of fulfillment of the voting pledge.

Hardly surprising, because for the professionals of the political trade, the prestige and electoral returns were palpable—possibly exaggerated; but PACT was a coronet to wear—no, a halo, more accurately, a band of sanctification that winners felt could be seen around their brows in no matter what situation, ready to be evoked as character testimony, including, as sometimes happened, when they ended up in a criminal dock for unsaintly practices. To be able to place *YoY* after one's name on a calling card—Chief the Dr. Sunmole, M.Sc., Dip. Ed., YoY—was already status enough to open doors, but to be able to add the once-a-year-only PACT tag was to enter the nation's Hall of Immortals, with a commissioned portrait in the National Gallery, side by side with those of members of the Council of States and a select line of national Founding Fathers. And it entitled any such winner, by public consent, to the right of generous plea bargaining, a presentence mitigation plea, and then, if all else failed, a secured benefice of the exercise of the prerogative of mercy, all sometimes in place even before the passing of a sentence. The right of permanent immunity for life for any crime was still a proposition of public controversy.

It was only to be expected, therefore, that this category was tensely contested. No endorsement from the public was too small to be courted, none too blotchy to be scorned. Each division equally extracted and maximized its own significance, potential, and recognition zone for its winner, be it in professional, business, or mere extended family circles. There were voiced misgivings about the inbuilt factor of unlimited sub-categories, their escalating tiers of unmerited privilege, most especially the slide towards comprehensive immunity for undeserving categories of winners, but these were easily resolved under the doctrine of popular condonation. Precedents were not lacking, or parallels, among them the reign of paedophiles and extortionists in legislative chambers and governors' lodges, immunized by religious attributions. Were they not expanding the happiness boom among even minors?

The pattern of conferment also underwent ingenious variations. There were instances where the winner could not attend the awards in person, and the reasons for such absences were myriad. A traditional ruler, business mogul, or governor might feel—rare, but it was not unknown—that it was lèse-majesté to be seen with lower creatures of the entertainment world, trade unionists, common agitators, the notorious and unpatriotic members of the Academic Staff Union, or simply junior local councilors. A finicky judge might feel that the dignity of office was imperiled by the garish ambiance of the gala night, or a bishop or mullah fear a loss in congregational attendance from puritanic elements and thus a reduction of tithes or zakat. The motivation of extending hospitality was also to be conceded and commended. The reasoning was obvious: absence justified a special ceremony in its own right, specifically for the private presentation. Chief Ubenzy Oromotaya had an accommodative temperament. At the event itself, the winner would be represented by a cabinet minister, commissioner, permanent secretary, first lady, or nearest available son or daughter. Afterwards the designee held a special, extra ceremony in his or her domain, dispensing happiness in normally neglected, indeed often hitherto unheard-of corners of the nation.

The much-craved super-category of the Common Touch Award was of course in a class of its own. It was presented by a farmer, market woman, factory line worker, or street vendor, plucked off the kerbside or market stall for the occasion, washed, clothed, and festooned in costume jewellery for the public presentation. In the case of an absentee winner, the bewildered representative of the people would be invited as guest of honour to the banquet hall or performance grounds of the exalted absentee, a public toast for the next twenty-four hours of happiness. The glory of physically presenting the symbol of popular acclaim, needless to say, belonged exclusively to the media proprietor himself, the effervescent Ubenzy Oromotaya.

Perhaps it is worth remarking that at inception, the in-absentia variation was not permitted—you were either present and honoured or absent and dispossessed—though this did not prevent the right to add a rubric to one's CV in the tradition of "Two/Three Times a YoY/PACT Nominee." For the proprietor and organizer, absenteeism also offered the advantage of presenting double awards in the missing category the following year. All that changed, thanks to the somewhat extreme conduct of an unusually temperamental winner, a governor. Later Oromotaya kicked himself, wondering why from the very beginning he had failed to think of the advantages of a distinct in-absentia category—*Don't budge, we'll bring the award to your doorstep!*

The advantages were delightfully obvious. For a start, this structurally turned YoY into a moving, all-year fiesta, spread all over the nation, as each winner took to celebrating victory in his or her own time, own milieu, own manner, and, if an office-holder, at public or corporate expense. How many could embark on the logistics of dragging a cow, even the odd sheep, ram, goat, or baby camel, to be slaughtered and roasted on a spit at the venue, which was the National Theatre on the semi-outskirts of Lagos? Of course, a number were only too happy to eat their cake and also have it—they basked fully in the glitter and glitz of the gala Night of Nights, then returned home to hold a mini-fiesta of their own—happiness outreach to the less privileged, who could not afford the time or transportation fare to Lagos. However, the defining moment for the formal change of policy—which had in any case evolved on its own into a most extravagant and economically robust mixture of variants—offered no glimpse of such prospects at the time. Indeed, it came rather close to tragedy.

It so happened that this expectant winner, a governor from north of the River Benue, Usman Bedu, had turned up in a motorcade of thirty "luxury buses" and motorized caravans. These ferried his entire harem of twenty-seven wives, plus extended families totaling three hundred and eighty-five and the State Cultural Troupe, including acrobatic horsemen with glittering lances and attire straight from the Arabian Nights. The last were lined along the final approach to the vast rotunda known as the National Theatre—a Bulgarian Palais de Sports import to the last bolt, knot, and cement blob—to welcome arriving guests. It was a personal contribution—a token of his appreciation, unsolicited. The same award had, however, been sold, democratically auctioned by secret ballot, and not for the first time, to the highest bidder the morning before the ceremony. The governor was not expected. Indeed, the excited young recipient had deliberately suppressed his real intentions. It was all designed to be a surprise, a spectacular, dramatic appearance. The cavalry was sent to stand in, a compensation for his supposed absence. The planned scenario went thus: they would canter to the airport to receive their governor, then lead his Rolls-Royce Silver Cloud in grand formation to the National Theatre. The factor of a notorious Lagos traffic jam was one that never even entered the head of the celebrant, such was the narcotic power of the people's Night of Nights. Usman Bedu's arrival was indeed a spectacular feat, never to be forgotten by motorists on that infamous Saturday. The young scion, who regularly spent his summer vacations in London, had seen the Trooping of the Colours at Buckingham Palace and had resolved to celebrate his win in a no less splendiferous manner.

Chief Oromotaya was not aware of his presence in Lagos until the cavalry clattered up the concrete drive of Entrance A of the performance rotunda. Accustomed to "regularizing" such minor blips in his own way afterwards, the sponsor had not expected the unsportsmanlike response that emerged from the celebrant. Among the governor's people, however, loss of face was not considered a trifle. When Chief Ubenzy tried to explain the "unfortunate mix-up" to His Excellency Usman Bedu in the VIP green room, the convivial atmosphere changed abruptly. The media proprietor saw the governor's hand disappear into the folds of his *babanriga,* to emerge with a jewel-encrusted curved dagger the likes of which he had seen only in Bollywood films. Ubenzy let out a scream and his knees buckled. He slumped onto the carpet, clutching his heart. It was the governor's turn to be horrified, believing that his gregarious host had died of a heart attack or whatever. He fled the National Theatre, headed straight to the safety of his private jet at Ikeja airport, ordering his aides en route to round up his caravan and herd its participants home to safety as best they could across the Niger. Ubenzy, now recovered after first aid administered straight down his throat from a Johnnie Walker bottle, spluttering and badly shaken, was rushed to a private hospital for a checkup. From there he took a decision to be "flown to Dubai" for full examination and recuperation.

That gala Night of Nights did proceed peacefully thereafter, Oromotaya monitoring and overseeing progress from his permanently reserved suite at the Intercontinental Hotel, Victoria Island, while the terrified governor was fed the latest health reports on his stricken host, supposedly in intensive care in Dubai, hanging between life and death by the sheerest thread. Before Ubenzy officially returned to his home base, peace, as always, had been restored. The governor had no choice. Intercessors ensured that he became aware of some sensitive material in the chief's possession that would be of public interest, ready to go to print in *The National Inquest*. This illumination enabled the governor to accept that there were limits to blood feud under the Nigerian constitution and that a community of interest had to be the deciding factor of business relations. The dueling pair restored accustomed diplomatic relations and swore eternal friendship. Governor Bedu was rewarded with a special individual edition of YoY where he accepted a newly created, personalized award—the People's Scimitar. They exchanged chieftaincy conferments, Udenzy in Bedu's hometown, Bedu in Oromataya's. Bedu threw a feast that featured, for the first time in Nigerian history, an entire stuffed baby camel—a specialty, it would seem, of Saudi Arabia. In addition, he became the Life Patron of YoY. Oromotaya was famous for his creative application of soothing Vaseline on what many would consider incurable tumours. That, anyway, remained the authenticated version of events, according to Ubenzy Oromotaya himself—but only when secure among his close circle.

The pursuit of that golden fleece, the YoY Award, was not, it would appear, an affair for the faint-hearted. Acts of sabotage and image neutralization, crude to sophisticated, were commonplace. Fake News expanded a thousandfold, with the ruination of marriages and friendships and the bankrupting of businesses. There were sudden, unexplained deaths. College cults were recruited and let loose on the neighbourhoods of aspirants, both virtual and physical. Nonetheless, many conceded that the contest for the Yeomen Awards, and most especially that of the Common Touch, brought out the creative and egalitarian spirit universally remarked among the Nigerian people. There were videos of a governor eating *amala*, the gooey Yoruba yam-flour staple, in a peasant's roadside shack, the okra dripping down his wispy beard while he licked the backs of his fingers with an out-sized tongue and belched into the camera—no elitist steel cutlery for him, thank you very much. And he drank only palm wine—from a calabash, not a glass or plastic cup. Another submission featured a senator ushering an aged woman into his BMW Sports Utility, which he drove himself, while his aides loaded her firewood into the rear space, its caption "Lending a Helping Hand." One notable entry was a photo of yet another governor hoeing a yam patch in unison with his workers, just another lusty voice raised in the traditional work song, in readiness for and stimulating the early arrival of expected rains, caption "Stomach Infrastructure." The more adventurous politicians were filmed participating in a break-dance contest at the famous Federal Palace Hotel, Victoria Island, caption "Rumble of the Humble." And so it went, with an enthusiastic followership sending in comments both verbally and in the shorthand literacy of emoticons.

There were critics, not unexpectedly. What happened to governance under a serial, cyclic fiesta hysteria? Such voices were easily silenced. Governance, as attested by flurries of releases from ministries and government agencies, was unaffected. Indeed, business peaked, most especially in what was called the informal sector. A journey normally of ninety minutes between two cities now took four, six, nine, twelve hours and sometimes spilled into the following day, especially in the rainy season, when lakes sprang up in the middle of the express-way, sucking even petrol tankers into their bosom. Such stagnations created instant road markets—more truthfully amphibious—shooting the nation's informal GNP to astronomical heights. Gridlocks brought reality to economic diversification. Culture itself profited, as there were new entries into the register of Nigerian names, a nation that had justly earned fame for inventiveness—Tonade, Bisona, Bolekaja, Toyota, Aderupoko,* etc., the nomenclatural celebration of infants born in public or private transport when traffic stood completely still and motorists were turned into instant midwives. The hunt after missing billions intensified, headed by the prime minister himself, who personally flew out to consolidate the repatriation of new discoveries of hidden assets, all announced with fanfare—Cayman Islands, Dubai, the United States, and Switzerland. These counters silenced the dissonant voices, kept the nation's adrenaline high and hope ever-resurgent. A few careless, overbearing party card-bearers were felled to establish the stamp of evenhandedness in the apportionment of justice. This rejuvenating cycle—missing, pursuit, whistleblower, and hyperactive agencies, lawyers, witnesses, no matter if they proved missing in action on their day in court—joined a list of enviable achievements. The breast-beating overwhelmed even the throb of the annual Drum Festival from one of the allegedly happy states.

It therefore came as a rude shock to the executive, legislators, and nationals when news broke that the nation had earned an unexpected—and unmerited—honorific from a former colonial civil servant as the Most Extraordinarily Corrupt Nation in the World! This laudation, which appeared to have been off the cuff, attracted far more prolonged and intense denunciation than the continuum of vanishing chunks of the national treasury. The day's business was set aside in both lawmaking houses to debate and condemn the utterance. What, the debaters argued, was extraordinary about a cultural norm? It was pure abuse of language—just because the language was theirs, was that a good reason to use it just anyhow? Did they think the Giant of Africa could be intimidated by such big words? The two-tier legislature tabled motions for a complete boycott of British goods, seizure of all British assests, expulsion of all British nationals and then a break in diplomatic relations with such an impertinent foreign power—yes, foreign! Did they think the nation was still under colonial rule to tolerate such insults?

It was time for a renewed world tour by the prime minister, Sir Godfrey Danfere, this time to dialogue with foreign nations who

---

* Landed en Route; Born on the Road; (Born Within a) Passenger Truck; (Born in a) Toyota; Excess Load.

haboured the same conviction, next to rebuild the image of an abused nation. Accompanied by an entourage that dwarfed the caravan of Usman Bedu, Sir Goddie commenced an unprecedented blitz. The charm offensive ended just in time for nominations for the next edition of YoY. It was a triumphant return. He looked forward to presenting his report first to the president and next to the nation in his State of the Nation address, that the denigrators and professional PhDs (Pull Him/Her Down Syndrome) were mere noisemakers, international nonentities. They were economic saboteurs acting against the diversification of the one-track oil-based economy. Sir Goddie would urge the creation of more Ministries of Happiness by states that had yet to jump on the bandwagon.

"I have been everywhere," he announced to the waiting media corps, success neon-inscribed all over his impressive frame, which had earned him his favourite nickname, the Presence. "It will be my great pleasure to report to the president when I brief him tomorrow that nowhere did I hear one dissenting voice. The nation is in no danger. We retain our number-one position—the Happiest People on Earth."

Seated in the comfort of the stretch limousine on his way to his power base, Villa Potencia, he tapped the shoulder of his chief of staff, seated next to the chauffeur. "Get hold of Teribogo. Tell him to ensure some—happiness—awaiting me at the Villa."

The chief of staff was expressionless. "She's there already, Sir Goddie."

3.

Pilgrim's Progress

Harsh were his beginnings, his trials and tribulations, long the journey, albeit interspersed with patches of lucrative relief, of the man whose origins remained a cause for endless speculation. At the time of the issuance of his second passport however, he was registered as Dennis Tibidje. His original document ended in a midnight bonfire in the backyard of his first home liaison, following his hasty return to Home Sweet Home. The multitalented youth had dropped out abruptly from overseas studies. He shook the dust of the United Kingdom off his feet in a fit of righteous indignation. He had received an invitation by his college dean to report and defend his honour against a charge of attempted rape, laid by a fellow student. Not even his closest college buddies knew of his departure, not even his landlady to whom he still owed several months' rent, plus some emergency borrowings while "awaiting his scholarship remittance."

Back home, Tibidje soon found a niche as a bit actor in Callywood—the South-eastern (Calabar) version of the national cinema flagbearer, Nollywood. There was a brand-new film village in the same state, a rustic, water bordered setting called Tinapa, with fully equipped ultra modern studios. It had been established by a film-struck governor with a passion also for Nature and her preservationist imperatives. Tinapa's technical facilities were utilized, but the practitioners shied away from branding their products with such a backward sounding name as Tinapa. They preferred to be seen as another foundling of the gnarled family tree that was rooted in a distant coastal state of the United States, known as Hollywood.

Tinapa's new entrant augmented the precarious livelihood of all actors through a position with a publicity and marketing firm. He had also artistic skills that enabled him to keep his head above water in those barren stretches between shooting engagements, which all professional actors undergo much too frequently. Such talents included, in his case, a natural ability to copy the handwriting and signatures of others and thereby provide vital documents in time of need. It was a proficiency, alas, that also led to the brevity of his sojourn with the firm. After failing to produce the promised original of his college diploma, a condition of his provisional engagement, he eventually presented a document whose authenticity was unfortunately suspect—not the artistry itself, which was impeccable, but a computer-generated contradiction on dates. The future, in one instance, seemed to predate the past. A small detail, but it caught the attention of an overzealous personnel clerk and avid computer geek. His employers summoned Tibidje, advised him to change occupation. They admitted being sad to be obliged to dispense with such talent and even provided him the bus fare to his alleged home in Lagos State. His explanation for claims of Lagos origin was that he was sired into a Lagos household. The culprits, however, were pure Deltan, of Itsekiri stock. Tibidje had one all-engrossing yet suppressed ambition, not always openly acknowledged—to reoccupy his preferred roots in Lagos ancestry. Not as a sentimental longing but as the logical facilitator of his desired occupational destiny.

For a while the venturesome youth remained where he was, in the bustling city of Port Harcourt, contemplating his future moves. A decision was not long in coming. The three months of his employment, as well as forays into the putative cinema community, were more than sufficient to enable more than a few helpful contacts. It was thus one easy step into the virtual world of internet entrepreneurship, focusing on accounts of his erstwhile associates. Barely escaping a police raid on an operational café for the yahoo-yahoo fraternity, as the internet scam artists were known, Tibidje decided that it was time for a change of environment and indeed a change of persona. Interception of an advance payment to his former company for publicity work required no more than a morning's intensive work, followed by its redirection to the coffers of a travel agency. It was his farewell exploit, dedicated to a return ticket to Houston, USA, via New York City, and a passport that passed immigration scrutiny. It did, however, lack a visa. Confident in his ability to persuade immigration officials that he was a victim of political persecution, he flew out, landed, and was indeed granted admission, but straight into a waiting federal bus that took him, together with a motley of international voyagers, straight to a staging station for illegal immigrants in Newark, New Jersey.

Nine months later, having battled America's Homeland Security to a losing standstill, he was back on African soil, the interim spent in a holding pen for uninvited visitors. His spell, however, netted quite a few new acquaintances, both within the detention centre and outside, through telephone calls and even correspondence with human rights defenders, charity organizations, and lonely ladies. The most valuable of these were the internal ones—the visiting Christian chaplains of indeterminate denomination but with links to a West African mission in Liberia. For a while the visiting ministry from the Nation of Islam occupied the detainee's sightlines. Those ministers of Louis Farrakhan's office for prison affairs were vastly interested in the Nigerian prisoner of conscience, and their chapter generously lavished the mandate of zakat on the martyred guest, over and above the call of scriptures. He strung them along, ensuring the dividends that came with the battle for his soul from two rival camps. The tussle lasted as long as his stay while he weighed his options, deciding in the end that the Christian fellowship came closer to his schemes for personal salvation. When the moment came and the federal bus returned to ferry his group to the airport, it was by no means a noticeably depressed illegal, unlike most of the other deportees, who was returned to his continent of birth.

He did not return to his precise departure point, however. Tibidje succeeded in persuading his captors to return him not to Nigeria, the land of persecution, but to Liberia, the land of liberty. He had discovered through discourse with fellow inmates and some light reading that Liberia enjoyed a special quasi-colonial status with the United States, and this worked to his advantage. Somewhere along that trajectory, the future minister of souls announced that he had discovered his true calling—evangelism. It had proved a most educative stay, he declared, a sea change in his life. The detention camp at that time was not entirely inhumane. The food was edible and sufficient. There was a small donated clutch of books and journals that passed for a library, mostly of a religious nature. These included, predictably, the scriptures of both the Christian and the Islamic faiths. The small cupboard also boasted Oscar Wilde's *The Ballad of Reading Gaol,* John Bunyan's *Pilgrim's Progress,* Khalil Gibran's *The Prophet,* Thomas Merton's writings, and other works of the spiritual quest and upliftment.

The presence of the Kama Sutra was intriguing. The favourite story was that it had been donated by one of the inmates, who succeeded in convincing the duty officer that this was the bible of a Hindu sect that was officially recognized by the United Nations. Thus it would amount to a violation of UN laws, to which the United States was a signatory, to exclude it. On leaving, Tibidje relieved the facility of its embarrassing presence. Inmates could also watch television to their heart's content, and even engage in pro bono legal consultations. His mind was kept busy, and he enjoyed the solidarity of the visiting prelate, whom he even began to assist in his impromptu services in the camp. His eventual arrival in Monrovia was thus straight into the warm embrace of the chaplain's associates, who again took him under their tutelage.

It proved a learning period. Among other assets acquired during his Newark internment, Tibidje was now able to assert—and in all truthfulness—that he had been to the USA and had indeed spent several months under the mentorship of a servant of Christ. He had an accent to prove it and could nasalize his syllables as persuasively as any native American—indeed, Dennis Tibidje's vocal register was no longer recognizable, not even by his former associates, the yahoo-yahoo boys. The wanderer had begun the long odyssey to homeland.

Misfortune dogged him, though. Hardly had Tibidje landed on Liberian soil than the civil war erupted, courtesy of a certain ex-sergeant major named Sergeant Doe. The accidental immigrant was not a rash youth. He escaped into nearby Gambia, then crossed over into Senegal. It was pure instinct and his strong point. Tibidje always obeyed when inspiration called upon him to move.

Senegal being a French-speaking nation, Tibidje's stay in that largely Muslim nation, which had a highly cosmopolitan temperament, was thus of the briefest. That made him sad, as he found the ambiance most conducive, surrounded as he was by a minority but socially upscale and accommodating Christian populace. He soon made his way into Sierra Leone, aided by the evangelical network that crisscrossed the West African coastland in a multiplicity of imperial faiths. The itinerant apostle made a decent living out of a career as "visiting" or "substitute" preacher. He even appeared occasionally on televised revivalist marathons as warm-up speaker to the resident star of the religious turf. Home Nigeria remained the ultimate destination, however—be it Delta or Lagos, home beckoned. Home was where he was resolved to cast down his bucket and found his apostolic realm. Each passing day, month, year, was a mere passage of apprenticeship, and Tibidje was a conscientious learner. More importantly, he was a network builder and an impressive preacher. Even in Ivory Coast, where the language was again French, such was the dynamism of his message—and delivery—that interpreters nearly launched a civil war in the contest to serve him.

Real war appeared to dog his footsteps—it was that era—but such unpleasantness only provided pertinent material for his pilgrim's progress, contributing to narratives of ordeal by fire. It enabled sermons of miraculous deliverance from the hands of warring factions, virtually at the point of death, horrors piled on horrors, salvation in complementary dosage. He held congregations spellbound, hallelujah-bonded for the preservation of a man clearly destined to propagate the word of God. His lasting regret was a failure to secure a slot in the pulpit of the imitation St. Peter's Basilica in Yamoussoukro, the *grande folie* of the erstwhile leader, Houphouët-Boigny. This was due to a sudden conflagration in the politics of Ivory Coast, an escalation of conflict that soon earned her laurels in the internecine bloodletting that now distinguished the once-peaceful West African states. Still, such grim vicissitudes merely provided further stirring material for eleventh-hour deliverance homilies. Who could fail to identify with the itinerant apostle on the very edge of being devoured by the pet crocodiles of the late leader, into whose residential moat the drugged commandants of an embattled faction had thrown him, just for the fun of it. Such reminiscences, alas, were missed by the majority of Ivorian congregations—Apostle Tibidje had already moved on. Next stop the Republic of Ghana.

It was in Ghana, a zone of comparative stability, that he would later declare he had his first epiphany. It happened in the middle of a reverberating delivery in a football arena in Kumasi, a revivalist crush of tens of thousands where he was again a last-minute substitute preacher. Right in the middle of an ecstatic peroration, he stopped suddenly. Something he had just said, something that had just slipped from his throat, compelled an instant sound rewind in his head. It took him back to the beginning of that very utterance, the root of the resonance, a moment that equated a lightning illumination from a clear sky. It left him dazzled and tongue-tied before an audience of equally riveted thousands. *Therefore, flock to the site of prophecy wherever you find it, seek out the prophet's site where dwells the spirit of the Lord* . . . and he stopped, stunned by the clarity of a message that slammed into his standard exhortation with the fist of inspiration— *the prophet's site.* Contract into . . . *prophesite!*

He looked nervously around, hoping that no one else had caught that creative slip, or at least that it had not registered with anyone in that audience with apostolic ambitions. The flash momentarily unnerved him, as it inserted profound doubts in his mind—could it be that he was after all the genuine article? That he had indeed responded to an authentic call to prophesy? *Prophesite!* Why had all his predecessors failed to formulate such an exquisite, indeed mellifluous name for a place of spiritual quest? Could it be that he was, unbeknownst to himself till now, truly . . . called? It took days of nerve-racking self-doubt before he fully reassured himself that he had not deviated from his true calling—a skillful, creative spiritual trafficker. At the end of that flash of illumination, he packed bag and baggage and hit the road. He was now the proud possessor of a Volkswagen camper, equipped with recording gadgets and a loud-hailer powered from the car engine, always prepared for an impromptu revivalist session. Accompanied by three faithful adherents, one of them a substitute driver, he headed east. It was time!

Not back to Port Harcourt, however, not immediately, indeed nowhere near the south, where he had made friends and acquain-

tances of starstruck celebrities. There was need to ensure that sufficient time had passed, that no one remembered him in his earlier home
emanation. He returned to the nation of happiness able to count on
a trickle of corresponding associates along the west coast, and even
southwards in South Africa, some of them notorious for spiritual remedies that included swallowing live snakes and mice for keeping the
devil at bay. On the home front, he renewed contact with a voluntary
array of scouts, enablers, and enforcers, some of them turned full-time
revolving clients of security forces and prison yards.

Men—and increasingly women—of God, even from rivaling
faiths, enjoy a remarkable status in the nation of happiness. There
appeared to be, at base, a willingness to join hands in solidarity of
purpose. Hardly had Tibidje concluded his first sermon in a converted
commodity goods warehouse than he found himself sought after in
upper-middle-class circles. One should also credit him with success in
creating an air of mystery that intrigued men and women of the faith
and eased his passage into the middling, then higher echelons of power.
Tibidje hardly needed to advertise his debut as a new entrant into the
potential arena of spiritual largesse. Before his departure from Ghana,
his scouts had fanned out ahead of his triumphal reentry and returned
with their findings. The recommendation was the city of Kaduna, its
population reputedly divided near evenly between two warring faiths.
The now full-fledged apostle arrived with a clean-shaved head, oiled
and gleaming. He grew a beard that brought his appearance closer
to a black charcoal sketch he had retained of the sage Nostradamus.
Each environment had its own needs, the people their special thirsts
and hungers. He felt "called" to preach the gospel of peace in Kaduna,
a city that was gradually evolving into a microcosm of Liberia, Sierra
Leone, or Ivory Coast. Kaduna was, however, none of these. In no
way could it be likened even to Maiduguri in the northeast, hotbed
of religious fundamentalists, permanently under siege. It was troubled, but it was comparatively peaceful. For a returnee in need of an
untroubled profile yet high on spiritual hormones, Kaduna was both
secure and promising. It did not take long for him to make contact
with the governor, who was young, untested, ready for any prospect
of conciliation for a divided city. A senior civil servant paved the way.

"If only we can in some way restrain these killers," lamented the governor, receiving Tibidje on a courtesy visit. The visitor did not miss a beat.

"Have you tried making contact and paying them off? Throw money in their midst and leave them to fight over it."

His credentials as a veteran of West African wars lent him authority. Within Nigeria itself—Tibidje knew that history—a governor of Kano State, known as the Suave Appeaser, had done exactly that, paid off a sect known as the Maitatsine, the undercredited predecessors of Boko Haram. The Maitatsine warred primarily against orthodox Muslims—these were the real enemies of man and God, who disgraced the black race by genuflecting to false prophets, the slaving apostles of Arab descent! The Maitatsine were incensed by all who rode in any mechanical conveyance. The punishment for all such infidels was strangulation with the bicycle chains of the two-wheelers on which they pedaled to work and worked the market. They waylaid workers, held up trains, captured the males and enslaved their women, fortified enclaves, and set up governance within governance. That governor's solution had been to dine with the devil, not even with the proverbial long spoon but directly across a festive board, with takeaway packages in tens of millions.

Indeed, in seven years away from the land, Tibidje found that much had evolved in that part of the nation. The forbidden fruit was no longer motorcars and motorcycles but books. The written word. Now armed soldiers sprang up everywhere, setting roadblocks with zigzag rites of passage for vehicles, passengers compelled to disembark, walk across a *cordon sanitaire* with bag and baggage while the emptied vehicles proceeded to the other side after a stringent overhaul. Martyrdom had taken on a new meaning, and to add to his horror, martyrdom was no longer content with willing submission to persecution and death or even self-immolation in a cause, but required the immolation of nonconsenting adults and children, anywhere, anytime, in motor parks, marketplaces, schools, and allied institutions, in leisure places and workplaces. Churches presented themselves as the most provocative targets, joined much later by spiritual fence-sitters, considered worse than the real *kafri*. Prudence counseled Tibidje to establish his contemplated temple on the southern side of the dividing bridge. The theme was visible, palpable, ready-made as if for the first conscious symbolist: the physical bridge was man-made and inevitably a symbol of separation. He would be the spiritual bridge, the messenger of peace and healing. It was convenient that those two problematic virtues, peace and unity, were also embedded in the national anthem. Tibidje co-opted the line, plus the snatch of tune in which it was clothed, into his opening sermon every Sunday and as dispersing doxology. The governor was impressed. Tibidje drew on the Newark internship of nearly a year's close confinement with the two religious streams. He was a godsend of an intermediary, the governor confided to his advisers, and a natural conveyor belt for appeasement funds. Millions exchanged hands, and perhaps a fair portion remained stuck en route. Suspicions flared. "We paid all that was agreed up front," wailed the governor. "Here are my witnesses, and I even have the receipts."

Tibidje smiled complacently. "It is exactly as I predicted. The money has divided them. They cheat one another and there is no more trust between them. Now leave the rest to God—He'll make them fight one another to the death."

Problems of like nature appeared to dog Tibidje. His timing could not have been more untimely. Boko Haram had designated the same period for the activation of its sleepers, pursuing its own unification agenda across the bridge of division. Other, not so religious voices claimed that it was not Boko Haram at all but frustrated protection racketeers who had lost patience awaiting the promised windfall from their elected governor. The consequence was all that mattered. The complacent lines of military buffers were breached one deadly night. Insurgents sneaked through, fanned out, and unleashed their pent-up proselytizing ferocity. Tebidje's headquarters, only halfway up from foundation but already in weekly service, was consumed in a baptism of fire. The governor hesitated. He was still upset by the funds that had inexplicably gone missing. In the end, however, he decided to leave everything in the hands of Allah and instructed his aide to send a message of sympathy—but don't overdo it, he ordered.

This much all conceded to Tibidje. He was endowed with one asset—a loyal following, an inner core, carefully cultivated, perhaps no more than between four and six at a time. He saw generously to their welfare and in turn they looked after his business. His early-warning system and instinct for survival were honed with every adverse situation. With his experiences along the ECOWAS—another unification project—he was not altogether unprepared when his yet unconsecrated church—ritually, that is—was razed to the ground and two of his lieutenants slaughtered. It was a gruesome setback, a violent deterrent. Tibidje was human, he did not pretend to be anything else, and thus he considered abandonment. Indeed, he had begun to contemplate a second incursion into the United States, this time on a one-way ticket. A new name. A new history. A new beginning. A new life. As emotions struggled in the soul of the repatriated son of the land, however, he looked back on the past and encountered a chastening spectre: a mission unfulfilled! A life in limbo. Deep within him, something rebelled. He recalled pledges, pledges of youth, made to himself and his peers.

The preacher's stoicism in reconciling himself with that adversity was nowhere more brilliantly manifested than when, not long after the violation, he stood in the middle of fallen roofs and tottering supports that had once housed his ministry, feet scuffing ashes and cinders, and preached his valedictory sermon. It was a never-to-be-forgotten spectacle. With a reflective pate bared to the diminishing light of dusk and a quivering beard that seemed to invoke the wrath of earth, he reminded his followers that destruction had shifted from Christian places of worship only and now embraced even mosques. The Muslim fanatics had begun to inflict even worse brutality on their fellow believers. There was only one response: the unity of the assailed. The wand of faith had fallen into diabolical hands and needed to be rescued, cleansed, and restored to men and women of good will, be these Christians or Muslims. That united will must rout the revelers, an undiscriminating plague that made one and all prospective victims, in spiritual mayhem. It was at this moment that Brother Tibidje sought and received his own counsel—out of evil cometh good. The solution, as a structured, sustainable birth, struck him in the face with such dazzle that he gasped for breath. He went down on his knees, even though wearing his best preacher trousers—straight from the Kaduna main street Souls for God Drycleaners Ltd., a black pair, striped dark grey—and rededicated himself to what was now his prime mission: the ecumenical pursuit. It was not quite epiphany, but it came close.

Tibidje's travails took on new meaning, new urgency. His year sojourn in the Newark detention camp had pointed the way, only he had failed to see it at the time. Until that moment in the scuffed ashes of his truncated evangelism, he had also been seized by Kaduna as the divided city, requiring the pious disposition of patronage. No, this was no longer sufficient. What the world—not just the happy nation—needed was a new, all-embracing religion! In his hands, offered on a platter of piety, he had at his disposal two main contending religions, united in victimology. The call for a religion of peace, genuine peace, not one of mere spiritual rhetoric, no! It strained for material birth. Adumbrations followed swiftly. A unique space for all faiths, a site for revered seers that catered for both religions in their united peer cultures, emerging beyond controversy, neutral and accommodative. Both sides boasted—indeed, marketed—prophets, and in overabundance. When he tried out the new direction on his surviving threesome Council of Elders, it was an instant hit. Inspired, they screamed, *You are truly called, Apostle Tibidje*.

One main ingredient the evangelist early seized upon was . . . bravura! His inward eye flashed to the overflowing amphitheatres where he had stood in for the modern-day stars of television ministry. Were they greater orators, better read, or more world-savvy than he? *The trouble with you,* he chided his reflection in the bathroom mirror, *is diffidence, that illegitimate child of memory. Go for chutzpah!* All around him were indicted governors, senators, permanent secretaries, bankers, some of them even returned fugitives, strutting boldly in accustomed splendor, manipulating the judicial system, fêted and fêting as if they owned the world and could not be called to account until the judges retired, were promoted and taken off the case, witnesses had died, or files were forgotten. They milked the courts for bail and adjournments on health grounds, rivals in the performance trade, since they often entered the court gasping for breath, carried on stretchers, leaning on crutches, bandaged head to foot like walking Egyptian mummies, yet the next day were seen cavorting on the beaches of Florida, hale and hearty. Not even with any sense of a decent interval or concern for the accommodating magistrates and judges before showing their faces in public. Several were already recruiting for their next foray into new elections, bribing, openly campaigning for YoY nominations. So? Who still took the trouble to recall a few peccadilloes that had sent him on an odyssey of self-apprenticeship to lesser talent that could not muster even a fraction of his oratorical powers? As for scriptures, he knew the Bible, the Quran, the Upanishads and Bhagavad Gita backwards and forwards—well, snatches. What mattered was to be able to outquote any aspiring prelate with pertinent passages. Or manipulate the narrative to bear on whatever had been retained in the mind from Quran or Bible. He had made good use of the mini-library in Newark, memorized the powerful declarations of originals such as the legendary Father Divine, the black religious leader.

Now that—and again, for perhaps the hundredth time, Tibidje shook his head in awed admiration—that was some dude! Father Divine called down the wrath of the Lord on the judge who had the temerity to sentence him for some arcane crime called "mail fraud." Yet the whole world knew that Divine's crime was simply that he mobilized his fellow slave descendants to demand that they be repatriated to their continent of origin and that the government of white slaveowners pay their passage home and even pay compensation for generations of enslavement. No one could obscure that truth. And so, as his sentence was pronounced, Father Divine in turn pronounced his sentence on the judge: "You will not live to see me walk out of those prison gates a free man!"

Whew! Wow! Caramba! Blood of Jesus! Lo and behold, that judge expired while Divine was at his morning meditations in his prison cell. The journalistic horde pursued him thither, eager to receive his reaction. Divine was learning for the first time of the judge's departure from mortal realms, but the charismatic son from the land of the blacks did not miss a beat. "I hated to do it," he said, and resumed his orisons.

O gbeleticos! That, determined Tibidje, was the alpha and omega of the prophetic enterprise, and that shard of history stuck in his soul like the forked stick of a water diviner. If he came even halfway close to such power of a bull's-eye, it would be more than sufficient to rank himself among the priestly immortals. Any judge who made the mistake of dusting up old files and annulling the statute of limitations would be guaranteed a like fate—he knew exactly how gloriously he would embrace the trivial martyrdom of a prison record as the price of fulfillment. It was the testamentary moment of Tibidje's formal rebirth. He felt himself a spiritual son to the son of slaves who were forcibly taken from the very portion of earth that he, Tibidje, had returned, just like Father Divine, to reclaim. The decision was already hovering on the spiritual horizon, but now he formally made the resolution—he would adopt a slightly altered version of his hero's name. If he ever came to trial for whatever and a misguided judge made a similar misjudgment, he would pronounce on his head a local version of Father Divine's counterjudgment. The Apostle Davina—yes, Tibidje had finally chosen, settled for the name change—Apostle, Prophet, maybe Papa Davina, would deliver nothing less potent than his adopted father's terrible pronouncement on the judge. The rest would follow swiftly.

The means? Time enough to cross that bridge when he came to it. Tibidje had no doubt whatsoever that Father Divine had organized a hit on the presumptuous, racist instrument of injustice. Thus he saw his preparatory mission as being no less than to ensure a capability to deliver a like riposte even from within prison walls if the prophecy took too long to fulfill itself. Not for nothing had he kept close contact with the denizens of his modest beginnings—the yahoo-yahoo boys, the Area boys, not forgetting the cultic proliferation of counterministries with outlandish names that straddled cultures as far apart as Scandinavia and the slum warriors of his own happy nation—the Icelanders, some called themselves, others Konudi, Black Axles, Dagunro, and other predators who ran parallel governments from Zamfara to Lagos, Bayelsa to Birnin Kebbi and back. The Apostle Davina felt ready to move. Papa Davina was in town, let all embrace piety.

In the name of justice, close to eleven full years had passed, after all, since Tibidje's unfortunate beginnings in Port Harcourt. The national character had become established in the exhortation known as *m'enukuo*, a contraction of *mu enu ku'ro*—take your mouth off it! Let sleeping dogs lie, etc., etc. Even those who knew, who recognized him, would simply shake their heads and—*m'enukuo*. It was time to move on. But in grand style. With bravura. No looking back. In the style of the brazen state governor who beat a twenty-four-count rap of financial finagling, took off for Dubai, and lived happily ever after, almost—an idyll that was truncated only because of an unprecedented clash of ambitions within the ruling heights and the proverbial morality tale of a falling-out among thieves. It was time, the evangelist estimated, to strike out for greater glory. He would move, yes, move further south, for greater safety. This time, however, every move would take place with unprecedented spiritual panache. Strike out. Act frontally. Beard the devil on his, Davina's, own terms. The coming relocation would reflect the nation's current dilemma. It was time to annunciate a ministry of tolerance.

Ministry? No, no, no, that would never do. The confusion between the secular and the spiritual would be insurmountable. Who, within the nation, had not heard of a Ministry of Happiness? Was he, the Apostle Tibidje, now Papa Davina, heir to the tradition of the great Father Divine, to let himself be saddled with such banalities? *Think different,* Davina chided Tibidje. *Think novelty. Think grandeur!*

Davina went into seclusion, wrestling with a flurry of projections, each of which contained at least a dozen options. He fasted, banning lunch in entirety. The thread of life was sustained by a breakfast of four *akara* balls and a bowl of *akamu* with some local fruits, then nothing till dinnertime, when he tackled a wrap of *tuwo* and/or fried plantains, with some *kilishi* on the side. He was, fortunately, abstemious by habit and a teetotaler—in public—his indulgences lay in other directions. At the end of three days there came a flash, to which Tibidje was uncommonly prone. The expressway, Lagos to Ibadan, on which he had not even traveled for over a decade, provided the setting.

That artery linked the most heavily populated city on the African continent, Ibadan, to the rest of the nation. It was an increasingly rutted dual carriageway of presumably two lanes on either side, sometimes three. Or four. Sometimes five—when last traveled, which was nearly a decade before, it had become impossible to count exactly how many lanes existed on either side. He could recall it only as serial death traps which progressively became home—on both sides!—to competing spiritualities. It seemed as if a starting pistol was fired on some day and a race commenced for the strangulation of traffic on days of religious feasts—Easter, Christmas, Ramadan, Id after Id, birthdays of prophets and avatars, or simply revivalist sessions on the whim or on days dedicated to a National Day of Prayers against drought, floods, diseases, corruption, locust invasion, epidemics, collapsed buildings, fires, exploding tankers, kidnappers, paedophiles, traffic carnage, ritual killers, etc., etc. Tibidje retraced his last ride, which had taken him through the two roundabouts-cum-flyovers which turned the expressway into a ring road skirting the city of Ibadan itself. It was that final section—the second roundabout and its quarter-mile approach from Lagos, a medley of every kind of motorized contraption and disoriented vending—that now preoccupied the calculating mind of Apostle Davina. He had never given it much thought—he was merely an occasional road user—but now it struck him as a transcendental divide: one part headed towards the ancient war and trading city of Oyo, the other to the spiritual fount of the Yoruba, Ile-Ife, home of the *orisa*.

The notion, he now realized, had been implanted by a long-submerged sighting of a dirt-blue two-storey building with a wide board across the railings of the first-floor balcony. On that board was painted, in lurid colours, four words: The Home of Chrislam. Strategically positioned at the expressway junction, it was as if its originators were pronouncing that spot both as meeting and departure point of spirituality and worldliness. Tibidje now recalled the controversy it had stirred at the time—was it at its launching? Or was it some years later, evoked perhaps by some purity-obsessed religionist? It did not matter in the least. In that single flash, Papa Davina summarized its history in one word: Timidity! Defeatism. A laudable, indeed inspired religious advocacy, but beyond that? Stagnation. Chrislam was a calling, but where was its dwelling? That was the yawning gap, pleading to be filled! But where? Where? A hard-boiled pragmatic soul, Tibidje knew that he was not yet prepared to take on Lagos itself. More research needed to be done and, more critically, accumulation of capital! Miracles were all very well, but even if water must be struck out of stone, the stone must first be procured, and that meant money.

Papa Davina ordered his lieutenants into action.

The results confirmed his recollection. Chrislam had remained in its poky little spot in all its decades of existence. Not one extra square foot of expansion, barely a grudging coat of new paint since the building had been raised, becoming increasingly squeezed as its surrounding plots of land were developed. It had been eclipsed by even later arrivals, minor sects and branches of lesser-known spiritual advocacy.

It remained uninfluenced even by an inspirational contrast—separated by just two kilometres. That contrast was situated just before the first of the two roundabouts, that is, on the southern outskirts of Ibadan. It was the vast, sprawling, ever-expanding estate of a self-styled Living God, the Guru Mahara Ji. This vast domain took off from the express-way on a manicured grassy incline, on which the guru's name and divine order had been florally sculpted by inspired horticultural hands and landscape hairdressers. On the plateau that sheered off the rim, the beginnings of an orchard, then the living and meditation spread of buildings, hidden from profane eyes. By contrast, the site of Chrislam was—not to mince words—a slum.

That projection of contrasts, yoked in unity of spirit—yet another flash of inspiration!—decided Tibidje in his search for an overarching structural motif, a two-in-one that would mean something to all—a fairyland located in a slum, feeding off each other, bringing the world of warring faiths together in amity. He directed his scouts to commence an exploration of the suburbs of Mushin, Oshodi, Ajegunle, Alimosho, all within the bustling city of Lagos but not of it. Papa Davina's mood was uplifted. Already he began to feel restored. The blueprint had begun to fill out. It only awaited fulfillment.

Render unto Caesar what is Caesar's . . . Tibidje ordered his aides into the idle precincts of land registry and company records. Lo and behold, the Spirit was again at work, and all was exactly as he had predicted. Chrislam was indeed registered as a religion, but not as real estate or business. All hesitation ended. Guru Mahara Ji had met his match. No, not as competitor; Tibidje abhorred such crude contests, was content to play his cards in conformity with the unforced dynamics of proselytisation. He applied for registration, patented the name. That choice was no more than Divine Prescience, a custom-made fit that most definitely constituted the Second Epiphany. The world's first-ever city of ecumenical worship was on its way—Chrislamabad!

The vision was complete. Now commenced the harder part—the mission.

His journey through his West African region had toned him. Impetuousness of youth had taken several steps back. Now a solid middle-aged campaigner, he was not rushed, neither was he diffident. Tibidje believed quite simply that while "a step at a time" was a counsel that merited notice, two steps in tandem were even more meritorious. Even the yahoo-yahoo boys knew that, but they lacked any sense of coordination. They worked internet scams, then dabbled in child-snatching on the side. That was a crippling deficiency in finesse. No sense of the big picture. They were creatures of the moment and would always remain cannon fodder. He would commence with a prototype, make it a launchpad while slowly constructing the landing pad—the permanent headquarters in, where else? Lagos, here comes Papa D.!

The rest followed in logical progression. His ministry would depart from Kaduna, move, for now, just a little further south, further away from the lunatic fringe increasingly consolidated by Boko Haram. Chrislamabad was a city whose birth was too long in coming. Only question for now was, where build the prototype? That was the sole dilemma. There had to be that tryout while the foundation of the headquarters took form, shape, and magnificence. Papa Davina brought out his constant companion of a ten-year itinerancy, his most reliable direction finder—the map of West Africa. As he smoothed out the traveled scroll, his eyes roving around the contours of his native land, his instinct-saturated eye, attuned to signs and symbols towards whatever task in hand, settled on the answer. There it lay prone, quivering right before him—Lokoja! The confluence of the nation's two major rivers!

The bombshell of sheer light exploded in his innermost soul. Christians, Muslims, as well as animists, had pursued their main occupation—trade—on the banks of the Benue for centuries, in above-average amity. The main city itself nestled snugly in the heart-shaped cusp of the two major rivers, Niger and Benue. Rivers are not known to take much interest in the plans of mere mortals; this, however, was one instance of unbridled favouritism—two historic rivers echoing the careers of two imperious spiritual streams! It was symbolism pleading to be turned into reality—the fugitive from hate came, saw, and committed. His instinct, he quietly pointed out at the first sermonizing opportunity, continued to serve him flawlessly. It meant that it was no instinct at all but direct spiritual coordination of vision and returns. He laid the foundation of his temporary church—bamboo and clapboard, plus planks from discarded canoes and fishermen's nets—on a quite substantial sandy island in the western armpit of the two rivers, approachable only by canoes. Tibidje was reasonably schooled in his nation's geography, but he went further than mere Nature's landscape—the town, Lokoja, enshrined much of the nation's history. There the explorers Richard Lander and Mungo Park had taken turns to founder in their search for the source of the River Benue, one getting himself taken prisoner or killed, or maybe both of them—he was no longer sure of details; school was already a decades-old basket, shaken and sieved for what it had to offer, the rest discarded. Neither of the two white interlopers pretended to be on any godly mission—it was all trade agreements with illiterate chiefs—so there was nothing in their legendary passage, as individuals, for him to build upon. But the rivers! Now these were different, rich, prostrate, and available.

The River Niger and the Benue! Their robust consummation neatly bifurcated Nigeria north and south before cascading to the coast to spread its veins all over swampland and create the Delta from which all blessings flowed in the form of black gold, the spinal cord of the nation's economic standing. Papa Davina reasoned that a fair share of that belonged to him. He had a fair mind, was equitable in human dealing, so he conceded the same right to all fellow citizens, but—and his face, whenever his mind was engaged in such thoughts, became irradiated ear to ear—he had resolved not only to have his but to deserve it. He was not that musically inclined, beyond of course the co-option of that powerful medium in the course of his trade. However, he did have one favourite singer and song, and the lyrics of that song floated around his head like a swarm of colourful butterflies at the onset of the rainy season after the long Harmattan drought when cocoons break loose and all manner of airy things came to life:

> *Manna's gonna rain, don't let the sky scare you*
> *It's darkness of plenty, ain't rage before the Flood*
> *Journey end sometime, ask the children of Zion*
> *Then harvest come, sweet manna from heaven.*
> *Manna from heaven, yeah manna from heaven,*
> *Sweet mamma, yeah mamma, sweet manna from heaven*

The chips were falling in place. He had only one commodity on offer—spirituality. All it required was creative packaging, and that was his forte. Nothing went to waste. His apprenticeship, albeit a short-lived spell, in publicity and marketing moved to answer its long-awaited call.

Such were the foundational stones upon which the launchpad for Chrislamabad was laid. That choice, Lokoja, was a picturesque, unworldly home of simple fishermen and canoe transporters, yet a busy intersection for road travelers. Davina hired a hall while he commenced the building of his own. The banner on the church entrance read, for ease of pronunciation, *Ekumenika*, whose calligraphy also carried a hint of ancient Greek, adding to the mysteriousness of the sudden inplant. He labelled his departure from Kaduna the First Exodus, hired fleets of canoes to ferry worshippers to his island church. The service began as a free ride, which soon drew worshippers from mainland churches to its island bosom. Papa Davina introduced modest fares. Soon he owned the canoes. The fleet multiplied. Next, they were no longer conveyances for the prophesite of Ekumenika but a commercial transportation system controlled by the site. It ferried market men and women, schoolchildren, workers. Gradually the site raised its own soccer team. The fleet, decorated in all hues of the rainbow, ferried the blessed soccer team from match to match on the mainland. From soccer it moved to festivals—a canoe regatta that turned into a mini-fiesta, with promises of annual sustenance by governors of the river-bordered states. A trickle of tourists began, swelled into a fair-sized stream, then became a torrent. Tibidje had found his niche. He was halfway home, to the national hub of happiness.

His city of choice was indeed tailor-made. It had centuries-old landmarks, all begging to be co-opted, but through a modern spiritual perspective—the true city of God and Allah, snatched from the unimaginative entrepreneur of the Lagos-Ibadan Expressway. Lagos awaited the Coming. For now, Lokoja was the container vessel for the ecumenical spirit. He moved to expand, consecrating every encroachment on the island real estate, quietly nudging out the shacks of "illegal squatters." Tibidje made material what till then had been mere spirit. His ministry moved swiftly, nearly miraculously, beyond the merely speculative. Chrislamabad covered all the grounds, spiritual and temporal, squeezing out competition—mostly Lone Ranger prophets with bell and cross—or absorbing it. It enjoyed the patronage of the state,

Kogi, of its middle-class and affluent, of government officials, business types, and politicians. In no time the Kaduna scenario was being reenacted but in a vastly improved version, and minus the menace of a universal plague called Boko Haram. It was inevitable that the governor found himself graciously accepting to be guest of honour at a cultural event, a reelection campaign having entered a critical stage. Enthralled by what he saw on stepping out of the site, he scooped up a handful of the Benue-Niger waters, poured it all over his face, and invited his entourage to do the same. Most did not even await orders; they had already stooped to follow his example. As he stepped into his yacht, he announced that a gift of a motorboat—not just a canoe with an outboard motor but a covered eight-seater motorboat—be delivered gratis to Ekumenika.

That official imprimatur was the final propellant. The island became dedicated to the service of "retreats." Business deals were negotiated under its spiritual aura. Academics and other fevered brains sought its calm before embarking upon or rounding off research. Artists favoured it for its serenity, and many were the painters' easels that sprang up in the evenings and weekends to blossom with rich images along the banks of the riverine landscape. Politicians knew where to go for discreet meetings, watched over by the eyes of God. The powerful from beyond Kogi borders heard of it and made it their discreet pilgrimage goal, to escape prying eyes for meetings requiring uttermost discretion. This was how, indeed, Sir Goddie, nominally the second most powerful leader of a powerful nation but in fact her most powerful individual, came to hear of it and sent his most trusted aides to check it out. They returned with glowing reports. When Sir Goddie visited, the entire island was cleared, but with professional discretion. No one heard a thing, not even after he had been and gone. The banner was sufficient: SPACE CLOSED FOR SPIRITUAL RENOVATION.

Lokoja fully consolidated, Papa D. commenced his move on his real destination, the national home of Ekumenika—Lagos. The decided sector was Mushin/Ipaja, on the road to Otta and Abeokuta, the latter being home to the first missionaries to plant the Christian gospel in the hearts of pagan Yoruba but now a melting pot for no matter what religious affirmation, including the marginalized *orisa* which Papa Davina had long decided was an economic basket case. Something is not quite right about that traditional religion, he once lamented, seated among his board of trustees. It is just like that expressway Chrislam—a calling without a dwelling. They needed to get their act together. *Orisa* was simply not worth quoting on the stock exchange, not even on a virtual one. Some tourist value for addicts of the exotic—beyond that, he would not invest one kobo in that antiquarian piece. Still, Davina remained open-minded. He invited *orisa* priests to the Ekumenika cultural fiesta and even lodged them free of charge in one of the prophesite chalets.

In preparation for the final coming, Papa Davina had taken possession of a "distressed" sector of Mushin/Ipaja with an incongruous hilly outcrop that served as an informal garbage dump. Street gangs and political thugs once ruled the space, released their excess energy by setting fires to a number of small businesses. They imposed protection fees on markets, dismantled the stalls of the recalcitrant, and organized accidents for their families. Papa D. infiltrated with his modernized successors, the yahoo-yahoo and cultic assassins, assigned them productive functions. Prophesite and surrounds witnessed unusual sights—a presiding prelate who changed attire from cassock and surplice plus bishop's crozier for one service, only to follow up with the "Touareg look"—turban, half to three-quarter facial cover, and a dangling jowl loop. He would follow up a week later with the Hare Krishna saffron robes and tinkle bells but interrupt the week every Friday with the plain Muslim kaftan and skullcap, ivory worry beads. Other chambers ministered simultaneously to other deities in different ways, presided over by his assistants. Gods and avatars, saints and demiurges of all lands were united under one roof, in images or simply manifested in song, chant, and incense across open spaces. Was there not, Papa D. struggled to recollect, a boast attributed to the jihadist Uthman dan Fodio that he would march all the way down from the Fouta Djallon hills of Sierra Leone to dip the Quran in the Atlantic? He, Papa Davina, would go one better. He would dip his chequebook in the Lagos lagoon and bring it up dripping with proceeds from the nation's petroleum flow.

This account is authoritative—and by none other than the pilgrim himself, pieced together from numerous sermons, confidentialities, and police records. Thus did the man once known as Dennis Tibidje progress from the eastern city of Port Harcourt to Lagos, of the same nation, via Newark, Monrovia, Dakar, Kumasi, Kaduna, Lokoja, until the moment ripened—a full eleven years later—when Lokoja moved to Lagos in ultramodern technological blaze. A rank outsider had hit town with one sole mission—to settle down, beat the established ones at their own game. Lagos was fertile, receptive. He had experience and resilience on his side. And he arrived prepared with a winner, a brand that he could sway in any direction: the Ecumenical River. Let all the envious, the obsessed of sterile purism, the unimaginative, deride or challenge the model! Hundreds of miles away, two mighty rivers attested to the power of the ecumenical vision. Let the hymners of the River Jordan and praise singers of the wells of Saudi Zamzam waters top that if they could. There was a river that beat them all hands down—the river of oil that rolled from a fountainhead that knew no division: *EKUMENIKA!*

4.

Scoffer's Progress

Let this cup pass . . .

It had been a long siege, aided by many of whom the hostage himself had scant or no knowledge, but finally, yes indeed, it was sweet victory to be savoured by the long-embattled spouse, Mrs. Jaiyesola Badetona. This was the icing on the cake of victory that had already been celebrated in multiple events, all framed devotionally—even down to the sumptuous feasting and souvenirs, grateful offerings by a spouse for a most unexpected upturn in the career of her life partner. That hitherto intransigent spouse, scion of a royal house, had eventually succumbed to her entreaties—and not even grudgingly. On the appointed day he would observe every schooled detail of his ransom, and with precision. He consented to visit the Apostle Papa Davina for a spiritual consultation.

Prince Badetona's elevation, on his own estimation, had been no less than seismic. Thus he had not hesitated to slaughter the fatted cow—he did pride himself, after all, as a traditionalist, nothing to do with being a scion of a royal house—so sacrifice was expected, and he was not averse to spreading the fat among friends, colleagues, and well-wishers. In any case, he could not fail to have been infected by years of association with the master party soul of his close circle—

Duyole Pitan-Payne, engineer and acknowledged leader of their eccentric Gong of Four—but that blithe spirit was in a class all his own. The prince even conceded a Thanksgiving service—it rid the home of a lingering tension between husband and wife. That feeling of domestic persecution, however, was the product of a series of mishaps, strange happenings over and beyond the elastic limits of coincidence, and of such persistence that even he began to lose confidence and permit chinks in his cynic's carapace. To make matters worse, such untoward incidents had followed the good news almost like a structured cause-and-effect, commencing so close to his career elevation that he did begin to wonder if there was not indeed a maleficent linkage. Good luck attracting bad, either through some quirky law of Nature's balance, call it karma, yin-yang, or whatever, or simply—as promptly concluded by his wife and extended family—enemy action!

Have you sought divine intercession? At the beginning he lived up to his nickname—the Scoffer. He preferred to knuckle down to preparations for the assignment at hand and his new status in life. Money he was prepared to spend for celebrations, but he balked at the idea of submitting himself to divine busybodies in his earthly failures, successes, both, or absence of any. After all, he had succeeded in keeping divinities at arm's length throughout a humdrum career—in his view, more accurately described as lack of spectacular recognition. He preferred it that way. It enabled him to indulge in his favourite hobby, which was simply problem solving, especially of the statistical kind. He had been and still remained a reticent mathematical genius. That had its compensations, its material perks. An internal auditor but with unaudited earnings. He saw no reason to complain or jubilate. It was all strictly business, and Badetona was genuinely possessed of a retiring temperament. Left to him, he would even have discarded his princely title, but that was now part of his existence, and it also had its advantages.

Jaiyesola, however, saw it differently. The position lacked public recognition. A prince without a throne—it would not be the turn of his royal line for another century. And then, despite the streak of genius that he had exhibited all the way from schooldays and into public service, in her own parlance, nothing to show for it. She looked at his close circle of associates, some of them members of the prestigious

Motor Boat Club of Ikoyi, or the Lagos Island Indigenes Club, Free-masons, and Rosicrucians, and felt that Badetona was short-changed in social entitlements. The title of internal auditor sounded in her ears like a life sentence in solitary confinement on a diet of *garri* and water. So she took her case to God, albeit without her husband's knowledge. Who was to tell her that it was not a wife's duty to boost her spouse to greater heights?

Then commenced a series of omens. Prayers answered, and in such generous helping, Badetona began to encounter a flurry of mishaps that moved, in her view, beyond mere coincidence. First his custom-ized computer crashed. That was unprecedented. Next he stubbed his toe against a protruding table leg—the left toe!—it was one of those ultra-modernistic designs that catered more to sensation than sense. Was it a coincidence that she had terrible dreams that same night? It did not take too long afterwards before the newly appointed chief executive director locked himself out of doors, having left his key wal-let in the office. Jaiyesola had also traveled for her Christian pilgrim-age, undertaken two weeks after her return from accompanying her Muslim friend to Saudi Arabia for the lesser hajj—both were follow-ers of the ministry of Papa Davina's Ekumenica. His phone battery also chose that night to run down—ah yes, the long-distance call from Jaiye in Hebron, with a protracted argument on why she should not fill her suitcase with holy water from the River Jordan, where her spiritual journey had next directed her feet.

The Scoffer slept that night on the back seat of his SUV, locked in the garage. He had returned late from yet another party in his honour, and his mildly groggy condition—he was a moderate drinker—wasted no time in sending him off to sleep. Opening the garage door for some fresh air the following morning, he heard a scrabbling in the top jamb. Before he could look up to investigate, a scaly creature dropped, landed on the balding middle patch of his head, its thin claws instantly trapped in the surrounding tufts of foliage. Bade's first thought was *Snake!* Next, *Scorpion!* He leapt out under imminent heart failure, uncertain how to deal with what he could not see, collided with the housemaid, who was just reporting for duty. She took to her heels, screaming for help against the intruder, before she realized who it was. The mystery squatter seized on the confusion to escape, thus finally identified for what it was—a lizard. The maid would later narrate "the scariest moment of my life" to Mrs. Badetona on her return from pilgrimage. Confronted with her report, Bade roared with delight and added it to the list of portents. His last contribution, a mere week earlier, had been the black cat he had found sitting on his car bonnet as he stepped out of the supermarket. He relished the rapidly changing registers on Jaiyesola's face, especially when he went into details over the one-sided confrontation. The cat refused to budge even after he had started his car and begun to inch forward. *My dear, that cat, I swear, kept staring at me through the windscreen as if to complain that she had been looking forward to the ride. I had to stop and engage the security guard to help shove it off, so I could drive off.*

Were all these little more than an occult buildup towards the *pièce de résistance* that was yet to come? That momentous day considerately awaited his wife's return from pilgrimage, so that news reached her within minutes of the occurrence. In Badetona's own words, *This one shook me to my binary heels!* While Jaiyesola rubbed her hands heavenwards on receiving the news, giving further thanks that she had indeed made that year's pilgrimage a dual-purpose voyage of devotion—thanksgiving and protection—the prince found himself compelled to admit that something appeared to have gone loose since his elevation. All the euphoria of advancement evaporated with the horror that unfolded at the bus stop along Ikorodu Road, just before the Maryland overpass. And he had been caught within that event only because he, recently moved from a humdrum desk to head a brand-new glamorous parastatal, chief executive director on the rare Level 17, etc., etc.—known nationwide as the super permanent secretary scale—had chosen to queue at that bus stop like any common worker, awaiting a ride to his housing estate. He could have phoned a taxi company or flagged down one of the ubiquitous *keke napep,* the Indian import tricycle taxi. He opted instead for the commuter. Badetona, one of the most live-and-let-live, self-adjusting humans one could hope to encounter in a field of reversals, felt tickled by the notion of himself, a prince and super-sec, doing a little slumming, mixing with local yet distanced commuters whom he normally viewed through the tinted windows of his air-conditioned, albeit battered, SUV. Never in his life could he have envisaged the consequence of that crackpot decision as he stood in line. For once, the hardened Scoffer was forced to revise his calculations on the law of probabilities.

Badetona followed a pragmatic mode of existence that left him very much attached to his ancient, creaky, but still serviceable SUV. A mere two days after his wife's return from Saudi—he lost that argument; her excess luggage bulged with outsized sachets of certified holy water from the River Jordan, plus other objects of veneration from the tourist arc of holy sites—his long-suffering vehicle broke down along Ikorodu Road just before the turnoff for Gbagada heading for Oworonshoki. It took the form of a multilayered, cracked china rattle that he had never heard before, as if a box of domestic discards was being sorted for a jumble sale. He sighed, irritated that this should happen on a day when he happened to be at the wheel himself, having granted his driver a three-day leave of absence to travel out to a village for the prelude ceremonies to a betrothal. His driver was taking a brand-new wife.

Bade manhandled the car into the slip road—fortunately, traffic was light. The loafing area boys emerged from nowhere, as usual, to lend a hand. His mind turned, by long habit, to predicting how his wife would read this new interruption in routine, and he smiled at the cleverness of a response that was already under formulation: *Well now, you've just returned from Jerusalem with a full bag of good-luck pouches, talismans, and reliquaries. You received predictions and prescriptions from the Senegalese marabout who scalped you and your Muslim friend in Saudi for nearly half your shopping budget. How come there was no prediction of the impending crack-up of my vehicle engine?* Definitely first round to him! And he was prepared for her retort: *Why should it take a marabout to repeat what I've been shouting all these years? Abandon that junk heap and get something befitting your position!* That was the moment he would deliver his coup de grâce. Before she could enjoy the vindicated smirk of a long-enduring wife, he would slam his hand on his thigh and silence her with his welcome surprise: *Quite right, dear—let's go. I was only awaiting your return to help me choose our new car. Ready?* Too bad the new status vehicle decided not to wait. Worse, what followed totally wiped out any carefully rehearsed banter, witty repartees and silly teases, all ingredients of a married life that did not lack for genuine bonding and affection. Bade truthfully regarded himself a lucky husband.

It did not take long for an itinerant mechanic to appear—this tribe seemed to know just when disaster struck, or perhaps they operated a roving network, an urbanized bush telegraph. As always, they beat the state's tow truck to the involuntary traffic obstruction. A quick inspection, and the expert confirmed what he had already sensed—the engine was "knocked," the affliction terminal. The private-enterprise, locally constructed tow truck was already in place even before the professional verdict was delivered. Bade emptied the car of briefcase and other contents, surrendered the car keys, crossed the road to the sleek bus stop, one of a series of implants whose sprouting had begun visibly to lift the body tone and morale of daily commuters. He took his place at the end of the queue, silently relishing his brief, voluntary demotion in social status.

His sigh exuded relief that this was the last week in his old office. He was in a relaxed, all-accommodating frame of mind when an event played out right in front of him, one that knocked out all mental rehearsals for a domestic playful interlude from the compulsive operations of his statistical mind. As he settled into position at the tail end of that long queue, a man came up with a flattish object under his armpit, muttered an "Excuse me," but simultaneously shoved him aside. He whipped off the brown paper wrapping and out flashed a machete. Badetona heard him utter a violent curse in some unfamiliar language, he heard a swish, and with that single stroke the man lopped off the head of the commuter next in line. The head fell against the reinforced plastic rain guard that curved halfway from the roof of the bus shelter. It bounced off the ground, while the trunk sprayed him as it fell with a red, thick, viscous fluid, just like an errant lawn sprinkler. Ignoring the pandemonium that ensued, the assailant fastidiously wiped the machete on the clothing of the prostrate trunk, calmly restored it to its improvised paper scabbard. A car drew up, again as if on a signal; the rear door flew open. In what some transfixed witnesses experienced as a coordinated slow and accelerated motion all at the same time, the vehicle swallowed the killer and zoomed off, weaving sleekly through the Ikorodu road traffic, heading east towards the town of that name.

A few moments for the prince to absorb what he had just witnessed and then, without further thought, he shook off his paralysis like the other commuters, took irrationally to his heels, and stopped only when he had rounded the first corner and felt safe from the immediate rampage of indiscriminate head cropping which all involuntary witnesses felt certain would logically follow. Such a blatant flash of lunacy did not seem destined to be a one-off act. Even those who had no idea what had happened did not wait to be enlightened. The screams carried their own unambiguous message—*Run!* They galvanized even the slow-witted into one concerted response—follow the trail of panic wherever it led, with a few variations to throw off the contaminating scent of blood. Badetona launched his limbs at full stretch, heading for nowhere, everywhere, simply as far as his reasonably athletic legs could take him; he was an irregular weekend jogger, and never was the state-sponsored jog-for-your-life campaign, and in accelerated tempo, more patriotically vindicated. He stopped only at the entry of the new supermarket just after Charley Boy's domain, stopped to look back for only the second time that morning. Still unsure of what he should do, he ran inside, vaulted the exit turnstile, and disappeared into a room whose half-open door was marked Staff Only. He inhaled, exhaled, and inhaled to some inner-dictated rhythm.

Safely ensconced in the safety of his home that evening, the event shared in all blood-soaked detail through a still shaky voice, wife and neighbours in attendance, the conclusion was inevitable, based on the unanswerable question *Why you? Ask yourself, why you? Of all the millions of people in Lagos, why you? Why did you have to be the one standing behind that victim, a total stranger? Normally you would be with your driver—how come you happened to be driving yourself today, of all days? Why did you decide to take a bus when you could afford a taxi? What brought you there at that very moment of his decapitation—you think it simply happened to happen?* It was plain reading. The untoward had become too frequent of recent. All voices counseled a visit to the healing ministries—any one would do, but the clamour was near uniformly for Apostle Davina. When Jaiyesola summoned the maid to recount to sympathizing visitors—for the tenth time at least—the lizard episode, all alternative or oppositional theories crumbled, the sequential logic was unanswerable. The garage lizard! It had landed on his princely head. A head had been cut off in front of him. Whose head did he think was primed to follow? No, no, no, did he have to be so literal? No one was suggesting it was a sign that he would also lose his head, but definitely someone was after his, Bade's, head, in some form or another. That was the message. If he failed to see that, to understand the generous warnings of Providence, it was pride, false pride, and what do they say goeth before a fall? Pride. And who was the proud one? Answer: the stiff-necked Scoffer.

If there had been an invasion of clan and long-forgotten family branches after his promotion, news of his "narrow escape" unleashed even more powerful waves of prayer counterattacks. The palace sent a delegation, headed by a *babalawo*. Long-forgotten relations who had recently surfaced to share in the bounty of service elevation returned in force, and they came with a supplementary canticle: *It happened because you failed to see the divine intervention in your life! Worse still, how do you know there isn't an even more glorious future ahead, one that, however, requires you to do this or that to consolidate present preferment? There are deadlines in these matters. You miss the deadline and everything is reversed—it's downward from then on. Only a few among the blessed few can pierce through the mystic veil and reveal all this to you.* If Badetona's nerves had been shattered by the event itself, instigating nightmares that terrified his wife, then moved to infect her to a degree that she even began to have them in her own right, the swarms of intercessors soon completed the rout. Could there possibly be something in what they preached? Reconsiderations of allied experiences that he had once instinctively waved off as comic incidents began to nibble at the edges of cause and effect or, worse, chain reaction.

And there was something else that even the wife did not know— the chickens were coming home to roost. Behind the calm, reassuring façade, Badetona was a much troubled man. Vague hints of storms ahead had accumulated lately, and these were not psychic storms. His pragmatic mind continued to string the seemingly mismatched pieces together—it all seemed extravagant, but he had begun to consider a grim possibility: the beheading, the time, the place, his presence, the victim—that none of these was an accident.

It mattered little from whichever direction it came, the prince admitted, he needed help. The saying among his people came to mind: *That the man is first to see the snake but the woman kills it—who cares, as long as the snake is killed!* So who was this man Davina anyway? What powers did he exert to hold so many in thrall? No disaster, no exceptional event, no routine happening, but he had predicted it in his end-of-year prophecy, an annual ritual that laid out all divinely premeditated events destined for fulfillment during the year ahead. Whatever was not fulfilled had some rational explanation—including fulfillment itself, but not quite in the literal way the uninitiated could understand.

Outside pressure could be shut out, ignored. When complemented by the silent protest and muffled sighs of a spouse across the breakfast, lunch, or dinner table, it became a burden. Each long-suffering sigh spoke daggers of rebuke—there were malignant, diabolical forces at work, it was evidently time for spiritual delivery. *I know you have nothing against psychiatrists, so why don't you look at it as that kind of therapy? Every day millions of your peers wake up across the world, look at their calendar to see when next they are due for a turn on the couch, even when they feel absolutely on top of the world. So take the plunge. Treat the visit as merely marking a watershed in your career—anything wrong with that?* It all fitted in neatly, a statistical punctuation mark on the wobbly spreadsheet. Finally the beleaguered man decided that he needed badly to be delivered from delivery. If that was guaranteed by a call on the devil in his lordly lair, maybe it was time he donned the cloak of veneration. He threw up his hands in surrender. *All right, dear, I shall go. The man intrigues me.*

PRINCE BADETONA MAY have been the wizard mathematician he was reputed to be, but Jaiyesola in certain regards vied with or complemented him in logic. Thus, when she followed him to the prophet's Oke Konran on the eventual day of consultation, it was not out of mistrust; no, it was because she wanted to cover him in her aura until the last possible moment, thus ensuring that the spiritual incense that emerged from her accompanied him all the way.

The rules were strict. Only the actual supplicant could climb the hill. So she chaperoned him to the base of the hill, her presence replenishing his deficiency from her abundance. Hopefully, this would last until he actually stood before the gate of the temple of Ekumenika, where, obviously, the overwhelming emanations from the holy man himself would take over, enwrap, and waft him into his presence, where he would again be topped up, like the fuel tank of a motorcar, for the return journey and for some days, weeks, and months afterwards. She redoubled her prayers as her eyes pursued him all the way up, even where a few scattered trees obscured her sight from time to time. She continued to wreathe him in this potency as palpably as she experienced the force of the choric "Alleluia, Blood of Jesus," a force that she knew was transmitted through upraised, quivering arms at those sessions of her prayer warriors when even the roof of the church seemed to be raised in ecstasy, albeit invisible to minds with depleted fuel tanks of faith. And hers was true partnership, so that wherever and however and in whatever one lacked, the other provided. Her husband, she did not doubt, was well primed for his meeting with the apostle, despite himself. No one could claim that he had defaulted in any way. She had followed him with eyes and spirit; her mind was at peace. He was playing his part, following instructions conscientiously up the steps to the temple of Ekumenika, the palace of piety perched atop the very peak of Oke Konran-Imoran. She turned back only when she had seen him execute the prescribed moves every step of the way—saw him stand beneath the neon-framed archway of the preacher's prophesite as, without turning round, he raised his arm in a wave that spelt a loving *Here we go, my dear.*

Halfway up Oke Konran-Imoran—though a few irreverent locals, spirited infidels of the prince's truthful cast of mind, soon renamed it Gethsemane—was a shoe depository, a cemented ledge. This was where the paved and pebbled steps began. From the base, where Jaiyesola parted from her husband, to that halfway stop, seekers simply picked and occasionally slithered their way up as best as they could, among pebbles and screed, garbage that sometimes featured both human and animal faeces. Quite a few eminent figures went to ingenious lengths to avoid recognition by both transient and resident scavengers; these would eventually qualify through sheer swell in numbers and resilience for a local government of their own. At the end of that hazardous lower half of the hill, away from the human soldier ants who prodded, turned over mounds, and bore their luck in sacks slung over shoulders, the chief executive director of a newly minted petroleum parastatal, rumoured to have been specially created to reward his past and ensure continuing "cooperation," arrived at the cemented ledge with a token enclosure of fencing wire. It had been created as a shoe depository, complete with disposable footgear for the finicky or simply tender of sole.

It was not unusual for a supplicant to find his or her consultation rewarded with a prescription that called for the partial consumption of such disposables after returning home. This required stuffing the used footgear into a gourd of palm wine or jar of millet beer, where it turned into an infusion—one spoonful three times a day as a general spiritual prophylactic, or a one-time liquid breakfast, downed in one gulp, to follow seven days and seven nights of fasting. Such gourmet variant was reserved as a permanent cure for severe body ailments or symptoms of malevolent spiritual forces. There were suggestions that this was a derivative from the superstitious awe in which the needle injection was once held by the former generation or two in the nation's then rudimentary Western medical practice. Those old-generation patients would arrive at their rural clinic, and later at modern teaching hospitals, not with a clear expression of where the health problem lay but with a mind set on their favourite curative—an injection. Pills or liquid agents were mere placebos or procrastinations—injection was the key, no matter the ailment. Badetona could recall the dismissive pronouncements of some of his elderly relations, on both sides of the family—*Oh, that doctor, he's useless, he doesn't give injections.* And they followed up by transferring their problems elsewhere. Or simply abandoned the modern clinic altogether, took their health issues to the local "dispenser." That could be a moonlighting nurse, a midwife, or the nearest patent medicine store owner with an eye-catching signboard, as long as such alternatives were equipped with an obliging needle and coloured fluid. Apostle Davina's injection—for high-maintenance cases mostly—was infusion from the plastic jerky, but only when it had absorbed spiritual healing potency from treading the pebbly twenty-one steps uphill. Many were those who went home crestfallen because the prophet had denied them the plastic prescription. The very thought brought the CED close to retching—not all the riches of the world would make him so much as sip the stuff. Any plastic-obsessed relation, his dear wife included, was free to drink it on his behalf, not he! Submit to the blatant emotional blackmail, yes, but further than that, the prince drew the line.

With no other than that modest demurral, the fugitive shook his head clear and brought himself back to his duties. He took off his shoes, his face twisted anew into a defiant grimace as he substituted a pair of disposables for them, as if that very motion yet again dared the apostle to prescribe any plastic discard or liquefied needle therapy. Then he changed his mind altogether. If he did not arrive wearing the disposables, there would be none to prescribe by the apostle. So he proceeded barefoot. When he emerged, Jaiyesola's keen eyes were swift to see her husband's unshod feet—it completed her sense of triumph; this was humility over and beyond the call of spiritual duty! It was certain to augment the store of redemption coupons she had accumulated on his behalf. The battle was three-quarters won.

She accompanied every remaining step with silent intoning of hymns of praise—this bonus self-abasement could not fail to contribute to the routing of those envious ill-wishers who prayed daily for her husband's downfall. After a further fourth or fifth step, the pilgrim himself, unaware of his wife's inner upliftment, began to lament his decision, discovering that the soles of his feet had become quite tender over the years from normal shoe addiction. It was too late to return for those protective aids—just in time he recalled that he was not permitted to return or look back. He gave silent thanks for not rewarding his wife with a day of wasted labour and lamentation after such a relentless campaign. Having come so far, he would never have forgiven himself. He completed the remaining sixteen steps up the pebbled slope, glossed by myriad feet in the quest for a cure, fulfillment, search for or celebration of a preferment, a simple remedy for any of the catalogue of human woes, cravings, and inadequacies. Or threats.

And the wife could now relax. She had been a little, just a little, concerned that he might turn back to wave, but no, he did not look back, did not risk being turned into a pillar of salt. Time was when, yes, the Scoffer would have looked back deliberately, just to prove to her that no force on earth or heaven could turn him into a pillar of anything, least of all salt. It brought a glow to her face that even in that final, no-looking-back moment of temperamental temptation, Bade stuck to the bargain and resisted the urge. It gladdened her heart, generated a renewed wave of affection. She waved, left her arm raised for the duration of a brief prayer as the gate was thrown open and the interior courtyard swallowed him. Her face was wreathed in contentment. She lingered for a few more moments in silent prayer, then turned reluctantly away from Oke Konran-Imoran.

Barefooted and only slightly winded, the prince had completed the ascent, arrived at his destination. Perched on the tip of Oke Konran-Imoran, the eyrie looked from the outside totally unimpressive. His mood was resigned, yet also expectant. For a few moments he merely stood and stared at the ponderous brass-studded gate, topped by an unlit neon archway inscribed

Welcome to the One and Only True Prophesite
EKUMENIKA HEALING MINISTRY
Oke Konran-Imoran
(Nothing on Our Living Earth Is Beyond Faith)

He indulged himself with a huge breath intake, expelled it slowly, braced his shoulders, seized the heavy brass ring, and slammed it against the entry. Motions from within nearly instantly produced two beefy security guards, girded in what seemed to be thick black protective armour. Their appearance seemed guaranteed to intimidate any humanity below mercenaries of Africa's civil wars. He was obviously expected. They took no more than a perfunctory glance up and down the full length of him, then beyond him, as if to ensure that he had not been escorted on the ascent by a hidden force of invasion, waiting only for the gates to open to crash past and overwhelm the apostle's sanctuary. Satisfied, they guided him across a well-manicured lawn, a geometric composition that instantly sent his mind flashing to where he had last seen such a landscaped garden in the country with that very design, only miniaturized here—yes, of course, Jos Plateau, an ancient British colonial residence and clubhouse named Hilltop Mansion. His ancient buddy Kighare Menka, one of a close foursome, last recorded cutting up bodies in Jos, had once wined and dined him in its staid dining room and oak-paneled lounge, so many forgotten years ago. Grimly he wondered what that surgeon would have made of the clean decapitation whose lingering effects had brought him to Oke Konran-Imoran, seeking help from the man named Papa Davina.

Before he had time to dredge up episodes in the eccentric career of their madcap foursome, Badetona found himself ushered into a special audience chamber reserved for just such as he, the rare ones whose life trajectory had raised the limits of the possible, spread the carpet of hope to accommodate even the most callused and often undeserving feet. On the right side of the entrance he saw a small altar-table. He placed his stuffed envelope on the altar, muttering inaudibly but with evident resentment.

News spread from tongue to tongue of those who had been admitted, however briefly, into the Prescience—a different order from the Inviolate Presence. Truly awestruck, they spoke of what they had seen or imagined, what transformation they had witnessed or conjured up in their minds, what profound revelations had emerged from divine discourse and the wisdom of the ancients, transmitted in modern modes and ingenious formulations. The word infiltrated all and sundry, but only the few were chosen for the ascent. The testifying parades at Davina's all-comer worship stadia nationwide were already more than follower-generative; when added to marvels that were reported by those who had been privileged to step within the peak of Ekumenika itself, followership could be accounted phenomenal. It became a gold rush that left behind multitudes. Badetona began to understand why. He found himself surrounded by a splendour that snapped his mind straight back to his primary-school introduction to the oriental fables of the Arabian Nights and the wonders of Aladdin and his magic lamp. An uncomfortable feeling, however, also crept up his leg, leaving him cold between his shoulder blades. He felt there were hidden eyes watching his reaction.

No sooner sensed than a man entered the room so quietly that he was nearly seated before the Scoffer was aware of his presence. A well-oiled baldness on a blunt cone, such as could be glimpsed in the centre of his open-top turban, was amply compensated for by a flowing beard that terminated in greased curls. In between was no more than a two-centimetre width of visible flesh. The eyes were protected behind a large pair of reflective sunglasses. The rest of the face was wreathed in camouflage that could have belonged to any of the cultures of sand dunes or simply that of a Muslim itinerant preacher. His main frame, however, was mannequin-sharp in a three-piece suit of grey-striped black but with an embroidered waistcoat that glittered with gemstones. He carried a gold-topped walking stick that seemed to have been tailored with his suit, and its orb carried clear football serrations.

"Please sit down, Prince. I hope the climb was not too arduous. You have come on the day of Arjunava, an Indian god, not much known even in his own land. Here we honour all religions. We join hearts in spiritual embrace on the holy days of others. Our mission is to celebrate the ecumenical spirit."

Badetona made what he considered the right noises, still overwhelmed by the contrast of this chamber with the squalour through which he had just struggled up the hill called Oke Konran-Imoran. His wife had not prepared him for anything remotely close. All he knew, like tens of thousands, was of the open-air venue adjoining the foot of the hill, the heaving, unassuming concourse of ecumenism that catered for everything that walked on two legs and sometimes four, including chickens and goats that wandered in from the neighbourhood.

The prince took the seat to which he was waved by his gracious host. The latter settled in the opposite chair, an imitation Roman consul chair, a design that Bade felt he recognized from Cecil DeMille's cinema annunciation of *The Ten Commandments*—or was it *The Gladiator*? Or *The Rise and Fall of the Roman Empire*? No matter, one of those lavish cinema renditions of the ancient scriptural or history classics.

"Needless to say"—the man spoke quietly, his voice assuming a near-spectral timbre, obviously cultivated through a long career of trial and error, testing and practicing, but never discarding its basic flavour of an American accent—"the purpose of your visit has been revealed to me. But I would like you to say it in your own words. Be as detailed as you wish. My mission is to listen, pray, and counsel.

Also to transmit any message, if any, now or later, from our Perfect Listener, for whom I am a mere intermediary."

Badetona needed no further urging. He was not one for wasting time on incidentals. Facts. Figures. Moreover, the startling contrasts in the day's itinerary had begun to fray his nerves. He was already regretting the visit, reflecting on how most of those hours could have been deployed far more usefully in organizing his new office. Crashing lizards and computers, even cars, he would leave to his wife if he succeeded in surviving the session. However, Ikorodu bus stop had shaken him to the core of his skeptical being. The assault had even succeeded in appropriating the national headlines for three days before melting into the staple pottage of a nation's daily feed. He made a point of putting the apostle on notice—internally of course. The herculean effort that had been exerted by his wife to bring him to that point of an unwanted encounter had better be worth his while, though in what way, he had no idea.

He plunged into his narrative, crisply, essential details extracted in advance. Papa Divina listened intently, nodding occasionally like one who knew it all already. Ikorodu had admittedly pushed Badetona's absorption quotient to the limit, but nothing, absolutely nothing in the entire gamut of his projections had led him to anticipate anything close to the effect his news had on the apostle, the dapper Afro-Asian Saville Row–attired figure who confronted him, both hands laid on the orb of his walking stick. Bade was startled. He could not believe what his hearing so clearly reported. Unfortunately, there was no way of affirmation by facial expression of the speaker, since his head was all swathed in the day's religious attire. Despite that, however, the prince was ready to swear on his statistical honour that behind the neutralizing turban and sunglasses, the voice exuded . . . rapture. A quiescent but most emphatic dissemination of rapture. Badetona felt a chill down his spine. He felt that the apostle's face became surreally transfigured; perhaps it was on account of his mummified head, which rotated slowly, just like an owl interrogating a night rustle. Then the slow drawl, and a voice that clearly said, "That was indeed a sign. A heaven-sent sign. You could not have asked for a more auspicious sign from beyond. I almost envy you, Prince Badetona."

Bade blinked, swallowed, shook his head free of the improbability of any lingering fumes from the rounds of the weeklong celebrations. It was, in any case, morning, and even the previous day he had had nothing beyond a glass of tepid white wine with his dinner. He stared into the apostle's glasses, leant forward to ensure that his pronouncement was clear, incapable of being misunderstood.

"I don't think you heard me, Papa Davina. I said I witnessed, right before me, a man decapitate another, at Ikorodu bus stop, just before Maryland junction."

But the man's comportment remained unchanged, and he returned Bade's boring eyes with the utmost calm. The words he had just uttered rang clear, with no possibility of distortion in that near-soundless chamber. Badetona shook his head and spoke, picking his words even more distinctly, ensuring that his own response in turn was not misheard.

"Apostle Davina, sir, I still do not believe that you quite understood what I have just narrated. I said, I stood at a bus stop. A man squeezed himself between me and the commuter in front of me— pushed me aside, more accurately. He whipped out a machete and before my very eyes slashed off the head of this stranger. It has nearly lost me my mind."

Davina sat back in his chair, nodded gently. "Yes, I heard you. A good augury, I repeat. A divine gift to you from the one and only, the Perfect Listener. You are indeed a man most blessed."

A pause followed, during which Apostle Davina threw back his head, eyes shut—Badetona could see that much through the reflective glasses—as if communing with some absent presence. Both retained their postures for what seemed minutes, then Davina snapped himself back to life, stood up, and gestured.

"Come with me, Mr. Badetona. I have something to show you. It is nothing you have not seen before now. Indeed, you came through it all in your ascent—yes, remember that—your *ascent*. From now on everything is on the rise. But I would like you to view the present with a completely new insight. You see, dear Seeker, it all has to do with one's perspective . . ."

Less than two minutes afterwards, a middle-aged man, eyes still distended in the effort to ward off demonic presences, was seen to crash through the gates of Ekumenika and commence a race down the steps he had earlier climbed so fastidiously. As he had passed through the doors to the main building, the same as his point of entry, his eye caught the envelope he had deposited at the offertory on arrival. Scooping it up, he fled Ekumenika. On arrival home, he threw down the envelope, poured himself a drink. Downing it, he announced to the emptiness:

"Fulfilled my part of the bargain. Brought back the consultation fee. There's enough in there to hire a brace of the finest lawyers in the nation and/or to corrupt the entire judiciary. Sooner those than that ghoul of Ekumenika!"

When the detective squad came for him the following morning, they found him dressed in his finest three-piece suit, resigned and waiting.

5.

Villa Potencia

Duyole Pitan-Payne, engineer and business entrepreneur, a compulsive glutton for "inside stuffing," would have wished that his assignation at Villa Potencia had been set for the previous day. That, of course, was out of the question. As it was, the villa had regained its normal placidity as he was effusively received at the first security checkpoint by a sprightly young ministerial aide who introduced himself as Shekere Garuba, "your equivalent at the presidency." A most inauspicious beginning, and Pitan instinctively dubbed him Uriah Heep, one of his perversely favourite Dickensian characters. Garuba was a stagestruck overgrown juvenile who had once described the mass funeral of slaughtered farmers by rampaging herdsmen of his Fulani clan as a media show orchestrated by the governor of that bereaved state. He mocked the Ebola epidemic as a creative opportunity for Nollywood video sitcoms, even as his fellow aide attempted to upstage him, wondering why widows, widowers, and orphans did not simply lick their wounds and adopt appeasing attitudes towards their violators for the privilege of staying alive. The fault was all theirs, the duo proclaimed. Their intransigence was responsible for any breach in their happy state, provoking renewed assaults on the survivors and the burgeoning culture of mass infanticide.

The political aide—official title SPECIAL ADVISER ON ALTERNATIVE ENERGY, as luridly emblazoned on his calling card—escorted

Pitan-Payne through patrolling peacocks whose abrupt, raucous cries belied their floral preening. He was swept through a corridor of archways designed to pay lip service to the reality of two dueling faiths professed by a religion-saturated nation. Pitan was a churchgoer by habit and imprecise conviction, but he bristled, wishing government should simply mind its real business and leave religions alone. Still, his engineering eyes instinctively evaluated the security turnstiles, electronic scanning frames, and other strategically positioned sentinels of the prelude rites of audience, including state-of-the-art camouflaged cameras. He mildly wondered who was at the monitoring end. More vetting security? Or Sir Goddie in person, also known as the Presence, assessing each approaching visitor ahead of their encounter? The peacock cries pursued him into the waiting room, short, sharp shrieks that grated on his preferences in the musical mode, more like the abbreviated bray of donkeys in heat. He marveled—not for the first time—how Nature could have been so cynical as to unleash on humanity such disparate creations as donkey and peacock in any associative vocal register, surprised that no one appeared to have considered inventing a modulator. Hung around the peacocks' necks—of course it would have to be decorative or the vain creatures would reject it—it would at least muffle the horrendous emissions from their vocal cords. Hmm, something to think about.

The special adviser spoke ceaselessly, but lost in thought of how else he might improve the approach to the main prime ministerial block if anyone were sufficiently reckless as to let him loose on the sprawling real estate, Pitan-Payne did not even have to make an effort to close his ears to the effusive welcome, the congratulations on his UN appointment, beaming enquiries about the health of his wife, children, and the rest of his extended family. His acknowledgements emerged from what he referred to as the auto-dispenser, all the way across the yard, through the halls and vast spaces of emptiness, caucuses, and conspiracies. Somewhere along the way, a white-overalled figure in a half-mask aimed the thermometer gun at his forehead, then pointed him towards the sink, where the regulation hand sanitizer invited. He readily complied. Another door slid open automatically at their approach; Mr. Garuba stood aside to let him enter, invited him to take his choice of seats. Only then did Pitan-Payne absorb his first intelligible communication from the effusive adviser. The latter bent low, winked as if in affirmation of a secret pact between them, and said, "It won't be long. The People's Steward will see you soon."

Pitan-Payne knew about him—the son of a local village head, he enjoyed the reputation of garnering privileges beyond his dues and was known to be under special grooming for greater things. One of a brood of twenty-three children, he had simply been handed over to Sir Goddie by his father during a political rally—*This is the smart one I told you about. Do what you like with him, I dash you.* The youth was entrusted with ensuring that the prime ministerial kola nut bowl was steadily replenished with that stimulant from a special plantation not far from Abuja. Trust the uncharitable national rumour mill—having tried and failed to find in his background any training in or knowledge of energy matters, the mill churned out a claim that this in effect was the real field of competence for his advisory portfolio—to ensure that the desk knickknack bowl of the People's Steward was filled with an adequate supply of that source of energy, the kola nut.

Whatever obvious deficiencies he was universally charged with, however, the lack of an instinct for mood assessment, specifically of his master, was not among them. Garuba had become adept at comput-ing the "right moment to bring this up, sir, if I may presume," learnt to assess Sir Goddie's mercurial moods with near-pinpoint accuracy. That talent had now earned him a delicate mission from his colleagues and superiors, prompted by the Pitan-Payne visitation. As if on cue, a languid, bored figure entered, who was introduced to the engineer as the chief of staff. The sole interest of the new entrant seemed to be to give him a leisurely once-over. He shimmered into the room clutching a pile of files, nodded what could be read as acknowledgement of his existence, leant against a wall, then stood watching, without a word. The normally sharp-eyed Pitan-Payne totally missed out on a glance between the chief of staff and the fidgety adviser: there was a slot, and that slot was now, just before the invasion of a new set of party bigwigs. As if the adviser could hardly wait for his guest to be seated, he fussed over him for a few token seconds, stammered his intent to inform the Presence of the presence of the expected, promised to be back very soon, and dashed out of the room. That silent message acted upon, the languid officer turned, melted through the open door, and vanished. The engineer found himself alone, enveloped by a silence that was sibilant with power, whispers, and intrigues.

Outside, the special adviser, remarkably nimble in motion despite the traditional leather flip-flops that occasionally lunged out from under his long kaftan, traversed the lengthy corridor, reached the massive, padded double doors of the prime ministerial office at the double, and applied invisible brakes to his propulsion. He hesitated, knuckle poised for a soft tap, and then, somewhat strangely, his demeanour changed. He had just recalled his recently published chart buster in the shape of the monograph *The Making of a People's Steward*. The in-house launching of that learned paper—departmental heads, ministers, party stalwarts, and a brace of diplomatic clerical staff—had earned him the unspoken right to ferret out the prime minister wherever he was, even if on the toilet seat—from which location the Steward had in any case answered a dozen or so questions to validate the adviser's narrative in the compilation of *The Making*. A follow-up—*Behind the Enigma*—was promised in a matter of months. Recollecting that he was now the albeit ungazetted house chronicler, another twenty-five percent hesitation melted away. Finally he recalled that today was today, not yesterday, when they had all moved gingerly about their duties, praying not to be summoned into the Presence even for the most routine chores. Yesterday was when it had taken only the bravest of the brave to cross the Steward in any manner of thought, how much more speech. The day had started out hectic but ended on a note of total mastery of a shaken political field. A new identity handle, formerly stolen, had been effectively deactivated by a robust substitution, now under trial throughout the villa. The chief of staff was right to nod the adviser on his way. The question must be posed, and the answers conveyed to his bewildered and resentful colleagues. What his superiors, more seasoned, more battle-scarred, did not dare, he would do. His earlier poised diffident tap was transformed into a confident rap.

"Who is it!" bellowed a voice that could only belong to the Presence.

"*Ranka dede,*" the Equivalent responded, and entered without further protocol. He trotted confidently towards the mammoth desk, shaped oval. A former incumbent, having heard of the world-famous

Oval Office, had ordered all possible furniture and interior decor designed to conform as closely as possible to the oviform motif.

Garuba executed a practiced dive downwards to rest on one knee, head inclined, right fist raised but its elbow cupped in the left palm in the traditional deferential salute of his part of the world, and repeated the terms of his people's traditional homage: "*Ranka dede.* The man is here, Your Stewardship."

"Go and keep him busy. We are still on emergency watch, I hope you know that. There is quite some mopping up to do."

"Your Stewardship, if I may . . ."

"What?"

"This is a matter for immediate attention, PS, sir. It concerns national security."

Sir Goddie perked up, slowly closed the file before him, and sat back in his chair. "I'm listening."

"It concerns the very man you wish to see."

TWO HOURS LATER, still awaiting his summons, Duyole Pitan-Payne felt his patience approach the teeth-grinding phase of all who wait and hope. Belatedly, he thought—this audience was still a squeeze—that the prime ministerial primaries were just five days away and that meant the nation was beginning to shut down. Now he remembered dismissing a glimpse of *The Inquest*'s tubby proprietor, Chief Ubenzy Oromotaya, the acknowledged brain behind the YoY awards, leading a flock of *agbada, babanriga,* turbans, red chieftaincy caps, and flaring female head-wraps—the troops were gathering. Consultations could still stretch into the night—more positioning for party slots in governance after elections that were already a foregone conclusion. The visitor began to feel contrite about his tendency to liberally bestow names from the fictional world—plus original concoctions—on business, social, and even brief acquaintances. He conceded a mild feeling of guilt—not much, admittedly. Still, he chided himself for having deflected a rising umbrage from the real cause, venting his spleen on every lawfully engaged occupant of the governance hub, from the hapless adviser to the peacocks' measured, proprietorial strut and their incongruous accompaniment of strangulated shrieks. The real Uriah Heep was none of these—the place itself was a heaving Uriah heap of oozing unctuousness. It was induced by the very nature of power. Silently he apologized to donkeys on heat. And to the unknown architect of the hypocritical propaganda designs of a cozy cohabitation between two religions which, a mere kilometre or two from that very spot, held each other by the throat to be piously squeezed or slit at little or no provocation. His problem, he decided, was a minor and personal one, and it only required a bit of practice—learning to wrap his tongue around the prime ministerial choice of a mode of address, a preparatory schooling into which his equivalent, the special adviser on alternative energy, had wasted no time in inducting him, quite unnecessarily, as he had received him at the very first, outer security gate.

"Remember to address him as Your Excellency the People's Steward. With or without Your Excellency. Or simply PS, with or without the 'sir.' It's not yet official, but it's already in limited use in the presidency, since last night. You're privileged—today is the first full day of the changeover. When he hears it from you, an outsider, you'll see, he'll be eating out of your hand."

Everything came together thereafter—the culmination of months of covert mobilization of manpower and material resources, all leading up to the coming dual contests. The image-building had begun. Even so, of all the choices! Duyole indulged himself in a mild grimace. *The People's Steward!* What would he not have given to obtain even a tiny snatch of the saga that had preceded its adoption, culminating in the frenzied sessions of the previous day! Opting not to strain his mind with speculations, however, he did not take long to doze off, his snores emerging in instant accompaniment despite his patronage of the latest promotion of antisnore aids that appeared to monopolize his mail cookies. It was the one bane of his existence, the engineer had long brought himself to admit—a career of stentorian emissions, sometimes even during a theatre performance, including operas, to which he equally admitted a modest addiction. The boom from his forty winks reached the receptionist's ears just on the other side of the wall. He woke to the clicks of her high heels.

She looked shocked. "Would you like the day's newspapers?"

"No, thanks. Covered them while waiting for my flight." And then it occurred to him to check his probable waiting time. "Would this be one of the, er . . . prime minister's . . ."

Smiling, the woman also corrected him. "Steward. People's Steward. It's supposed to be in-house for now, but it would please him no end to have his guests subscribe to the new protocols."

"I am not a party member," he reminded her.

"All the better. It makes it even more exciting for Sir Goddie. It's in the trial stage—you know. Today's callers are all our guinea pigs, so to speak."

"Young Garuba already inducted me—I don't mind. So—His Excellency the People's Steward, right? Do I address him as Your Stewardship? No, don't bother, let me work that out myself. I was about to ask, is this going to be another full day? Coming in, I thought I recognized a few bigwigs ahead of me."

She hung her head. "It's always difficult to tell. You're lucky your appointment was not yesterday—I wouldn't have encouraged you to wait, quite frankly. Today is simmer-down, and I know he does wish to see you. Very much so. It's just the . . . well, you know . . . party matters. And when you think one crisis has been solved . . ." She threw up her hands.

Duyole sighed. "Wish I'd known that."

"With party primaries raging all over the country? Even here, it's been more a war office. But he insisted we must bring you over today—he said you have a reputation for moving fast and suddenly, and may be off before we know it. Today—well, just the final touches to the manifesto—that's the main agenda. The nation is in for some pleasant surprises."

Duyole did his best to look interested. "I'm on tenterhooks, but I won't encourage you to spill state secrets. So now the question is, just how does that affect my engagement? Do I still expect to return to Lagos today, or shall I book a hotel room while waiting? I've been here over two hours already."

The woman bristled. "His Excellency the People's Steward *will* see you. It was an appointment he made himself. He knows you're here. I have already sent him an administrative nudge."

"What is that?" His innocent curiosity appeared to have a mellowing effect. She made an effort to recover her smile.

"That's our trade secret. Try and be patient, I know he will see you. Are you sure you wouldn't like a soft drink? We could also do tea or coffee."

Pitan-Payne shook his head. "No thanks. Don't worry, I had a feeling it might be a long wait. Yesterday's marathon meeting is all over today's papers, but as usual no hint of what it was all about."

She sighed, the recollection appearing to disarm her even more. "Yes, yesterday was crisis day, round the clock, but it's all sorted out. I'll check the list from time to time and let you know how it's going." She pointed to the coffee table. "There are some recent villa publications in that pile. Not yet officially released. In fact, that top one is mint-fresh, straight from the villa's press. You're having a preview, free of charge, Mr. Pitan-Payne. You can't complain we are not treating you royally."

"Thanks, I shall explore the privilege."

Off she went, disappeared into her office, and that was the last he saw of her for the rest of the day. They all seemed to take turns at appearing and disappearing, including a cleaner who appeared with a fancy feather duster, flicked off nonexistent motes around the room, grinned at him, and then melted away. He was beginning to feel like Alice in Wonderland.

He shrugged. It was a commitment, and he would outwait every delay. No less than his wife, Bisoye, could have extracted the concession from him—and then not even on her own. There was much that puzzled him about the government's sudden interest in, indeed adoption of, an enthusiastic proprietary posture towards his United Nations appointment. He was sufficiently immodest to know that he had earned it on merit; he was more than qualified to be offered a place among the UN elite family of specialists, as a consultant to its Energy Commission. The blessing of the government was totally unexpected, suspect, but not objectionable. Sir Godfrey O. Danfere—known variously as the Presence, Sir Goddie, the Chief, Leader, Mentor, Godfather (sometimes Godfadda), and now Steward—had contributed a late, superfluous, but nonetheless determined boost. The marching orders were delivered directly from the horse's mouth to the head of the Nigerian mission to the UN, the Chief himself thundering down his mobile:

"I don't want to hear of any last-minute hitch, especially one created by those half-arsed so-called sister nations who still don't know their bums from their brains. They can't even balance their budget, yet they insist on an equal vote at the General Assembly. Or quota in UN positions. Some of them still vying with us for Africa's slot on the Security Council. Put them in their place, do I make myself clear?"

"Don't worry yourself, Your Excellency." The momentous day of the official name change was then still months away.

"Kick arse or stuff arse, whichever or both, you got it?"

"The brown envelopes are already stuffed for distribution."

There followed a sharp breath intake. His Excellency Sir Goddie was a frugal man, and his emissary's instant acquiescence had sounded a little too enthusiastic for his liking. "Don't overdo things. More kick than stuff. Many of them don't deserve a cent."

"You may rely on this office, Your Excellency. We constantly update the sliding rule. And of course we make their secretaries sign receipts."

He was rewarded with a familiar sigh of relief. Sir Goddie had indeed approved—quite legitimately—a fair-sized portion of the nation's "diplomatic offensive" budget, but he hated to see it frittered away, even mildly depleted, since its primal dedication belonged to the principal's personal revolving imprest for foreign trips. It was crucial that the appointment was not derailed at the last moment, through either rival lobbies or mean political intrigues within the UN's tortuous bureaucracy. Member states were notorious for throwing a spanner in the works at the last moment, simply for lack of anything substantial to report to their home governments, and sometimes simply from boredom, a bit of peevish gamesmanship just to delay the inevitable. In Pitan-Payne's case, his government's intervention was merely—to borrow a spicy turn of phrase from the demilord of the villa himself— pissing in the river under a heavy rainfall. In this respect, a blissfully unaware Pitan-Payne did benefit from the stout backing of the Steward's foreign advisers. They remained averse to missing out on what in diplomatic parlance is known as "opportunity splurge."

In between bouts of dozing, flicking idly through the coffee-table journals, taking calls from his wife, Bisoye, who needed to ensure that he had not quit his post in any sudden fit of pique and reassure him that there was twenty-four-hour room service at his provisionally secured hotel with a guarantee of his favourite cow-leg pepper soup no matter how late, Duyole did his best to while away impatience.

He was in the midst of his dozing intermissions when the chief of staff reentered. Beyond looking him over once again, making no pretence at disguising his mission of inspection, he offered nothing in the way of greeting, recognition, or even acknowledgement of a visitor in waiting. He made a show of looking round, however perfunctorily, as if he expected to find the reception room empty, or host to a different occupant. He vanished just as noiselessly.

The intrusion, whatever purpose it was meant to serve, merely renewed Duyole's sense of resentment. He resented being stuck in distant Abuja, waiting for a never-never summons, when he would rather be back in Badagry organizing his own grandfather of all sendoff parties, navigating cooking pots, beer barrels, flying corks, lamb on the spit, maybe even fresh venison from the game market . . . Duyole Pitan-Payne's eyes lit up, his tonsils dilated. The engineer took extra care to ensure that the whole world knew the family motto: "The love of food is the beginning of wisdom." The *Otunba,* Pitan-Payne Elder, countered that the family history had no record of any such wisdom, but his son merely responded that he read it in his genes, which perhaps leapfrogged the patriarch's generation. In any case, would the old man please remember that Duyole's claims were restricted to his own narrow brood, not the Elder's family, and if he contradicted him once more, he would secede and form his own dynasty.

Originally designated the "Bow Out Blowout Rout," the invitation card format was yet undergoing revisions that would continue, as always, till the very final tantrums of the long-suffering printer. Even in Villa Potencia, a coffee-table monograph on the art of the Nok had provoked thoughts of an adjustment that would designate the two-faced Esu, the Yoruba god of chance, as special guest of honour. After all, it was chance, nothing but chance, that had led to his adoption of a logo that in turn had brought a Greek art enthusiast into his factory, a journey that resulted so fortuitously in his now imminent journey to the United Nations. Not a bad idea, and he began to reach for his mobile. No. Wrong step. He discarded the notion. Much as he would enjoy riling up both Christian and Muslim bigots, he was fearful it would also choke up a few throats—nobody wanted that! What was the point of dazzling his guests with his inventive culinary deftness, then putting a crimp on their gastronomic gusto? He might as well feed them dry *garri* and send them home! The company logo would take its usual place on the card. Nothing would be permitted to mar an event that was intended to fête, not just his joining a club of international scientific thinkers but, more crucially, his definitive severance from government consulting. *Won't be back for five whole years—try and remember that! Not for nothing was Pitan attached to the colonial name I bear. Pitan—you know the meaning? Legend! So let the blowout be one for transmission down generations. Never asked for this, not sure if it's merited, but undeserving does not mean underserving—that's another family motto, of course—so let's make it one for the* Guinness Book of Records. For the self-declared all-rounder, his hands-on party ethic was that of a creative general factotum, indefatigable. He applied it as meticulously to electronic designing as he did to the provisioning and micro-management even of a small-chops stop-by catering for a minor office reception.

"Mr. Engineer Duyole!" Bisoye once exploded. "I can do my own catering."

"No question, no question. But catering is not the same as curating. I am merely helping out with the curating."

"It is my private get-together. It does not need curating."

"Wrong there, girl, wrong. I won't let your guests think badly of your husband."

"Yes. Glad you remember that—*my* guests. Not yours. For my former classmates! A small get-together. Go curate for that four-headed mascot of yours, the one you think is a gallery all by itself!"

"Isn't it? It's responsible for the family business."

"But not for my private party!"

"Mascot. Good-luck charm. Business logo. Brand of the Land—come on, girl, that's already four art galleries in one."

"Lucky for you I didn't hear my private get-together on that list."

"It brought me you. One brought-together deserves—"

"That line won't work. This is a girls-together only."

"Okay, okay. Offer not appreciated, offer withdrawn. If you need anything . . ."

"I don't. Take off. And you're not invited."

"What? Can't look in just to say hallo?"

"No!"

"Oh, all right. I'll ask Scoffer. If he's free and willing."

"Yes, he is. I didn't even have to check, because Jaiyesola is with us. He's taking you out—I've booked a table for the two of you. It's a newly opened place, so you can tell me all about it afterwards."

"Oh, you should have told me. Who wants to stay around you old hags anyway? Where's this place?"

She flounced off. "I'll get the name and address. Don't move."

A miracle of heroic sufferance, Bisoye could not wait to package him off to the United Nations. First there would be fewer opportunities for his labour-intensive social binges. Next it did not take her long to acknowledge—and fervently appreciate—that New York was a safer environment for the temperament of her partner—fewer chances of getting into squawks, becoming entangled in political and other incomprehensible intrigues, and without him being remotely aware of it. That was what scared her the most. As they sat together in their living room watching the UN delegate read out news of the unique appointment to cameras in the Foreign Affairs Briefing Room of Villa Potencia, his wife committed the fatal error of asking him how it felt. Duyole did not disappoint.

"I have that strange feeling of . . . I don't quite know how to describe it. It's like a gentle, intoxicating rush, like imagining being in the middle of organizing a party for all of the United Nations." Bisoye gave a heartrending sigh and kicked herself.

The wife knew when to leave him alone with his organizing mind in permanent upheaval. She could tell it was already at work sorting out the implications of their relocation. She was equally adept at choosing the right moment to insert the fly in the ointment.

"I hope you know that you'll have to drop in on Mr. Prime Minister."

His response was instinctive. "What for?"

"Form, dear, just form."

"I don't see why. He had nothing to do with this."

"I said form. For form's sake. Oh, and also to reduce one's natural quota of enemies. We still have a few weeks before we leave—at least I do—and we are returning home sooner or later."

"Who tells you he'll still be in office when we get back? Even ignoring rumours of a fallout between him and the president."

"Duyo, they never leave. They merely substitute themselves."

"Well, this consultant has left. Completed his assignment twenty-one months ahead of time, and that was nearly two years ago. Got to the bottom of the mess and left him a sizzling folder. He never asked to see me. Never a word of acknowledgement. So what business do I now have with him?"

Bisoye threw up her hands. "Form, Duyo. Or protocol, if you prefer. The way these things are done. I never said it was anything else. You did your job . . ."

"I haven't even received the rest of my payment!"

"Well, suppose that's why he wants to see you? Someone may have reminded him that you were leaving the country soon and that the government still owed you. Maybe he's not to blame."

"Someone is."

"No one is asking you to visit that someone, and you don't know who it is. Look at it this way—I mean, you yourself showed me that report. Wage-earners who haven't received their salaries in ten months. It's the same system. Just think what's happening to them and their dependents. How are they coping?"

She was rewarded with a grunt. The engineer sensed that the argument was slipping away from him. "Serves me bloody right anyway. I should have stuck to my earlier policy. No dealing with any government."

"Or cash before delivery. Except that the man simply hates parting with money in any case. Before or after makes no difference."

"Heads you lose, tails he wins. Maybe I should send Pop after him. They're both Rosicrucians, after all. That should embarrass him into paying up."

Bisoye stopped. "Now why hadn't we thought of that? Shall I ask him?"

"No way! That is what is known as an expensive joke. Don't even think of it. To borrow his favourite line, I'll go quietly."

At the beginning—yes, that much he could assert—a policy of keeping governments at arm's length—private, business, institutional clientele only. Right decision? It proved too limiting; worse, unfair to his workers and partners. In the end, albeit warily, always with a rapid exit plan ready to be activated on the instant, he succumbed to "testing the waters." State governments to begin with, and finally, inevitably, the centre itself and its hydra-headed ministries and parastatals, those indefinable quantities that were never quite meat nor fish. Nor vegetable. But ravenously omnivorous. Degree and duration of the breakdown were unprecedented even for a nation accustomed to a culture of total blackouts. Rural areas or urban centres, it made no difference. Yet the dedicated billions kept vaporizing, to be annually replenished at budget time, not forgetting supplementary budgets. Factories died, small industries folded up. Each new government blamed the last, then appropriated even heavier funds. His partners fretted. Finally it became a personal challenge—it was time for the Brand of the Land to make a bid, he half hoping, guiltily, that they would lose. They won. Abuja, here we come. It did not take too long to discover—with some chagrin, he would reveal to his "twin," the surgeon Kighare Menka, that there was a strong work ethic in control, indeed a pervasive hands-on ethic, near identical to both theirs, with unintended literalism, just a slight slant—a prime ministerial finger in every pie!

Only the twenty-million-dollar question remained: How long would he last? Thus came the pact with Bisoye—first three months, I'll stick it out, no matter what. Agreed? After that, a choice of his single-malt whisky, always a different brand, for every month survived, plus a night out followed by a bed in, no holds barred. The nation never knew how much it owed to the blissful athleticism of the couple, and Duyole did come close to earning a full case of Islay malt, Collector's Reserve—just one bottle short of a full case. In the display cabinet he conspicuously left a gap in the row of twelve, a silent accusation of Bisoye's ungenerous spirit. Was it his fault he completed the task so far ahead of time?

"So, that report—foolish question—but did you name names?" she asked one day.

"Of course."

"How high up?"

Duyole chuckled. "The trouble with you, girl, is that you think I am suicidal. The inferences are there—all clear. The buck stops somewhere—left it like that. What more could one do? Beyond taking my quiet leave, of course!"

"Quiet? A full-day street party?"

"Needed something to do with the excess talent. A thirty-six-month assignment rounded up in fourteen. That's a lot of bottled-up, unused talent. Dangerous. If it didn't find release, you would have put me away in some institution."

"And what did you think they would make of that in the villa?"

Never was parting more mutual. Pitan-Payne heaved a sigh of relief as he withdrew fully into his more congenial zone of private manufacture. His blood pressure, attested by his doctor, promptly dropped to survival levels, and flesh returned to the hollows of his face. Bisoye was always quick to insist that this had nothing to do with her cooking, in which—as the entire household could testify—the engineer often took more than perfunctory interest, becoming more insufferable after leaving Abuja. He suddenly found more time on his hands, time formerly spent shuttling to and fro, increasingly overnighting in Abuja to slay elusive, invisible, yet incendiary dragons and trouble the sleep of smiling, regretful, and deferential bureaucrats. They were so schooled in procedural stagnation, bowing, scraping, solicitous Uriah Heeps—"with all due respects, sir," "if I may make so bold, sir," "but perhaps you would like to take this up personally with Mr. Prime Minister," ad infinitum. Uriah was everywhere, somehow ensured the disappearance of crucial files, the evaporation of pages in contractual agreements, and often the prolonged to permanent absence of crucial facilitators—those simply posted medical certificates of a sick leave to silence any heartless complainants. *Did they ever claim to be anything but human, Mr. Pitan-Payne? They fall sick, just like you and me. Their turn today, it may be mine tomorrow. Or yours, Mr. Payne. None of us is superhuman! Please exercise patience.*

All good things come to an end, as did this. The engineer signaled the termination of his association by hanging up a banner to proclaim the deed of severance—*Fourteen Months, One Week, Nine Days, Seven Hours—Still Breathing!* Always one to look on the bright side of experience, using his operatic voice, he decanted his gratitude for the opportunity that departure provided to scale new heights in dissolution rites: a mini-Oktoberfest—he had trained in Austria but mostly wassailed next door in Bavaria, and never let any opportunity pass to evoke it. The truth was, he had missed that year's Oktoberfest, with his 24/7/12 schedule, had chosen not to step out of the country until the assignment was complete. It would be a waste of time and money, he swore, since his mind would be elsewhere, even a day's absence being sufficient to unravel all the gains he had made and set the clock back several years. And so Engineer Duyole rewarded his long abstinence with a street party with cooks, waiters, and usherettes dressed in Bavarian costume, hastily constructed beer barrels that were rolled into Badagry from the Students' Union of Lagos University, situated on the road halfway between Lagos and Badagry, escorted by the union's Palm Wine Drinkers Club in regalia and the mincing androgynous *gelede* masquerades of Badagry. The severance party spawned at least two musical additions to the repertoire of Lagosian social praise compositions—unfortunately not assigned to posterity as recorded performance. Duyole heard of the plans, bought up the master tapes, and promptly destroyed them. Personal laudatory art conflicted with Pitan-Payne's "terms of enjoyment" as captured in yet another family motto: "Eat, drink, but be wary!"

That severance spectacular should have been the end of the association, but parting was fated to endure a slight extension, the terminal act of which—a mere courtesy call—was now taking all afternoon and extending into the evening. The prime minister was not part of this call-up, so why the courtesy call? Unknown to either Sir Goddie or to the engineer was a "discovery note" dropped on the desk of the under-secretary for science by a complete stranger from UNESCO two years earlier. The collector had returned from an artifact hunt in Badagry and Benin that had led to Pitan-Payne's factory. Two years later the United Nations was recruiting, member states nominating, lobbying, and backstabbing. The note surfaced. Pitan-Payne was contacted. Then began the fun. His own embassy had other ideas. Other preferences. Eager nominations. And then, surprises, and—horror of horrors to some!—from the least expected quarters, the People's Steward himself! Sir Goddie was body and soul for his recruitment!

The bitter pill was passed from mouth to mouth and swallowed. The culprit consented to a visitation tuned to minimal protocol. He would return to the lion's den on the requested date, after which all agreed to accept that he thereafter became body and soul property of the international clan—their servant, as in serving their agenda and none other, with no obligation to any government. He would do whatever peace of departure demanded—after all, he was bound to work with the embassy on some level from time to time, and he did agree with his spouse that there was no need to make enemies. He swore to her that he would give credit to the Presence for the privilege of serving the nation on the international stage. Now he was here, and he was not sure whether he was in Villa Potencia, Nigeria, or in Wonderland—his intermediary hosts all kept appearing and dissolving in thin air, including his own Mr. Equivalent of the energy world. Said he would be back shortly, and that shortness had already stretched into one hour forty-seven minutes.

Where in the world of Uriah Heep was he, anyway?

6.

Father, Is That You?

Uriah Heep Junior? Actually, prosecuting the very business that had brought the engineer into Abuja to meet the prime minister in person. The Equivalent was seated opposite the Presence, primed to execute a collective mission with which he had been saddled. It fell neatly into his portfolio, as adviser on energy, and he was not especially averse to demonstrating that he was now installed in a position of influence, a new arrival admittedly, yet he had cornered the good ear of *oga patapata*.*

"Your Stewardship, sir, yes, we think that this involves national security. And with all due humility, sir, I would like to phrase it in the form of a question. It's a question, sir, that is agitating many minds among your loyalists."

The Steward perked up at the word *loyalist*. Taken in tandem with the earlier-evoked *national security,* this was clearly not a session to be rushed. "Are you sure you don't need more time? If you prefer to wait till later, when I'm done with other matters. Today is a lighter day, but for instance, I still have to see your man—the engineer."

"Exactly, Your Stewardship! That's why it cannot wait. It has to do with him. It's probably too late, but at least, sir, before you receive him, which will be like the final endorsement . . ."

* Top man at the top.

"And what's wrong with a final endorsement?"

"*Ranka dede,* sir, it's this way. We know you must have your reasons, but we cannot work it out. The question on our minds is, why him? Why this man? That is the question, PS. A well-known saboteur. Everyone around here celebrated his departure, and just as well we did, Your Stewardship. Because what he did in Badagry was to celebrate it himself, noisily and disparagingly to the office of the prime minister itself. The man is a walking insult to this government."

The insult would have rankled even deeper had they known that Pitan-Payne had refused to even consider the offer until he was assured, by a letter from the secretary-general over his signature, that the choice had been made on merit, after in-depth enquiries into his outfit and operations, that it owed nothing to any government nomination or intervention. However—the response also carefully explained—international relationships benefited from protocols of consent, and better still, whenever possible, reinforced by national endorsement. The UN had routinely requested these of the government, and—wonder of wonders!—a response had been provided, and with a sizzling seasoning of alacrity that frankly confounded the secretary-general's office. Usually internal wrangles on the home front of the nominee delayed the process. Sometimes it even resulted in the nation's loss of a prestigious slot. Thus it was that, on the Pitan nomination home ground, heads were shaken, chins wagged, as expectations were shattered in debates on the reasoning behind such an incongruous official endorsement. The party, it seemed, was especially incensed.

The People's Steward studied his ward closely. "Wait a minute. Are you suggesting that the party has other candidates in mind?"

The Equivalent's pulse quickened with optimism. Other candidates in mind? What a question! His hand closed on the sheaf of papers—CVs and references—burning a hole in the pocket of his kaftan. "We have made a small compilation, Your Stewardship, sir. Perhaps you will like to see . . ."

There was no need for Garuba to reassure Goddie that most of these, boasting not the sheerest connection with the world of science, or their nominators, were ready to contribute generously to party coffers. They would blow up one another and engage local herbalists,

Muslim marabouts, Indian fakirs, Jerusalem pilgrims, etc., for super-
natural influence to ensure their selection, so why should the government support a basically disinterested, unappreciative, marginal,
purely business bird of passage—no party obligation, indeed no obligation to anyone except his egotistical self—who had proved impossible
to work with, had poked his nose where others had sworn affidavits
to a clean bill of health, a busybody who insisted that files be dug up
that had been consigned to oblivion? Pursuit of the nation's energy
needs had undergone at least several dozen master plans, empow-
ered two generations of generator billionaires. And had it not also
spurred consumers into the solar age, bringing the nation, no matter
the spotty minority, into the ultimate world of modern, clean energy
supply? The last atrocity of this rank outsider, they protested, was his
attempt to reopen closed files, such as the mystery of an explosion at
the nation's major electricity distribution station, which threw at least
five-sixths of the nation into three days of total darkness. Unprecedented, admittedly, but was it worse than what had happened in
New York City—the city of lights—some years ago? Hundreds were
trapped in lifts—called elevators over there; even hospital surgeries
were immobilized right in the midst of operations. They were unprepared. They had never experienced such a breakdown. Which side
was better off? They didn't know what to do; we had standby generators. People say the explosion blew up a handful of workers—three
of them top-level engineers—terminally. Who can confirm that? What
does his report say? We know that part of it. Sabotage was not merely
suspected, it generously voided any alternative theory—not simply the
thumbprints of guilt but the palm, sole, facial, and faecal imprints
were on full forensic display, and so on and so forth. How do we
know? Some of the report had been leaked. Why? For what purpose?
Who leaked it? I ask you, People's Steward, sir, what is your own
candid opinion? Why did he send a copy to the president? Exactly.
So as to make sure it leaked. Was it the president who commissioned
his firm? No. It was merely to make sure it got leaked to the press.
We found the trail. The man from Badagry claimed he had uncovered
several million-dollar turbines, transformers, and distributor units
abandoned at the wharf, mothballed for over three years, shrouded
in tarpaulin, some cannibalized, even as invoices had been issued for

a further batch, shipped but diverted on the high seas—not by gun-toting Somali or Bakassi pirates—to an ECOWAS partner, a nation that had paid for that same consignment. No one had missed the turbines, so no one was complaining. Their eventual destination did not appear to exist in any installation blueprint. What is our business with that? The Central Bank did not express the slightest interest in the fate of the purchase—CBN, the ultimate authority, authenticated the receipts. Those receipts had been tendered, vetted, and audited. That account was thus legitimately closed, so what exactly was the problem of Engineer Pitan-Payne? He had been brought on board to solve the problem of an epileptic power-supply affliction, not dig into moribund issues that offered no practical value to the living. And now that individual, providentially excluded even from the elastic "ruling family," a misfit who publicly celebrated his dissociation with a street fiesta of hoodlums and student cultists, had successfully lobbied, no, bribed his way, unquestionably bribed, we all know about his family wealth and connections—they bought him a position that amounts to the nation's energy ambassador, he is being made emissary to the prestigious club of experts on the United Nations Energy Commission! The nation had only that one slot, and it had to go to some Pitan-Payne-in-the-neck? Sir, our people are asking questions.

Primaries were close, to be followed by elections. A substitution from the right constituency—all it needed was to view and present the profit margin in the voter calculations . . . It was not as if they were not all versed in what was lightheartedly known as "administrative adjustments." Under his kaftan, the Equivalent continued to caress the folded sheets of paper, ready for presentation to the Steward if he betrayed just the right amount of inclination to reconsider. He liked people to have done their homework. They had, even overabundantly. The CoS had provided him all the facts, most of which he had easily regurgitated—he had, after all, the proficiency of memory from his training in the Quranic system. The affair had to be settled that very night, the pesky engineer sent back where he belonged, empty-handed . . .

"Your Stewardship, sir, the consensus is that it was a mistake to have nominated him in the first place. It's never too late to revert, sir."

Sir Goddie's mood changed dramatically. He leapt up from his chair and snarled, "Who told you I nominated him?"

Hastily the special adviser rephrased, also rising out of respect. "No, sir, no, sir, I never said you did. We know those people in the UN, how they like to dictate. But why did you allow it, PS, sir? That's what is worrisome. We have people even more qualified, and more dependable . . ." Again he fingered the list—was this a good time to flash it?

The prime minister barked, "Sit down."

Instantly the adviser slammed himself into the seat. Had he gone too far?

The People's Steward looked him up and down, his scorn increasing with every word. "You know, I sometimes wonder what report to make to your father about you. Because sometimes you can be stupid. Very, very stupid. You don't even know when to do something in your own interest. All you know how to do is to keep complaining, whining, complaining, whining and complaining."

The adviser shrank even tighter into his kaftan, wishing he had never accepted the brief from his colleagues. "PS, sir, we lack your wisdom. You have to be patient with your children."

"You are slow learners, all of you! That is your problem. I have to do everything myself, look after all of you. Including the too-knows of the party. Those who think they know it all. And sometimes it leaves me with no time for my own interests. Or even for governing the country."

"Ah, Allah forbid, People's Steward. Allah forbid anyone here should become responsible for such a crime against the nation, sir!"

"Allah forbid this, God forbid that. Has no one ever told you the story of 'Ah, Father, is that you?'"

"Never, sir. Never heard of it."

"No? The story of the Reverend Father, the sexton, and the communion wine?"

Shekere Garuba grinned. It was a full-fledged grin that celebrated redemption, relief that he had not misjudged. The People's Steward was indeed in a post-crisis mood, which meant expansiveness, which meant there was even room for other matters on his private shopping list, which meant there was a story not only for instruction but to regale to others as proof of a special intimacy. The protégé's eager-listener posture was food and drink to Sir Goddie, who now rocked himself back in his chair, let his *agbada* overflow the armrests. He chuckled, his face as radiant as that of a loving father who took delight in the learning zeal of his adopted son.

"All right. Pay close attention. Pass me that kola nut bowl."

The adviser quickly leant over and lifted the crystal bowl that housed an assortment of kola nuts, *orogbo,* and alligator pepper as well as wrapped toffees and mini-cookies, all testimony to the minister's solicitude for the plurality of visitors' tastes and cultural preferences. His fingers hovered between the kola nuts and *orogbo,* decided on the former, took one out, split it neatly along its faultlines, dug his fingernail into one wedge to cut off a piece. With a practiced flick of the wrist, he tossed it up, tilted his head backwards at the same time, caught it neatly in his mouth, and commenced a slow, relaxed chewing. The young adviser was delirious. This was going to be a drawn-out session, and he promptly consigned his waiting equivalent to whenever. The hospitality imprest would cover his hotel bill, if needed.

"So listen carefully. There was this priest, and he noticed that each time he prepared to celebrate communion, the level in the wine bottle had decreased since he last celebrated Mass. He did everything to solve the mystery, but it all came to nothing. He strongly suspected it was one of the choirboys—in fact, he was sure it had to be one of them—but there was no way he could catch the culprit, so he decided to recruit outside/inside help. An outsider, but one who knew the insides. Most important.

"The choice for that mission fell on the sexton. Very conveniently, the fellow lived near the church, so the Reverend Father charged him to drop into the vestry in and out of his working hours, and most especially in the evenings when there was a choir practice. He rightly suspected that it was during the choir practice that the potential alcoholic member slipped into the vestry to lubricate his throat. Makes sense, right?"

"Oh yes, PS, sir, absolutely."

"And he was right. Before long the culprit was caught *in fla-*

grante. In fact, it was none other than the head choirboy. You know that age—teenager heading towards manhood. The sexton followed instructions. The moment he caught anyone sneaking in, he was to switch on the light and give a shout, so there would be no escape, no cover-up. That's how they caught the head choirboy, exposed and disgraced. Are you following?"

"Oh yes, sir. Very much."

"The young man was punished, of course, and that was the end of the matter. All returned to normal. Everyone forgot about it, except one. The sexton himself. As far as he was concerned, it was an assignment for life. So whenever he had nothing better to do, he still went and hid in the vestry, hoping to catch any other culprit. It had become an addiction. No one knew they now had an addict on their hands—no different from a drug addict. Sometimes he even fell asleep in the vestry—his wife would go round looking for him. Sometimes he would not wake up till the following morning when the cleaners came to work. That's how bad it was.

"Well, it turned out he was also right. It was not only that choirboy who had developed a taste for the communion wine—there were others. So one evening this overzealous sexton found his way again to the vestry during choir practice for his fix. He took up his accustomed position by the switch and waited. He heard steps. He followed his routine, waited until the intruder had actually picked up the bottle, poured out a good tot, and was tossing it down. *Gbaram!* Sexton switched on the light and gave a loud shout. The choir broke off in the midst of a cantata and rushed into the vestry. The poor sexton was transfixed, appalled. All he could do was gasp, 'Ah, Father, is that you?'

"You can picture the scene yourself. In that vestry, all the hubbub died instantly. No one knew in what direction to look. Yes, there was the Father, bottle and silver goblet in hand, the wine leaving a red splash down the front of his dress while the sexton remained there, finger pointing, unable to utter another word."

The People's Steward bit into another piece of the kola nut, took his time in measuring out the pregnant pause that had made him a much-sought-after raconteur.

"But you know," he resumed, "they don't become reverend fathers for nothing. You know I belong to the church myself, and I can tell you this—don't mess with our reverend fathers; they will trounce you any day. They learn how to recover fast from bad situations. So the father drew himself straight up, furious, and pronounced something in Latin, maybe a curse. Anyway, he followed it up in the language everyone understood. 'Of course it's me, idiot! And you've brought down the wrath of God on your head by spilling the blood of Christ!' "

"*Wayo* man!"

"Ah yes, you could say that. *Wayo man* indeed. Those rev fathers? They think fast. They think on their feet. He dashed off some more Latin, made the sign of the cross, upbraided them all for desecrating the most solemn moment of priestly duties when he must finish off left-over wine and swallow the remaining communion wafers with only Christ as witness! Did they know that? Did they think they were worthy to share that moment with him? Had they been confessed in the past twenty-four hours? Hmm. I can just see him standing there, with that wet red stain on his shirtfront, intimidating everyone in Latin. Of course all the young choristers were fooled, but not the grown-ups, like the choirmaster and the organist. You see what burden the priest had to carry for the rest of his life?"

"Yes, PS. That's a terrible burden of conscience."

The Presence lost his cool, hit the table with his fist. "I knew it. Who said anything about conscience?"

The pupil scratched his head, shook it violently, but received no help from that unit. The People's Steward looked at him, contempt all over his face.

"I obliged your father by finding you a position to occupy here, but thank God I never expected you to advise me on any matter. I keep you here only so I can keep an eye on you. What has conscience to do with it? Now, pay attention. Ask yourself, doesn't the priest make his parish rounds? Doesn't he go knocking on doors to ask after the welfare of his flock? Doesn't he drop in at events unexpectedly? Or don't people run into him suddenly? And so on and on. Now imagine you are inside your house, someone knocks on the door and shouts, 'Is anyone home?' You recognize the voice, and you want to return the greeting. What do you shout in response? Think carefully."

The adviser frowned, thought hard, and enlightenment descended. He grinned sheepishly and intoned, "Father, is that you?"

"Exactly!"

The adviser doubled up with laughter. "Ah, People's Steward, sir, you are too much."

"Not me. It is the father who forever found it much too much. From that day on he knew no peace of mind. Conscience, what is that? Peace of mind is what counts. The question he kept asking himself forever afterwards, whenever he heard that greeting, was, is it a genuine salutation? Or are they making fun of me? People would put on a straight face, or decorate their faces with a fawning smile and say, 'Father, is that you?' And the wretched man wouldn't know what to think."

"He should have transferred that sexton."

"Straightaway! Now you're using your head. Assignment over, presence terminated. No hanging around. Promote them out of sight or send them on special courses. They can't resist that. They collect travel allowances. Everyone likes money. This terminal departure was handed to us on a golden platter, and you dare complain? And you can pass that on to all those who egged you on to come and ask me the stupid question—you think I don't know? You are all so dumb. Tell them I said they should be grateful you all have someone who knows the ropes and looks after your interests. Now go and keep him occupied. When I'm ready, you'll bring him so I can wish him godspeed and good riddance. Come on, get out. He's unpredictable, just like his father. I know the family. So make sure he doesn't leave the premises. Get him anything he wants!"

The adviser gasped, then turned radiant. A grateful smile lurked around his lips, and a distinct body lift attended his departure. But for his flapping slippers, he came close to skipping as he opened the sanctum doors, half jogged the few yards along the corridor into the waiting room, and startled the engineer out of his distant rumination zone. This time he took a seat beside him, settled in comfortably.

"It's all arranged. The People's Steward will see you any time now, I promise you. If need be, I shall interrupt him personally, whatever he's doing."

"Just how late is soon? Our appointment was for—"

"He knows, Mr. Pitan-Payne, he knows. He sends his apologies. He's extricating himself as fast as he can. In fact, any moment now."

It was time, Duyole decided, to be difficult. "I need a drink. A real drink. Is there anywhere I can get a beer?"

Uriah panicked, but only for a moment. He had his orders to keep him, and this appeared—so soon—as the first test. He squared his shoulders. "Any particular brand, sir? I think I know where we may be able to get some."

"As long as it's chilled. Thoroughly. I'm dehydrated. That tends to affect performance. And you know one needs one's wits around one when meeting with power. Any form of power. Not to talk of Sir Goddie in person."

"It must be the air-conditioning," Garuba proposed, and he sounded immensely relieved. "Sometimes even I feel drained of moisture. Then I find I can't think straight."

Duyole smothered a snigger. "Actually, just between us, I think it's my snoring. In fact, I'm sure it's my snoring. The guru who advertises my online remedy was emphatic. Did you know that? Snoring affects one's level of dehydration."

The adviser stared, open-mouthed. "You mean there are remedies? Among my people we think it comes at the discretion of Allah. Like belching. No one should attempt to stop it."

"Really?" And for the first time Duyole really *looked* at his equivalent, with genuine human interest. "You are not making that up?"

"No way," Garuba reassured him. "You should hear the snores at night in our family compound. I think some people snore deliberately so others can think they have been touched by the special wand of Allah."

"Interesting." Duyole appeared to think it over. After close to a four-hour wait, he felt urged towards recklessness, even relishing the near-certainty that the room was bugged. He leant forward and in his most confidential voice enquired, "What of farting? Is that also considered divine intervention?"

As one who simply stated universal possibilities, the energy adviser replied, "It all depends. For instance, if the People's Steward were to fart . . ."

That was more than the engineer had bargained for, and he quickly retreated. "No, no, don't let's turn our noses in that direction. What about that beer?"

"Give me a moment. I'll dash over to the residential quarters. His Excellency the Steward said you had only to ask and I must deliver." He grinned. And off he went.

7.

An Intellectual Property Heist
The Inside Story

Pitan-Payne settled back into the overstuffed chair, leaned forward to pick up a magazine, and sharply withdrew his hand. There it was, right on the top of the pile, as the receptionist had indicated— *The Making of a People's Steward*. He picked it up by the edge—it did feel warm. Perhaps the woman had not exaggerated after all. His eyes flew over the pages—mostly glossy pictures—and snorted. Well, some people are so easily satisfied! Duyole Pitan-Payne did not fall for the glib, bowdlerized stuff. Unabashedly avid for the "nitty-gritty" and "juicy morsel," he made it his business to pump even the most marginal source until he had pieced together a riotous version of the most insipid anecdote and entered it into his private repertoire—factual base and details intact, but somehow ending up a nearly unrecognizable original in the retelling. Parturition of the *People's Steward* was no different, a drama occasioned by one of the most daring intellectual property heists, he would insist, for which the felon deserved either a national medal or a direct hit from the aggrieved. From all the signs he had received since his arrival, it made no difference. They could commit mutually assisted destruction for all he cared. Right then the engineer merely drooled with anticipation. Adoption of "the People's

Steward" as the new prime ministerial identity label appeared to have set a seal on that unprecedented crisis. But what on earth had actually taken place behind the scenes?

A virtual unknown, the political miscreant had defected from his own political party, then in opposition at the centre but in the seat of power within his state. His ambition was to be governor. Denied his party's nomination for that seat, he defected—that was normal—and joined the party in power. *I listened to the yearnings of my people as befits a true leader, obeyed their call, and have now moved into my true political family.* His reward was instant—governorship nomination from his new political home and now contestant against his former party. *Shambolic, sham ballot, shame of a nation,* screamed the losers. Kidnapping of party agents, in daylight glare and in the presence of international observers; decapitations, flying ballot boxes, and riverbeds lined with the same UFOs; acid rain through slits of the chained-down replacements; a display of scant respect even for the virtue of originality—same scenario, same identifiable hands: the pasted and broadcast result was the ultimate decider. International observers had their say, then went home to document their findings. What difference did it make? mocked the victorious, lamented the losers. Seventy-five percent of that year's elections ended up at the tribunals anyway. The state set an all-time record for election hits, boasting no less than a hundred and eighty-five fatalities, most of them administered in broad daylight.

So far, so good. All that was public property, but how many people could claim to have obtained even a whiff of the real insider stuff? That, Pitan-Payne boasted, was what separated the men from the boys! And here he was at the source. If nothing else, he would extract the real *fabu* from that pinhead of an equivalent.

The rapid *slap-slap* sequence of the flat-soled leather sandals between the wearer's heels and parquet floor, and he found his tongue already running over his dry lips—it had been a long wait, and he did yearn for that beer! If the god of success had indeed sat on Garuba's explorative shoulders, he promised, he would never again call him Uriah Heep. The footsteps came closer and the door opened. The prime ministerial guest did not attempt to disguise his eagerness, his eyes fastened on the distinct shapes, even in their brown paper disguise—and not just one, but two! Small cans, but he could not wait to savour their liquid contents.

"Thanks. No need to have gone to such lengths to keep them chilled," Pitan-Payne gratefully reassured the bearer.

Shekere Garuba was baffled. He raised one of the brown paper shapes as if he would pierce through the wrapping. "They came straight from the fridge."

"Yes, I appreciate the care. Here. Let me touch it." Pitan-Payne touched, then unloosed the wrapping and placed a palm directly against the can, grinned his satisfaction. "Thank you, Mr. Garuba. The wrapping retained it at fridge temperature. May you outlive even Villa Potencia."

The penny dropped. "Oh, no, the wrap was not to keep it chilled. This was just so people wouldn't start getting the wrong image about the presidency."

"Image? What kind of image?"

"One doesn't wish to make people think that all we do here is drink."

"Oh, of course. I keep forgetting. This was the arena for the recent battle of images, right?" He tapped the monograph. "Wish I could have been here yesterday." He prised up the small top lever of the can, took a long draught, and asked, "Is Sir Goddie a teetotaler?"

Garuba giggled. "Who? The People's Steward?"

"I thought not. And this is not a mosque?"

The liaison was instantly on his guard. Sir Goddie was right, the man was simply a mischief-maker. He looked warily at him. "This comes from the private fridge of the first lady—I went directly to her residential quarters. In fact she had learnt you were here through the People's Steward. I didn't know you were family friends."

"We are not," Duyole firmly corrected him.

"No? She spoke as if you are."

The engineer shook his head firmly. "No such thing."

Now the emissary stood confused. "She even asked me to let you know you are welcome to come over for dinner if the audience drags on till late."

Duyole shook his head in the negative as he treated himself to a second gulp. "It's looking that way, isn't it? We may not even meet today after all. I just hope you all remember I'll be flying out of the country in a few days. And once I return to Badagry, I'm not coming back here."

"Of course, of course, that's why the Steward rushed the appointment—you know he only got in a week ago. Look, Mr. Pitan, he will definitely see you. That's why I'm here. He told me to keep you company."

The engineer settled more comfortably in his seat. The key to the locked room of the full story lay in that publication, so he picked it up again, ostentatiously.

The liaison could not resist. "That's my latest. Very latest. Actually straight off the press. How do you find it?"

"I hadn't quite started reading."

"The original cover read *The Making of a Nation's Servant*. You know that story already, I'm sure. Everyone does. But not the trouble it caused for us here. I had to rush to stop press the day after that infamous rally. This new cover—you can't imagine—we kept the press open all night, just to change the cover. Plus the few pages which bore the original *servant*. The villa is really blessed with a dedicated staff."

"Why the rush? Pulping goes on all the time in governance. Pulping and shredding is all part of the business."

"No time to waste. Independence Day ahead. Elections round the corner. And need one mention the festival itself? Luckily the villa has its own press—it can turn out thousands of copies even of the entire Quran without outside help if we wish."

Duyole whistled. "Impressive. Or the Bible?"

"Or the Bible. Any book you like."

"Really. I am impressed. Can I keep this?"

The young man leapt up. "I'll get you more copies. You may like to share them with your friends—your scientific colleagues and others over in the U.S. In fact, we're shipping bundles to embassies. Fortunately the former version had not been distributed—not that it matters. We can always recall."

Pitan-Payne gave his best muckraker seduction grin. "Is it all in here? The full story?"

"Not yet, but soon. Everything. The People's Steward is an upfront leader, you know. Tell it like it is—that is his philosophy."

"It should make riveting reading. Thanks. But don't trouble yourself about the extra copies. I can share this copy with others."

"It's no trouble. No trouble at all. I'll see to it. I am glad that it caught your interest."

"Interest? I'm dying to go through—once I've got this audience over with. A magnum opus like this requires concentration, not something to be tackled while waiting. Talking of which . . ."

"Any time now, Mr. Payne, any time. Just give us a few more minutes."

"A few more minutes? Why not? I'm not rushed. I left my home for the airport at five a.m. Just to be sure I caught the first flight out—that's always the most reliable. I've only been in Abuja"—he raised his watch-bearing wrist ostentatiously—"for over four hours. I can wait another four."

Wasted sarcasm; his equivalent was simply elated. "That's the spirit. The People's Steward appreciates that. Let me get you those copies."

"No, no, what's the hurry? I can take a package when I'm leaving. Plenty of time." He smoothed the slim publication against his thigh, bent over confidentially, and offered his own vintage Uriah Heep ingratiation smile. "This must have taken some doing. Digging for facts. Analyzing. Then putting it all together, thinking, *Ah, job well done*. Then having to redo it all over, all in one night? I bet you're already thinking of a sequel."

"What?"

"A sequel. A follow-up. Something along the lines of *The Steward No One Knows*."

Shekere Garuba's delight was boundless. "How did you guess? Actually, I'm giving it the title *Enigma*. Something *Enigma*, or *Enigma* Something Something. Because that is what he is—an enigma."

Pitan-Payne put on his most solemn face, nodded gravely. "You've said it—an enigma. That's what that treacherous governor failed to appreciate. He did not know who he was dealing with. I'm sure this work is a revelation." And he patted the pamphlet anew.

"It was not even my department, really, but I felt the story had to be told. People don't appreciate him. They simply do not appreciate what they have. The Steward, he is a godsend. He's a genius. He's our father-mentor-prophet rolled into one. People misunderstand him."

"I know, I know." Duyole's pursuit shifted into a renewed confidential gear. "Take a seat—that is, if you have no urgent national emergency sitting on your desk. That strange man, that governorship candidate—what a character, eh? Did you know him personally?"

A satisfied air of achievement settled all over Shekere. "Well, you see, it wasn't really my doing. The man brought it on himself. He was a snake who finally swallowed an apple too big for his gullet—if I may quote the Steward's own words."

Duyole's roar of delight brought the chief of staff from nowhere. A door whose flush existence with the wall had remained unnoticed pushed outwards and a face briefly occupied the gap. It was with relief that Pitan-Payne actually heard a voice emerge from it.

"Is everything all right?"

The engineer waved him away with exaggerated cheerfulness—the beer had put him in a good mood, but even more important, he was on a promising trail and was even getting attuned to the tempo of this restricted environment. "Go away. My equivalent and I just found that we have some things in common. Thank you, but we're doing fine."

Puckered eyebrows of the chief of staff registered disapproval of such boisterous violation of the solemn ambiance of the nation's power hub but withdrew. Duyole gestured the adviser to come closer.

"Fill me in. I'll be away quite a while, so I'll be missing all the fun. Something to recall and console myself with when I feel homesick over there. You must have gathered lots of material."

The young man hesitated. "Well, it's not as if I did anything in particular. The man was a loose cannon. When he jumped ship and came over to us, to our great party, the Steward asked me to stay close to him. Bring him into the inner circles of the party but also keep an eye on him—those were his instructions. You see, our leader is very shrewd, very, very shrewd. He doesn't just take anyone at face value. His very words to me were 'I don't trust turncoats, so watch him, in case he turns out to be a rotten apple.' I promised him I would be the rotten worm inside that rotten apple if he proved to be one." A smirk of self-satisfaction and he continued. "*Oga* smiled over that, you know. He gave me that big smile and slapped me on the back, just like an equal. He said, 'You're learning fast—I'll let your father know, he'll be proud of you. Good. You be the deadly worm inside the apple. When he bites into it, I want to see his teeth corrode.'"

This time Pitan-Payne stifled his struggling burst of delight. "I like that. I like that! You know, the way I've heard people talk about that governor's takeoff, it's the proverbial case of the man the whole community wants to roast. So what does he do? It's Harmattan weather and on the chilly side. So he rubs palm oil all over his body, wraps himself in blankets, and sits next to a roaring fire."

"Exactly. Our man wasted no time in carrying out his election promise to hit the ground running. He didn't even wait to hit the ground before starting to run—he was already pedaling in midair like one of those circus performers from China. Writing postdated cheques on the government treasury, to be settled once he took office! I mean, he has yet to take office, he has yet to take the oath of office. But he arranged it all with the outgoing governor, the one who is still sitting there right now. Beat that if you can. I mean, match it!"

"But he is quite wealthy. He has lots of money."

"Elections cost. Elections eat money. And then politicians like to play big. In my four years with Sir Goddie, I have seen it happen. So that is what I'm telling you. Say it anywhere that you heard it from me. I said, this character Akpanga, governor-elect, has already signed postdated payments on government chequebooks. *Wallahi!* Write it down that I, Shekere Garuba, said so!"

"Why not a straightforward prosecution?"

Garuba laughed. "Who will be prosecution witness? His opposition partner in crime? Outgoing or incoming, this crosses party lines. Who will agree to testify?"

"Too bad he has immunity. That means four years in which to cover his tracks. Case files get lost. Witnesses disappear."

"Good. Now you understand the whole thing. As long as you don't cross the line, you can do what you want. Nobody really bothered their heads about that. But what the man did at the rally—that was the real sabotage. Sir Goddie will never forgive him. All day yesterday we were still at it. And nearly all night."

Pitan-Payne sat up, leant forward eagerly. "Even more serious matters?"

"Heavy. All yesterday. It was one hot session after another. Only top party members, the very top, allowed in. Even I was not invited. Until after they had all finished, then I was summoned to carry out their decisions. Can you imagine? It's not right." Garuba had turned resentful, even maudlin. Pitan-Payne consoled him with the smarmiest tut-tutting of fellow feeling he could muster, patted him on the knee with consoling gentleness. Garuba felt a genuine warmth for this earlier execrated thorn in the flesh—he seemed not a bad fellow after all, indeed a sympathetic ear and willing confidant. His eyes roved cautiously round the room, lingered a little on the wall through which the apparition of the chief of staff had emerged and vanished. Satisfied, he drew his chair yet closer to Duyole Pitan-Payne, whose impatience from the long wait had again changed texture from angry resignation to that of the insatiable story harvester. Already he could hear himself narrating the crisis meeting of the POMP caucus "from the inside," larded with voice mimicry and variations from his own special effects. He heard his equivalent commenting, "One thing I can tell you, though, the People's Steward got the best part of the bargain. He always does."

Just then, extracting from the engineer a loud expletive of frustration, Duyole's mobile phone rang. He moved to silence it, thinking it was yet another check call from his wife, Bisoye, who wanted to make sure that he was still at his post. Then he saw the caller's name—Kighare Menka, his acquired twin. The engineer slid instantly into a playful, indulgent mode as he tweaked the Answer button, raised a hand in apology to Garuba, and rolled out his name in his best lord-of-the-manor theatrical drawl: "Aduyole Muyomi Pitan-Payne, engineer, head of the Pitan-Payne dynasty, speaking. May I ask who the hell are you?" Meant to be followed by a plea to give him some half hour or so and he would call back. Not even his inseparable companion from schooldays, the surgeon Kighare Menka, would be allowed to jeopardize the delicious stream of confidentiality that teetered on the edge of delivery—not unless it was a matter of life and death.

Pitan-Payne cut himself off midstream, a heavy frown on his face displacing all the earlier frivolity. Kighare Menka had just spoken in a language he had not heard in years. It was reserved only for emergencies, an internal SOS known only to a foursome whose student antics had resulted in the famed brand now known as Brand of the Land. Without even bothering to mutter a polite excuse, he stood up and moved slowly away from the man on whom he had been working so unsubtly to fullfill his lust for "insider stuff."

"Kiln ready stoked," Shekere Garuba thought he heard the engineer respond to whoever it was. His hearing had not deceived him.

8.

Jos

For any wanderer into Hilltop Manor, Jos, in the Plateau State of Nigeria, all claims that the sun had set over the British Empire would appear to be premature.

For now, none of the regulars—mostly locals, but with a sizeable foreign sprinkling—in the private members' lounge of the prestigious Manor Club had the sheerest premonition that this would be the last sunset they would celebrate together at that sturdy legacy of colonial occupation. It was indeed a nostalgia-inducing countryside implant, an imposing, stately granite home set in ample, symmetrically man-icured grounds, lulled by a temperate climate that seemed divinely ordered for the former British overlords. That entire oasis was known as the Plateau, a name to be later adopted by that portion of the north-ern region of the nation when it was split into several pieces by one of the post-independence military dictatorships.

Conversation that evening, during preparations for the nation's Independence Day celebrations, did turn unusually heated, and per-haps the residual cinders, when all the members had retired to their homes, simmered through the night, then burst into flames at the very onset of dawn. Several of the expatriate population, woken up by explosions, cautiously tiptoeing to peek through the louvers of their tropical windows, would later confess that when they glimpsed the distant spurts of flames through the early-morning haze, they mistook the glow for rehearsals of Independence Day fireworks in the state. It would have been just another day of routine ceremonials, but its governor had also sworn to show Boko Haram, the psychopathic warriors of fundamentalist Islam, that nothing would stop citizens of Plateau from sharing in the "dividends of democracy." It was thus projected as a feat of defiance and the conquest of fear. A few feared that Boko Haram itself was sending yet another signal that it had a different agenda for Independence Day celebrations. Such pessimists were proved wrong.

Preparations were certainly in high gear, and the army appeared to retain the upper hand against the insurgency. Enemy infiltrations did occur—there had been one that very morning, a female suicide bomber—but they had become infrequent and blunted in deadliness. If the escapist sanctuary of Hilltop was indeed burning—the rumours were not long in filtering through—damage would be confined to some minor detritus of the past—not to be regretted, shrugged a handful—and such futile flickers would soon come under control. The stone sentinel would survive intact; the rhapsodies of expatriate sun-worshippers, whenever the sun was simply setting up shop or closing for the day, would continue as one of those idiosyncratic traits that the locals found bemusing. It was a favourite topic also among the elite, an affliction to which the British appeared especially prone. What those locals would have thought, had they known that such displays once featured, right up to the sixties, in special dispatches of the local district officer to the Home Office—that is, the colonial desk of the Ministry of Home Affairs—was probably beyond speculation. The exceptions—such as the resident surgeon Dr. Kighare Menka, senior civil servants, technocrats, school headmasters, and a handful of other sophisticates—were those whose schooldays had featured musical concerts with a repertoire of songs that vowed that the sun would never set on the British Empire. Such cynics probably wondered if their rulers' obsession with the sun's private business was a confession of nervousness over the hubristic prediction. After all, wasn't it the same sun they had watched setting piecemeal over those possessions ever since even before 1960? One after the other, members of that empire appeared to delight in jumping off the fiery chariot.

Much had changed in that colonial redoubt, but not to such a degree as would permit the members to recognize, for instance, the existence of any such aberrations as Yeomen of the Year or its crown jewel, the People's Award for Common Touch. Keeping one's feet on the ground was one thing; ostentatious slumming transgressed the limits of tolerance. The superficies of colonial presence required only minor adjustments here and there, not a wholesale substitution by nationalist buntings. The temperate climate was a balm that seemed specially designed also for successors to the departing mandate. It was cool, most especially in the evenings. In the main, the sun's antics were lost on them.

Once upon a time it had indeed provided the erstwhile administrators a measure of consolation after the restless sleep that capped each arduous day of running the affairs of a restive populace and the prospect of more of the same—another day, *sigh!,* among the thieving, devious ingrates, *sigh, sigh!* Not anymore. The lucky expatriate residents whose bedroom windows overlooked the east could luxuriate in the admittedly generous pyrotechnics that made up for their daily imposition of awakening, signaled by the muted entry of the uniformed steward. In impeccably white uniform, he shuffled in on apologetic feet with a tea tray to be served in bed—unless of course he had watched "Master" staggering home after midnight from an extended night out with the boys at the clubhouse, or in the redder spots further inland, the Sabon Gari zone, conceded to alcohol-swilling strangers and infidels. That had tutored him to expect a hangover the morning after, so the faithful steward pulled back the curtains with extra solicitude to gradually let in both view and refreshing air, also now freed of mosquitoes. The agonized Beauty Awakening shielded his eyes at the first incursion of light, gingerly opened one after the other behind spread fingers, blinked rapidly, then solemnly yawned the day's ritual consolation: "Gabriel, just look at the colours of that sky."

"Yessir. I look am just now."

"Don't you find it simply exquisite?"

"Yes, Master, just like every day."

Still, masters and vassals were all brought down to earth by that very earth-shaking event whose memory would continue to linger in mounds of charred masonry, cracked, blackened, and broken china, and twisted metallic rods that disfigured the landscape for years afterwards. It was all that remained of the sturdy legacy of a love-hate relationship from the colonial era in that northern part of the nation, a proud, majestic outcrop that had dominated the region for nearly two centuries. For the local population, mostly traders and local workers simply carrying on with the exigencies of the hour, their faces turned resolutely earthwards, it was hardly surprising that it was they, who lived far from the mansion in an area known simply as GRA— Government Reservation Area—who first noticed the overnight disappearance of the imperial squatter. These early spotters consisted of early risers, many shuffling to the motor parks, bicycling to work, or awaiting the vacant taxis—motorcycles or *keke napep*, the Indian-constructed tricycle taxis, increasingly reproduced locally.

Even when the cantilevered hill—only one of a range that stretched, with substantial breaks, sloping and sheer, over a hundred and eighty kilometres in the direction of the capital, Abuja—was shrouded in mists during the Harmattan season, there was still a view—no, views!—worth an early rise by the painterly inclined, as witness the framed poor man's Constables, Turners, etc., lining the reading room, bar lounge, and ample corridors of Hilltop Mansion—different faces of a plateau masked by mists, a sun pressing valiantly through, patches of shifty shrouds as if the hundreds of mosquito nets in the GRA had billowed outwards through the broad windows to be progressively shredded into willowy scrims.

That was then, seasonally predictable, almost to the calendar dates. Like everything else, however, there crept, then accelerated a transformation that earned the name "climate change." There were other changes, unacknowledged, some far more deeply penetrative and malignant than even desert encroachment, itself a prolonged, phenomenal exercise in denial. Sometimes the resident surgeon Dr. Menka feared that the change would infect the hills themselves, that he would wake up one day, the mists would have cleared but taken the hills with them. So far, however, they seemed to have defied all such prospects. Menka was loath to lose his own consolation fantasy, which accompanied his contemplation of the hills, that all he had to do was take a short stroll along the rim, then slide down a natural chute on the other side and he would find himself in his own village, Gumchi, located in one of the hollows, yet boasting heaps of sheer granite that rose to dwarf the surrounding hills. It made no difference that he knew it would take no less than six hours of driving through a twisting course to arrive at a village into which he had not stepped for as many years and over.

More striking—perhaps because somewhat incongruous—than the amateur Constables and Turners, occupying pride of place in its florid glory of crocheted lettering, was a maxim that had endured all the way from the mansion's initial occupation. It was a survival that presided over the spacious fireplace of the main lounge, having outlived generations of Hilltop tenancy. This eighteen-by-fifteen-inch wall décor bore the inscription *Manners Maketh Man*, often jovially invoked by members as the Triple M—or simply MMM—Club mani-festo. Despite constantly provoking irreverent variations, depending on who and in what state of lubrication, it was an inviolate touch-stone for membership conduct for which even the physical structure appeared to serve as prelude. Maintained under its near-pristine con-dition, a monument to arrested time, the historic mansion indeed also testified, as a corollary, to the principle that environment conditions manners. A librarian's dream of an interior of glazed wood paneling, absorbent carpeting, browned, outdated British journals, and ornate chandeliers took over from an approach of geometric hedge configu-rations, conspired with an exterior of lichened walls and stained glass architraves to imbue in members—and guests—a comportment that was merely and superfluously summarized by the framed Triple M, conditioning the movements of the domestic staff, the placement of objects, the vocal level of exchanges, and even accompanying gestures.

It all collapsed, alas, during the countdown towards that memora-ble Independence anniversary. British décor and decorum presided for the last time over the Hilltop landmark, an unprecedented shattering for which the actual fire was a mere spectacle of affirmation.

Within its walls, all had proceeded as always—safe, measured, and predictable. Members conceded nothing beyond a dismissive acknowl-edgement of the madness that still engulfed wide swaths of the north-ern part of the nation, the northeast most notoriously. True, it was indeed those events in a nation partially under convulsion that ignited the evening, but ultimately it was none other than the conduct of their very celebrant, Dr. Kighare Menka—a gross MMM violation—that held them all riveted and anxious, confounding their incredulous hearing, wrenching minds over what to make of—perhaps even do to—the bearer of bad news. *Manners Maketh Man?* The opposite, and intolerable, side of that was *Bad Form.* You simply do not make members and guests uncomfortable on club premises. And the solitary medium of Bad Form, ironically, was the man they had trooped by to honour. It was not a formal event—the usual notice had been sent to members: *Drop by on your way home from work. One of us—and from a little-known corner of our host state, Plateau—has brought distinction to the club, bagged the prime national honour, the very first member of the club to so much as make the Honours List on any grade. Drinks on the house between 6 p.m. and 7:30 p.m., half price thereafter till nine, after which back to membership rates.*

The reception was all impromptu, but it followed the age-long pattern, with a few trivial variations to pay homage to local tradition—the breaking of the kola nut and the pouring of libations to thirsty ancestors—the variations themselves having fused over time with inherited rituals. Nothing really out of the ordinary. A welcome speech by the social secretary, a few reminiscences, eulogies, and rambling jokes. A vote of thanks. The evening proceeded along familiar, ritualized observances that would have earned approval from their British predecessors. Then came the turn of the honoree, the eminent surgeon Menka, to respond. Nothing startling expected, nothing unique, nothing ponderous or provocative, nothing controversial. A measured *Thank you for the honour of this peer recognition, etc., etc.,* rendered especially significant for its season of national rejoicing. Hopes that the next would witness the terminal exit of religious fanatics, etc., etc., pietisms delivered with genuine sincerity, from all appearances. The formal event was soon over; the club reasserted its ambiance of British genteel bonhomie.

The guest of honour had even assumed his favourite position at the bar, beer mug in hand. When the eruption occurred, even to his hearing his voice sounded odd, as if it were coming from somewhere outside himself. Only afterwards did he acknowledge that it was a long-repressed catharsis that had only awaited the moment of detonation. He admitted to himself, however, that on reflection it still offered a glimpse of some emerging brightness. All was not lost. What these colleagues—and strangers—were admitting, despite their discomfort, resentment, and even outrage, indeed on that very account, was that, MMM notwithstanding, some deeds stood outside even moral outrage, indeed that the emotion itself still had validity, that it implied a moral discrimination—a possession that he had begun to consider was merely presumptuous.

None of this diminished the unexpectedness of the outburst, or the impact. Menka was not conscious of its approach. He had no explanation, and he offered none. He only knew that something blew apart inside him, as if that morning's explosion in the market had occurred deep down within the recesses of his own guts, which then involuntarily spewed out all its contents, drenching Turner, Constable, Ruskin, and club injunctions in their bottled-up ferment. He could only conclude that he, Kighare Menka, famous Dr. Bedside Manners, lost his cool and violated the founding principle of *Manners Maketh Man,* replaced it with *Bad Form* in a hitherto unprecedented manner, and through revelations that would have churned the stomach of the founders of Hilltop Mansion Club.

Embarked on stock-taking afterwards, the worthy surgeon did feel unjustly put upon. After all, he was not the initiator. He had played his role, gracefully acknowledged plaudits from his peers, accepted their packaged gift, which he had declined to open on the spot, and was quietly gathering up his physical self to join his thoughts, which had long preceded him to his bachelor apartment in the same hills. Along came Kufeji, the club treasurer, with whom he maintained a quite unremarkable but cordial relation. In Kufeji's hand was the day's newspaper, his eyes glued to its contents.

"Get a load of this, Doctor." He chuckled. "It seems you have some stiff competition."

Menka raised his head from staring at the array of bottles on display, asked quietly, "What is it?"

"The country is full of aspiring surgeons. Just take a look."

Menka waved him off. "What else is new under the sun?"

"No, no, no, this you have to see. Listen." And he began to read: "'Thirteen—take a good note of the number, we've never had so many at one sitting—*thirteen* suspected ritual gang members and their patrons, made up of herbalists, a church pastor, Islamic clerics called alfas, have been arrested by operatives of the Inspector General of Police Intelligence Response Team (IRT) in—' Hey, wait a minute, I hadn't noticed that. It's in my state! Oh my bleeding ancestors! It's in my own bloody state! Damned if I'm going to disseminate this with my own mouth."

"Come on, no censorship. Read it all—leave nothing out!" The reader was unaware how far his voice had carried, enabling occupants of a nearby table to overhear him distinctly as he read the headline, "Thirteen-Member Ritualist Gang Broken Up, Reveals IG Police." Other members begun to gather, eager for the lurid details. By all accounting, the number was unusually high. Mostly such groups operated in smaller units. This was one for the record books.

"No way!" Kufeji protested. "Why should I expose my own state to your kangaroo trial? How do I know it's not Fake News?"

That predictably drew haw-haws of derision. "Oh yeah? Until now there was no mention of Fake News. Don't stop. Read it all out."

He ignored them, blocking their voyeuristic efforts by resting his back against the bar counter and holding up the newspaper against the pressuring lineup. "I was addressing the doc, not you mob . . . Here, here, all right, I'll read it out. 'Thirteen arrested for allegedly killing a thirty-year-old housewife, Mrs. Abosede Adeyemi Iyanda. The suspects are Segun Olaniyi, forty-two years old; Adewole Oluwafemi, forty-one, aka Pastor; Mustapha Iliya, aka Alfa . . .' It names all thirteen of them, let's see—thirty-seven-year-old, fifty-six, forty-eight, etc., all seem to be in the range of between thirty-five and sixty."

He lowered the newspaper and surveyed the lounge. "Imagine, about the average age of our elite membership. For all we know, you all could be part of those still at large." He shook his head in mock dolefulness and tut-tutted, then resumed.

" 'Another eight of them have been identified but are still at large; the IG has threatened to place them on his Most Wanted list. The victim's daughter was said to have written directly to the inspector general after her mother vanished on her way home from the office. The herbalist has confessed . . .'"

More and more listeners were drifting towards the reader. Menka tried to change seats but found his exit blocked.

"No, no," Kufeji pleaded. "I'm just coming to the part that really caught my attention, the part that concerns you. Listen . . . yes, here it is. Just get hold of this. 'According to the ritualist's confession, the victim was once his lover but was now married to someone else. Some clients had approached him for a money-making ritual, so he tricked her to return, saying that he had seen a vision of danger to her and she needed delivery. He then contacted Ayo Adeleye to come and do the slaughtering. After sending for food for the woman, Segun put some drug in the food so that she would begin to feel sleepy. She was then told to go and wash in the river for ritual cleansing. She proceeded, having taken off her clothes, so that she was completely naked. While Abosede was washing her hair, Ayo pushed her head into the river, brought out a pocket knife, and killed her. Both he and Segun then pulled out her body from the river—' Now wait for this, Doc, wait for *this!* 'He dismembered the body, separating the flesh from the bones as directed by Segun. Some of them allegedly roasted the meat and ate it with hot drinks. Among the items recovered by IRT operatives were decomposed human breasts, burnt human flesh mixed with liquid substance in a bottle and calabash, one complete human foot, pieces of dry human skull. A Laura SUV with registration number . . ."

By now the trickle had swollen to a sizeable group, successfully peeking over the shoulders of the reader, joining him with their own tidbits glimpsed from the paper, punctuated with exclamations of disbelief, imprecations, and proposals for summary disposal of the arraigned or implicated. For some reason the police had been unusually generous with details—clearly one of those breast-beating instances provided by detective success, and of an especially sensational nature. Photographs of the captured accused adorned the page, most squatting on their haunches and made to hold up placards bearing their names, others some of the recovered implements deployed in their crude surgery. Even the registration numbers of vehicles trapped during the raid featured in the bulletin. Individual profiles—address, occupation, local and other connections—graphically filled out their profiles as if in an effort to dispel all incredulity, affirm that these were indeed no more than next-door humanity. The facts had been volunteered by the suspects, in such detail that one could only wonder if they had been administered the so-called truth drug, last rumoured during the interrogation of one of the nation's failed coup-makers, the infamous Colonel Dimka, trapped in a brothel in Asaba after his flight from a doomed attempt to overthrow the regime. The papers all reported that he was singing like a canary, virtually in a state of euphoria.

ADMITTEDLY IT HAD BEEN an abnormally stressful day for Dr. Menka, shuttling between the emergency wing of the hospital and the operating theatre—a slightly above-average haul of human forms, sometimes unrecognizable. The women quota had been especially unnerving—the bomb had been planted in an onion basket in the vegetable section of the main Jos market. It was over ten hours without a break since his summons from bed, wave on wave of casualties—on bicycles, trolleys, pushcarts, and motorcycles—before he was able to hand over the minor wounds and shock cases to his assistants, then call it a day. He showered and changed at the hospital, then drove to the club reception gratefully. He did need some unwinding before finally heading home. The club fulfilled that function; indeed it seemed specially tailored for such crisis days, as if human carnage had been factored into the mansion by its departed proprietors. That halfway house was efficacious therapy, to be followed by a quiet dinner on his own, needfully and entirely on his own. After the groans of the injured and the expiring gasps of fatalities, he needed that spell of solitude, the restorative silence of the hills. Thereafter, hopefully, an in-depth crash into fathomless, uninterrupted sleep. In the morning, substantially refreshed but never fully recovered, he was back to the hospital on ward rounds. That routine had earned him the nickname, bestowed on him by appreciative patients and colleagues, Dr. Bedside Manners. There was certain to be some time before another assault shot him back to the surgical theatre. If that happened, he simply psyched himself and moved among the dead and mutilated as one born to that occupation and none other. Menka had attained a level of detachment that made him feel sometimes that he was no different from the media voyeurs who wallowed in body counts and lurid headlines, not forgetting image harvesters of disasters whose phone cameras, obsessively poised for internet voyeurism, pursued dazed survivors meandering sightlessly, walking through debris, propelled by some inner beckoning destination, oblivious to their surroundings, or even to their own fatal hurts, simply dragged forwards on some inner momentum until the frayed, invisible thread snapped and they collapsed in a totally unaffected neighbourhood, dead on arrival.

In the midst of this unpredictable yet constantly anticipated brutality, it was the domestic, noninsurgency wounds that most depleted his reserves. Something appeared irreversibly unhinged, turning the human terrain that he felt he knew so intimately into mere maceration fields. It remained the most tormenting encroachment on his professional latitude. Victims of that undeclared internecine warfare, mostly one-sided, consisting of the most vulnerable, unsuspecting of society, often jostled for space, their conditions demanding precedence over the urgency of terrorist carnage. The flashes came unsolicited—the eight-year-old "housemaid" driven into the emergency section that very morning, after a ride that lasted over an hour on rutted roads. She arrived wedged between the rider and a hysterical aunt. The girl was already halfway dead. There was hardly a moment's hesitation as her loose wrapper fell off and he glimpsed the gruesome mush between her thighs. It was instant priority on the surgical roulette. She died anyway, right under his hands—a merciful end to prolonged serial rape by a businessman and his nineteen-year-old son. Each such abuse merely sealed up channels of emotional response except one—rage, murderous rage. It accumulated behind the neutralizing surgical mask and beneath the swift interventionist hands, always hovering over decisions of life and death where the hopeless made room for the dubious, the dubious for the clamorous—his hands schooled in parameters of designation, unwelcome but essential.

That was the hardest part, he openly conceded—to immunize himself against horrors that did not emanate suddenly and violently from the demonism of religious fanatics and deluded millenarians but from the civilian demonism. That seemed even more determined to win the grim contest in human desecration, physical and mental. As he led his team of equally blood-caked assistants through shattered humanity, honed instincts to the fore, his mind actually found relief in trying to make sense of beliefs that justified such scenes, to configure visions of that future whose gateway some could only glimpse through mangled humanity.

And the bombastic self-attributions among the contestants in the race for paradise. Their identities had long ceased to matter—deadly nomadic herdsmen or the latest aspirants to the mantle of the Chosen, apparently sprung from the regions of Burkina Faso—they called themselves ISWAP. Or perhaps sleepers from the same unsuspecting home front, suddenly galvanized into action through some mystic telegraph, intoxicated by the fumes of religious rapture that the Harmattan wind blew over the Sahel and along the Niger and Benue Rivers, imposing an all-engrossing reign of morbidity over sleeping villages! Who cared what name they were called or called themselves? Their calling remained the same—morbidity. Doctors were trained to deal with river blindness, but river madness had simply never featured in his medical curriculum—there was no such registered ailment in the known repertory of diseases since the earliest known shamans, sangomas, *babalawo,* so to what did one ascribe this affliction that appeared to be river-borne from the Fouta Djallon hills? How to diagnose, then prescribe for it?

The madness of civil society was in a class of its own, and it sickened him. Haunted him. Like the wide eyes of the mutely accusing three-year-old violated by a grandfather of seventy-six. If only it remained—as it did for millions—mere fodder for the lurid pages of the media, easily exorcised by immersion in activities, occupations of one remedial kind or another! Alas, it did not. The body count from such wars of rivaling human ruinations might be lower, but the inner ravages exceeded both stalking bombs and gleefully swiveling AK-47s, and didn't all meet at one common point—the negation, at least the prospect of the end, of humanity?

It had been quite a while since he had begun questioning the difference, then finally decided there was none. When the deviants were caught, interrogated, and paraded before media cameras, the public had learnt to expect invocations of the routine extenuating influence—*The Devil! Please, I am very sorry, the Devil made me do it. I don't know what came over me, but I know the Devil was behind it.* And then the crowning insolence, the plea for attenuation of abhorrence—*If people can just forgive me, I promise not to do so again. I'll dedicate the rest of my life to Jesus, to Allah, to Jesusallah.* The rapist duo, father and son, did not disappoint. *The Devil pushed me,* wailed

Rapist Senior. *Check with my priest, he will testify. Ask him how often I have gone to him to be delivered.* And your son, Chief? What of the heir apparent? *He caught me in the act, so he joined in. The Devil is no respecter of age.*

And indeed, were there not others, even more authoritative, versed in theological niceties—the governor paedophile leading the charge, attesting to the culpability of that universal tempter and, by logic, exoneration of the human perpetrators, to be seen as mere vicarious agents of the Devil's machinations? But what a brilliant variant in demonologic from the gubernatorial pulpit—it was indeed the Devil, argued His Devout Excellency, but operating through absence. Never was self-applause more resounding—acquittal through demonic absence, one step only, in effect, to beatification of the Devil! A serial stud of the underaged, augmented by cross-border trafficking of that vulnerable grade, he perched smugly, unassailable, on the saintly minaret! *The Quran does not forbid copulation with the girl-child, nowhere is there such an interdiction, so who are you to accuse? What the Quran does not forbid, I am free to do.* And for good measure: *The Prophet himself*—trust His Excellency the Punctilious not to forget the ritual "peace be upon him" tripping from the lascivious lips of immunity—*did he not espouse the underage Aisha?* End of discourse. End of innocence. Beginning of vaginal fistula.

And that, Menka silently raged, is where we are summoned to clean up the mess of appetites for fruits that should set teeth on edge.

Not forgetting the ghosts of those he had never met, would never know—case histories tucked among his predecessors' handing-over of notes in the cabinet marked Extremely Confidential. The cryptic warning that read "Handle with Care," handiwork of the Untouchables. The graphic photos. Precedents are efficacious teachers. Restored to life, triggered awake, those case files burst through the scrim of time no matter how effectively the seductive environment imposed itself between viewer and pulsing replications, clambered over the insulating range of hills—sunsets or sunrises, mists, social clubs, or whatever—where many continue to seek escape. Images on surmounting images—how many did one take into account in a week's tally of ritual imbecilities, now being slobbered over by these colleagues luxuriating in the haven of a colonial refuge whose ancient walls, burnt brick chimneys and framed precepts merely evoke images of the altar-hearth of a distant church, a presiding priest in full regalia, pious hands raised to harvest God's blessing. In those hands, alas, a silvery axe raised above a trusting head bowed in supplication, her superfluous pieces destined for burial beneath the altar in a ritual—predictably the same illusion—to make millionaires of the guardian of the lambs of God and his anointed cohorts, vital portions served as communion among them.

Images in pursuit of images of a ten-year-old—only that was no image for Menka but a flesh-and-blood patient, leg amputated for fleeing home from the eighty-year-old groom to whom she was betrothed in settlement of a debt. And who carried out that surgery? Her own enraged father, to whose home she had returned as sanctuary from the unwanted nuptial. *She dishonoured me,* the indignant papa lamented, and returned her minus one leg to the love-stricken octogenarian. She was back in Menka's hospital a few weeks later, this time minus the other leg. The ingrate had again fled, this time to nowhere, just hobbling as far as she could on crude crutches and alms but not far enough to escape a now incandescent father, invoking Allah as witness of righteous restitution, of patriarchal honour. Right on that dirt road he slashed off the other leg for humiliating him before man and God.

And then—and Menka shook his head from habit, not that it brought relief or remorse—his own past haunted him; that much he found himself compelled to concede. Again and again it rose in accusation. He looked through the same prism at his own special community of peers, skilled, trained in an envied run of proficiencies—could they presume to volunteer for the angelic hosts that would assuage the self-inflicted trauma of the world he inhabited? No, not even the micro-community in which they strutted around, privileged among the herd. It was, after all, from the same implanted nurseries of presumed enlightenment that new profanities, hitherto unheard of, had emerged, from nurseries that nonetheless did breed dreams of transformation. Year after year, one after the other, those dreams had faded, drooped, or rotted. Year after year he had deferred his modest—well, somewhat on the ambitious side, but attainable—dream for Gumchi, a modest return of privilege, nothing more. How did those youthful claimants to allied professional nurturing attune themselves to the supremacy cults that plagued such sanctuaries of knowledge—weren't they products of the same ennobling rites of passage? Was it really too much to expect of them—no, no, not even a plausible, futuristic dream, just avoidance of devouring the dreams of others? They strutted in that dark alley of power fixation—or was it simply the thrill, the sheer thrill of killing? Oh yes, more mimic surgeons, indeed the elite of those elites, theirs was a shorthand primer to brain surgery, a simple arrival point with that feudal proceeding: *Off with his head!* They could pride themselves also as belonging to an elite corps of innovators, their feet set upon glazed paths to recognition. It all ensured reputation of a kind, the recognition of the dead end of innocence!

His mind attempted to dialogue the minds—if they had any—of the midnight soccer games whose originality had riveted and outraged the nation. Four freshly severed heads stuck on poles; they had once belonged, and not so long before, to members of a rival cult. The players did not lack recourse to their own empowering devil—trade name Tradition, perhaps? Universal Tradition. College fraternity tradition with a local cultural flavour to enhance the awakened, aggressive sporting spirit of a continent? And so they stuck the heads of their victims on poles and played soccer between the totemic goalposts, the field lit by headlamps of their expensive, indulgent-parent-donated motorcars. The screams of outrage and condemnation were to be expected, but Menka shrugged; it all sounded hollow, insincere. It was all of a tune with the cross-border paedophiles, the promoters of vaginal fistulas, infant mortality, and proliferation of street girl beggars. For this was where they ended, thrown out of marital homes when their malodorous emissions became unbearable to the once-triumphant groom who had basked in the adulation of his peers, fellow legislators, for a job well done—yes, theirs was a tradition stoutly maintained.

Pilloried by the public, did that lawgiver not receive a standing ovation as he resumed his seat in the senate chambers? The mere student campus was the state breeding ground for such future leadership. It shared borders with pulpit, minaret, and senate. The students deserved their initiation grounds, no different from the kidnap gang not far from that governor's state, post-modern vampires who kept their victims in designer cages, some for upwards of a year, pending ransom. The ghoul leader's complaint—hubris eventually led to his capture—was a study in reversed culpability: *Their relations were not serious about ransom. I had to kill some so I could drink their fresh blood.* What was the public outcry all about, anyway? Tradition under co-option, albeit unvoiced—echoes from time past resounding in the present from neighbouring palm oil estates turned slave kingdoms. In those ancient times of trade and glory, forebears of today's human commodities of cash and carry, progenies of historic exemplars in action. Eager to impress on visiting naval officers their control over all within their territory, did not the kings lop off the heads of a few slaves and play polo with them, skewering and tossing them from one lance point to the next? So why the rage? *Why do the nations so furiously rage together, and why do the people imagine a vain thing?* In vain he also tried to recall where he had last heard the anthem, gave up. The outrage was pure sentiment. The football fiends did no worse than play modern variations on the old tunes. A new generation of the digital, democratic, informational age. The students should be honoured for offering the World Cup an original idea in totemic culture—those goalposts should have been adopted as the nation's emblem. His Independence Day national honour belonged to them, not him.

Drop in on the Hilltop clubs, proliferating under whatever name, on campus, off-campus, debating joint or clusters around news vendors, enjoying their free morning read—sooner or later the same consensus was reached: comb the desert, sweep the Mediterranean, bring back the migrating hordes, load them into capsules and fire them into space, to discover and settle new habitations where, just maybe, redemption awaited. They would subjugate the galactic natives and perform daring feats like the old colonial explorers, just like the ancient European transportation of bankrupts, highwaymen, mountebanks, prostitutes, atheists, reprieved suicides, chronic antiestablishment dissidents, press-ganged vagrants, and nomadic soldiers of fortune. And yet others proposed the establishment of dedicated killing fields—perhaps the first of their kind—as a conscious, deliberate social relief facility, to be patronized entirely by the willing to kill or be killed. After all, it was already happening, had moved beyond rhetoric or palliatives. Each day seemed empty, incomplete, and even unreal without competing news of yet another gross human depredation.

There was so much that Menka had long wished to push in the faces that crowded him in that club. He saw his own face among theirs, and its scattered clones, wherever he happened upon such hubs of complacency, but always he felt inhibited, even strange. And there was the fear of conflating nightmare with reality—Hilltop Mansion with the National Hospital, surgery wing. Which was the nightmare, which the testable reality? Even his award swam between, a slithery eel, morphing into human anatomical parts—were these all parts of the nightmare? The jury was out, but did the jury know of his history, and did they approve it? Excuse it? Dismiss it? Rationalize it, as he had done? Being fêted that evening perversely brought it all to the surface, a long-repressed bilge, and he felt his gorge rising. The trouble, he wanted to scream, is that it always happens elsewhere, far from this Hilltop observatory, ancient or sleekly, breathtakingly modernized, scattered countrywide. It only happens elsewhere, even when it takes place close by, even if at a short distance, just below these hills, on the built-up plains; it happens grimly, explosively, all the time, where my overworked staff on duty can testify to its palpable immediacy—that is the difference. It still remains elsewhere, even if the sounds occasionally carry uphill from the advancing northeast corner of the nation—Borno, Yobe, Taraba, Adamawa, Benue, overwhelming sections of Kaduna and sister cities, once remote from the madness, coming nearly within reach of our nicely lubricated gathering in this secular cathedral. Conversation remains measured, predictable, detached, faithful to inherited decorum that appears to cling to these Victorian portraits, the restraining décor, and MMMs, just like the one-and-a-half-century-old creepers cling to the outer walls, dispensing the soporific balm of a British countryside, the original mythical inventors and custodians of sangfroid. And of course we are only too grateful for those interjections of the rhetoric of learned detachment, even escapism, the exonerating transfer of grim reality to ideological paraphrases—all that so conveniently subsumes even the most accusing horrors, dispenses them in neat capsules we can pop down the throat and feel vindicated in our lofty indifference and pompous impotence. But we can explain it all we want; we still cannot wish it away.

It suddenly burst out in the open. The bouillabaisse of multiple ingredients, the devil's pottage, finally completed the rout, and Dr. Kighare Menka's Gumchi stomach rebelled. He began to sense his very presence within that environment as self-inculpation, even as flaring hypocrisy. Did he wallow in an unfair advantage because he was a doctor and thus thrown right into the consequences of decades of hideous derelictions? It was too late to ask, to call himself to order and sense of balance. Something snapped. Memory pointed accusing fingers at his own self. Suddenly the famed bedside manners, so lavishly lauded at the ceremony of the world-televised National Preeminence Award, crumbled under the protesting assault of a deeply embedded Gumchi idyll, their debris flying out of the stone-arched, wood-trellised British windows. It caught his innocent tormentors unprepared, right in the midst of a new round of banter over do-it-yourself unregistered members of the Order of Short Knives, who dissected their patients by the riverside, having anaesthetized them with potent *ogogoro* for lack of chloroform. Not forgetting the rest of the motley fraternity, also doctors in name—the government spin doctors, the cosmetic surgeons of national image, the specialist doctors of financial ledgers, the self-protective ascendancy of body-part combine harvesters and transplant specialists of reality, the appropriators of the vital organs of social survival who displaced and replaced at will. Like himself, albeit not so technically, they exercised powers of life and death, more inclined, however, towards those choices that defined them first and foremost, no matter their professions, as social morticians.

It was one of those days when Menka would wish afterwards that he could reverse the hands of the clock, or else that he could have found a way of reconciling the imbibed mores of childhood with the pragmatism so necessary for adult adjustments—one lived among others of the species, after all. Failing, he simply wished he had never left the hills of Gumchi, almost wished he had never set foot below the severity of the eternal self-sufficient rocks, never even met his bosom friend, the irrepressible Duyole Pitan-Payne, and their Gong of Four, never even approached the gates of a college of medicine. Usually such moods did not last long; duty and the needs of others were ever-ready to remedy the feeling of impotence.

But there he was, seated at the bar, his back turned to the main body of the lounge, and he woke to a realization that his beer mug appeared to have slammed itself on the bar, spilling its contents over the intruders and soaking the newspaper whose contents had sparked off the new round of self-savaging. He spun around on the high stool to confront the voices that had been united in his *laudamus* barely an hour before and were still luxuriating in a share of their member's public recognition. An out-of-body experience? Without question, he was indeed conscious of watching himself at one, even several removes. All that belonged in the purely academic realm or—resorting to his own people's summative formulation—medicine after death. Even he could not explain it, but yes, there was a crack in that mostly expressionless face, an additional streak to the cicatrix that somehow succeeded in not disfiguring his appearance. All he heard was his own voice in top register: "Cut it out! Yes, just turn it off—that tap! That's more than enough. What do you know? All of you, what have you seen? I said, where do you all live? Hypocrites!"

At the beginning of the outburst, no one knew it for what it was— the enraged kind. They thought he was entering into the spirit of the game. Then they saw his face, and all chattering froze. Eyes turned on one another, furrows dug deep into foreheads, a few raised glasses hung suspended halfway to destination. There was nothing more immediately forthcoming, so they remained confined to swiveling faces and bodies, seeking explanations. A handful, including Muktar, the club secretary—he had personally presided over Menka's induction into club membership—scrambled to recall who had sponsored him in the first place. Maybe he could explain, and apologize on the man's behalf. If not, both memberships would be a matter for review. The ensuing silence could not have been more convulsing if Dr. Menka had merely announced, "Isn't it about time we granted YoY laureates automatic membership in Hilltop Club?"

Finally a voice, a drawl in genuine concern. The voice belonged to Costello, the Italo-Nigerian, one of the older fixtures. He had been sitting close to the bar, enjoying the mildly rowdy session. "What's the matter, Doctor?"

Menka's response flew off without a pause. He flung his arm all round, his voice rising in contempt. "You. All of you! I don't believe any of you. You're either all hypocrites or . . . ignorant! Whichever, you are part of the nightmare and I say I don't believe you—that's all there is to it. And I am sick of listening to all this pointless babble."

Costello's voice grew even more solicitous, anxiously exploring. He considered Menka a friend. "So take it easy. They were just teasing. Did anyone say anything bad?" There were frowns and gestures of puzzlement around the room. "Menka, we came to celebrate you. What's gone wrong, my friend?"

The celebrant was no recent admittance, but few had ever found inclination or occasion to get close to him—not that he appeared to be in need of friendship or acceptance. He was not one of the regulars. A doctor's calling card was all hours, so no one really expected him to be a frequenter at club events. Just as long as he paid his membership dues and settled his monthly consumption account.

But there he stood, pinned against the bar by the small crowd, and the scorn on his face was unyielding, indeed hardening with every passing second, as if winding itself up for a terminal explosion. It was not long in coming.

"I don't know which is worse"—and he was near yelling—"these morbid jokes or the moral pontifications. That was a human being who was butchered, perhaps the hundredth this year alone—detected, that is, reported—and you all think it hilarious. And then the moralizing—I don't know which is the worse of these nightmares. Someday we'll all be grateful for one nightmare that knows itself—even one will do. But not now. Not yet. So all I ask for now is, how much does any of you know? Even the best informed—just how much do you really *know*?"

Another voice, again not hostile, not yet, attempted some oiled restraint. There had to be an explanation. It was unusual, unprecedented. "All right, our Dr. Bedside Manners," the voice virtually cooed, "this is unlike you, so tell us what we don't know. What's eating you? I don't know about others, but I am baffled. Can't we joke anymore? How do you think one keeps sane in this country? It's known as gallows humour, in case you never heard the expression. As a doctor you should even prescribe it. Gallows humour, good for digestion."

A member offered from across the lounge: "Maybe something terrible happened at the hospital, something we do not yet know about. Apart from the bomb, I mean."

"Is that it, Kighare?" Costello joined in. "You should have said. We could have postponed the party."

It was as if a blowtorch had been adjusted to its fullest suddenly and thrust in Menka's face. "Don't you all eat meat?" he yelled. "Which of you here has been to the meat shop lately? Or maybe you'll tell me you've never been?"

"What's the man talking about?"

"You. Me. All of us yapping away our souls in this palace of self-deception. That's what I'm talking about!"

Kufeji picked up the soggy newspaper, squeezed it and threw it behind the bar, headed back to his table. "Sorry-o. Someone seems to have got out of the wrong side of the bed this morning."

Dismayed murmurs spread across the lounge, creeping towards alarm. Had their own in-house, state-honoured doctor finally blown a gasket? Here and there some sniggering had begun to emerge. It was the secretary himself, Muktar, who picked up the gauntlet, his voice rising steadily with resentment. "What are you talking about, Mr. Surgeon? You haven't earned the right to come here and lecture members. Many of us here are senior to you! We avoid politics here, and also any holier-than-thou posturing. We are all Nigerians—no, we have some expatriates, we don't even remember that, they've become part of us. We have members from all over the country. No, wait, let me remind him"—he brusquely brushed aside a restraining hand from his seated neighbour—"I've had enough of this. Others can speak for themselves, but rules are rules." He raised his arm and pointed in the direction of the mantelpiece. "MMM—it's all there. I hate to have to invoke it. Never had to since I became secretary, but if that's what it takes . . ."

Menka looked in the direction of the latest interventionist, then began to move in his direction, parting with both hands the small crowd still standing around him. When he reached Muktar's table, he stood squarely and faced him. "What of you? You're local. Haven't *you* ever visited the meat shop?"

"What has a meat shop got to do with it? My wife buys all the food for the house. But I can tell you I'm not a vegetarian."

"Being a vegetarian has nothing to do with this."

"Then just what has to do with what? Why are you blowing hot over nothing? Come out straight with it, man! Cut out all the roundabout."

A new entrant said brightly, "Oh, I've got it. Pork! Is that the problem? Did someone suggest we scrap the club's no-pork-on-Fridays policy?"

Menka did not blink. "No one that I know of. But I am talking business. Simply business, do you understand? That's how far things have degenerated. And just because I come from the north, that does not make me a Muslim. I eat pork."

Muktar snapped back, "Then make yourself clear. First it was meat. Now it's business. What business?"

"You haven't answered me," Menka retorted. "Have you been to a meat shop lately? Clean, sanitized, well regulated by any standards—even bar-coded? It will pass any international standards—its products are branded, freshly packaged. Yes, that's what *I* am talking about. Specialized. Not pork. Or mutton either. Not even beef or poultry."

It only made matters worse. Sniffles competed with sniggers. The man was clearly disorientated. Something had gone wrong at the hospital. Part of the throat-clearing could have emanated from empathy or embarrassment, but it filled the lounge with unease, and a premonition of impending disaster. Chudi, owner of the cooing voice, appeared to have misheard. He shook his head mournfully and moved towards the club secretary, who had remained standing. "Menka, if you have turned vegetarian, just say so and leave us alone. No one is stopping you from launching a vegan campaign. Put up your posters or whatever you want."

It appeared to act as a signal for regrouping. Most moved back to their tables, but a trickle gravitated towards Muktar, mainly the club officers, Kufeji in the lead, perhaps propelled by a growing feeling that this somehow constituted a veiled attack on the competence of their executive. It required both solidarity and counteraction, possibly suspension. At least a fine. Kufeji leant close, whispered in the ears of his colleagues, but it was clearly a stage whisper, intended for everyone's hearing. "I think the Pre-eminence Award has scattered his Gumchi head." The mood was turning distinctly hostile.

"Maybe he would have preferred the populist YoY? You want to cross over, cross over. The club will sponsor you for Yeoman of the Year, category any which you choose. Even PACT. We'll come round and campaign for you. Don't take your frustration out on us."

Guffawing loudly, Muktar latched onto it. "Is that true, Doctor? All this sudden posturing on account of a national award? What happens when you get the Nobel Prize for Medicine!"

"Wissai? From which village? There's no quota system in Sweden!"

Unfazed but with studied emphasis, as one who was educating retarded pupils, Menka persisted. "Listen to me, I am not speaking of cow meat. Or goat. Or venison. I am not speaking of rump steak or veal cacciatori or pork chops in a fancy restaurant. Just the same, that establishment observes the same meticulous checks. The local inspectorate visits the premises and storage to check on quality, ensure that flies have not laid eggs in the meat and cockroaches are not scampering all over the floor. You will not find a single housefly buzzing within that shop. Standards are strict. It's all official. And impressive."

Muktar turned and resumed his seat. "I don't know about others, but I am tired of this rigmarole. If this is a campaign to involve the club in some new project of yours, you know the routine. The mission box is over there. Write down what you have in mind and drop it in there. We'll place it on the agenda at the next meeting. Now is not the time for it. We came here to celebrate your award, and I apologize to others for the mistake. It will not happen again."

The gruff sounds of dismissal were, however, cautious, unsure. Even the formerly disinterested had perked up and were keenly scrutinizing their guest of honour turned mighty irritant—but over what? Whatever the answer, this qualified for the grossest violation of MMM present and past officers could recollect in their combined tenures, an ominous display of Bad Form. The surgeon seemed embarked on a relentless course. Something unusual, even abnormal, was taking place in this in effect second home of theirs. Looks of apprehension were fast turning into flares of outright repudiation. The surgeon felt doused down from his fiery heights, drained. All commencing spontaneity defused, he eased back into a quieter stance.

As his gaze swept round the room, identifying individuals as if for the first time, his eyes caught, through a split curtain, a figure within the small alcove next to the swing doors that led to the kitchen. One of those stranger-recognition flashes that could be a mistake or taunting semi-recall. Not that he could claim to have met all the members, but the figure struck him as simply not belonging, yet he felt he had seen him somewhere not unrelated. The man stood idly chalking the tip of a billiard stick while assessing the relative positions of the balls on the ponderous table, perhaps as old as the mansion itself but in its prime, well-preserved condition; obviously it enjoyed regular renewal of its green baize. Instinctively Menka raised his eyes up the walls to see if the alcove also held a dart board—he had never really explored the club for its facilities, he reminded himself for the thirtieth time and some. He sensed, strangely, that the figure, whose features he could barely discern, had been paying far closer attention to exchanges in that lounge than to the billiards table. Come to think of it, he had not heard one click of the cue against a ball, no sound of collision of careering balls, or one that signaled a drop in the bag. The presence of a suspect stranger may have contributed to his feeling of exposure, even a mild feeling of foolishness. He had begun as the star attraction and now, within less than an hour, was being viewed as a pariah. The presence of an eavesdropping, suspect member further eroded his sense of a deserved, even overdue call to order, left embarrassment in it place. It was time to head home. The final therapy for the day's stress and excitement, dinner with his now thoroughly isolated self, beckoned.

As he slowly returned to the bar to pick up his present and leave, his gaze also reversing its line of observation, the figure was gone, as noiselessly as it had earlier filled the alcove while supposedly preparing for its next stroke. In the lounge itself, his interlocutors had drifted back to their interrupted exchange clusters, but only partially. The whispers varied. Some dismissed him as a crank or long-hidden bipolar; the rest remained simply puzzled by the abnormality of it all, the hostile accusation over something they could not yet fathom. Menka decided to pass through the billiards room, perhaps conjure over the dart board a few villainous *in absentia* figures that had contributed to his brain storm, then drill them full of holes—one of his secret modes of stress relief. He ordered another beer, downed it, turned to leave.

And then, just as abruptly, he changed his mind. Irrational though he found it, the disappearance of an outsider, albeit so presumed, decided him. It was no more than an intuitive flash. This lurking figure—could he be the one who had failed to deliver the crucial message that had thrown his hospital callers into a quandary? The visitation had taken place only a few days before. Someone was to have delivered a message, to prepare him for the visitation itself, and hadn't they mentioned something about this being a fellow club member?

THE VISITATION HAD FOLLOWED swiftly on the public announcement of the Independence Honours List, a bare three days after the award ceremony itself. Perhaps his callers had even watched the event on television, then met and decided to strike before others obtained allied ideas and netted their prize catch. Unlikely, but why take a chance? They certainly moved fast with the timing.

Recalling that day of his attempted co-option, Dr. Kighare Menka could only marvel at how incongruous yet logical it had been. The day had begun so quietly, almost lulling in its prospects. It promised to be a light workday. Just two minor surgeries, and he had begun to look forward to one of his rare early-closing hours. The usual rounds to check on his inpatients, then a drive to the club. That was his favourite hour, daily craved, grudgingly granted—the hours just after the departure of the business-lunch crowd and before the launch of the evening buildup by the thirsting faithful. They drove—or were driven—straight from offices, tugging off ties and abandoning jackets even as they strode through the oaken manorial doors. Today he would be one of those early birds.

Three men were seated in the corridor outside his hospital consultation room, obviously awaiting his return. That irritated him. It was not his outpatients day, and he had taken pains to give no one an appointment. Intuitively he felt that they were not patients. That assessment had nothing to do with the immaculate business suits worn by two of them, nor with the formidable polished leather briefcase sported by the younger-looking of the duo in bespoke suits. Menka's quick eyes assessed its leather hide as being nearly an inch thick, as if specially built to withstand a bomb assault, festooned with an array of combination locks that stood ready to frustrate all but the most seasoned code breaker with a whole night and day at his or her disposal. Nor did the splendour of a full *babanriga* worn by the third, the flowing, ornately decorated formal wear of the northern part of the country, play any role in his quick assessment—it was simply his customary intuition. Whatever brought them to the hospital had nothing to do with their health, or indeed any health emergency. On the other hand, he felt a distinct, uneasy tremor over his skin, along the spinal furrow, whose reading was that the visit had everything to do with his, Menka's, own well-being. It was again all intuition, he would later insist to his friend and confidant, Duyole Pitan-Payne. *My spine tingled. So I grimaced inwardly, shrugged, then braced my shoulders and said, "Gumchi Kid, here we go again, let's see what the cat has brought in today."*

On their part, the cats grinned most affably as he drew near, defeating Menka's effort to ensure that they at least glimpsed something of his displeasure. If they did, it did not appear to faze them in the least. A seemingly coordinated beam split their faces, as if they were bearers of unseasonal but nonetheless good tidings.

"Were you waiting for me?" he asked. They had positioned themselves so that he could only squeeze between them to gain entry into his office. The youngest stepped slightly forward, his spare hand flashing a card that had remained invisible until the moment of presentation. The voice emerged in a practiced executive delivery, businesslike yet accommodating. "My card, Dr. Menka. Yes indeed, it was you we came to see."

A cautious frown on his face, Menka ran his eyes quickly over the card. "Did my secretary give you an appointment? Today is not my outpatients day."

The spokesman's smile broadened. "We know, Dr. Menka. Today is your surgery day. We presumed on your indulgence. But we were also careful to check, and we saw that today's surgery schedule was light." He waved his hand. "May I introduce my colleagues?"

The admission merely increased Menka's irritation. "Well, if you know so much about my routine, then you also know that this is when I make my ward rounds. I am now on my way to do that."

"Of course, Doctor. We came prepared to wait. It is a matter of great importance, one that we believe will appeal to the love you have of your very profession. But Doctor, may I first present"—again he extended his arm to indicate his two companions—"my superiors. First, my immediate boss and head of our northern operations."

The indicated superior bowed, his card sleekly on offer. "Dr. Menka. We have heard a lot about you, even long before your recent state honours. My chance to say Congratulations, Doctor. Your great work among our wounded . . . we can never forget."

Menka shuffled his feet in accustomed embarrassment, received the card, shook hands. The young master of ceremonies turned to the figure in the *babanriga,* whose card had also emerged from the folds of his attire. "You won't recall me, Dr. Menka," he drawled, "but we have met. A very long time ago—when we were both young and . . . eager. Idealistic also, if you prefer. We did our youth service together in the state. Even at that time you stood out among our batch. The rest of us—well, we were just part of the herd."

Menka did not try unduly hard to task his memory—his batch had numbered over two hundred and fifty at induction, and he had served his sentence mostly in the hospital, interacted throughout with perhaps no more than a dozen or so of his inducted bunch. They were assigned from all over the nation and similarly dispersed after induction. He read the name on the card—Larinwa Odumade—and it meant nothing. "To be honest, I don't recall . . ." he mumbled. Then, briskly, "Well, hadn't we better go into my office? "His hand gestured towards the blocked entrance. They stood aside while he extracted a bunch of keys from his apron, opened the door, ushered them into his office, waited for them to be seated, then took his place by the side of his desk, standing.

They deployed themselves in what must have been an instinctive pecking order—Odumade in the only armchair, cushioned, into which Menka habitually sank after hours in the operating theatre. A straightback and a high stool served the other two. Menka then sat, half-arsed on the desk, one leg dangling. The obviously senior of the suited pair plunged into the order of events.

"Doctor, we know you're a busy man, and please accept our apologies for the intrusion. We are not here to waste your time. Or ours. But first let me add my congratulations to those already expressed by our young manager. We've come to invite you to come on our management board. That's it, sir. The decision was taken quite a while ago, but we were waiting for our chairman to return to the country. He has been on a world tour, broke it off specifically to be able to join us in this approach to you. We've been extending partnerships across the globe—"

Menka raised his hand. "Wait, wait, wait, Mr. . . ." He quickly shuffled the cards to refresh his mind.

His guest assisted him. "Rakuniwe. Dr. Rakuniwe. Professor." He gave a self-deprecatory smile. "Not a real doctor like you, I'm afraid, just the usual PhD. My real field is agronomy. I specialize in agric economics."

"Yes, Professor. I was about to say that I still do not know what partnership in what. I am completely in the dark about what has brought you here, gentlemen."

Rakuniwe's startled gasp was followed by a prolonged silence. Stopped in stride, baffled, the trio looked at one another, then at their equally baffled host, their faces gouged in frowns as deep as their commencing beams had earlier marked their confidence. The opening interlocutor, the young executive, rose slowly to his feet, the shiny briefcase sliding to the floor—he had forgotten that it rested on his lap.

"Dr. Menka, are you saying that you have no idea, no knowledge at all, regarding what has brought us here?"

Menka shook his head. Firmly. "Not a clue."

A medley of deep sighs ensued. The trio went into a huddle, from which eventually emerged a protesting voice, the young executive's. "But, Doctor, our intermediary assured us that he had spoken to you. Not made an offer—that was not his brief. We are here to do that. But the nature of the business, surely . . ."

"I know nothing. This is all very strange." He held up one of the cards. "This is my first intimation of what this may be about—'Primary Resources Management.' Coming across it for the first time."

"United Against Waste," the professor intoned, almost with a touch of solemnity, tapping the card at the bottom.

"Yes, I can see that. Your mission statement?"

"Precisely," said the young executive, relieved and eager, as if, despite the earlier setback, they were finally on common ground.

"That is what we do, Doctor. Prevent waste. We engage and maximize resources. Human resources."

After which all three kept silent, as if no other explanation were necessary. Dr. Menka glanced at his watch, looked up at his visitors, and found all three pairs of eyes on him, boring into him as if the guarantee of their entire purpose of existence were hidden somewhere within him. But he equally awaited elaboration. None was forthcoming. He decided to break the silence.

"I'm sorry, but I really have to do my ward rounds now. If you'd like to explain how you do that—this initiative against waste—and what you really want of me . . ."

The director of projects glanced at his chairman. He received a nod to proceed. "Doctor, it's all rather awkward. You see, we were assured that you had been duly briefed. Someone was sent to see you, one of your club members who knows you very well—at least, claims to. He was supposed to have laid the grounds for this meeting. Now we find ourselves in a difficult situation. We don't quite know how to go about this, and we were wondering . . ."

The chairman decided to take charge. "Why don't you come with us, Dr. Menka? I mean, come and see our operations for yourself. Then you can decide. It is not one of your run-of-the-mill businesses, not something you come across every day, but it's gaining ground. It's spreading. Expanding all the time, and it is highly profitable. You'd have noticed on that card that I'm an economist, so I know what I am talking about. And I can predict that it is only a matter of time and it will be quoted on the stock market."

Menka tried to interrupt, but Odumade persisted. "I know, I know. We shall take you to the site of operations so you can see for yourself. It all falls squarely within your profession. Where you come in is simply . . . your professional expertise. Prestige. And position. Our mission goes beyond waste management—you could even call it waste prevention. Right now it might seem that we are moving too fast for our time, but believe me, we have assessed the way society is tending, and we know this to be the business of the future. We have placed ourselves at the forefront of that future."

The doctor felt he had had enough. "Gentlemen, my staff are waiting for me."

"Ah yes, of course," sighed the man called Odumade. "We should release you now. How long do your rounds normally last?"

Menka's short fuse came to the fore. "Excuse me?"

"Your ward rounds. How long would that take?"

"I'm sorry, but I do not see why I should predict that to total strangers."

"I am not a stranger to you, Dr. Menka. I am not approaching you as a stranger."

Menka was startled, then angered by the abrupt change of tone. Did he sense a tinge of menace? Instinctively he responded in kind. "You are a stranger. I do not remember you from anywhere or anytime past, and frankly, I prefer to leave it that way." He rose. "And now, if you will be so kind as to excuse me . . ."

"Sit down, sit down, Dr. Bedside Manners," the man shot back at him. He swept the air with his wide sleeve, signaling a clear intention of staying put. "Or, if you prefer, why don't you go off on your rounds? We'll simply wait for you to be done and then we'll resume where we left off."

For a few moments Menka stood, stunned. Aghast. Then he burst out, "You will do what?"

"Wait here for you. We came with an offer. A partnership."

"And I am not interested. I don't care if you came to offer me the presidency."

The man chuckled. "No-o. Something a lot more modest. But definitely of interest to you. Please, go on your rounds. We have a long afternoon ahead of us. We're taking you on a ride—oh, sorry, bad choice of expression. Not that kind of a ride. Just a physical ride. On the bumpy side, but that's only a small stretch of the way, and even that is being taken care of. I promise you, Dr. Menka, it is one ride you will never regret."

The surgeon, known for outbursts that made acquaintances wonder how he ever acquired the title Dr. Bedside Manners, finally found his voice. "You will have something to regret if you do not leave my office—now! All three of you—get out!"

Odumade settled back in the chair even more comfortably. "Regret? I like that word. Do you sometimes think back on things you regret, Doctor? Have you any regrets at all? Anything in your entire existence that you regret? Think back, Doctor, think back. Take your time. We are in no hurry."

And now Menka found himself bereft of speech. Blackmail? Was this a blackmail session? His mind flew backwards over the years, wondering what immense crime he could have forgotten, of such weight that it armed his uninvited callers with such confidence. Try as he could, he could dredge up nothing. Then he saw the one whose card read "Director of Operations" move towards him, his tone placatory.

"Permit me to intervene, Dr. Menka. I apologize. I am truly sorry that things have taken this, er . . . rather hostile turn. That was not our intention. Totally at loggerheads with what we anticipated. I think it all has to do with, obviously, the missing link. We expected to meet you already in the know. Apparently not. The chief has just flown in from a prolonged tour, so, if I may say so, Chief, that made you somewhat irritable. Professor, am I right?"

The professor mumbled something incomprehensible but appeared to be simmering down. Menka did not feel the least bit mollified.

"You came into my office to blackmail me? Over what? Blurt it out! I dare you."

"No, no, no," the peacemaker persisted. "Dr. Menka, please, take my word for it. He spoke out of turn. Let's do it another way. We'll take our leave now and leave you in peace. I'll give you a call, Doctor, then come back and see you in person. Without the chief. He resumes his tour tomorrow, so it's just we, the locals, with whom you'll need to relate. We know the score. I'll take you round our operations and you'll see for yourself."

The other partner had also risen. "Yes, let's do it that way, Doctor. Please. I add my apologies to his. There has been a misunderstanding. We can still make this happen—it's a matter of mutual interest. Right now we need also to have a word with our failed intermediary. We need an explanation from that partner. And a new date for the ride. We'll clarify everything."

"The sooner, the better," Menka agreed. "I'd like to know what this is all about."

"Is tomorrow soon enough? It's a Saturday."

Menka shrugged.

The executive picked up his briefcase. "Can I meet you here tomorrow morning? Same time as now?" He looked at his watch. "Eleven a.m.?"

Stone-faced, Dr. Menka nodded agreement.

THAT VISITATION AND its morning after fully on replay, Menka fell completely in tune with his decision—he would finish what he had begun, take his leave, and never return to the club. The certainty destabilized him somewhat—a phase in his life had come to an end. He was spending his evening at the Hilltop Mansion Club, partaking of that ambiguous fellowship for the last time. As he rose, he heard the sound of a coin rattling down the metal chute of a jukebox in the recently abandoned alcove. The nearly totally forgotten relic, retained as an antique curio, found itself resurrected and recruited—perhaps to preempt a resumption of hostilities by the guest of honour? Or maybe to restore the ruptured ambiance of the club. It was an incongruous object in such a setting and was clearly tolerated for its very oddity, rarely played, a modern acquisition in its time that lingered on to augment the pub veneer already established by the billiards table and dart board. Suddenly given voice, the neglected jukebox rose to challenge the routine of Hilltop Mansion for the second time that day. Menka paused, his gift parcel in hand, then began to walk slowly towards the secretary, making it plain that that was his destination, for all the world unfazed. Arriving by his side, he waited the few remaining minutes for the track to end. In any case, it was a soothing melody, nostalgic and appropriately scratchy. It sang of a vale somewhere in the rusticity of the homeland of the original owner and donor. Against the weaving hills of Jos, that exile had perhaps sought to project the lulling evocation of someplace called Derry Vale in his nostalgic mind. Its strangeness momentarily tempered the generated heat and also gathered together the scattered shards of accustomed cordiality. Menka arrived at the secretary's table and stood beside him, the only way he was certain he would be accorded attention; even placed a hand on the man's shoulder and glued him to his seat with a pressure that was anything but hostile.

As he sensed the approach of the last violin whine, Menka raised his hand in the direction of the alcove to forestall a repeat. If necessary, he was resolved to raise his voice above any renewed din and generate a clash of decibels. His determination alone, he felt confident, was sufficient to floor any jukebox of twentieth-century manufacture. However, his voice remained under control, evenly modulated, conciliatory, but paced rapidly also to prevent the insertion of another disk or any dissenting effort to shout him down.

"One moment, please, just one moment. I owe you all an apology."

It worked. On the word *apology,* the putative disk jockey—it was Chudi—stopped, other heads turned in his direction, and ears perked up. Menka further placated them with a shy shake of the head, his hands raised shoulder high in a gesture of peace. "I agree. I should have gone into the mission box. I didn't even remember its existence." He expelled a mild snort. "Mission box! Most appropriate. Some of us have been bitten by the missionary bug, excessively, and I am speaking of both the main waves of religious exporters—yes, *those* missionaries. Anyway, there it is. We all know the society we live in. I just happen to be one of those who actually bathe in its offal. On a daily basis. Child rape. Child sodomy. Mutilations. I'm a doctor. I treat cases. I have studied victim and violator. But mostly all those derive from a sickness. They are the sick ones. Perverts. Plus the quota of morons who have simply abandoned conscience. They believe that sleeping with a three-year-old will change their lives for the better. Will win the American lottery. Or local elections. Or that sprinkling their food with powder from a smoked human kidney will make them live longer. We have overtaken South Africa on the index of casual rapes." He paused. They were still free to suspend him for breaking club rules—it was his valedictory speech, his parting gift of something to take home to wife and family.

"Yes, I should use the suggestion—sorry, mission box. But I have just remembered also that it is my night." His smile was self-mocking. "I am the guest of honour, right? Club rules entitle me to certain privileges. I'm nearly done, I have just one more question, and then I'll go home and leave you alone." Again he paused, cleared his throat. "Have you asked yourselves why it has been so difficult to stop rhino poaching?"

Again a puzzled silence. He chose not to prolong it, offering the answer himself. "Of course the answer is obvious. The horn. And for that, you must first shoot the rhino. Pass all the UN resolutions you wish, the Japanese will pay astronomical sums for a pinch of rhino dust. And you all know why, don't you?"

The atmosphere changed, shed a large wedge of hostility; the tension eased and the laughter turned salacious. Virility jokes and gestures passed from mouth to mouth, snigger to snigger, then petered out as a voice quietly admitted—a voice upped at last. "I know I must be slow, but I still don't get the connection. What have rhino horns to do with this?"

"Myth. Just myth." Menka sighed. "Medically it's all nonsense. There is no ivory component in Viagra or any of its effective predecessors or successors. It's a myth. So is the heart or scrotum or pubis of a human, pounded or stirred into pottage, in this rampaging obsession to get rich. But there are hundreds and thousands who believe it. And a handful take it sufficiently seriously as to lose all human compunction."

"So? What's the issue for us, Doctor, please?" It was Kufeji, the one who had started it all. "And this time, to the point."

"Supply and demand. The law of supply and demand comes into play. And that is what, frustratingly, most of us refuse to contemplate. Both the state and ordinary citizens like you and me. We keep talking about the sick ones who would kill anyway. But what of the sane ones, at least the ones we call sane? Look around. You need to take a very good look around. Don't we all look sane? We get drunk, but eventually we sober up, we return to sanity—agree? But who knows where some of us do our shopping?"

Menka waited. He seemed perversely resolved to ensure his complete isolation, and in that he was clearly succeeding. The response was not long in coming. It was Muktar.

"You have something to urge on the rest of us, Doctor, right? Well, just say it. You are the guest of honour. You have the floor, but don't overdo things."

Menka's voice turned nearly pleading. "Yes, I do have something on my mind. It's been growing in me. Call it a nightmare, if you like. Over and beyond the tumours I have to examine, then decide upon—leave well alone or take it out. I sometimes feel that everything I read in the media is addressed to me. Personally. Yes, that's the truth. The hypocrisy we all live. And the nightmares. No, no, no, this is not an accusation flung at anyone here, no. I have no grounds for that. But you see, this club is not the entire world. It is not even the real world. I look around and yes, we all look so safe, it makes us complacent, underestimating what is out *there!*"

Menka held up his hand to quell the rising murmurs of renewed protest. "Only a few more minutes and I'm done. It's about time you learnt something outside your professional stockades. I just want you to know that some places exist that many of us know nothing of. Maybe the club can play a role, maybe not. I don't know, but I must make sure you cannot claim ignorance after tonight—call it the missionary in me. If I fail to bring you into this . . . well, just say I couldn't live with myself after tonight. After all, this is not supposed to be a club of ostriches—please, be patient. You see, your men of power, your sanitized community leaders, moralizing from soapbox to pulpit and minaret and back again—you should try and get to know them better. You might meet them coming from strange places, places you don't wish to know of. Places where they do their shopping. But what kind of meat do they buy? Kufeji, you began all of this—that's what I am talking about. It's all there, in that news item. I've been there. I was taken there. And at such times I wished I believe in a god, so at least I could have some entity to blame for abandoning humanity. The rest of the time I wish I had taken to a different profession."

"Oh, come on," protested Costello.

"That's God's truth," Dr. Menka stated, his voice matter-of-fact. "Not that I believe in him. Or her. Anyway, that's the end of my spiel. I wish to thank you all again for honouring me. I am going home now to open my gift."

Menka walked away in the silence, passing again through the billiards room, perhaps in the hope that the lurking figure would emerge. He was increasingly convinced that it was the missing emissary. There was only the disk jockey, Chudi, and he hurriedly skipped into the main lounge, unsure how to deal with any further outburst from a seizure that he could not quite diagnose. The doctor took a deep breath, took out his mobile phone, and dialed his "twin," Duyole Pitan-Payne. His shoulders seemed to loosen as he heard the voice at the other end, his face slackening in relief for the first time that evening, from the first sound of the familiar rumble. Any chance listener would have been confounded by the cryptic exchange that followed, since it did appear to transmit sense between the two. It was clearly responsible for the mood change that overtook the surgeon at the Hill-top end of the exchange, a change that was in stark contrast with that of the recipient at Villa Potencia, Abuja.

"Kiln ready stoked." It sounded like an identification sign.

"Matchstick and kindling."

"Gumchi Kid, that really you?"

"Gong of Four."

Aware of his location, Pitan-Payne gave a quick look around. Nothing abnormal appeared to have been stirred into action. There was just Mr. Garuba, his equivalent. He continued on a more sober register: "That really you, Gumchi?"

"Who else?"

"Nightmare or what?"

"No fun. Crack in the mould. Stand by to receive."

That elicited a sharp breath intake from the distant end. "Skin or deep?"

"Skin."

"Dense or fluid?"

"Both. But not desperate."

"Neither bone nor marrow? Be candid!"

"Light bone. Just hairline. Metal fatigue. Nothing cooling kiln won't heal. Mingling with a few old faces instead of total strangers. Often with no faces. Sometimes even better off without. Takes its toll after a while."

"You'll never guess where I am—tell you about all that later. But I watched the ticker tape. The news seems bad today—the market blast. Is that it?"

"Never anything specifically. But it takes its toll. Adds up with other things. Not apparent, but it takes its toll."

"All right. Firing time?"

"This weekend. I'll book my flight tomorrow and call you."

"Advance stoke?"

"No, not on your side. Maybe mine. I plan to look up one of

ours—Bade. The fearsome foursome rides again—wouldn't that be great? Seen him lately?"

"Hmm. Bothersome item. He also seems to have taken to iso. Like Farodion."

"Faro is a special case. I think we've lost him completely. He's migrated—let's hope not terminally. Not to the Great Casting Kiln. The company diminishes, I'm afraid."

"Bade is around, but not quite firing. He ran into some kind of trouble. Ironic, isn't it? It was Faro one expected to provide that kind of gripe."

"That's sad."

"I know. He's getting back on his feet. Very slowly. He's been keeping to himself, that's all. Maybe he feels he's let the side down. Doesn't take calls."

"The Gumchi Kid doesn't take no for an answer."

That drew a chortle from the other end. "Doesn't the world know it! Right on, and good luck. A big reunion dinner. I'll alert Bisoye—no, maybe I'll simply set up a surprise. No, best to start all over again. Elevate Bow-Out Rout to something else—have to think up what. See what you've done?"

"All that trouble? I'll cancel."

"Write your will."

"On my way."

"Whichever way—war or peace. Dead or alive. Be on the plane."

"As the crow flies. Will chirp."

"Kiln on stoke."

"Cross my bones."

"Gong of Four!"

"Gung-ho!"

"Four for one."

"One for four-o."

The celebrated surgeon Dr. Menka looked quickly around the alcove, checking that no one had been listening. A childlike, mischievous, but contented grin. He replaced the mobile in his pocket, squared his shoulders, executed a high five all on his own, and moved to continue his passage home, his stride transformed into a Richard

Rowntree *Shaft* swagger, better known as stomping. As he pushed the curtains open, he surprised a small group gathered on the other side, obviously awaiting his exit. None of them failed to notice the mood transformation in the man who had harangued and implored them just ten minutes before. Tormented and tormentors alike, they stared at him in disbelief. Menka, at first startled by the reception committee, recovered before they did, winked, and moved towards the exit.

Blocking his way, however, was the Old Man of the Desert, flanked by Costello. He looked at the gift parcel under Menka's armpit and read accurately that Menka was taking his leave. He shook his head.

"Doctor, you can't just leave us like that. Some of us have questions that need answering." He stood aside. "Come and join us at our table. Away from the rest. Where we can talk seriously."

AT THE OTHER END, in Villa Potencia, Abuja, Pitan-Payne slowly replaced his mobile. Looking up, he saw Equivalent staring at him with a mixture of surprise and suspicion.

"Is that not some secret cult language?" he asked.

Cheerfully Pitan-Payne reassured him. "Of course it is. Only four of us in the whole wide world speak it. We've lost touch for a while. Now talk to me about this masterpiece you've written. Fill in the missing nitty-gritties. I feel ravenous—your boss has proved most inconsiderate of my time, but that's nothing to beat the way I feel starved for some insider stuff. How did you deal with that Bushman?"

The special adviser looked disgruntled. "How did we? I don't know. I was telling you—they kept me out. Top party hangers-on only." His voice rose higher and higher with resentment. "I was only called in afterwards to be told by that Dr. Merutali—he's the Steward's official speechwriter—that I would have to make changes to my work. Only two hours given me, I couldn't even go home for dinner. That is no way to treat an author. Writing a book is not the same as just writing speeches. I worked till midnight to make the changes. But that's all right. If the Steward hasn't signed off, who is anyone to go to bed? I like the way he leads by example. But that governor has a lot to answer for!"

9.

The Rumble of the Humble

Who could ever have entertained a thought that a rookie politician, recently brought into the ruling party of People on the Move, had the ability to generate that stressful day for the Number-Two official resident of Villa Potencia! That assailed incumbent was none other than Sir Godfrey Danfere, Knight of the Order of Templars. Pitan-Payne was right—he had indeed spied a gaggle of party stalwarts, as well as the maverick proprietor of *The National Inquest,* filtering through security checkpoint number 3, but the crisis was over. What he had glimpsed on arrival was the team of party coroners moving in to take orders on designated lines of public damage control, report back to their chapters, set the ball rolling for the final set of primaries, armed with newly crafted party slogans. Chief Benzy had been summoned to affirm his role in the changed picture—the prime award of the annual Night of Nights and its prime feature, PACT, the People's Award for the Common Touch.

Normally unflappable, Sir Goddie had been badly shaken, his carapace of invincibility cracked—in an open field, and under the full glare of the public. A mere political neophyte, and a defector at that, had stolen his identity handle, and in the most brazen, matter-of-fact manner, as if the culprit had no notion of the commission of any crime, nor of the consequences of such an affront. It was difficult to believe, but when eventually called to account, the man was reported to have looked bewildered. He did not deny it, having heard of the adoption of that nom de guerre from the knight himself, yet he blithely proceeded to appropriate it as if it were just another lump of discard in a junkyard. And he continued to cry persecution all the way to his village and to any listening ears along the way.

Pity, Sir Goddie's handlers had failed to check the reasons why, despite his popular appeal in his constituency, the defector's opposition party had denied him the governorship ticket. The ruling party was only too delighted to receive him, guarantee him his heart's desire under its policy of SAT—"special automatic ticket." As a party wag was wont to explain it, that policy assumed that you had sat—and passed—all the required tests and were thus qualified for whatever position was under negotiation. The party leader, Sir Goddie himself, candidate for a renewed tenure, had personally received him into his ruling party at one of the most intimidating rallies ever witnessed in the constituency of that very ingrate. The affair was thus an open event, not a deniable glitch that could be shunted out of existence or memory, having been witnessed by a cast of millions and a few more million viewers on television. Sir Goddie had suffered the humiliation—all by himself and with a handful of his image-makers in the know—of personally handing over the party flag to the miscreant, anointing him the party flag bearer and inevitably the winner of the approaching governorship elections. Goddie rose from his elevated seat on that rally podium, symbolically handed over the party and state control to this upstart in his own state, raised his arm in a victory signal, jointly waved the enormous flag up and down and west to east, and chorused the party name and slogan combination, "People on the Move." Then he was compelled to listen to the most treacherous acceptance speech in his entire career. He watched the crowd go into ecstatic applause for the blackguard, not one jot of suspicion on his mind that this anointed son was about to steal his identity, his political image stamp, in his very presence, to his own face. After handing over the flag, he returned to his seat, already bored by the familiar ritual, his mind only on quarter attendance at the rest of the proceedings. All of a sudden his wandering wits were jerked back onto the teeming plain of reality by an unprecedented rhetoric of pure perfidy: *Once elected, I shall jettison the elitist title of governor and all its derivatives, connotations, presup-*

positions, circumlocutions, and other concomitants. I shall contest the elections not to govern but to serve. I therefore declare, fellow citizens of our beloved state, that I shall interact with you as your servant, not your ruler. On assuming office, I shall choose to be addressed as your Comrade State Servant—CSS for short—not as Your Excellency the Governor.

Even the annunciation flam was copyright, stolen, claimed Sir Goddie's team, nearly word for word by the scallywag—though that was somewhat unfair. Chief Akpanga never did see any such script, which was tightly guarded by Goddie's chief image-maker and scriptwriter, Dr. Merutali, sometimes known as Dr. Fix-it. He insisted that the speech was nowhere near a duplication of what he was preparing— not even yet finalized—for his paymaster. Nonetheless, bemoaned Sir Goddie, this was a stab in the back, just the kind of slithery conduct expected from a green snake in the green grass. Akpanga was just like the palm oil he marketed—greasy—an unscrupulous opportunist—no wonder he kept jumping from party to party, the plundered knight raged. *I did not know it at the time, but I had taken a snake to my bosom! That male Jezebel stole my image!*

Governorship primaries took place routinely before the prime ministerial, with the presidential tucked in between tenures since that event took place only once every six years. Maybe it was time the process was overhauled, with advance vetting of all acceptance speeches. All that for the future. For now it was a successful pre-emptive strike, a public relations coup, and the prime ministerial camp was justly miffed and disoriented. This was identity theft, plain and simple. By public proclamation, symbolically endorsed by the topmost figure of the party structure. Copyright now belonged irreversibly to the first open user. There was nothing his superior could do except grin without and grimace within, commence plans for Akpanga's death from a thousand tiny cuts while simultaneously embarking on brainstorming to leapfrog the pesky footling a rung or two down the humility ladder. An internal emergency was declared. Orders were issued for a one-day retreat, at the end of which . . . ! Or else!

The Image Task Force was reconstituted. Debate commenced in the early morning after the historic rally, with the aggrieved leader himself presiding. This was brainstorming at the highest pitch, no time for peanut brains who merely filled up party-allocated slots in his government. When Shekere Garuba walked in, blithely assuming that his place at the session as author of a twenty-five-page biography, half of it full-page portraits and action photos with captions, was a foregone conclusion, Sir Goddie sent him out to go and fetch his bowl of kola nuts, then sent his secretary after to instruct him to hand over the stimulants to her and not bother to return. A firm believer in delegating, Goddie nonetheless entrusted weighty matters of state to no one but himself—he would stimulate ideas and cut out drivel. It was a difficult choice; he would have preferred to preside over yet another emergency session that was taking place simultaneously within the same power precincts, to turn the screw himself and watch the felon squirm. This was of course the trial of Candidate Akpanga for antiparty activities, identity theft, etc., etc. However, it did offer an opportunity to make a virtue out of necessity. So he invoked the principle of *nemo judex in causa sua*—never a judge in your own cause. He assigned the case to a reliable party stalwart, only incidentally an unapologetic Goddie diehard, while he presided over the more creative arm of damage control. The rapporteur for the trial was the versatile party intellectual and general Fixer Dr. Merutali. He was also the link for the antiparty tribunal.

The transcript of the trial would become a party classic. It made for some soul-searching, not merely within People on the Move but indeed as a reference, cautionary document for other parties in their eagerness to field electoral "sure bankers." Treasured excerpts, especially those that raised Akpanga's stock as an underrated political orator—officially leaked, some alleged—escaped party censorship and eventually found their way into the notorious social media. While there were undoubtedly suspicions of doctoring here and there, the main extracts were generally agreed to be authentic, based on Akpanga's own account of his ordeal when he returned to a hero's welcome in his village and was formally fêted by the chairman of his local council.

Akpanga, it would appear, stood trial on two counts.

Transcript from the Trial of Chief Governor-Designate Akpanga for Antiparty Activities and Conduct Bringing the Party into Conflict, Indiscipline, and Disrepute: Count I. PLAGIARISM AND IDENTITY THEFT.

"Chief Akpanga, you know why we have summoned you to this meeting, don't you?"

"No, I don't. You say I commit crime against the party. I still don't know what crime."

"You have done great harm to the party that welcomed you to its folds. You have repaid the party openness with malice and ingratitude."

"This is persecution. You know I am popular. I am the only one who can win that seat in my constituency. Why are you people persecuting me?"

"With all due respect, Mr. Akpanga, we will ask the questions."

"All right, I am here to hear you. Ask your question."

"Good. We shall go straight to the point. First, do you deny that you paid a visit to the leader, Sir Goddie, to formally thank him for approving your admission into our great party?"

"Yes, is that not customary? Is that not what our culture tells us to do as Africans? I went with full entourage. And I took him four baskets of yams, two rams, a coop of guinea fowl. Go and ask them at the security gate, where they took charge of everything."

"They were duly delivered—please, let us avoid digressions. We want to get to the point quickly."

"All right, continue."

"When you met the leader, Sir Goddie, what did he tell you?"

"He welcome me like his own son. He serve me kola nut and I take oath over schnapps. He give me his special telephone number and tell me to call him day and night. Anytime I want to talk to him, he say, just call him."

"Yes, go on."

"I thank him. I tell him I am ready to serve People on the Move body and soul. I tell him my loyalty was now fully with People on the Move, not with those useless people—"

"Right, Mr. Akpanga, very good. Do you recall how you addressed him?"

"Yes. I addressed him with all respect. I say to him, Your Excellency, I have come here to—"

"Stop there, Mr. Akpanga, stop right there. You addressed him as Your Excellency, right?"

"Yes."

"And then what did he say?"

"He stop me, just like you do just now. He said, No, no. I want you to address me as National Servant. That is how I intend to be addressed. I want to do away with Excellency. No more Excellency this, Excellency that."

"Yes?"

"So I address him National Servant, sir. I say, National Servant, sir, I have come here to thank you. I add sir because everybody know he is a sir, and also he be my superior."

The trial jury looked at one another, their eyes alight with relief—and surprise. They had expected stout denials. This made it all easier. The prosecutor flung his arms upwards.

"So you admit it."

"Of course. What is there to deny? From then on I address him National Servant, sir. At home, after the rally, I even refer to him as Our National Servant."

The party prosecutor now proceeded to give every word full gravity, stabbing the air in the direction of his chest.

"And yet, knowing that, the following week of party primaries, in your acceptance speech, fully aware that that designation had been taken by the leader, you proceeded to appropriate it to yourself in your acceptance speech."

Akpanga turned from one persecuting face to the other in mounting disbelief. *"What is wrong with that? I wanted to show loyalty. Is he not our leader? I like the idea, so I follow his example. Are we not the same party? Where is the problem? He is for centre, we are just state, so there is no confusion. I think everyone should do the same thing."*

There was silence in the trial chambers. Finally:

"Chief Akpanga, have you ever heard of identity theft? Do you know the meaning of copyright? Legal or moral, it doesn't matter. Copyright is copyright. Are you aware of copyright?"

"Oh, you mean I didn't copy it right? Is that what you call anti-party activity? Eh, we can always make correction. If it is a matter of grammar or spelling, nobody is above mistake . . ."

At that point, it is reported, the chairman of the trial panel called for a recess. The jury went into a huddle to consider the disconcerting turn that the trial had taken. When it was time to resume, the chairman recused himself from further participation in any trial that involved Chief Akpanga, pleading health reasons.

IN A SEPARATE CHAMBER in the same wing of the presidency, around a ponderous conference desk, the more cerebrally strenuous exercise attained fever pitch—a search for a substitute for the now-compromised designation. The machinery was ready; the graphic artists awaited the logo to move into action with images. The printing press yawned for fodder—time was short, and Sir Goddie on the impatient side. Glad he was that he had chosen to preside, because no sooner was the session open for suggestions than a primed, overeager voice proposed "the Nation's Serf."

One look at Sir Goddie's face was sufficient. The peon tried to recast, refine, etc., but it was too late. The bellow "Take your yam pottage brain out of here!" found him already at the exit, fulsomely apologetic, to be formally banished and confined to his office until after re-inauguration. *Slave* as a proposition—"Slave of the State"—fared only less suicidally. The proposer raced to place it within a rhetorical frame—"I stand before you, a Slave of the State," etc. It did sound less repellent than Nation's Serf, but Sir Goddie pronounced it slithering too slimily obviously down the chute of self-abasement—to be expected only from Pharisees and Sadducees. The proposer suffered the fate of his predecessor, with just a few refinements in administrative castigation.

The "People's Valet" was next to surface. It rated very high—so many angles to it, it struck an exotic tonality, and after all, did the party election promises not include a cleanup undertaking? When taken with "Grooming the Nation for the 21st Century," it became even more acceptable.

The American-trained member of the Image Task Force, however, wrinkled his nose—it did not smell quite right. In the U.S. of A., he reminded his colleagues, the valet was the garage flunkey. He relieved clients of their limousines, stacked them, brought them out of confinement when the clients were done with their business lunches, dinner dates, shows, or shopping sprees. Was the prime minister of the most populous black nation to be conflated with a mere parking attendant who earned a living from tips? What did it matter if some of the more upscale valets were so snooty that they refused coins—even if the coins exceeded the customary tip—insisting always on the "rustle of green-backs"? A rustle would be strange to his compatriot big men—notes rustled mostly in isolation, and local players were more accustomed to the *thwack* of landing packs, high domination, mint fresh, always in hundreds. Only then did counting make sense and save labour. And so on and on, the arguments swayed this way and that. In-house, much-traveled professors were summoned to join the discourse. They trooped in from the Ministries of Culture, Education, Mass Commu-nication, Business, etc.—drop everything and report to the presidency immediately! Over coffee and *akara* bean cake, crunchy *chin-chin* snacks, alligator peppers, kola nuts, and other instant energy induc-ers, they strained to find the perfect fit within the adopted twinning of service and loyalty. "General Factotum," "National Supervisor," "Overseer," "Field Worker," "Foreman," "Attendant General" . . .

Finally, towards evening, a timorous voice belonging to a Youth Corps intern just graduated from the Institute of Theological Studies piped up: "*Steward,* sirs? How does *Steward* sound?"

There was silence in the conference room. The eyes of the princi-pal himself lit up like twin fireflies. "The Nation's Steward," the hesi-tant voice further amplified. The brainstorming paused in stride. Each expert checked other faces for reassurance—somehow it sounded a reasonable fit—finally resting on Sir Goddie's face, awaiting verdict.

Independently of desperation for leftovers after intellectual larceny, there was, Sir Goddie felt, a finely adjustable, double-, even triple-decker signification about the consolation title—the Nation's Steward. It suited a governance source from which orders emerged, yet insisted on acting subordinate, and with plausible dignity. *Steward* dispensed that faint suggestion of being in charge, unlike *Servant,* the very func-tion of which the intended beneficiary, Sir Goddie, temperamentally detested, though he had not really found it untenable before it was stolen. It went beyond sour grapes, however. It had to do with his knighthood—a *sir* was a contradiction of the servant's functions. The notion of serving brought out his most irritable moods but also the most colourful, memorable declamations, of which perhaps the often-

est cited was "I prefer to sock it to them rather than suck up to them."
That enjoyed the liveliest retransmission from desk to desk among the
villa staff. "Didn't I order you to kick some arse?" came a close second
favourite. It attested also to his familiarity and identification with the
reported sally from a past American president during that nation's
ritual of televised debates—*Hey, did we kick some arse?*—unaware
that the microphone was still on.

Sir Goddie silently wrapped his lips around the proposed designation, chewed it a little, and found that, yes indeed, it was palatable. A
creature of deep religious convictions, he found it immensely evocative. There was a theological redolence about stewardship that he had
already begun to mentally explore—*Let us remember that one day
we shall all render account of our stewardship on earth, etc., etc.*—
that suited a full-time commitment to the management of property
and possessions in the here and now. The leader was lost in a reverie,
a parade of images of those stewards of scriptural chronicles, sometimes entrusted with the total control and management of households,
thrones, and commercial empires. The icing on the cake, however, was
summed up in its popular, nonspecialist understanding—stewardship
as camouflage for power under the servant's livery. He especially
delighted in the implicit dissembling—stewardship. So, he knew,
would his campaign manager, the party caucus, and all. The spin doctors would be enraptured. It was a clear case of having one's cake and
eating it, currants, trimmings, icing, and all. And of course he would
nod bashfully when they all came to congratulate him on his choice—
genius, Sir Goddie, pure genius.

"Out of the mouth of babes . . ." he began, only to raise his hand
to restrain other hands poised for relieved applause. "But not quite.
Close, very close, but not right on target. The People. Change *Nation*
to *People* and what do you get?"

A cementing chorus filled the chamber: "The People's Steward."

The newly employed domestic beamed. "Nation? State? You
leave that to the internationalists. On home ground, always give pre-
eminence to the people. It doesn't get more grassy-rootsy than that!"

That same evening the theology student was moved from internship into a permanent position in the ministerial office. It contributed
to Shekere Garuba's general disgruntlement.

The most pressing business of the day had ended in triumph, a dangerous outsider checkmated. Re-designation settled, the task of organizing supportive images could begin in earnest. There was much catching up to do—a different yet related tournament was at hand, and other contenders had enjoyed a clear run so far in acquiring credentials for that contest. Sir Goddie's mind had already shifted—it could occupy fifty different planes at once. Now it raised itself up to an even higher level of aspiration—PACT! The annual People's Choice Awards. Alas, there also lurked the same stalker, the ubiquitous Chief, now Governor-designate Akpanga. Accustomed to being on the side that dished it out to others, Goddie began to wonder if he had not become a victim of undeclared persecution. Was Akpanga's defection to his party genuine? Or could it be part of a cunning design? The man had to be a plant! It was not simply that he quit, he was sent! His mission was to undermine the ruling party through a frontal attack on the leader's accustomed state of being in charge.

Designed as the people's answer to the "elitist" Independence Day Honours List, the alternative event was nearly as good as an election ace in hand. That it should fall in the wrong hands at election time was not a welcome prospect. It went beyond the award itself. The maverick media proprietor exerted such influence that he was assiduously courted by no matter what government was in place. His journal, *The National Inquest*, was a fearsome weapon of subjugation that made even the powerful occasionally pause before taking a dubious plunge. Oromotaya's award Night of Nights was, without argument, the event to beat. In Sir Goddie's campaign strategy, it stood to reason that his new identity as the People's Steward would constitute a distinct advantage in securing nomination for the most coveted of the awards of the People's Choice—Dr. Merutali himself had not failed to stress its importance at strategy sessions. It was not, he was quick to point out, a matter of life and death. However, the role of *The Inquest* in swaying votes at election time was ignored only at the candidate's peril, and a YoY Award was the most visible evidence of endorsement by that institution. The party had done its "arithmetic, cashrithmetic, and thuggerithmetic," courtesy yet again of Sir Goddie, and would still win without it. Nonetheless, it was a feather that deserved its place on the knighthood cap—actually the elongated gondola-shaped hat of the Knights Templar. The first and major step was to secure nomination, and from a prestigious source. That done, the rest was easy.

Governor-elect Akpanga, in all innocence, had no notion whatsoever of the full extent of the grounds on which his servility gambit had so blatantly encroached. Nor was he even aware that he had been scouted and was now shortlisted for that same apex award. Akpanga was simply one of those products of Nature upon whose heads the wand of recognition lands, without any effort on their part. An oil producer and marketer—the palm oil of human, not machine, consumption—Akpanga was accustomed to working arm- and knee-deep in the gooey cholesterol-saturated product, noted for its deep red-purple intensity. He had laboured side by side with his workers ever since he had first learnt, as a barefooted, semiclothed urchin, to extract the precious colloid, easily the densest cooking oil humanity ever forced from spiked clumps of kernels that ringed the neck of the palm tree. Even squirrels, whose favourite snack it was, found negotiating the spikes to sink their snouts into the kernels a sometimes thankless exercise, the harvest hardly worth the labour. Such a parable of Nature made for irresistible promotion images and campaign copy—it was a predictable leap from "from a nest of thorns, the kernels of life" to "from a nest of thorns, the kernels of wisdom"— words that his party would come to regret as each public appearance became a source of escalating embarrassment on every occasion that Akpanga left his comfort zone. At the time of the find, however, he was the political catch of all time! A godsend. The oil man was a natural, and soon pithy comments wrapped in folksy renditions found themselves attributed to the successful oil merchant, sometimes with his head emerging from a penumbra of kernels. His presence at campaigns guaranteed a down-to-earth dimension, a public relations dividend of minimal labour investment. Akpanga's own election trajectory was one of a constant shoo-in—beginning as a town council member, unchallenged in his own milieu of a once-overlooked constituency. From there, all proceeded exactly as Nature prescribed. Palm oil had furnished him with all the wealth required for each succeeding step. Akpanga became a rallying point for others. Soon he found himself referred to as Godfadda Junior—the position of the godfather of all being conceded to Godfrey Danfere by universal consent, even across party lines. With the first taste of office, and with prodding from calculating interests, came the state of addiction. From local councilor to chairman, then House of Representatives . . . Finally, at the approach of the next elections, Akpanga declared, *Governorship or quit!*

The ruling People on the Move Party, proudly known as POMP—*We are the people of pomp and majesty, Guardians of the people's sovereignty, etc., etc.,* went the party anthem—desperate for a foothold in a tantalizing zone that controlled a fair percentage of the other, more potent oil deposits, offered it to him with no strings attached. His departure was a mixed relief for his original patrons, and they wished his new party the best of luck. *They'll find out, all in good time,* smiling behind their hands but of course condemned to endure the jeers and taunts of the sour-grapes morality tale. How right they were after all, lamented Sir Goddie, the man had nothing in that skull but clotted palm oil. No matter, his punishment awaited him, governor or no governor—if he cared to look up, his neck would twitch from the dangling object known as the Sword of Damocles. Right now it was time to concentrate on the main target—the Festival of the People's Choice, and its highly prized awards of the Yeomen of the Year. Sir Goddie had his eyes on the prime prize, and if the palm oil tycoon chose to act spoiler just one more time . . . !

Engineer Pitan-Payne! In the day's to-ing and fro-ing, he had forgotten all about him. Feeling genuinely contrite, he had already reached down to press a button underneath his desk when he heard the knock on the door.

"Yes?"

The caller was Dr. Merutali, the image-maker, fresh from the Chamber of Inquisition on Chief Akpanga's misconduct. There was a sly look on his face like one who was trying hard to suppress a smile, and Goddie instantly bristled. Only a handful of individuals, of the caliber of Teribogo and Dr. Merutali, enjoyed the right to walk in on the prime minister without first checking in with the chief of staff.

"What have you got to smile about?"

A calm, not easily ruffled operator, used to handling clients from bilious monarchs to wheedling entertainers, Merutali moved to the

Steward and laid two neatly typed sheets of paper on his desk, took a seat, and helped himself to a kola nut.

"I think all competition is over. We can proceed to elections."

The People's Steward pulled the folder closer, opened it. "This had better be good."

Transcript from the Trial of Governor-Designate Chief Akpanga for Antiparty Activities and Conduct Bringing the Party into Conflict, Indiscipline, and Disrepute: Count II

Acting Chairman: "Let the records show that hearing by this Special Panel resumed at 4.30 p.m. under a new chairmanship. My name is Ogusuigbe. The former chairman has requested to be relieved owing to an attack of migraine. Everything else remains the same. Chief Akpanga, are we ready to resume?"

The accused, Chief Akpanga, having indicated his readiness, the acting chairman continued.

"Chief Akpanga, we have also been delegated to look into an incident that took place at your home two days ago, in which the police had to be summoned and arrests made."

"Good, I am glad the party has noticed how I, number-one citizen of my state, am being persecuted."

"You are not yet number-one citizen, Chief Akpanga."

"By God's grace, I shall be. Just a few more weeks and I shall take office. God has said so. The promise of God is a pledge that will not be broken."

"As loyal party members, we share your hopes and prayers. But right now we are here to ask you some questions about how truly loyal you are to the party, especially where its public image is concerned."

"Fire on. If it is a matter of image, try my loyalty and see."

"Do you consider yourself loyal to our leader, Sir Godfrey Danfere?"

"If I am not loyal to him, who else will I be loyal to?"

"Do you accept that you have a duty not to tarnish his image, or the image of the party?"

"As far as I am concerned, the leader is the leader. We must all queue up behind him."

"Good. Now take your mind back to last week Friday. Did you receive some visitors in your home village?"

"Oh yes, many people came. They came with camera and made video all over the place."

"Did they tell you the reason they were doing that?"

"Something about the Festival of People's Choice. They said they wanted to put my name down for an honour. Some prize they want to give me on their gala night. They were liars. They just came to look for my trouble."

"They came to look for your trouble? Isn't it the truth that they came to film you at home and at work?"

"That was what they said. And I let them do what they want. They make video everywhere—me and my family. My workers and so on and neighbours. Then they come into the house and start asking questions. That is when trouble start."

"What sort of trouble, Chief Akpanga?"

"They insult me, so I tell them to leave my house."

"They insult you. How come?"

"They take their photos, come into the house, then come and insult me. They said they want to award me because I am a common man."

"You're talking of the YoY Awards, of course. The Yeomen of the Year, with the Common Touch Award at its apex."

"Yes, that is the one they mention. That one is insult. I am a governor-to-be. Just because I come from the village, is that why they should come and give me a common man award? I tell them to pack their things and get out of the house. I tell my people to chase them off my land and they must never come back."

"Mr. Akpanga, these were people from The National Inquest. *They were offering you nomination—"*

"You were not there. I was. They should not come and tell me I have a common touch. Would you take that kind of nonsense?"

"But did you have to be violent?"

"Who was violent? It is my house. I cannot take that kind of nonsense anywhere, how much more in my home. Just because I follow my leader and call myself Servant of the State, is that why people should forget I am going to be governor? Is that a common rank? What is wrong with special award—that is what I expect, a special award. What business do I have with a common one?"

Danfere looked up slowly and keenly inspected his caller. "You realize, of course, what I would do to you if this turned out to be Fake News."

Merutali shrugged. "I was present. I had this typed out quickly from the transcript so you could see it yourself."

Goddie chuckled. "Talk of casting political pearls before village swine. But are you telling me he knew nothing of the YoY Awards?"

"We-e-ell. You could say he, er . . . sort of."

"What do you mean, sort of?"

"I made sure he did. Modu is a romantic." A sharp gasp of shocked disagreement escaped Sir Goddie, but Merutali quickly raised his hand to plead for patience. "Yessir, believe me, he is actually a romantic. Of course he's all business, a hustler, but he's a romantic hustler. He actually believes in some of these awards. Don't underestimate that. So he gets excited when he finds someone like Akpanga. It gives the authentic touch to his scams. He loves to inject exceptions into the entire process. In turn, that legitimizes the cynical parts."

"Especially when they have money?"

"Exactly. I keep an eye on competition, so no sweat. I learnt he planned to bestow the Big One on our man. So I paid Akpanga a visit. I said, 'Look, my job is to look after the party image. That means you are now my charge. Some people are trying to rubbish you, to reduce you to the level of a common man, just because you come from a village and you don't talk big grammar.' You see, you have to study the raw spot for a man like Akpanga. I have. So I said to him, 'If anybody comes to you talking of a common prize, reject it. Don't even let them say it twice. Throw them out.'"

Sir Goddie gave a long, low whistle. "Merutali, you are the devil!"

"No sir, politics is the devil in all of us. Including you, my friend. I actually enjoy my role. It brings out the creative in me." He rose. "So now, the rest is up to you."

"You mean . . . ?"

"Between you and Oromotaya. I've done my part. I told him you might need to see him today. He's in one of the reception rooms."

"He's a scalper. How much do you think he'll want?"

"Does it have to be cash?"

"With Modu, it had better be."

"That's where you are wrong. I've just told you, he's a romantic."

"So what do I do? Find him a girlfriend?"

Merutali laughed out loud. "You can only try, you cannot match Akpanga. I can actually hear him saying exactly that! No, try National Honours. Independence is round the corner. Do a swap. He'll lap it up."

Sir Goddie shook his head and smiled in a rare gesture of admiration for any object outside his mirror. "You know, I'd never have thought of that."

"The two big awards brought together in his own person? This year's YoY will be one for history, you'll see."

Sir Goddie sighed, pushed the crystal bowl towards him. "I think you deserve another kola nut."

10.

The Audience

This time it was the silent chief of staff who came for him. Pitan felt a presence even in his dozy state, woke up with a start. There was the man standing over him, simply studying him without a word. Pitan rapidly restored his senses to his actual location.

"The People's Steward will see you now."

Pitan glanced at his watch; it was close to seven o'clock. Next he glared at his taciturn escort, then followed him wordlessly. The Presence was indeed awaiting him, right by the open, leather-padded double doors.

"Come in, come in." Offered his hand for a welcome handshake, then propelled him to his desk. "Take a seat, Mr. Pitan." He strode to his own chair and pushed the eclectic bowl of snacks towards his guest. "So you're abandoning the entire country this time, not just our inadequate government."

"Your Excellency . . . excuse me, I mean, People's Steward, sir—"

"No, don't bother your head with that one. One simply wishes to set an example, that's all. Call me whatever you want. People do anyway, and they're not always flattering."

Uncertain, Pitan managed what he hoped sounded sympathetic. "Oh no, you mustn't think that, sir."

"It's true, it's true. But who cares? Once you are in this position, you must expect all sorts. So, off to the UN, eh?"

"Yes, Sir Goddie. And I know what effort you put in to make it happen. It's an honour. My family and I are most grateful for this support."

"No, no, no, everything is God's doing. Let us thank God, who put me in a position to be of help. That is a much-coveted portfolio. I would have been sorry to see us lose it to some other nation."

Duyole tried to unscramble his mind and access his rehearsed speech, found that it was lost somewhere among the past recollections with which he had whiled away time in the reception room. No choice but to follow the lead of his host and simply respond to whatever.

"I was perhaps the most surprised individual on earth. I had no idea I was even under any consideration from anywhere until I received a letter from the UN under-secretary."

"Well, I know you know your Bible—seest thou a man loyal and diligent in his works, he shall stand before kings and not before mean men."

Duyole's smile grew weaker. Even his vaguely conceived speech, whatever direction it took, had not prepared him for such an encomium. He thanked the delighted figure once again, this time for forming such a high opinion of him during his consultancy. He hoped that whatever little achievement he was able to contribute would be built upon, leading to a steady supply of power for both domestic and industrial needs. The People's Steward assured him that no effort would be wasted, no resources spared or squandered. Rural electrification was at the heart of his regime's power manifesto, and they were determined to carry it out, nationwide. He slammed his open hand on the desk—"with or without the help of the World Bank or IMF."

Duyole blinked, tried to work out what those two institutions had to do with the project that connected him with the Ministry of Power. None. If anything, his detailed blueprint had stressed that the nation required the help of neither body; all it had to do was maximize existing local resources and involve the private sector, resuscitate mothballed equipment and distribution stations rusting all over the nation. So much for the labour of fourteen months. Duyole sighed.

As if Sir Goddie read the engineer's thoughts: "Oh, by the way . . ." He opened a drawer beneath the desk and brought out a red dossier, neatly tied with a black ribbon. The lettering SECRET was stamped diagonally across the cover. The People's Steward patted it with touching gentleness and leant forward as if to stress confidentiality. "I must thank you for this. I know you must have wondered why I never sent for you all this time." He raised his hand to forestall what he assumed would be the engineer's protestation. "No, no, in your position I would feel the same. Quite understandable. I just want you to know, this"—and he gave the file yet another gentle pat—"this is what we call an active file. Active. There it lies looking innocent and still, but take it from me, Mr. Pitan, it is a most active file."

"I am most relieved to hear that, sir."

"Thank you. I need say no more. You shall yourself feel the impact of this report, even from far away in the United Nations. Take my word for it."

Duyole smiled his appreciation.

"You have no idea, simply no idea what you have done for me in that ministry. I am handling it personally. The follow-up has started, and it is not pretty. Heads shall roll—no, heads have begun to roll. Until you came in, no one had succeeded in getting to the bottom of the rot in that sector. And then, of course, solutions! No one has gone that far in all these years. Criticism is easy, the nation is full of carpers They are professional. But when it comes to solutions . . . suddenly they are missing in action!"

"I am glad to have been of some help, Mr. Prime Minister."

"You are modest. What I did not understand was why you chose to leave so abruptly. You were not even halfway into your contract. What was the hurry?"

"Mission accomplished, sir. There was nothing left for me to do."

"Don't say that. Never ever say that. I could have done with your help on the next phase. This is only the beginning. If you had not left, we would have moved into Phase Two by now—no, we would have finished with Phase Two and moved into Three."

The engineer smiled weakly. "I am beginning to feel guilty."

"No, no, no, that was not my intention. You did what you undertook to do, and the professionalism was impeccable. I know there were difficulties. I know what traps were set for you. Those fools didn't know who they were dealing with. They know nothing of the

Pitan-Payne stock. Oh, that reminds me, how is your father? Does he still find time for his favourite ballroom dancing?"

"Mostly by himself these days, Sir Goddie. Then he even dances to hymns."

Sir Goddie laughed. "Including 'Rock of Ages'?"

"You know that nickname, sir?"

"Of course. We belong to the same lodge."

"He's well. Very well. And active. I've even tried to entice him into the firm."

"That's good. Very good. Some people prefer to let age go to waste. That's a pity."

Duyole laughed. "I promise you, sir, he's not the kind who lets himself be wasted. He'll always find something to do."

The Steward smiled. "But best to involve the family wherever possible. I approve of that. When next I see him, I shall let him know how much you've done for the nation. Up to us to pick up where you left off. That process has begun. You can safely leave the rest to us. Completely. You may take it that you have left this in safe hands."

Duyole inclined his head to convey diffidence and appreciation.

As Goddie returned the dossier to its home, he jerked up his head suddenly. "Oh, I nearly forgot. I owe you one more apology. The government owes you an apology. We owe you money. It was when I called for your files that I discovered that embarrassing lapse. Can you imagine? It shames us. I have given orders. That unacceptable lapse shall shortly be a thing of the past. I have seen to it."

"I do appreciate that, Sir Goddie. I was of course going to mention it."

"You would not be your father's son if you left without mentioning it. It's all settled." Goddie pushed the crystal bowl towards him. "Take some kola nut. It's special. Comes from a tiny plantation not far from here. The flavor is unique. Many people don't really know kola nut. They don't know that it has dozens of flavours, each one different from the next. This one is truly exceptional. I like to use the coffee analogy—what the Blue Mountain coffee is to most other coffees, that's what this is to the majority of kola nuts. And I mean anywhere on this continent."

"Thank you, sir." Duyole stretched his hand toward the treat.

"The man who owns that plantation makes a delivery to the villa every fortnight, with his own hands, the kola nuts still in their pods. His own idea. My housekeeper calls it the prime ministerial pod. Comes from a little village not far from here—it's called Gumchi. Go on, take more than one. Take some home with you."

Duyole's outstretched hand stopped abruptly, frozen. He looked questioningly at his host.

Dr. Goddie looked puzzled. "Anything the matter?"

"Did you say Gumchi, sir?"

"Yes. You know the place?"

"I should hope so, Your Excellency. My bosom friend is from that village. A surgeon. Presently in Jos."

Again the PM sat back, marveling. "Is that so?"

"Yes, sir. We were that close, we once made plans to help him build a small clinic right there. Four of us."

"Really? What a small world. And an even smaller village, from all reports. Where were you going to put the clinic? There's hardly any space in there. It's all rock formation. Apart from that small kola nut patch, a few citrus, not much else. I sent the agric minister to go take a look, in case we could help with developing the kola. He brought back photos. Rocks. Nothing but rocks."

"That was the challenge, Sir Goddie. As an engineer . . ."

"Of course, of course. If anyone could, you can. Just don't touch my kola nut trees, or we shall fight-o!"

Duyole joined in the laughter. "I'm sure they will be preserved, sir. That is, assuming we ever get round to that project. It was one of those youthful schemes, over two decades old. We formed a kind of mutual assistance pact. But we've all gone our different ways."

"Ah yes, that is life for you. Humanity moves, but the rocks remain."

"And the kola nut trees also, I hope, Your Excellency."

"We hope. We all hope. Change is all very well. And development. But some things should remain the same. We all need a sense of something permanent."

"I cannot agree more."

"Oh, that reminds me. Well, I don't have to tell you. You, your company, you have acquired quite a national clout. Your name—my

God!—that **Brand of the Land,** it all resounds as something extra. The name carries weight. And with this UN recognition . . . well, no question at all, yours is a name the nation must reckon with. I know you will always use it judiciously—in the interest of the nation."

Duyole tensed, sensing, *Here it comes!* Sir Goddie did not fail to notice the sudden guardedness, having years of experience watching out for just such dangerous reactions when dragooning a "volunteer" into non-voluntary missions. Goddie had no appetite for rebuffs and smoothly back-pedalled. "Hm. Let's see now. Has your old man spoken to you?"

"About what, Your Excellency?"

And Goddie burst into laughter. "He's a cagey one. I thought he would have mentioned it before our meeting. So I'll tell you what's the best way I think we should go about this. Well, I'll give you a hint—we think the nation has a duty to promote Brand of the Land. Make it ours. A national heritage. That's just a hint. When you get home, talk to your old man. There is just one small, connected service you may be able to perform before you leave—but I'll let him explain." He slapped the table. "Yes, we'll leave it at that. He has something to discuss with you."

"As you wish, sir. But if you prefer—"

"No, no, no hurry. He'll explain. He and I speak the same language. Oh, here comes trouble."

The door was pushed open softly and the PM looked up. It was the chief of staff. Duyole now deliberately fixed his eyes on the man and kept them there throughout, returning the compliment for his earlier discomfort in the reception room.

"I'm sorry to interrupt, Your Excellency."

His Excellency the People's Steward looked up in surprise, looked at his desk clock. "Good God, are they here already?"

"I've kept them in the main reception room, PS."

"Too bad." And he seemed genuinely regretful. "Our conversation was beginning to get really interesting. All right, in a minute."

The receptionist's "administrative nudge." Audience over.

"That reminds me, CoS."

"Yes, People's Steward?"

"Mr. Pitan-Payne's security detail—I assume that was withdrawn when he left us?"

"It's routine, PS."

"Well, see that it's restored immediately, and it stays with him until departure."

Duyole instantly launched into protests but was stopped by a very firm, no-argument gesture from his host.

"I'll see to it, sir," assented the chief of staff.

"His safety is even more crucial now than when he was consulting for a single government. He is now a world acquisition, not just ours. Big as we are, we can't compete. We don't want to incur global infamy if anything happens to him."

"Understood, Your Excellency."

"And of course anytime you visit home, Pitan—all right if I just call you that instead of your double-barreled name?"

"Honoured, PS."

"Good. So be sure to notify the chief of staff in advance. I don't trifle with security—ask the CoS, he knows me."

Duyole shook his head, visibly upset at the turn of events. His severance from the system was intended to be final. He made one more effort. "Your Excellency, there is really no need, I assure you."

His host stopped and faced him squarely. "Yes, there is need, Mr. Pitan-Payne. There is every need. We cannot take chances. The security situation is what it is, unfortunately, so it is a responsibility we just have to confront."

"Leave it to me, sir," the chief of staff reassured his boss. "I'll take care of all the necessary."

The People's Steward readjusted his *agbada*, swept round the vast desk, raised his wide-sleeved arm around Duyole's shoulders. "You must come and see me anytime you return on leave or for whatever reason."

"That really is kind of you, People's Steward. I'll be sure to do so."

"We hate to lose you, but, well, you know what the Good Book says—in this case, Nigeria loves you but the UN loves you the best. Thank goodness you have the stamina. Your stay with us bore that out. You have no idea how tortuous their operations are in that place;

it's a marvel that any decisions are ever taken or carried out. I hate to say it—don't quote me, but the UN is a madhouse. It needs shaking up. If you really want to achieve anything, you'll have to give them your full time."

At the door he again offered his hand. "At the risk of repeating myself, the nation loves you, yes, but others, the UN especially, not only love, they *need* you more."

The special adviser was waiting on the other side of the door, his face somewhat distraught, his voice apologetic.

"Yes?"

"Your Excellency, I'm so sorry, but my assistant wasn't ready with the package."

"What!"

"He didn't know that we'd brought forward Mr. Pitan's appointment to this afternoon. We shifted it on account of yesterday's marathon."

"He must be an idiot. Does he think they're laggards at the UN like all you useless people around me?" Sir Goddie turned to Duyole. "I'm sorry. I told them to prepare a package for you—something to show the government's appreciation, and of course our pride. Just a token."

"If Mr. Pitan-Payne could wait a few moments . . ." Garuba began.

"If Mr. What could what what what? Send it after him. Take his address and see that it is personally delivered to him before he takes off for New York!"

"Apologies, Your Stewardship. We shall do exactly that."

"Now see Mr. Pitan through security and bring yourself back here. The night is not yet over, so don't disappear with him."

"Will take care of him, Your Stewardship."

Engineer and Equivalent departed, leaving Sir Goddie alone—at least, so he thought. As he shushed close the heavy door after him simply by swiveling round and resting his back on it, he scowled at his reclining chair, seeing there the ghost of his predecessor. He rewarded that dislodged occupant with a further snarl for having bequeathed him a possessed scientist by the name of Duyole Pitan-Payne—yes, talented and all that, no one denied it, but what the hell! Was that why he should keep making trouble for everyone? Well, good-bye to bad rubbish. He heaved a sigh that resounded through the labyrinthine corridors of power. Then he clasped his hands, rubbed them together, interlocked the ten fingers to support his chin while shutting his eyes tight and pursing his lower jaw upwards—it was his terminal sign of satisfaction. If the engineer carried the same mentality to the UN and they kicked him back home, it no longer mattered. His impact thereafter would be considerably diminished. This was Nigeria's own slot, and they would have no problem filling it with someone more deserving. The nation was not short of experts in every field, and nobody would accuse the government of sidelining or suffocating talent—every inch of the way, they had done everything to make full use of him. Records don't lie.

He had forgotten the presence of his chief of staff, who had stood to one side of the departing pair. He coughed discreetly to make his presence known. Sir Goddie was startled.

"Oh, you still here?"

"Sir, you said you would give instructions about his outstanding fees."

"What fees? He knows what to do, otherwise it's lapsed. I expect to hear from his Old Man latest tomorrow night. He at least doesn't encourage throwing government money back in the government's face."

"Very good, sir."

"And we have one of his close cronies in our clutches—corruption network. We've checked—the fellow is not really part of his business outfit, but they are close. They are not only close, the criminal is a founding member of this overreaching Brand of the Land. All we have to do is tag them a secret cult—we have the full story of the founding members and what some of them have been up to lately. A bunch of drunks to start with—can you imagine that? I have the lowdown. The social media will do the rest. He cannot afford a scandal, not at this stage. The UN won't stand for it."

"Your Stewardship is absolutely right."

"I'm letting his father handle him. Nothing directly from me—I don't trust his kind. He strikes me as capable of anything."

"We know that type, Your Stewardship. You can rely on us to do the needful, sir."

"You do that. Is Oromotaya still waiting?"

"No, he left, Your Stewardship. Together with Dr. Merutali. Said I should let you know that they're having dinner with the first lady."

"I'll join them later. I'd hoped that engineer would also join, that's why I kept delaying him. But he's too pig-headed for his own good. Either his old man brings him round or you make sure his file is lost in the system. I'll deal with the useless file he sent me before he quit—as if the nation doesn't have enough on its hands as it is."

"Very good, sir."

"The only problem is that he managed to get a copy to the president. That's not convenient. Our president often forgets he's a party member. All this non-partisanship nonsense once you sit on the presidential chair—he actually takes it seriously! All right. If needed, we'll just have to remind him that all shit may smell different, but it still smells. But he's in good standing with Oromotaya. Keep that in mind. It means Mr. Benzy now has a copy. Has had one for years." He clutched his head. "I don't know how I am supposed to deal with all these nasty variables."

"We're mopping up the copies, PS. And we can always denounce them as forgeries. Dr. Merutali knows how to handle that. The president knows how he got elected, sir, so I wouldn't waste much sleep on him, Your Stewardship. Everyone knows how they got where they are."

"They'd better. That'll be all. Oh yes, send in that numbskull as soon as he returns. Oh, anyone else waiting?"

"Just the Indian, PS."

The People's Steward slapped his forehead. "The geologist, right?"

"Yes, sir."

"I can't see him. Not today. He had a bad experience in Zamfara and I don't think I want to cope with that right now. When gold—the real thing or the black gel, doesn't matter—when it gets mixed up with religion, prospectors must learn to expect the worst. Tell him I can't see him today."

"If I may humbly suggest, Your Stewardship, maybe just shake hands with him? He's been waiting longer than the engineer, and he did have a very unhappy experience. But he is not deterred and wants to return. All the reports show he's a genius at detecting gold deposits. I think he's a useful man to know, PS, sir."

Goddie became thoughtful. "All right, all right. Bring him to show face. Just a few seconds."

"Very good, sir."

One moment Goddie was waiting impatiently at the door. The next moment he swiveled and bounded back inside, making a straight dash to his desk. He grabbed two kola nuts and made it back to the door as his chief of staff returned, the Indian prospector in tow.

"Sir Goddie—so kind of you, Your Excellency, so kind."

"I am so sorry that this has been such a bad day at the villa. And I hear you had an even worse time in Zamfara. But you must come back. There are places my own experts can suggest to you. We certainly need you here."

"You are most kind, Mr. Prime Minister. I have to fly out tomorrow, but I shall be back. I shall be back because I know there are rich resouces within your soil, and we wish to do business with the country."

"You will be doubly welcomed. My CoS will give you the numbers to call. And here"—thrusting the kola nuts into the bewildered hands—"you know about kola nuts, don't you?"

"Absolutely sir, absolutely. I see them in the markets. They were all over Zamfara."

"They are a symbol of friendship, among other things. Take them with you. Have a safe flight and return soon."

Bowing in great elation, Dr. Mukarjee was finally ushered off, all his terror of days in Zamfara hived off him as if they had never been experienced. He had been briefly kidnapped but was quickly rescued by the civic vigilantes. "Most daunting experience," he continued to declare for weeks thereafter. "But the deposits are even more daunting."

The pair were replaced almost immediately by the special adviser, breathless from his semi-trot back to his boss.

"Is that preacher still around?" Sir Goddie demanded. "What does he call himself these days?"

"Teribogo, Your Excellency."

"Ah yes, Teribogo. Send him to me"—indulging in his broadest, unquestionably his most self-rewarding smile of the day. "There's no harm also soliciting some, er, divine intervention over this one. I think Mr. Pitan-Payne's case calls for multiple insurance."

Shekere Garuba relaxed, sensing that the day had worked exceedingly well to his boss's satisfaction. He felt sufficiently emboldened to take a parting liberty: "Bishop Teribogo? Ah, Father, is that you?"

For a brief moment the People's Steward hesitated—was he letting the young rascal become too familiar? No, he decided. His upbringing ensured that he knew his place. So Goddie threw him a conspiratorial wink, which he followed with a kola nut, The young man caught it, then prostrated himself full-length in gratitude. This was indeed the ultimate sign of acceptance. Uriah Heep finally felt himself absorbed into full family membership.

11.

The Hand of God

Teribogo, known more affectionately as Papa Davina, was now fully established in awareness as not one of your common run of preachers. He was a study in difference, and innovation. Indeed, the prestige media, in their dedicated pages on spiritual pursuits— published Fridays and Sundays—often lauded him as the future of the Call, if God himself were to survive and Satan driven to his primordial hole. Satan is a Bushman, Papa D. was fond of preaching, and together, with the force of our prayers, we shall shame him back to his jungle lair! For a class of followers, such heady imprecations would sound crass and insensitive, but Papa D. was nothing if not combative and controversial. He reserved such rhetorical flourishes for his open services at the base of his operational hill, Oke Konran-Imoran, which, translated in the true spirit of canonical—twin to poetic—licence, meant the Mountain of Faith, Counselling. In ecumenical alternation, encouraged, indeed enjoined as an article of expectation for all true believers, was its equally revered version, Oke Ariran, the Mountain of Vision. Propagated as one and the same, they were united at the spiritual confluence of the supervising ministry, registered in the Company Affairs Commission (CAC) as Ekumenika Ltd. Papa D. led by example. In the tradition of officially bilingual nations such as Canada, Papa D. was famous for never completing even the tiniest phrasal fragment of any pungency or mysteriousness without ensuring that he had given it utterance in more than one language.

Services at the mountain base took place in a vast outspread Y-shaped space, whose stem was open on all sides to wind, rain, beggars, goats, and chickens as well as hawkers of snacks and multinational gadgetries, including motorcar spare parts. By contrast, at the remote end of one arm was a nearly soundproof aboveground bunker. This served as vestry and meditation space and housed individual prayer cubicles. The other arm terminated in a special soundproof "confessional," dedicated to Papa D.'s famous ICDs—Intensive Care Delivery rooms, where extreme cases were delivered of the devil and all his works. Delivery could involve prescriptions such as self-flagellation and other forms of self-mortification, including but not limited to sessions of cold baths in the central sit-in, larger-than-life baptismal-cum-redemption font. The sit-on ledge onto which the faithful descended from floor level was a solid marble block from Jerusalem, reputed to be from the same marble deposit that produced the covering slab of the Jerusalem sepulchre. It was a replacement of the former, lighter slab, which had served faithfully until it was smashed by the descent of one of his more ponderous followers, known as prayer warriors.

The lady drowned, in full sight. The weight of her transgressions obviously smashed through the flimsy marble top despite the scientifically supportive buoyancy supposedly provided by the water. The same oppressive weight of unexpiated sin prevented her from raising her head above the merely three-foot-deep waters, certified imported from the Lake of Galilee. She choked and drowned, flailing in what the small gathering thought were ecstatic motions. Teribogo gave several media interviews on the cause and effect of that event, contrasting it favorably with the toll of over three hundred pilgrims from across the continent incurred by the Church of the Blessed Saints whose new building, then under unlicensed construction, collapsed over their heads. The substitute marble block, evidently impervious to no matter the weight of future burdens of sin, was gladly subscribed by his grateful congregation at one single session of pledges, all promptly fulfilled on the next bank working day.

That powerhouse, as it was widely known, directed the affairs of the ministry. The rest was simply the all-comer open space, roofed by tarpaulins and corrugated iron sheets, occasionally demarcated by bamboo and raffia stalks. The space could accommodate a cast of thousands, doubled and tripled, even quadrupled during religious seasons. Services were round-the-clock, often conducted by well-trained subordinates. But mostly the apostle himself presided, preached and ministered to all humanity without discrimination as to gender, age, class, profession, ethnicity, nationality, or *spiritual erratism*—a term that Papa D. respectfully applied to all who commenced with different faiths but had come to realize, or were on the way to accepting, the error of their ways and had begun to grope their way towards the one and only truth—ecumenism.

It was no secret that Papa Davina's distant model was the charismatic Father Divine of the black American Peace Mission, early twentieth century, who, Papa D. was convinced, had died with the stigmata of martyrdom on either palm and both feet. While he adopted a tweaked version of the name, he did not thereby discard his own, Teribogo, which may or may not have been his real name anyway. Perhaps even he no longer recalled the name that had been conferred upon him at birth, or it had gone through so many incarnations that it no longer mattered, nor did he care. Some claimed that Teribogo, the sobriquet on his calling card, one that offered him a tenuous hold on identity with Yoruba-speaking parts of West Africa, was possibly not his own but a product of malicious conferment at one of his earlier evangelical bases in a different part of West Africa; Ivory Coast was mentioned.

One of Papa D.'s envied talents was his ability to convert even the most negative event or mere imputation into a positive asset. Thus what was rumoured to have originated in some scandalous past became a thing of treasure and emulation as he migrated to a new location and reinvented his ministry. All preachers worth their salt have their signature tune, a sound bite or exhortation trigger. Teribogo was the one that became thoroughly identified with Papa Davina: *Bow your head into glory*. His confident attachment to the name gave the lie to malicious versions that were peddled about its origin—would any sane man parade, including on his gold-lettered calling card, a name of dubious, especially salacious, antecedents? The name gave power to the word, most especially during "delivery" sessions. Nonetheless, that irreverent version of its origin persisted, spread by skeptics and prurient revisionists. Papa D. remained indifferent. Let them continue to imperil their souls by tarnishing a product of divine inspiration. Papa Davina, self-repatriated to the grotty suburb of Lagos known as Mushin, was aka Teribogo, and this became a household name for all who sought divine guidance and intervention, despite being a victim of the profane proliferation of apocryphal lore instigated by sinful tongues.

It had all happened, it was claimed, during one of Papa D.'s exorcist sessions—that is, in the presence of more or less a five-thousand-strong congregation. The crucial event took place out of view, in the special, privileged section, but not out of hearing of an assemblage that had itself attained that level of paroxysm of worship to which, as in all things, while all may partake, only a few are called. The most common cause for spiritual intervention that Papa D. handled was, as might be expected in a society plagued by rabbit envy, childlessness, a condition that stigmatized women, very often without just cause. Slowly, and with enduring skepticism, scientific explanations were permitted to percolate through, including the blasphemous theory that the cause of this condition could possibly emanate from male deficiency.

The history of the afflicted woman followed the accustomed route. It resulted in its apportionment to the portfolio of devilish possession—her womb had clearly been seized upon by the Devil, squeezed dry, and blocked from germination. The Devil himself had been contracted, no question whatsoever, by a neighbour enemy. Papa D., a seasoned raconteur, acquired fame—or notoriety—by his in-depth knowledge of that affliction, a knowledge that he imparted through illustrative tales that were uproarious, disarming, and thereby satisfied the yearning of his audiences for a rational explication of the mysteries of diseases. The woman's predicament became the anecdotal vehicle that transported his audience to distant lands and back, even while the remedy itself lay in the inner sanctum of Teribogo's Mushin prophesite. Papa D. took his audience on a ride from reality to virtual reality and back, leaving them fluttering like butterflies in a wind stream. With a deadpan, unemotional mask over his face, Papa D. plunged into the Lagos lagoon, resurfaced in the African diaspora of the West Indies—Jamaica, specifically—dispensing laughter and merriment along the way, until it was time to explode presumptions of cause and effect.

This reminds me, dear followers in Christ, of an expatriate from Jamaica who for days had been experiencing acute pain in his urethra. The problem was diagnosed, and he was ordered to drink gallons and gallons of water. For our poor sufferer, this was worse than the ailment, since he had a great aversion to any water treatment except under the shower. Titters. *This in turn made his wife wish that his aversion to water was total and all-inclusive. Why so, you might ask? I shall tell you. Once he was under a shower in our notoriously hot, humid weather, it became a problem to get him out!* Laughter. *It was worse when he chose the bath, because by the time the bath was half-way filled, the water supply, which was usually little more than the average of a cupful for each household, totally dried up. It led to petitions that he be assigned a special hour, after the entire block of flats had had their turn.* [Don't we all know it? Tell it, Papa. Let the Water Corporation hear it!]

Teribogo paused. He smiled. He raked in the entire prophesite with an indulgent smile. Only those who had never heard of Papa D. committed the error of thinking that he was ever contented with extracting only one moral lesson from one story. The homily was yet nowhere complete.

No matter. Mack—that was the name of the gentleman—finally bowed to the doctor's prescription and drank ceaselessly. His stomach bloated, but finally he felt the beginning of a redemptive flow. More laughter. Clapping interruption. *The process was painful. If you ever have a choice between expelling gallbladder stones the natural way and doing it like a pretence Caesarian, don't be brave. Just tell them, bring on the surgeon.* By now the audience's eyes are streaming tears of laughter. *His wife was present. She held his hand and urged him to persevere. Mack did his manful best. In the midst of his anguish, however, he screamed, squeezed his wife's hand till it bled, and threw accusations at the poor lady.* "Betty, why you doing this to me? Why you trying to kill me? I told you to always make sure you pick out all the stones from the rice before cooking. See now how you going to emasculate your innocent husband!"

Then, as the congregation's laughter and exchanges roiled round the divine arena, the voice of the Worshipful Bishop Teribogo, yet another superb calculator of the dramatic moment, thundered across the arena and wiped off the smug countenances of his female listeners, focusing, from long experience, on an already selected two or three women seated together. Teribogo held his listeners in the cup of his hand. Changing vocal register, the superlative performer roared, *"You find it funny now, but think for a moment. Sooner a million particles of stone in the gallbladder than a devil-stone in a woman's womb. You can expel the gallstone, but where is that most brilliant of the followers of Aesculapius that can deliver you from the devil-stone in the uterus! Where? No, tell me. You know of one, point him out here and now! So there are those unbelievers who say barrenness is a medical condition? No sin is worse than ignorance. The ignorance as of that poor liberated slave from across the seas, who blames the stones in the rice grains for the stone in his gallbladder. Between one agony and the anguish of the devil-stone in the uterus, is there any difference?"*

In a concerted voice that nearly brought down the tarpaulin roofing: "No-o-o-o-o!"

"I said, is there difference in ignorance?"

And Teribogo would thereupon throw back his head and go into a laughter convulsion, then break off abruptly and resume the voice of the patient teacher.

Immerse yourselves in the story of Sarah. What sin did Sarah commit? Did you read in your Good Book that she was wayward? Did you read that it was a punishment for unseemly conduct? Was she disobedient? No! Did she turn her back on God? No. But she was guilty of envy. Aha, you think you know the story? You think you know that story better than Papa D.? Yes, she was guilty of envy. She stirred up envy in others, and those others became enemies. They had something to avenge. They envied her status. Envied her success. Envied her demureness. Her humility. Her industry. Her family. Envied her very existence. And what did they do in revenge? Placed the devil-stone in that sister's womb."

A devil-stone in the womb required deep penetrative ministration, administered by the physician of souls, aided by the church entirety as supporting cast and chorus, albeit unwitting, but in deep fervor. As ecstasy mounted, Papa D. would lead his child-starved supplicant into the multipurpose side chancel which served as private offertory, for registration of tithes, private prayers of "deliverance," personalized sessions of blessings, consultations, and sometimes all-night vigils of the personal kind, where the supplicant might be advised to spread-eagle himself or herself stark naked before the mini-altar, on the cold cement floor, all night, sometimes for three or more successive nights, subjected to mysterious lashes in the dark by malevolent spirits. Occasionally these sessions were relieved by brief communions with the angelic touch with milk-white gloves. They shimmered into place, lifted the head of the seeker, administered a sip of "Jerusalem water" to the parched lips, which they then wiped daintily clean, and took their departure.

On the memorable day, to the fervent chants and prayers of the congregation, Papa D. led this especial case to the miracle and delivery sanctum. She knelt on the padded stool, head bowed. Papa Davina went through the liturgy, intoned prayers, and liberally cursed the enemies who had inflicted such misery on his client. In the main arena, organ, choir, and congregation grew increasingly ecstatic. Papa D. placed his hand on her bowed head, most conveniently level with the storehouse of male procreative energies.

It was a day of miraculous happenings. The preacher's fervor, even his greatest enemies admitted, was unusually charged and infectious. If this was not spiritual arousal, said one faithful, then nothing ever was or could ever again be. On that day the prelate found himself in the throes of possession. The wand of blessing rose to the occasion. As the supplicant bowed her head, she knew she had encountered a rising obstacle and instinctively recoiled. This was not to Papa D.'s liking, and he placed his hand on the back of her head, pulling it towards the energized zone. The more she attempted to retreat, the more determined he grew, exhorting her to *t'eri b'ogo!* Again and again—*t'eri b'ogo, t'eri b'ogo.* It was a contest of organs, the musical pump artist equally possessed, perhaps in mystic empathy, while the spiritual carousal of *Praise the Lord* from thousands of voices continued to rip apart the sanctified air. The organist, accustomed to such bouts of possession and exorcism, increased his pedaling and pulled out all the organ stops, his eyes popping in a head that darted from vestry door to the assembly and back again. He knew what might be happening as even the heavy breathing became audible under the laboured *t'eri b'ogo* that emerged loudly from the ministering sanctum. And so, under inspiration, even possession, he continued to pump until suddenly the door burst open and the supplicant, all disheveled, burst through at the very moment when the priestly command, staccato and urgent, changed completely into an unbroken, ecstatic cry that would never be forgotten by a congregation, since all were instantly stunned into silence by the apparition that burst through at the very moment that Teribogo gave voice to that impassioned culmination: *"T'eri b'ogo-go-go-go-go-go-go-go-go-go-o-o-o-o-ooooooo!"*

It went down as a day of miraculous delivery. Papa D. made an Oscar-winning appearance, microphone in hand, and what appeared to be scratches, a reasonably deep gash on his face, and a swollen eye, staggering only a little but in the main triumphant, as one who had wrestled and prevailed, a contest that he instantly captured in ringing outburst: *The Devil was strong, but God was mightier! Alleluia!*

The congregation went frenzied. Revelation was imminent.

Praise the Lord! Hallelujah, praise the Lord! Glory to him forever and ever.

It was a day that turned legend, hailed as that blessed day when all skeptics were silenced. Were there not several thousand eyewitnesses to testify how they had seen the Devil, having taken possession of the woman, turn on the preacher in the seclusion of the vestry, pummel him with his own crozier, and reduce him to a pulp? But he fought back, the valiant prayer veteran that he was. Seeing what he was up against, the Devil reentered the woman, and what they saw was not the woman at all but the Devil which had taken her shape and voice in a bid to escape. Emerging, she stumbled and fell and promptly collapsed in a faint. The proof was incontestable: the Devil had been chased out of her, and the congregation went instantly into the triumphal mode. She struggled against their restraining hands, desperate to say something and attempting to point in the direction of the priest, but who was interested in what the Devil tried to say? The more she struggled, the more evident was the Devil's continued presence. Her husband was the most fervent and inflexible. He gave her a huge punch across the breast which knocked out the rest of any breath in her sternum. She went limp and was carried into the recovery room by Teribogo's uniformed wardens. The Devil was vanquished and—so goes this version—Teribogo was born.

SIR GODDIE WAS at his most affable. This was his last engagement for the day, and by preference he liked to end the day on a spiritual note. He had his own chaplain and chapel—it went with the position—but if the proprietor of Ekumenika was available, that prelate of many parts was his choice for intoning the day's vespers. All staff was now dismissed. The pair could hold communion without a fear of profane ears or voices.

"Come in, come in, Your Eminence. I hope you'll forgive us the long wait, but it has proved one of those long days."

"I understand perfectly, Your Excellency. I understand. These are hard times."

"Take a seat, Papa D. Relax a little." He pushed the crystal bowl towards him.

Teribogo shrank back instinctively. "At this time of the night? The caffeine won't let me sleep."

The People's Steward grinned. "It's from the prime ministerial pod."

"Ah well, to please you. I'll keep one for the morning." And Teribogo helped himself to a nut from the crystal bowl.

Sir Goddie went straight to the point. "Bishop, we may have a problem."

"Our mission, Your Excellency the People's Steward, is to solve your problems."

Sir Goddie leant back. "Are you sure that in doing that, you are not creating other problems for me?"

Teribogo expressed shock. "Impossible. Your interests and those of the Lord's ministry are too deeply intertwined."

"Does that include what happened on Ikorodu Road?"

Teribogo nodded understandingly. "Ah, that. I did have a feeling it might alarm you. The moment I heard, my mind went to you. Indeed, I confided my concerns in God, I prayed to him, *Don't let our prime minister be unduly alarmed.*"

"Not unduly alarmed! What do you think I am made of? An atrocity like that! In broad daylight! Well, at least you don't deny the divine hand was involved?"

"A hand in what, Dr. Goddie? These weak hands of mine?" Teribogo spread out his hands, leant forward confidentially. "Sir Goddie, I know you are not a soccer fan. But at least you do follow some games."

"Soccer? What's this about soccer?"

"I shall remind you. But first, do bear this in mind. Apostolic work, no matter which religion, strives to bring all human beings closer to God. To Allah. If we succeed, we have done the work of God. In the process we may achieve other things, but basically our life mission is simply to bring the erring mind closer to the Almighty. Sometimes it takes effort. Planning. What matters is that it should succeed. We must never disappoint our Creator."

"Are you going to get to the point? I have been here since seven this morning! And yesterday was even worse!"

"I know, Sir Goddie. I've been here nearly as long. Now, I was talking about soccer. You see, Sir Goddie, what happened on Ikorodu Road—I did hear of the awesome event, who hasn't? Well, what I learnt was that on the one hand, a sinner was brought closer to God. At the same time, a lesson was also served on those who think they can impede the work of God. An open lesson. Not hidden. Two events coming together, the principle of confluence—do you get my meaning, Sir Goddie? But to achieve that confluence, it required yet another confluence. The confluence of time and place. Bringing two things together to form one. The police theory is that the victim had been followed all day, perhaps all week, until time and place came together as one. The confluence of confluences. That took some diligent work. I ask you, Sir Goddie, do you recollect the match between the United Kingdom and Argentina? Remember the controversial goal?"

"No, I don't. As you've observed, I have no time for soccer."

"There was a goal. Some cried foul. And so it seemed. The moment was caught on camera, played and replayed afterwards. How come the referee, the two linesmen were so positioned that they did not see the foul? The ball had indeed been handled. The goal remained validated. And what did Maradona call it?"

Again Goddie conceded ignorance.

"The hand of God."

12.

Boriga or Bust

They were waiting outside the billiards room when he emerged—Muktar; Costello; Baba Baftau, the one everyone called Old Man of the Desert; the treasurer Kufeji. While he was on the phone to Duyole, a faint glimmer, not too far off the mark, had begun to percolate through to the lounge. Not all but at least a few of them had heard stories, difficult to believe at first but increasingly attested. They had come to invite him to join them at a table in a secluded corner where a half-dozen other members had already gathered.

"We need to know more," Baba Baftau pleaded. Until then he had not taken part in the discussions, though he had listened to every word from his prayer corner.

"I need sleep," Menka protested. "Let me get my things and go to bed."

"Just a few more minutes," Baba insisted. "Not more than half an hour, I promise. Take it as a hospital emergency. We are patients. We need some reassurance."

Menka took a deep breath, capitulated. He liked Baftau. After his phone call, he felt buoyant, liberated, as one who had finally taken a decision that was irreversible. Nothing else mattered. He sank into the seat that Baba had pulled out for him. They went straight into questions. His answers were given clinically, without emotion or commentary. He told them of the visitation of the corporate threesome and where it had eventually led the following morning. The suburb was known as Boriga.

"Yes, I saw it myself. I was given a guided tour, all businesslike. The goods were on display. Rows and rows of body parts—thighs, ankles, necks, breasts and fingers, hunchback tissue, well preserved. Foetuses and reproductive organs. There were entire rib cages suspended from hooks—that was strange to me at first. But apparently if you imprison an infant within the rib cage and leave it there to die naturally—yes, that was the word—naturally, that is, from starvation, the baby's vital organs produce a double, triple potency for something—I forget what precisely, but it had to do with longevity. Yes, all neatly arranged in refrigerated glass display cases. Preserved in alcohol. Sometimes in coconut oil. Professionally labeled. They even have a vault. Access granted to a very limited clientele."

"They have a vault?"

A loud spluttering as Muktar nearly choked on his drink. A spell of racking coughs as his laughter competed with speech till he managed to expel his contribution. "A vault! Did you hear that? A vault. I warned you people it's a waste of time. This man has been doing the pilgrimage rounds. Visiting all those vaults and catacombs of Europe and Jerusalem. A vault? What else?"

Baba Baftau gave him a vicious look and pointed the way back into the lounge. "I thought we agreed we were to have a sober talk here. Ask questions. If you came on simply to have yourself some fun . . ."

"No, he should stay." Menka smiled. "A vault, I said. Like a bank vault where you keep private boxes with important documents and prized jewelry. Massive steel doors. Round-the-clock refrigeration. That is where they keep the heads. Both fresh and in various stages of desiccation. When I visited, I counted fourteen fresh skulls. All human."

"Did you ask how they came by them?" Kufeji queried.

"No. I didn't need to. They volunteered that information. You remember the luxury-bus crash at Lokoja, the media screams over a secret mass burial? Visit that supposed gravesite and see if you'll find one single body beneath the disturbed soil."

Again, for Muktar it was too much to take. The man was raving! None of them denied that the media was an obliging source of prolonged banquets of sensationalism as the occasional grave robber was exposed, paraded, and prosecuted, but as organized business? His cranky guffaws threatened to resurface, so he quietly left the group, shaking his head. He had long come to his own conclusion for the seeming derangement—the doctor was a glutton for attention. The national award had merely fueled his hunger. Greedy for publicity, he needed to make himself interesting over and above his newfound fame.

Kufeji decided to bring matters to a head. "Very well. The solution is easy. You say this is business? I am the treasurer—I'll accompany you on your next shopping spree. We both report back to the club members. Agreed?"

That made Muktar pause in stride, listening. A calm response, however, sliced through the air behind him. He turned round, incredulous.

"You shall. Tomorrow?"

Muktar retraced a step. "Is the man serious?"

"After this morning's carnage in Sabo market," Menka pressed on, "we are likely to have a few weeks' respite. So before I get boxed in by the next emergency, no time like now. Let's do it tomorrow. Crack of dawn. Shall we say six a.m.? It's a two-hour drive from here, and their opening hours begin at seven, before the general office hours."

"I think I'd like to come with you both." It was Costello's voice.

As a few other voices mumbled in the volunteer mode, the surgeon stopped them. "One more, maybe. Two at the most. They don't like a crowd."

Kufeji looked at him intently. "If what you're saying is true, don't we have to be members—I mean, like a shoppers' thrift club?"

"No. Obviously you can only be introduced by an existing member. And you swear an oath of secrecy. You are obliged to take that oath. And you'll have to make a purchase, no matter how small. Even a fingertip can be expensive—it all depends on your desperation, what your ritualist has prescribed, the timing and all that. Age. An infant's finger may be more expensive than an old woman's today, tomorrow the positions are reversed—and so on and on. The purchase is to commit you, to bind you as a participating member."

A voice piped up from the end of the table. "So what part did you purchase, Menka? Or perhaps in your case, what did you supply? I mean, given your profession . . ."

"Exactly. That is why they approached me in the first place. I told you—maybe you weren't listening! They offered a business partnership. As plain as that."

He was no longer an attention-seeker. A sizeable flank of curiosity had taken over, tinged with some element of fear. There was a common resolve not to miss another word. The self-detached group around the table leant forward, eyes boring into Menka's face from every direction.

"They came to you. But why? Because you hit the headlines? This Award of Pre-eminence? Was it recent?"

"He's a surgeon." A thoughtful mind had obviously been working at it, quite conscientiously. "That would make sense. Steady source of supply. Those parts they cut out of patients. It's obvious."

Menka sighed, looked round the clubroom, feeling increasingly clear-headed. He began to massage the back of his left hand with his slightly cupped right palm, beginning from the fingernails, past knuckles, and up the forearm, up to the elbow and back, stopping to nurse his fingertips one by one, as if engaged in the preparatory motions for drawing off an elbow-length glove.

"Yes"—his voice taking on a thoughtful tone—"because I was a surgeon. Was. That career is over. I've decided to quit. When things reach that stage . . ."

That seemed to shake them all, disbelief on every face. Kufeji broke the silence. "What do you mean, quit?"

"Quit the job," Menka replied quietly. "Quit the position. Even the profession. I need a change." He allowed himself a smile. "After all, you said it yourself. Too much competition. I never could stand competition."

Costello appeared the most shocked. "Why? For heaven's sake, why? On account of this business? Is the fault yours? What has it got to do with you?"

"It's time to quit, that's all. Leave Jos. Leave Plateau State altogether. To start with, I need a change of environment. It's been building up for quite a while."

"Where will you go?" Kufeji protested, his erstwhile levity turned into genuine concern. "You think anywhere else is different? You're allowing something like this to upset you?"

"No, no, no. You wouldn't understand. It's a long story. But I do need a change. It's time to go. I haven't decided where, but I think it's time for a kind of semiretirement. Maybe go back to my village. Think things over."

Costello walked over and confronted him. "Stop me if I seem to probe, but was there something else about this business? Something you don't mind sharing with us?"

Menka hesitated. "No-o-o. Unless you wish to take into account my injured professional pride. Those callers wasted no time in laying their cards on the table. They even left me with a price catalogue, assured me that the pricing was all negotiable. You see, they were confident about me—that was what rankled, still does, if you want to know the truth. I don't believe they would have gone to any other doctor, at least not in the confident manner they adopted—as if I were already part of them! Mind you, I could hardly blame them. I learnt a lot."

"Like what? What else?" Kufeji demanded.

"Like the cost of clipped toenails, especially if the patient ended up dead. Or pre-operation shaved-off hair. Or pubic hair, especially the female. Or menstrual pads—you'd be astonished at cleaners, even nurses, who scavenge those things from disposal bins, offer them to the highest bidder! My callers assumed I knew all of this, even assumed I took a cut. Their conviction was so total, so unquestioning, I decided to change my tone and pretend I was only playing hard to get, trying to place myself in a strong bargaining position. Do you understand? My staff, my own staff, had been selling body discards all these years, right under my nose. They sold even the washed-down blood from the emergency room—and this in the season of HIV! Just think of that for a moment! I found I had been compromised for years without even knowing it. It was that sudden, shocking realization that decided me. I decided to play along. At the supermarket I acted interested. Asked questions, like a prospective partner. But by then I knew I'd had it."

Costello shook his head, frustrated. "So they came to you? Who else would they approach? How many surgeons do we have in these parts? Mostly the surviving Pakistanis from the first wave of foreign recruitment."

"And were those dedicated killers or what!" The voice belonged to Baba Baftau. He had been chaperone to scions of rulers, the emirs especially, during their tutelage at British public schools—Eton and Harrow topping the list—even before the runup to independence. And he had supervised the selection of trainees for post-British bureaucracy in the north. All eyes turned towards him.

"Well, don't look at me as if you didn't know it. It's public knowledge, we never hid it. With independence on the horizon, we were so anxious to get rid of the southerners, we recruited specialists from everywhere, including even from our former masters, the British." He snorted. "Those British! They went out through the front door, then returned through the back. Who brought them back? Our own leaders. And they were given special contracts. Nearly bankrupted the regional treasury. We're still paying emoluments to some of them, even now!"

"Now, now, no politics, Baba," Costello teased.

"That's not politics. It's history." He turned to face Kufeji. "You southerners were dangerous people, so we were warned. It was safer to recruit from the British—and other Commonwealth countries, like India and Pakistan. It wasn't just the medical services. We preferred to import every kind of expertise—railway engineers, teachers, surveyors—all the way from India and Pakistan, the latter most especially. Expatriates were safer than people from down south. Dangerous people. Too clever by half. And don't forget the economics of it. You could get rid of expatriates as their contracts expired. But imagine if we had allowed ourselves to get stuck with people like Menka."

"What do you mean? Am I no longer from the north?"

The Old Man roared with laughter. "The worst kind. Better a straightforward southerner than your type. We call your kind expatriate northerners. All right, just take what you've been digging up, for instance. Why you? I'm a full-blooded son of the soil, born and lived here all my life, and I never heard of this meat mall till now. I knew all about the Pakistani, but this one? Never heard of it!"

Chudi brought him back, looking his sternest. "Why bring in the Pakistani, Baba? Why do you call them killers? It wasn't they who killed us during the pogrom."

Muktar, who had returned to the fold, was on his feet. "No, no. None of that, gentlemen, certainly none of that!"

"Thank you, Sec. And I wasn't referring to all of them. I'm talking about the quacks! Quack doctors. They performed surgeries. One of them, he was just a ward attendant. He never went beyond cleaning the floor and carrying stretcher cases. But he arrived as a certified doctor. Remember, I headed the civil service. I was in the midst of it all, and hmm, what didn't we uncover! It took too long, much too long before we noticed how people were dying under the knife. It was like we were hit by Ebola."

Dr. Menka nodded. "I was taken to the grounds where the hospital buried most of the victims of that quack. It's painful to think of, but over here the powers did largely what they wanted. A malpractice charge often meant nothing, as long as it did not exactly conflict with the laws of Sharia. That was the reality."

"There was the Commission of Enquiry, Doctor. Go and read the report. I was secretary to the commission. In fact, if you're interested, come to think of it, I'll bring my own copy here. I'll leave it in the reading room."

Chudi chipped in. "I'll remind you, Baba. I want to see that report."

"So do I, but the real question is, was anything acted upon? Was the fake doctor prosecuted?"

"No, he was merely deported. And you won't need to remind me, Mr. Librarian. Time I transferred some of those files for safety into this fortress." He raised his voice, pointed a finger in Menka's direction. "As for you, *touranchi!* Yes, you. You are not going anywhere. Let me tell you something, something you don't know for a change. Or do you know how you got nominated in the first place? This national award of yours, you know how it came about?"

Menka shrugged his shoulders in the negative. "No idea. It came out of the blue. I had no idea anyone took notice of what we try to do over here. Except of course when Boko Haram pays us one of their deadly visits."

"Quite right—and that is exactly where you came in. Your work on the victims. The state took notice. Time and weeds may have covered up the cemetery where those poor victims were buried, but the records are still there. So is your own record, what you've been doing. We owe you. You wiped out that memory of a time when we legitimized butchery. The powers that be in Abuja finally listened to us. So you owe me a drink. Come to think of it, you owe us all a drink, disrupting our celebration mood like that. Couldn't you have picked a different time for your gruesome revelations?"

Whatever remained of the tension evaporated. Baba Baftau was one of the most dedicated patrons of the bar, not that it stopped him breaking off when it was time for any of his five-times-a-day regulation prayers. Baba Baftau would break off in midconversation or mid-swig—it made no difference—repair to his dedicated corner, spread out his prayer mat, and perform his orisons. Then he rolled up the mat, replaced it in the cupboard, and resumed whatever he had interrupted. And he never missed his annual pilgrimage—neither the lesser nor the greater hajj.

Menka looked at Baba, shook his head sadly. Baftau was one of the two or three members he would truly miss.

"Repeat, you are staying put!" the veteran bellowed. "This state won't let you. You are also forgetting our neighbouring states, who come to borrow you when they have those complicated cases. If you're thinking of escaping to Dubai, forget it. I have deep contacts there and I'll see to it that you never get a visa!"

A huge cheer rose from the table, causing the excluded body of the lounge to wonder what new event was being launched. It was as if a dark shroud had been lifted and a new spirit abruptly injected into the evening. They began emptying their beer mugs and glasses, moving out to crowd the bar for refills. Only one person did not move. The mood had turned jovial, camaraderie was in uproarious emission, but it did not seem to have found a stopover where Menka sat, shaking his head dubiously.

A changed Muktar stood up, slapped him on the back. "Cheer up. You heard the Old Man."

For a moment Menka was startled. Recovering, he forced himself to smile. "I wish it were all that simple. Anyway, tomorrow?"

The secretary nodded. "Let's meet here. Six a.m."

Menka warned, "Just you, the treasurer—he was the first to volunteer—and Costello."

.   .   .

THE EVENING WORE ON, slipped stealthily into night. The company gradually reduced, mostly in a haze of euphoria. Accustomed harmony was restored and the seeming derangement of their celebrated member nearly totally forgiven, if not forgotten. The guest of honour who earlier could hardly wait to retire to his solo dinner found himself still stuck to his stool at the lounge bar, strangely reluctant to leave his accustomed corner, unable to prise himself clean of a niggling dialogue with the past.

Arguments soon petered out. There was one final surge, its provocation owned by none other than Baba Baftau. First the veteran insisted that he must accompany the agreed team of three to the meat emporium. He felt a personal sense of guilt that such a business should exist on his own doorstep, and for no fewer than five years—even if Menka's deduction was merely approximate—yet he knew nothing of it. He had to be part of fumigating the stench or it would be to his everlasting discredit. The argument raged fiercely. Baftau swore he would use his "inside powers" to track their movements, follow, and arrive at the secluded destination with a convoy which would include a busload of *almajiri*. In the end, Costello "bowed to the combined privilege of age and unfair citizen priority rights" and yielded his place to the veteran. It delayed departure yet again, since Baba then had to reciprocate by buying drinks for all the interventionists. The more difficult task was to wean him off yet another source of personal failure. How could he, the oldest club member and a deep-rooted "son of the soil," with reaches to the highest branches of the power tree, fail to hold down this restive scion of a small, obscure village called Gumchi? Unknown to the others, he had even included the cause in his last prayer session.

"What will I tell the council?" he wailed. "They all worked so hard to bring this honour to the club. They insisted I must be here to celebrate on their behalf—as if I needed persuading! Now some lazy good-for-nothing hospital down that way will harvest the glory!"

"Baba, I don't even know where I'm next headed," Menka tried to reassure him.

"Don't tell me! With your new fame, they'll all be after you like flies around rotten *kilishi*. Dubai, America, England, Germany, and all those *touranchi* countries."

Inconsolable, he reminded the teasing crowd that he had lived through quacks for so many years, he recognized the genuine item when he saw one and could not bear the thought of losing such a catch to others, least of all when he had worked to turn him into a national property. It was like a personal robbery, and he did not know quite what to make of it, and no one should attempt to tell him that this was the will of Allah or he would crown him with a full bottle of Guinness stout and send him prematurely to the bosom of Allah. He implored, cajoled, promised new employment conditions strictly created for Menka—he would see the governor the following day and have a letter signed and sealed, with a new contract and unique salary structure.

Finally Menka argued, "Look at it this way, Baba, just follow it along its logical progression. To learn that a limb, an organ, something you've cut off as a medical procedure, becomes a sought-after commodity for others, with negotiable market value! And not for stitching onto the body of some beneficiary—maybe the victim of a motor or factory accident, the usual organ donor practice now commonplace everywhere. You see, we never know where we all encounter our wake-up call. That procuring visit, then my follow-up visit to the meat mall—I needed to, of course. I didn't require any persuasion to visit the depot and see for myself—and all those questions finally homed in on target. Pursue it to its logical conclusion, consider all the ramifications. Just place yourself within a society—this very region—where they actually cut off a man's wrist, arm, or leg for some offences. Isn't it one step away from imposing and strictly enforcing such sentences? No option of fines or imprisonment—just amputate! And the Medical Association can do nothing about it. Disfigured for life. How do you stop the deliberate imposition of such extreme penalty whenever demand exceeds supply? That is my question, Baba. In what direction can one predict the laws of supply and demand?"

Baftau's voice rose, high-pitched in scandalized dismissal. "*Haba,* Doctor. Are you not beginning to exaggerate? Islam does not permit such abomination."

"No, not Islam. But human. We are no longer living in the world you once knew, Baba. Just check the daily media. Check the court cases. We are ringed by new abominations every day, acts you never could have contemplated in your youth—all have become commonplace . . ."

Finally occupation was down to just the dedicated night huggers, from whom even the last seep of reputed stamina had been drained. The unexpected revelation itself, terminus of a distempered moment, appeared to have pronounced its last word. They drank, turned to other subjects, set down their mugs and wineglasses, downed their final shot of whisky and soda, gin and tonic, stubbed out cigarettes or lit their accompanying final drag for the road. One after the other they began to drift away, some casting glances of uncertainty, puzzlement, even ambiguous protest at the initiator of it all. Baba Baftau dragged himself away, muttering morose imprecations. Gradually the clubhouse fell silent.

The night waiter locked up, shut the windows, leaving the last stragglers to close up shop whenever they pleased. The evening, Menka felt, had finally healed itself—well, left him a residuum of contentment for a decision taken. He was already looking forward to the interim stay with his Badagry family. He looked up suddenly to find himself virtually the last occupant—in a sense, that is. There were still two or three scattered around, but they were out of reckoning. They had no further interest in what happened around them, being slumped in armchairs or over the drinking tables. Despite himself, Menka continued to linger. A creeping regret—he would miss the place, the company, he would miss even the fireplace lit in the Harmattan cold with fake glowing coals, miss even its mantelpiece, over which hung the framed injunction *Manners Maketh Man*. Come to think of it, he would miss *everything*.

The surgeon lingered until the lounge was virtually emptied of the last member—it had to do, he tried to persuade himself, with a wish to avoid running a gauntlet of ambiguous good-byes, or any drunk sentimental talk of desertion. Eventually the silence translated into near-emptiness. He finished his drink, again picked up the present from the club, still in its wrapping. Suddenly he had an urge to see what was under the wrapping. So he gingerly tore off some of the paper. It brought a smile to his face. He should have guessed—a miniature replica of Hilltop Mansion. He signed the honour tab for his account and rose to leave.

Dr. Menka was close to the door when he heard the soft sound of clapping from the adjoining alcove, which he thought had also been abandoned. It threw him off stride, startled. For at least thirty minutes after the last slurring voice, spasmodic movement, or cranky snore, he had lulled himself into believing that he was alone with only his thoughts for company, and the hypnotic silence. Also, those thoughts, being largely reminiscent of the good old days of innocence and promise, had left him in a fully tranquil frame of mind, so he was jolted. The owner of the applauding hands was framed against a window, a mere blur in place of features, since he stood with his back to the window, through which an outside lamp cast a powerful beam, leaving his face just a shrouded oval. The beard created a penumbra that lent the face further mystery, and it was not the kind of mystery that made Menka comfortable. In a corner, virtually invisible, another figure slumped in an armchair, apparently one of the fully incapacitated members. Menka's emerging paranoia rose to a level where he felt that the figure was not merely awake but was somehow connected with the window silhouette. The thought of a bodyguard flitted across his mind. The clapping hands from the window slowed to a stop, and a voice replaced them.

"An impressive exposition, if I may comment. But can I ask one question?"

Menka hesitated, squinted, tried to make out the features. "What exposition? In any case, who are you?"

"All of it—I've listened all evening. But especially your final allocution to the old man—I was riveted. Doctor, just take it from me, we are acquainted. I'm referring to your revelation over the supermarket. The human meat mall, to use your own expression. It has been a most informative evening. And as I said, your final argument with Old Man Baftau. The issue of merchandizing the rewards of punitive extraction, such as amputations. I admired your style, Doctor."

Menka's immediate instinct was to walk away from the intruder—he was certain the man was not a club member. A mixture of irritation and curiosity, however, made him linger. He decided to challenge him instead. "You don't strike me as being a club member."

The man's arms spread in agreement. "Quite right, Doctor. I am not. You may consider me a club follower, though. I'm one of those who hang around places like this, where all the problems of the world are solved. And I really would like to ask a question. In the public interest, if that makes it easier. Very much in the public interest. I know the media, and especially the social media, would be most interested in your answer."

Menka felt a sudden queasiness, a near-premonition, but his face showed no sign of it. "Go on."

"A simple one, Doctor. How does it feel to cut off a man's arm?"

If there was silence before, the lounge now felt as if it had turned into a tomb. For the longest minute he had ever experienced, even during the most critical moments of surgical intervention in a human form that lay helpless on the operating table, Menka found his tongue turned leaden in his head, motionless as in that nightmare that he always prayed would never leave his hands paralyzed in a life-and-death moment of incision. Then he sensed a slow, creeping wave of anger, but he pushed that away quite abruptly and braced himself. The ordeal of the day was clearly not yet over, not by a long stretch. He sensed it, felt quietly enveloped in a cloud of resentment. Why this persecution? Wherever it might lead, he would at least put this intruder in his place.

Menka put on on his best clinical voice. "A very simple operation, as a matter of fact." He spoke clearly in an even, expository tone, one that had contributed to his earning the title Dr. Bedside Manners. "How does it feel? There is no feeling involved when we operate. A surgeon is trained to permit none. It's all technical. You've eaten stewed or grilled goat knuckles before, haven't you? Or pig knuckles, if you happen not to be Muslim. Our people in the U.S. call it soul food. It's gourmet cuisine even in some European restaurants. The Chinese, of course, specialize in the delicacy. Same process, separating bone from tissue and gristle. The only difference is that in one case you use your teeth and fingers, in the other forceps, scalpel, etc."

The figure appeared to grin. The face could be mistaken for a death mask, except for the elongated chin, the effect of the beard. "Take a seat," his voice invited. "Join me for a final drink."

"The bar is closed," Menka pointed out matter-of-factly.

"So it is. You're quite right. Well, simply for a few minutes' exchange. I know you've exhausted everyone with your disclosures—

except of course that you chose not to credit personal experience. All objectivization. Once or twice you came close. I thought, *Ah, at last,* but no, you slipped away. Still, they all appeared to have been fully satisfied. Most. More or less."

"But not you. You had a question to ask."

"Actually, some of the members know me quite well." He pulled out a chair and gestured. "Are you sure? This could be an illuminating exchange."

Menka hesitated. "What is your interest? Are you a medical doctor? Or human rights activist?"

Somehow Menka sensed another death-mask grimace within the dark patch. "No—my vocation is not unrelated, but no, there is no *Doctor* before my name. And I do not belong among those noisy agitators on human rights." He pushed the chair forward, his palm upturned in a repeat gesture.

Menka declined. "No, thank you, I believe I've said all I wished to say for the night."

"Are we quite sure about that, Dr. Menka? I read all about that affair at the time—how the years fly past! Over twenty now, I think. I was left suspended, have remained curious ever since over many aspects. I not only kept asking myself what the patient felt, but attempted to run through the thoughts, the state of mind of the surgeon himself, the one who took off the arm. Most fortunate for me being here tonight. Meeting you. Listening to the toast of the nation. But please . . ." Again he gestured to the chair, again Menka declined with a curt head gesture. The shadow capitulated.

"Of course. Perhaps inconsiderate of me. It has been a heavy day for you—the suicide bombing. You must be dying to get home. Oh, that reminds me, at least your work has been recognized by everyone, and I have yet to add my congratulations. Please accept my small contribution."

Menka nodded thanks, turned to leave. The voice remained quite polite, clinging. "Mind you, I still wish you could have indulged me. What was that like? I've been asking myself that. The Hippocratic oath, etc.—after all, any school pupil knows all about Hippocrates."

For the first time that evening, Menka actually smiled. The gloves were off, and he preferred it that way. "Well, to begin with, the Hippocratic oath never envisaged a society where you would cut off a man's arm for stealing a goat, so the oath is silent on that score. For me it was just a medical procedure. You looked at it like a gangrenous arm that had to be removed. You followed your training. Standard practice. It was painless. No cruelty involved."

"I am sure there wasn't. He would be under anaesthesia."

"Full anaesthetic, quite right."

A sigh emerged from the shadow. "Vastly different, far more humane than those civil war atrocities along our west coast—short sleeves or long sleeves? I'm sure you've heard the expression."

"Heard of it? It haunts me. Merely listening to you makes me shiver."

Despite the blur, Menka could almost see the man's theatrical grimace. "Ugh! Sadists. And children are involved. Child soldiers. Their commanders make them carry out such butchery, and worse. They drug them. Imagine what that does to a child. They overrun a village, and out come the machetes. They give their captives a choice—do you want short or long sleeves? Meaning at the wrist or at the elbow. Plain sadism."

"Part of our task as doctors is to rehabilitate such children. It's an endless task."

"Joseph Kony—that so-called Lord's Resistance Army chieftain—he handled his own mutilations personally, from all reports. Slit nostrils, sliced lips—he seemed to think up new refinements every day."

"The type proliferates throughout the continent. It's a real tragedy for us in Africa." As he spoke, Menka remained undecided—to move closer to the man so as to scrutinize him openly or continue to pretend disinterest in whoever he was? Moving closer would only encourage him, and he wanted to bring the encounter to an end. In any case, he had become quite certain that it was the same vanishing figure he had earlier seen in the billiards room—something about the man's posture—again, familiar yet estranged. And the voice joined to give off the same feeling of someone he had encountered before. Unlike the actual provocative questions, the tone appeared to labour not to sound aggressive, not to convey any tinge of disapproval or implied judgment. It was all highly theatrical, affected a clinical enquiry embarked upon in full sobriety, as if the questioner were propelled by nothing beyond average human curiosity. Menka shrugged—none of that made a difference to him. The stranger's mission was to place him on the defensive, place him on notice for one purpose or the other. Then something struck the surgeon.

"Oh. Were you the one who went missing? The one supposed to pass on a message."

"A message?"

Menka was not sure, but he sensed a hesitation. "Yes, I had a visitation from your business partners. You were supposed to have delivered a message ahead of them. What happened? Lost your nerve?"

"Dr. Menka, I assure you I do not know what you're talking about."

"Well, whoever you are, I do not believe you. Everything tells me you are the same person."

"We'll leave it that way," the stranger said. "Perhaps when we become further acquainted?"

"I doubt very much that that will ever happen," Menka said firmly.

"There I must disagree with you. But let's see what the future brings. Can I ask you just one more question?"

Again Kighare Menka was pulled both ways—leave or stay? He felt certain that if he kept up the exchange long enough, the penny would drop. He would unravel this shadow and end the advantage of the stranger's anonymity. It was too one-sided an exchange, and this made him seethe. The tug of war was short-lived, resolved in favour of curiosity.

"All right. Your question?"

"What about the thief? Do you have the same objection to talking about him?"

"What about him?" Voice as level as he could, but hard.

"Well, his feelings? Did he hold it against you? I used to ask myself that question. I mean, how did he feel? One assumes that even goat thieves have feelings. I imagine him finally waking up, discovering that his arm was gone. How did he feel?" The speaker's arms again emerged from the shadow, sweeping the dark. "Man goes to sleep with two arms, wakes up with just one."

Menka turned thoughtful, as if intent on recapturing moments of his first encounter with the felon the morning after.

"A strange society, ours. I was born in this region, in the Plateau, not far from Jos itself, but even here, quite distant from the Quranic equivalent of what is known elsewhere as the Bible Belt, I often find things very strange. I mean, improbable. Fulfilled my youth service in Kano—but you know that already, I am sure—which is where it all happened. Now, your question, I believe I can answer that. Naturally I saw my patient the following morning, with the full hospital team. That's routine. Now, this may surprise you. I don't know how it is with others, but by the time we began the rounds, the man had already been visited by the village head, the community worthies, mullah, even the emir. The village was under one of the junior emirates, I'm sure you recall. They brought all kinds of items to enable him to start a new life with one arm only—I mean, useful presents, including foodstuffs."

"Any goat?" With the laughter of one in control.

Menka managed a modest semblance of mirth. "No, nothing alive and bleating. Fresh clothing. Seeds for planting. A machete and a hoe. Requirements of that nature. The basic principle was, we mustn't let his becoming one-armed now push him deeper into a career of crime. But you know what? Let me tell you what outsiders—like yourself, I think—would find most unsettling. Me too, but then I schooled in the south and finished my studies abroad. So you could claim I had become . . . deculturized?"

"But you still carried out the sentence."

"Do I have to remind you I was on my youth service? Compulsory youth service. The thief was convicted under Sharia law. I received a directive to amputate."

The man gestured dismissal. "Oh, come on, you were a trained doctor. Full-fledged. Graduated from Bristol University, United Kingdom. The Nigerian Medical Association took a position—"

"And found they had no choice but to drop the matter. Different laws operate, and not only on medical matters."

"Weren't you struck off the register?" Again the man affected a neutral, disinterested voice. "Yet here you are, still practicing. Receiving national plaudits."

"Struck off?" Menka laughed out loud. "I don't know who you are or what you're up to. I know you're not the press, or your approach would be different. Whatever or whoever you represent, you should know—it's quite elementary—you have to put an offender on trial. Otherwise you lose when you're sued in court—the principle of fair hearing. Basic. I made myself unavailable, on orders. I was ready to stand trial. Things are different up here—and not merely in the north, by the way. Remember we are speaking also of that north, the north of that time, both pre-Independence and even till now for quite a few states which have yet to cross that regional or religious barrier. You want me to remind you of the boastful paedophiles whose victims we treat all the time. Some of them damaged for life. Never one prosecuted. On the contrary, the criminals shuttle between governorship and senatorial immunity. So which law exactly are you talking about?"

"Your own personal self-regulatory laws, Doctor. That's what I'm talking about. What do your ethics preach, Dr. Menka? What did your professional ethics dictate?"

Menka remained unruffled. "Law and ethics often clash. That comes to all of us, sooner or later, and in the medical profession most often. And some have that dilemma thrust on them much too early, under unjust circumstances. But we do make choices—there you are quite right. And sometimes those choices are not the most elevating. Doctors are not supposed to chop off a healthy, serviceable part of the human anatomy. Yet it happens. It's happened here, and the law prescribes it. Experience counts. And maturity. What is known as human development. Reviewing one's early givens. Asking who pronounced the givens in the first place. And under what state of human development? I hope you do not think so little of me as to imagine I have not given it any thought. Don't doctors supervise the execution of the condemned where capital punishment still obtains? Yet capital punishment is considered primitive in other nations. In the U.S. doctors administer the lethal injection to the wretches. And then priests. Those who minister to the condemned before execution—what do you have to say about them? Have you tried to reason it out in that context? Is there any difference? Regarding what views I personally hold today, that is my own affair. I am not willing to share that with a stranger."

"Be so kind as to indulge me with just one very last question, Doctor. As you have surely decided, I am not here by accident."

"Quite right. I've been waiting for you to disclose just what this is all about."

"Of course. So now the man himself—how did he take it afterwards? You're right, sir, I have nothing to do with the media. My curiosity is quite genuine. Personal. But also related to my occupation. In good time, as we become further acquainted, perhaps you will understand. Right now I suppose I must sound presumptuous."

Menka's face was squeezed in a puzzled frown, but he had resolved to see it through, wherever it might lead. *I opened the can,* he reminded himself, *so I shall also be the one to close it.* He felt unusually relaxed.

"How did the man take it? That was what baffled me the most. I expected him to be bitter, angry, or self-pitying. Not he! That amputee remained one of the most cheerful of the human species I had encountered throughout my student course. He was beaming from ear to ear, slurping down his *akamu*—it was breakfast time, and there he was breaking his fast like a chieftain, as if he had not a care in the world."

"Well, maybe surrounded by all those gifts . . ."

"No. Only partly to do with his new cotton smock, rough sandals, kerosene lamp, and sorghum seeds, plus a little cash. It was he, he himself, his demeanour. He felt nothing adverse about the loss of his arm. I remember his words—*It's the will of Allah that this should happen. I am glad the arm was cut off. It will remind me not to steal anymore, and that is what Allah wishes for me.*" Menka again shook his head as if to free it from decades of disbelief. "That's right. He was not in the least distressed. I'll stake my profession on that."

"Amazing."

"Isn't it? Ah well, goodnight." And then, as if he now felt that he had been shortchanged in the exchange, Menka turned and waved a hand in the direction of his interlocutor. "My turn to be curious. You haven't really told me what you do. You're not a club member. You are not the media. Your curiosity is . . . let me just say, it strikes a different tone from the exchanges I've been having. I think I have earned the right to be inquisitive."

The blur appeared to hesitate, then drawled, "I did give some kind of a hint. You could say I am also a doctor, but only of the spirit."

"Ah, a churchman? Preacher?"

"Sort of. Same business. Maybe I am closer to being a farmer, though not what I would call a rounded one. I am at the parasitic end of that vocation. I harvest. Harvest souls. Others do the planting, I harvest. I try to be honest."

A pause hung between them. Then the stranger said, "Goodnight, Doctor." He detached himself from the window, walked towards the service door. He made no attempt to hide the fact that he hugged the wall, avoiding the light pools to frustrate recognition. And then he vanished into the night.

Menka stood for a while longer, his eyes roving round the recumbent figures still littering the lounge. Not one of them appeared to have moved or showed evidence of having been conscious of a single moment of the strange encounter. The doctor shook his head to clear it, or perhaps simply to force the exchange into rational pockets of his brain.

All accumulated highs dissipated as he finally gained the familiar seat of his Nissan Patrol in the parking lot. He remained there a few moments without moving, running through the reel of the weird coda to an already strange evening out. He could make neither head nor tail of it all. The most unsettling part was, he could not even begin to seize upon any remarkable feature of the stranger, yet he felt reasonably certain that it was someone he did know, someone he had encountered before. A vague outline, yes. Beyond that, no features. He could not begin to guess whether the man was swarthy, light-skinned, bald, walked straight or stooped, was short, tall, or average. It seemed it was only a silhouette that spoke, walked, questioned, and dodged questions. Ah well, he would enquire from Baba Baftau when they met the following morning—he seemed to know Hilltop denizens inside out. And with that dismissive thought, he turned the ignition key.

Lo and behold, Mr. Silhouette reappeared, shimmered into position on the driver's side, leaning over the door frame. This time Menka did not attempt to disguise his irritation—it was so sudden, and the park being unlit, he was again startled, even frightened. The quadrangle was deserted, never mind how safe Hilltop Mansion was reputed to be. His reaction annoyed him more than the intrusion—he hated to concede fright under any circumstances. The very rites of passage he had been made to undergo in Gumchi before his very first departure from home, to join a boarding school, had been based virtually on the ability to control even the most instinctive responses to the sudden or unexpected. Yet there it was, twice already within minutes the same evening, and caused by the same mysterious intruder, so he felt a heavy wave of aggression welling up in his gorge.

"You again? What is it this time? I need to get some sleep."

"I'm sorry I startled you. I forgot something important—I would have remembered if we'd sat down even for a moment, but then our conversation also turned interesting, not quite the way I had anticipated. So I forgot."

Menka waited for him to continue. The voice was self-assured. "You won't need to keep that appointment," it said.

Menka was momentarily lost. "What appointment?"

"In the morning. The visit to the meat mall."

Menka snapped, "And why not? What is it to you?"

"It is no longer there. The meat mall has relocated."

"What! When? Where to?"

"Its location here was no longer viable. Economically. Some problems of security have also arisen. The board of directors decided it was time to move."

Menka sat still, speechless. Loudest of the alarms in his head was the fear that no one would believe him now. No one.

The stranger accurately read his mind. "You don't have to worry about your club unbelievers, either. I assure you, you can ignore them."

"Ignore! How do I do that? Would *you* believe me if you had participated in those exchanges?"

"No. Obviously not. We are all born with that Doubting Thomas gene. Still, I assure you, that is something you do not have to worry about. Tomorrow your club members will be too preoccupied with more important matters."

Menka's impatience had now reached its zenith. He engaged the gears and the car shot forward. The man's lethargy vanished; he leapt backward with an impressive athleticism that consoled Menka somewhat—at least he had forced the man to do something unexpected. The stranger's parting words would, however, ring in Menka's ears for days afterwards: "Trust me!"

Within minutes, such a drastic extension of the more than already oversubscribed, unprecedented revelatory evening! So what for an encore? Perhaps a rockfall from loose boulders lining the Plateau hill! Menka braced his shoulders, drove home, thoughtful and resentful at once. Sure, he had lost his cool, but was that sufficient to generate this spectral intervention? For a start, the man's presence was clearly no accident, so who was he? Despite his theatrical attempt at self-effacement, there still emerged something from him that triggered recollection. It was there, elusive, constantly slipping from grasp, but Menka had no doubt about a linkage somewhere in the past. At the beginning he had thought, ah yes, a blackmailer, come to squeeze him with the threat of denunciation after the lavishly publicized award. A connection somewhere with that operation, the excision of the thieving arm? He strove to conjure up the various participants in that twenty-year-old event, in whatever role, however minor—the judges, the mandatory witnesses, the attendant nurses, the pursuant rehabilitation officials. He ran the reel over and over in his mind—the youth corps commander, a soldier who had handed him the assignment at the clinic, casually passing on instructions as if the operation were of no consequence. Just a wave of the hand—*Your patient is waiting for you in the emergency theatre, Corper Menka. Let us know when you are done.* None of the emerging sketches quite fitted the intruder of Hilltop Mansion. He appeared to be a sinister force propelling, shunting events into predetermined channels, but all leading—exactly where? For once Menka seemed to finally understand the full impact of the word *vortex*. That was his location, yes, a vortex. No sooner breaking loose from a sneak undertow than another surged, attempting to suck him under.

A second shower, then the late, lingering, always restorative solitary dinner, his table set against the window looking tangentially downward across the hills. Not too far distant, he could make out, as always, the contours of the clubhouse, a few interior lights kept on all night, the solitary lamppost of the parking space that now lent the ill-lit quandrangle a sinister ambiance—the first ever such emanation since he had taken up residence in the hills. He caught himself observing more keenly his steward clear the plates, close the kitchen door, as if every gesture, every motion held a clue to the events of the day but particularly to that final encounter on its own. The entirety appeared to have played out in two movements. They stood apart from each other—with perhaps his phone exchange with Duyole the sorely needed interlude of clarity between the brawl with his disorientated club members and the intrusion by Mr. Silhouette. Clarity because it lent affirmation to a decision already taken—to take a break from the turbid atmosphere of Jos. He felt relieved that he had kept back something from Duyole—his letter of resignation, submitted only the day before. He would share that with him only after his arrival in Lagos, perhaps after the sumptuous dinner he knew awaited him—he did not need to be told—Duyole would plunge straight into plans for him in heaven alone knew what direction. He would arrive in Lagos and find consulting offers already awaiting him from some private hospital or business. Definitely from the university teaching hospital. There was also the pending visit to the meat mall—how would that change options still under consideration? The stranger wanted to keep him away—for what purpose? He was proceeding with that anyway, saying nothing to the others about the attempt to dissuade him. Backing out now was out of the question. Even if on arriving at the location they discovered it had been razed to the ground, the signs of a structure would remain. Then—pursuit? Or abandonment? Let the morning decide.

Sleep did not evince any volunteer spirit of cooperation in bringing the much-needed relief. Leaving the only other place he could rightly call home was strangely troubling, and surprisingly, the prospect also filled him with regrets. He tried to take consolation in his approaching reunion with Pitan-Payne. Perhaps they would even rouse other surviving members of their comatose fraternity—all four prodigious members, no less! His smile was a mixture of self-deprecation and nostalgia, not quite sufficient to light up the built-up gloom from the unexpected tail to an evening of long-restrained monstrosities suddenly let loose. Well, Lagos/Badagry beckoned, and never did the prospect of an interlude seem more enticing.

It promised more than an interlude, more a descent of packed transitions between multiple phases. Much had changed, Menka now consciously admitted, since those days of student idealism, with all their eccentricities. Even his own select quartet of dreamers, who wore T-shirts combatively emblazoned with *The Gong of Four* across the image of a Benin royal gong with four conjoined heads—even they, he ruefully conceded, had undergone irreversible changes. The group had formed around Duyole, the restless engineer, friend, and adopted family from the very earliest days of embattled idealism. Now the Gong members had gone their different ways, pursued by or confronting impositions and choices of sheer survival that ballooned by the day, by the hour. And now he found himself in the most drastic vortex of change, at fifty-seven, celebrated, yet faced with an indeterminate future.

His situation, he feared, now approached the surreal. One moment an overworked and largely overlooked medic, virtually unheard of outside his immediate professional milieu, just another slave of commitment. The next a national reference point, honoured by his peers for the nation's Independence Day Award of Pre-eminence. Now, barely a week in the role, he had turned fugitive, albeit not from justice. But it all came to the same thing—an urgency to get as far as possible from where he was. He felt hunted like any common felon, already detached from his habitual awareness of Jos as a friendly, ruminant space, a city that was evocative of the landscape and tempo of his own Gumchi—of course with vast differences even so. All in all, Menka had begun to taste the beginning of existence in limbo.

Hardy like the terrain itself, the Gumchi people eked out a rudimentary existence from the sparse patches of moisture and foliage that punctuated their vertiginous rocks. Early-morning commuters largely ignored the lines of Gumchi women, slightly stooped, waiting to cross the expressway. They emerged out of scanty huts to thread the spiky pathways on their way to markets for all the world like soldier ants, with water pots, firewood stacks, yam tubers, and other farm produce balanced on submerged shoulder pads, bead bracelets around shaved heads, a human formation that appeared to replicate those precariously poised boulders. The sight was a contrast to their counterparts of the southern tropical belt, city vendors and other supply chains of urban life who used their heads—literally, that is—for porterage. Summary of assets: one primary school wedged at rock base on the miserly plain; one charcoal-making homestead; a bead-making foundry only a little bigger than a domestic hearth; and the farm patches, which included a micro-plantation of kola nut trees, whose flavor had found favour on the discriminating palate of the head of state. There was ultimately nothing there for a freshly minted doctor, specialization surgery. In any case, there were the terms of his scholarship to fulfill—five years of service to the state. The Plateau called. Friendship tugged. The former won the tug of war—but that also enabled him to eat his cake yet keep it. His fast friend Duyole, the commencing link for a surrogate family, had equally turned homewards—in his case, southerly to Lagos and Badagry. For an orphaned survivor from an orphaned village—which in effect meant an occupied unit bypassed by the rest of society—Menka luxuriated in a friendship that cushioned the schooldays rites of passage. It grew only stronger during the period of castaway stressing on an inclement island known as the United Kingdom, its bond remaining intact as each came to terms with every fresh starting point called, nonetheless, home.

When Menka was first assigned to Jos at the end of his year of compulsory youth service in the city of Kano, Jos was an envied posting, a languorous place—at least for those who could live without the frenzy called Lagos, or increasingly Kano, Kaduna, Calabar, Enugu, and a handful of other state capitals. Then suddenly there were human bombs everywhere, bombs strolling into markets on human feet, often of children as innocent carriers, around village squares, hawking food or queuing for a place in motor garages, liberally donated even to infant schools. Churches and mosques lost presumed sanctity—it was difficult to decide which of the two rivaling sects attracted the deeper venom of the black-flagged redeemers. And the daylong, week-long flight of bullets, tracers, a full carnival of projectiles—audible, but still distant from the oasis of Hilltop Mansion, always creeping closer, beaten back, the treasured relief of relative silences and then the resumption of ominous whooshes and thuds of deadly pods. The townspeople even learnt to distinguish between the lethal subtleties of sounds. As for the assailants—it became a constant question with him—what did they want? What god did they worship? Finally his encounter with the marketers of human disaster, invading his clinic, bold as you please—well, after initial prospecting—to offer shares in their morbid merchandise. It was time to move. It had to be fate!

Menka prided himself on not being superstitious—he needed this constant self-reassurance—but this did look as if something akin to fate had taken a hand. But first, to get away, if only for a few days. Then?

The descent into the dense fog of human malformation in which Menka felt trapped called instinctively to past promises and designs of life affirmation, if only for the preservation of his sanity, or perhaps simply surfacing as the very material of nostalgia. It evoked memories of originating input into joint projects that belonged to a time of uncomplicated youthful vision. Skirting disdainfully round the outworn media language of a dream team—no sporting nation would be seen dead without one!—he and his fellow gladiators once settled for the adaptation of the Master Dream Collective! Nothing less grandiose was worthy of the summons from the realms of idyll as they were smitten, like most overseas students, with the transformative wand inscribed *Get back and make a difference!* After multiple trials and rejections, augmentations, winnowing, shameless plagiarizing and originating with equal fervor, the trigger word ended eventually on *branding,* more expansively *rebranding,* plucked—such is the logical irony of emptiness—from the prodigal jingoism of governments for whom it was merely a grandiose playword, banalized, mindlessly appropriated under junketing ministers of this and that on an everballooning entourage of worldwide missions to rebrand the nation. Well, if rebranding, what do you rebrand? Let there be some stuffing in the shell, ideally something unique to the rebranding entity. Offhand rejection of the first comers' "brand of rebranding" was predictable—where it led had become an embarrassment and a challenge. So out they leapt with their counter: *By all means, let's rebrand, but let the product do the rebranding.* Then, once vetted, guaranteed, ennobled, its standard proved sustainable, on comes the branding. The world would come to terms with, come to reckon with, the national brand!

It led to the creation of Brand of the Land. However modest, the term's resonance would echo across the national landscape—continental also, why not?—leaving its mark everywhere, cross-referencing and mutually enhancing through sheer brand recognition and penetration. Quality tests would be paramount. Innovations, expertise, delivery promise, follow-up services pulling in sustainability, etc., etc., irrespective of project and product. It was only on a whim that one of them—it would be Badetona the Scoffer, the practical, finance savvy conspirator—proposed that they head for the patent office. *You simply never know,* he warned. *Let's brand the brand before reprobates take over.* Every innovation would be the benchmark model, against which all other products—or undertakings—would be measured. No matter how disparate the products, they would be linked together as a master brand! Nothing out of the ordinary, simply unique, establishing its distinct, inimitable pedigree—BRAND OF THE LAND.

Dreams happened to them all, provoked by that tenacious bug loosely labeled "giving back," a ravenous tick among rookie graduates in the more productive fields of the learning adventure. National Independence Day found many still within or just across the Channel from the colonizer homeland, the United Kingdom, but that absence from the site of celebrations (of potential only, had they but known it!) just fired the eagerness of such overseas birds of passage. If they could, they would have altered the homeward migration pattern, redirecting even the motions of the trade winds so they could leave straight home from the convocation venue. The company diminished—that was predictable; many were there solely for the conviviality and by-products, not least of them local sex hospitality. By graduation, only four were left standing among a commencing group of a dozen or more fluctuating enthusiasts, determined to keep faith with the bug that had bitten deep and entered their bloodstream. It all seemed fated. At the time the nation was divided into only four regions. Duyole recalled a family heirloom, a four-headed conjoined Benin bronze, and that was it. Adopted as the brand logo! Was all this really a mere thirty-odd years ago? It felt like an eternity had passed. Each military coup seemed a lifetime.

Menka was nothing if not susceptible. Duyole Pitan-Payne was already showing signs of becoming the irrepressible, restless, and inventive engineer with a modest register of clientele. All acknowledged that he held the group together—of course, he had the funds to travel and reach out to all of them; he came from a wealthy family—but a special bond existed between him and the boy from the hills, right from the start. Perhaps it was the differences that attracted them to each other—one, sophisticated scion of Lagos colonial aristocracy and with a double-barreled, biracial family name. Duyole's bonding with the lost-looking pupil from that obscure village was instant. A fragile, accident-prone stripling who had never stepped out of the outcrop settlement where trees grew mysteriously from rock clefts, the outsider was clearly in need of protection from the rest of the claques of all too savvy city-bred schoolmates. The cicatrix on his face marked him also as an instant outsider, stamped him with the stigma of a hinterland excrescence. Unlucky for his earliest aggressors, the instinctive bullies, his restrained bearing hid a stubborn temper constantly on recoil.

On the euphoric morning of an autumnal seaside clime, to the clicking of official and family cameras, the white jacket was ritually slipped over the shoulders of the youth from a central highland in Nigeria, followed by the presentation of the lacquered box containing the silver scalpel and forceps. His shaky but elated voice recited the Hippocratic oath, plus other ritual affirmations of his membership of the "guild of butchers"—Pitan-Payne's irreverence penetrated any role or activity. Menka silently added his own secret "Gumchicratic oath"—he always did his best to match Duyole's deflationary improvisations. But Kighare Menka was anything but dismissive.

Next came the unofficial but profound ritual finale—*the real meat on stiff bone*. Did that really follow? Menka interrogated the night. For that was the dusk-to-dawn shindig at the class nocturnal "mortuary," where bottles of multinational breweries and distilleries breathed their last. A Nissan shed for stadium equipment at the southern end of the football field was transformed on Convocation Day by fairy lights, the revelers outfitted in extreme team-supporter attire complete with scarves almost the length of the distance between the twinned goalposts. There he openly articulated, in between hiccups, his oath that, come coups, come nation dissolution, secessions or bankruptcy, come marriage or family, he would build a first-class diagnostic clinic with his own hands in Gumchi village. The rest of the diminished band had no special agenda of their own, their graduation being between a few months to a year ahead. In any case they had only come to celebrate with him, so they formally, solemnly laid hand over hand and swore to join in bringing the dream of the Gumchi Kid to reality—*One for four and four for one, ever the Gong o' Four forever!* (Repeat four times, slap thighs four times, bump bottoms four times, drain the tankard in four gulps, and clink upended tankards four times. Repeat till only one contestant left standing.) The entire ritual could have emerged only from the sadistic mind of Duyole, though he took pains to admit that it was only an adaptation of a far more ancient drinking ritual from roistering Vikings in the ninth century. No matter, it was then flushing down student brains at their union bars, dedicated to a mysterious Cardinal Puff—*I drink to the health of Cardinal Puff for the first time tonight, etc., etc.* Duyole had traveled down from Salzburg to a warmer Bristol. He mulled over Kighare's dream for less than the disposal time of one pint of beer, promptly offered to design and build the clinic in a place he had never even visited, only heard of—and only through its solemn-minded overseas ambassador, Kighare. Once he had established his engineering practice in Lagos and had it running, Gumchi, he promised, would taste the weight of his dedicated genius. All ended up with a commitment to visit Gumchi within the first year of their return to the homeland.

The other two remnant members, recently elusive, chipped in, adopting portions of the scheme as suited skills or temperament. Badetona, suave corporate finance trainee, would generate the funds, extracting loans from stingy banks. Farodion—Menka again shook his head, mystified. What on earth had happened to our fourth member? Duyole might have been the hyper-efficient organizing mind; Faro was the live wire, heart and soul of the group. Talking of dreams, now there was a dreamer! Tended towards speaking in riddles, nonetheless dreamt big. His ventriloquist turns, acutely rendered, made him the performing star of gatherings, indeed once earned him a cameo voice role in a Disney cartoon. Mention popularity with the fair sex: the common wisdom was, stick with Faro and at the worst you would get to console his rejects. Strange, he had dropped out of sight completely! Simply vanished. A smooth talker, he dreamt of launching a film industry long before the thing called Nollywood. That man of many talents undertook to equip the Gumchi clinic with state-of-the-art electronic marvels, digitalized to the last disposable injection needle, guaranteed to bring Gumchi ancestors, in whose names he took his participant oath, back to life with one virtual jab. *Space-age health delivery? Watch this space!* Yes, that was Farodion—back in Sierra

Leone perhaps? He did claim his mother was a Saro, a descendant of the Yoruba slaves who were replanted in the soil of Sierra Leone after rescue on the high seas by patrolling British antislave ships. No matter, who ever succeeded in checking any of Farodion's multiple claims? They changed all the time, and sometimes in the most contradictory manner—which biography did he occupy at that moment? Perhaps the Sierra Leone internecine inferno had consumed him?

Hopefully, nothing worse than dispersed, like the others of course, just like their vision of youth. Careers, marriages, families, a civil war, military coups, religions—all took their toll. No one actually said, *Blow the dream,* no. It simply faded, receded into the mists of idealism. Abuja, Menka thought, with pointless resentment, played the largest role in the sabotage—too bad Gumchi was saddled with a neighbor that eventually became the choice for a "nation-unifying capital," the choice of a military dictatorship. To start with, who would now go seeking diagnosis and treatment in Gumchi when the nation's capital had moved close by from Lagos, just a stone's throw from the village? Even that loyal scion of the rockery settlement had to admit the problem. He bit his lips in disappointment, swallowed his pride of birthplace. There was no need for words—it was all understood—the Gong was released from its pledge. Life proceeded normally, staidly, profession- and opportunity-driven. If fulfillment and/or commitment required extra stressing, Boko Haram was gestating round the corner, readying to test Menka's skills and resilience in the theatre of emergency operations—pun definitely approved, he vigorously nodded.

But now—and for Menka it was truly the final straw—a different kind of awakening, a different turn in the rites of passage: the unexpected call by the unusual business consortium and its proposition. It was already happening. It had become routine under him, right under his professional punctiliousness. It all contributed towards the startling outburst by the Gumchi outsider in gross violation of the norms of propriety of a British former colony-within-a-colony, the ecumenical city of Jos. By then the stubborn Gumchi streak had melted into, then become inextricable from the surgeon's ingrained discipline—everything thereafter went into a spin. That vortex threatened to swallow him; it was something he sensed. His medical instincts prescribed a breathing spell . . .

At which point both body and brain had taken enough. Dr. Kighare Menka finally fell deeply asleep.

EARLY THE FOLLOWING MORNING, it was not his phone alarm, set for five-thirty, that woke him, but a pre-emptive call, about twenty minutes before the alarm was due. The caller Duyole Pitan-Payne, and with no trace of any Gong o' Four banter.

"Did I wake you?"

"Duyole?"

"Yes, it's me. Turn on your television."

"What's going on? What's the matter?"

"Just turn it on. Get the news."

"What channel? What's happening?"

"Any channel. Your club is on fire. The Hilltop Mansion."

"What! Where are you?"

"Still in Abuja. I was up early to catch the first flight back to Lagos. I switch on the TV for news and what do I see? The old club engulfed—the entire hill seems to be on fire."

"The hill? What hill?" Still trying to shake off inadequate sleep.

"The Hilltop Mansion, Club, whatever you call it. Where your club is—or was, from what I'm seeing." Duyole could hear Menka scrambling awake, perhaps trying to locate the remote control. "I imagine this will affect your plans, no?"

Menka's voice was now tinged with anxiety. "But that's where I live. I'm here . . . where's that damned control?"

"You live on the same hill? Where the clubhouse is?"

"That's what I said. My apartment overlooks—"

Banging suddenly erupted outside the bedroom door. Menka raised his voice. "Just a minute . . . Hey, Duyole, there are people at the door. Are you still there?"

"Yes, I'm right here. What's that noise?"

Towards the door, Menka bellowed, "Who is it? Just hold on, will you?"

Duyole's voice became anxious. "Maybe you should answer the door, Menka. This early morning—were you expecting anyone? It may have to do with the fire."

The banging intensified but was now joined by multiple raised voices in full-throated panic register: "Doctor! Doctor! Are you awake? We're evacuating. Everyone, out!"

"Menka, what's going on there?"

"Coming, coming . . . Hold on a moment, Duyole."

Duyole's voice brooked no dissent as he shouted, "Go and answer that door, Kighare. Call me later, but answer the door. Now! Right now!" And he switched off his phone.

IMMEDIATELY OUTSIDE, on the segregated lawns, were fearful batches of humanity, coverlets wrapped around them against the cool mountain air that was turning quite warm with wind blasts coming up from fires that seemed to strain at the leash from a yet safe distance. A short perimeter beyond the flames were also rudely aroused forms, but mostly in silhouette, framing the hillsides. Menka moved instinctively to his customary lookout position, from where he would sometimes confess, I feel lord of all I survey. This time, however, he would confess later to irrational moments when he felt that the fire actually took the shape of straining bloodhounds already primed with the scent of the very clothes he had hurriedly put on, so that they seemed to be headed straight for his bungalow, and specifically for his person. As a spectacle, the fire lacked nothing. It appeared to have a mind of its own but a mind of focused malice, with a quality of elemental force, indulging itself in serial morphing, just to confuse the watchers about its real intention. It certainly held the gazes of the hillside residents, dislodged from their homes, not to mention those in the plains below who had been aroused by the unusual crackles that carried far, as well as human agitations at that time of the night. Sometimes the flames appeared to race at a crouch, bent double by the very firestorm they raised along the tunnels formed by the ranges, as if they planned to encircle the buildings and trap the watchers, then consume them in one concerted, omnivorous sweep, only to change tactics, spring upright to full height, then lick the granite bowls clean towards the rims. Abruptly the outbreaks changed formation, swirled like colourful, performing masquerades, and at a signal bore down the mountain slopes at a speed designed to mesmerize, intimidate, then overwhelm their captive audience gathered below. The fire seemed humanized, orchestrated, malevolent. What appeared to be a series of cavalry charges down those slopes turned the flames into a phalanx of pennants that melted into one another, separated and regrouped, then whirled around at astonishing speeds down different inclines, disappeared into deep gullies only to levitate virtually under the noses of the hastily improvised firefighters and the two dilapidated trucks that had nonetheless set up a heroic line of resistance to the onslaught. Unfortunately, they lacked water. Again and again the resistance fell back. And then this demonic horde paused, as if surveying the rout, smacked its lips in satisfaction, then turned its back disdainfully and virtually strolled off, dwindled away in innocuous flickers, only to break out at a different compass point in a calculated feint, forcing the two-piece fleet of trucks to change their defensive line and select yet another line of resistance. Never did symbolism aspire so heroically to potency since, lacking water, it remained a mystery what difference their "tactical" change of position was designed to effect.

At one stage Menka thought he could count three separate fires on the leash, working independently, ravenously exploratory. Then, even as he tried to recall if anyone he knew lived in those locations, they moved on in opposing directions, consuming what appeared to be the line of domestic staff quarters, which also contained sales shacks and a poultry farm. He saw the cages encircled and dissolve. The units then converged, compared notes, separated once again, and resumed probing lunges, belching hot wind as they advanced. It was the turn of the white-collar homes. For that sector they appeared to have adopted a pincer movement straight out of military textbooks. Skeletal frames in the car park already signaled the scale of devastation, and he could almost follow the fiery traceries along the ivy that had once covered the mansion frontage, including the porch to the massive doors. Just beyond, as if to confirm the execution of a well-laid strategy, the cavalry of flames that had lain camouflaged at the deepest inlets of the valley, the same cavalry line that had retired out of sight along the further valley trough, sprung its ambush, pennants ablaze. With a triumphant roar it levitated and charged up the lower peaks, gathering strength, then swept towards the main water tank, where a uniformed figure struggled with a rusted faucet that appeared to have been sabotaged ahead of the invading force. Menka looked at those flames and it was as if it were a personal thing, a unilateral declaration of hostilities over a piece of real estate that he had not been aware was under dispute. After all, he had never claimed ownership. It was all government property, and his monthly rent was automatically deducted from his pay.

He watched the futile line of residents passing buckets of water from hand to hand, turned back to his bungalow, and began desultorily to pack his possessions.

13.

Surgical Transplant

The early-morning call did not resume until midmorning, as in between, Pitan-Payne was airborne. More calmly, against the remote backdrop of a charnel house that was once known as Hilltop Mansion, Dr. Menka, the night's reminiscences totally forgotten while the club exchanges of the previous night resounded with total clarity, the house now stood charnel for a lot more. Such as perhaps an entire era. The panic and evacuation exchanges of the early hours were also forgotten. Roles reversed, the engineer accurately diagnosed the doctor's dilemma. He moved to prescribe for it in the only way he knew how. It was no longer sufficient to bring him into mere reconciliation with a move from Jos as inevitable. The man from Gumchi needed to be cajoled into a state of mind that saw that the turn of events, even while signaling an end, also aligned with the dream they had all shared from youth. He had to be persuaded that the move was in fact a base for fulfilling pledges, bringing closer the core vision that had driven them over decades.

Impatience racked him throughout the flight to Lagos, which of course seemed endless. No sooner landed than he dashed into the VIP lounge, tucked himself into a corner, and dialed. Menka's report was straightforward: "It's all gone, Duyo. The Hilltop Mansion is gone."

"But are you all right? Your bungalow?"

"No, we were never in serious danger. A bit of a threat, yes, but not much. The mansion was the real target, and that was thoroughly consumed."

Silence followed. "Any explanation? Suspicions?"

"Nothing yet. But it was clearly a case of arson."

Another silence followed. "No reason to change your plans, is there?"

"Not in the least. I need that break more than ever."

"I'm thinking beyond a brief break, Kighare. On the flight, I couldn't help thinking—maybe it's time you made it permanent."

Again silence.

"Are you giving it some thought?"

"Everything has moved rather fast. Haven't had time to bring you up to date, but much shit has been hitting the fan of late. I don't know how soon we'll all get spattered."

"Then move, Gumchi. Just move. Do a transplant."

"A what?"

"A transplant. You're a surgeon. You do it all the time."

Menka was thrown. Transplants? It sounded as if Duyole had been at the Hilltop Mansion when the recent waves of body adaptation had come up for that impromptu, bitter airing. For one fleeting moment he almost wondered if Duyole was the vanishing figure in the alcove, listening to the exchanges. The absurdity of it made him fear that the events of the past twelve hours had unhinged his mind. Almost fearfully, he probed, "What are you hinting at?"

"You. Or rather, Gumchi. It's fate. Do you believe in fate? Bring Gumchi to Lagos. Do a transplant. That's what I'm talking about."

Menka's sigh was leaden. "No, no! Not Lagos."

"Where then? Tell me, where? Where next?"

"I hadn't given it a thought. Still trying to absorb what has been going on around here. Around me."

"Well, start thinking."

"You know me, village boy. Your Lagos . . ."

"No, not quite Lagos. This is the village next to it, my Badagry."

"What's the difference?"

"Lots. Listen, kid, you're still mentally locked in your primitive Gumchi stiff-neck prejudice. All right, suggest another location. You need a fresh start. Clean break. You've pieced together enough Boko Haram victims to earn you full retirement. And now this!"

"Don't think it hasn't often crossed my mind!"

"Good. So, do the transplant. Take yourself out of there and reattach elsewhere. I'm an engineer. I'm trained to adapt. It's the idea that counts. Suited to time and place. There's a growing population of amputees, mangled sleepwalking ghosts. Children. Hundreds going into thousands. With no prospects but to join the hordes of *almajiri,* those wretches who later become easy conversion fodder for Boko Haram. And now ISWAP. So we set up a model rehabilitation centre—the latest in prosthetics. Give them a new life. A different form of counseling. New direction. It's along the same plans you've long nurtured for Gumchi."

"Gumchi has no amputees. For a start, we don't wage war. Just have the nature-inflicted diseases. Boko Haram was not even born when we were in college."

Duyole caught himself just in time from reminding him of Boko Haram's predecessor, the Maitatsine—they had made Menka an orphan. He would never have forgiven himself for raking up that wound, one that continued to suppurate, Duyole knew very well, in his innermost organs. Nearly swallowing his tongue, he quickly changed tack.

"Stop trying to be literal. The idea, Gumcheeky, the idea! We all adopted it. Hand over hand, remember?"

"Yes, *four for one* and all that student crap. We are all grown, Engineer Pitan. Times have changed."

"Precisely! And you are getting old. Don't tell me at your age you'll be asking for transfer to another government hospital."

The response was prompt and definitive. "No way!"

"Good. That's settled. Unless, of course, you're going to join the queue for contracts. Mind you, I admit, maybe with your national honours, you won't have to queue. You just show up."

"Quite right. I can hawk the medal and live on the proceeds."

"It's only gold-plated, don't kid yourself. It's tin inside."

"And I bet it's other people's tin, not even from our own Plateau mines."

"The gold is elsewhere—actually not far from you. They're killing one another for it, pretending the killing is about something else. Religon, as always the scapegoat. Well, it's part of it, don't get me wrong, but there is gold, real gold, up there. Zamfara, for instance. And the whole fundamentalist shit began there. All that Islamic reform crap. It's the gold rush. I've seen sneak photos."

"There is gold mined everywhere—are we changing the subject?"

"Not me. So that's settled then. But of course I know you do have other options. There is this small settlement along the Benue plagued by river blindness. President Carter once visited. He might find you a job."

"Stop being caustic. What do I know of ophthalmology?"

"Good. So, when in doubt, home ground. Badagry, why not? A brand-new centre. Specialization changed. It's the idea that counts—the idea, Gumchi, the idea! And the idea isn't all yours, remember that. It belongs to the full house—all four still-subscribing members."

"Four? I thought we were down to three. When did you last hear of that man of all seasons?"

Duyole chuckled. "Farodion? He'll show up. I don't know why, but I just sense that he's gainfully active somewhere around, preparing to spring a surprise and show up the rest of the quartet. People like him don't just vanish."

"Ever the optimist."

"Why not? But always right, no? Well, nearly."

A huge sigh from Menka, one that the engineer could feel halfway across the country. "All that is past history, Duyole. Days of high optimism. We're done with that. Scattered all over the country—and perhaps overseas. End of Big Dreams."

"No way. We simply never got round to Gumchi. And no fault of any of us. It was not the country we left to which we returned. Abuja did not exist as Abuja, yet it's also played a role. Mostly counter to the Gumchi dream. Why should anyone go to Gumchi when Abuja is just round the corner? Did we think of that? Capital was Lagos at the time, now Abuja is all in all. They've even named the main specialist hospital after the most brutal and thieving head of state the nation has ever known. And after all the nation endured before getting rid of him. I still find it difficult to believe."

"Maybe that's the attraction. Our beloved compatriots have exotic tastes."

"And the major highway into Abuja itself, the nation's modern capital? Also named Sani Abacha Avenue?"

"That's the star attraction."

"You're just in your contrary mood. Pure Gumchi rock stubbornness. Anyway, bugger all that distraction. I was pointing out that the original blueprint never stood a chance. Misplaced. Sentimental location. I'm an engineer, but was not at the time. Now I am one, and I tell you—wrong location. So keep the blueprint, change location. Simple."

There was silence.

"Hey, are you still with me? Can you hear all I'm saying?"

Wearily, Menka acknowledged his listening existence.

"We can't fight reality. And right now you are jobless, right?"

"Who's denying it?"

"So you settle for Lagos. I'll make you sing for your supper, don't worry. I'm not just an engineer; I've become a businessman. I've developed the business killer instinct. I'll raise the funds, you'll do the hard work. Why fool around? You know I've made it—yes, that ugly expression, but accurate. I *have* made it. With solid hard work. Without compromising. My money, and I can invest it as I wish. Timing couldn't be better. Spot the silver lining? In any case, it will pay for itself—you'll see. I have it all worked out. Been working on it since your first call. Had nothing else to do while waiting for Godot! Oh, you know, that just hit me—what a coincidence. Tell you about it later. The man eats kola from Gumchi. And did he keep me waiting hours! Never mind, back to business. We'll even make a profit, which was not originally on the idyllic card. Everything then was pro bono. Amazing how generously youth volunteers what it hasn't got, eh? Well, stuff that. As for Gumchi herself, we'll do something for the old crabby lady—in proportion, of course, in proportion! A mud-and-wattle clinic in your bush village, tucked somewhere within your skyscraper floors, with hook-on ladders. Nothing fancy. Your people won't know the difference. So what say you? What better time than now?"

Menka was only half listening. He was all too familiar with Duyole's instinctive thoroughness—everything would have been worked out in that churning mind, in detail. That was what powered his business, drove it to its startling success. He heard Duyole's voice rising above his thoughts.

"You've nothing ethical against cosmetic surgery, I hope? God knows what primitive taboos you people still follow in that place. There are many of these wrinkled old lechers wanting a facelift—they don't ever want to age, man or woman. That's where we'll make our money. Listen, Badagry adjoins Lagos—I know you hate that word, but it does. That means an overflow from the Lagos clientele. Thank goodness for the internet—we'll work closely over the net, designs and everything. While the structure is going up, with you telling me where to insert this room and that facility and whatever else, you'll be consulting with any teaching hospital of your choice. Or private clinics. Even without your new status, you can pick and choose. I mean, how many surgeons do we have left? All gone to Dubai. The University Hospital is nicely situated between Badagry and Lagos—you can do the rounds among them, always assuming you are not kidnapped en route, of course," Duyole's voice ended cheerfully.

Or indeed within the hospital premises, Menka added silently, while making routine ward rounds, or even in the operating theatre itself. That last stage of refinement had yet to be recorded, but others had. His profession was fast replacing clerics as an endangered species, prized targets in the new epidemic of myth-busting—*no more sanctuary, the altar next time!* Ah well, sooner or later everything becomes once upon a time. Plateau or Lagos, Maiduguri or Yenagoa, who was he to place a wager on which was less or more vulnerable? The nation greedily partook of this communion of the wafers of development. No one could swear anymore where sanity lay. Or safety. Or sacrosanctity.

"That reminds me, G-Kid, I know these things don't count with you, but you know, we still have to wash that award of yours. There isn't much to celebrate these days, so why not a genuine deserving and— Shut up! No false modesty or I'll arrange your kidnap myself. How many Pre-eminence Awards are shelled out every year? No, tell me. One. Just one. When last did anyone from your—what did you claim was the name of your village?—snag one? So all right, that's by the way. A quiet celebration, anyway. As for the centre, I've ear-marked a site by the lagoon, beautifully situated. It was meant for one of our branch workshops, but we expanded in a different direction. Overgrown so repeatedly that the government threatened to revoke my certificate of occupancy—we'll go into all that when you arrive. Business with reunion, just the family. And—oh yes—you remember Damien?"

"You must be getting senile. How could I forget?"

"Well, just wanted to be sure, since it's such a while since you helped resolve that small issue. He finally showed up. Returned to the family bosom, wife and two children. See? Haven't really celebrated the return of the prodigal son, so that's another cause for slaughter-ing the fatted calf. Celebration goes with celebrity, and that's what you've become—big celebrity! Don't be shy. Pop complains we'll have to make double appointments to approach you now."

"All right, all right. I'm thinking."

Duyole sensed victory, moved to consolidate. "You need a break anyway. As your unsung and unpaid psychiatrist, I prescribe a break. Don't overdo things. You don't have to decide right away, just take that break. What does the Good Book say? Physician, heal thyself—right?"

Before the fire, Duyole would not have expended one moment's breath trying to entice him south, not for the sustained period his scheme demanded. Brief consulting clinics, yes, while overseeing construction, but to actually take up residence there? The south for Menka meant Lagos. Lagos meant Purgatory. Badagry was simply a euphemism for Lagos, a contiguous neighbour for the latter's over-flow of manpower, and a relief valve for a highly charged existence. The native son of Gumchi had been mentally ready for the one-year National Youth Service anywhere, even Lagos. It was a duty tour across the board for which he was fully prepared, even if Lagos proved to be his luck of the draw. That mandatory stint over, however, the five-year scholarship service bond was more flexible. There one had a choice, and he made sure he exercised it—no Lagos. Anywhere but! No amount of inducement could make him serve out that sentence in Lagos, not even closeness to his lifelong friend Pitan-Payne. Yet those were indeed halcyon days when "too frenzied" was the most disparaging charge he could raise against the metropolis. He settled for Jos, the closest on offer to his own craggy Gumchi hills, whose people kept so much to themselves that they were known as the invisible tribe of the nation, internally discovered, then allocated arbitrary population figures in each self-canceling census.

Pitan-Payne saved the *pièce de résistance* but *sans résistance* to the last. He had measured it all carefully. He was used to assessing the Gumchi Kid's temperamental tie to his village, one that could work in the contrary direction to Duyole's incessant schemes. He had been feeling his ground, endeavoring to assess what actually *happened* to the mind of Menka, only knowing what happened in Jos. That last by itself was sufficient for him to exert every measure to get him out of that heated zone without delay. Then there was his newly acquired profile—that surely could open the door to him outside the country. Was it not a similar process that sent him, Pitan-Payne, hurtling in the unsought direction of the United Nations? They had this uncanny pattern of leapfrogging or leveling up with each other. He let a few seconds pass in silence and then he threw in the prize bait—after all, even symbolic ties sometimes prove more effective than actual.

"By the way, Bisoye and I discussed a name for the rehabilitation centre." They had not, there was hardly time since the events of the previous day, but this was no time for fidelity to merely supporting facts. "What do you think of Gumchi Rehabilitation Institute? GRI to challenge GRA. Or Centre—no GRI much closer and more annoy-ing than GRC. But whatever. It's your call. You decide. It was your idea in the first place—more obsession. Those ancient times known as salad days. You know something? There are lessons to be learnt from that barren rockery of yours. Like survival. Extracting a living virtu-ally from nothing, etc., etc. So there's already a point of attraction. It would even make people curious to know, why Gumchi? *What's in there? Let's go find out. Was it what brought the Greek fellow to Badagry? Where did that logo come from?* See what I mean? Where did Gumchi come from? And they'll go look. Nothing wrong with a little tourism on the side. We could work on that, you know. If only Farodion were around . . . that would be meat and drink to his yen for promotion."

"You still count on him showing up."

"We'll find him. I feel it in my bones. Back together, eh? That will be some feast. All Bisoye's idea, so you can't turn her down. That's your chance to make up for the first time. What do you say?"

Menka mulled over his situation. Plans change. A crazy outburst can bring down an edifice or terminate a lifelong dream—it all depended on timing and context. What happened that day was sufficient on its own as the prelude to a seismic life change. Duyole, as always, had been instantly there for him. The idea of Gumchi in Badagry-Lagos did not seem much of a contradiction. Everything still appeared to favour his old battle cry, repressed but never abandoned—*Gumchi First!*

Yes, Gumchi first, but first Gumchi's unfinished business. Settle down quickly, then revisit Boriga, only this time better prepared. How? As yet Dr. Menka had no idea, only that it would involve careful, discreet, and perhaps even dangerous research. Pitan was on his way out—foolish to expect the United Nations to grant him a leave of absence before he even took up his duties. That left just the prince, the one they called Scoffer. Definitely, first stop in Lagos would be a call on Badetona. He moved in business circles, had connections of whose existence even the gregarious Pitan-Payne knew nothing. It seemed strange, but Bade had his ears closer to the ground than all the others—except perhaps Farodion.

And just then Kighare Menka paused. Strange, his mind returned to that post-convocation night which, thanks to Farodion's semantic objections, began as a pledge but ended in a wager. Admittedly the drinks flowed freely and the night grew increasingly contumacious. There is a difference, Farodion continued to insist, between *Gumchi First* and *First, Gumchi*. The former spelt a closed project, pure ego, while the latter indicated a mere starting point, with intimations of many things, and others, to follow. A hanging promise, he called it. *First, Gumchi* kept the project infinite, permanently exploring. It included both the known and the unknown, elastic. *First, Gumchi,* then . . . See?

No, Menka did not see. More factually, refused to see. Or hear. Theatrically plugged his ears with his fingers and shook his head. Even the U.S recognized the justice of affirmative action, he argued. Gumchi was the home of underprivileged natives, the black indigenes in the midst of affluent white settlers pretending to be black, calling themselves Badetona, Farodion, and one half-and-half known as Pitan-Payne—perfect giveaway expatriate camouflage. And so, *Gumchi First*. Over and above any other condition. A simple case of reparations. Agreed?

It was all a familiar, inebriated raillery, but Badetona was the one who noticed, and later remarked on, something he found troubling. There was not the slightest wisp of banter on Farodion's face when he retorted, "In that case, let's all begin on the same playing level. Then we'll see who eventually gets to brand the land."

It struck the prince, even in his state of impaired absorption, as being unusually heavy!

14.

Badetona

It took a long spell of patient silence, perhaps two hours of Dr. Menka's presence in the swish home of the failed financier of the Gong of Four, but finally something pierced through to Badetona's refuge, that hitherto impenetrable distance that he had placed between himself and the world. He glanced up suddenly, took a long look at his visitor, Menka, as if to make up for his days and weeks of withdrawal. He sat straight up, and his habitually slouched shoulders seemed to find support. They were the shoulders of an overweight seventy-five-year-old retiree, but he was only three years past sixty.

"The more you recall," he sighed, "the deeper this darkness that envelops you."

Kighare Menka gave no sign that he had heard, yet he tensed in every hopeful fibre of his body and waited for him to continue, but there was nothing more. Badetona had always been a man of few words anyway, more at home with figures and spreadsheets. A half hour later, his wife entered the room, picked up the emptied glasses and settled them on a tray, plus the untouched saucer of her home-made *chin-chin*, his favorite cookies. She made no attempt at pretending that she had just arrived—it had been agreed that she would remain in the anteroom, listening, the door left just slightly ajar. It had been an agonizing thirty minutes since he had spoken, but she held herself in check. She had left them together, hopeful that the company of his old comrade, albeit some five years younger, would stir something in his mind. She took her time picking up, arranging, and rearranging the glasses, wiping off nonexistent smudges on the glass top of the designer coffee table, but nothing more was forthcoming.

She took the tray away, resumed her place at the listening post, but finally reentered the living room. Badetona had sunk back into that dark hole of the mind from which he had briefly emerged. There would be nothing more, it seemed—at least, not that day. They spoke freely, as if the husband were not present. Over the past few months she had learnt that it did not matter what went on around him.

"And he has remained like this throughout? Ever since his release?" Menka asked.

She nodded. "Ask Duyole. He'll confirm everything."

"Did he say anything about what they did to him?"

"Nothing. Not a word. As you know, he was with them close to eight months."

"Any hint of . . . torture? I mean, how they treated him?"

"There is no mark on him. No sign of ill-treatment. If only there was . . . at least . . ."

"Yes, I know." Menka sighed. "Sometimes one actually wishes for . . . anything—you know, anything to which one can point . . . physical. Even a small bruise or whatever."

"What we do know is that they kept him underground. Everyone knows the place. They call it the Strong Room." She stopped suddenly, placed her finger across her lips. As Menka made to turn to see what had caused the change in her, she signaled to him to keep still.

Badetona had indeed stirred suddenly. He rose fully to his feet, looking vaguely around, perhaps for a mind that had been spirited away, one that he now convinced himself was in that room.

Wife and friend watched him. Badetona paced out a measure of the room, as if sectioning it to conform to a dimension that only he appeared to see. Over and over again his eyes slowly traversed the walls, and in short, brief spurts like a wall gecko's. The eyes climbed up slowly, descended, then scurried around and came to a stop, appeared to explore a crevice, a stain, only to dash to yet another walled-in secret, then resume in a sudden spurt of speed. A sigh emerged from him. Then, after a seeming struggle, his eyes prised themselves away from the walls. He turned, almost as if he had become aware that he was being observed, but then smiled, as if to assure his watchers that he did not really mind.

"Floor to ceiling," he said. "Floor to ceiling and all stacked. Day after day. After a while I couldn't count any more. I told them so."

The wife threw an anxious look at Menka. He understood the question and nodded eagerly. The woman girded herself and urged, "Yes, dear?"

Tears began to well in his eyes, then streaked down his face. As if in empathy, the words also came out in a torrent, but gently. "We counted them," he murmured, and his voice assumed a level, explanatory tone. "No, I counted them while they watched. They worked—that is, they watched—in shifts. Sometimes they brought their own drinks—hot coffee mostly, but sometimes soft drinks. Food, of course. Then they would point to my tray. At the start I refused to eat. I said I would count first, then eat after I had finished. They seemed to find that amusing. But that was at the beginning, before I knew what they had planned. Every day they would ask me what I wanted for lunch. Or dinner. They were so polite. Then, when I refused, they pleaded with me, saying they couldn't start eating until I had had my meal. I told them to go ahead and have theirs, that I would follow at my own pace. They complained that I was not being fair to them. They were only carrying out orders and they were just as much prisoners as I was. So I resumed eating."

Bade's voice took on a sense of wonder. "Over and over again. They would say to me, 'Are you sure you didn't mix up the currencies? Your figures differ from the last. Perhaps you should give it another try.' I looked around and asked, 'Which pile?' They merely shrugged their shoulders. 'How do we know?' one of them would say. 'You are the one to tell us.'"

It was now close to three months since Badetona's release, almost a year since they had finally come for him. He was waiting when they arrived, dressed in his executive-office suit. When they knocked, he did not immediately utter a word. Not even to ask who they were. As soon as he opened the door that morning—"Just after our morning prayers," the wife revealed in a voice that almost accused God of being in the know—he *knew*. He emitted a huge sigh, and it sounded like one of relief. He heard the voice of his wife from the kitchen, where she was preparing breakfast. "Who is it, dear?" He continued as if he had heard nothing, opened the door wider, stood aside, and led them quietly into the house.

"Yes, come in, gentlemen," he virtually whispered, like a well-trained English butler, steeped in impeccable manners. He indulged himself only with a brief glance across the three figures that confronted him, did not wait for them to speak, not even to introduce themselves, state their business, or ask any questions. He merely sighed, turned, and led them without a further word along the corridor that terminated at the door of the main guest room. He gestured towards the closed door—"Some of it is here." He stood aside as they entered, opened one wardrobe after another. After that it all proceeded nearly wordlessly. From the guest room he led then to the marble-tiled mezzanine, which was formerly the children's playroom, but of course they had all grown up and gone their different ways. Across his mind briefly flashed a vision of his own order of childhood—was it ever a place of innocence? he wondered. No matter, this room of his scattered, successful children was now filled with innocent-looking boxes. The school texts and exercise books had all been thrown out for more valuable contents—who used exercise books these days anyway? He recalled the first conversion of that room to yet another storage space. As each stack came in, needing more space, and he encroached on the deserted expanse, he felt his first twinge of regret that morning. It was brief, perhaps the only moment there appeared a flicker in his eyes; otherwise it was all calm acceptance. Even relief. It was all over, the years, even decades of deceit, of false appearances. Mostly he had no expression left. They were his guests, and he was showing them round the house.

The leader took out his walkie-talkie and spoke to someone. A few minutes later the evacuation team came up the stairs, smoothly efficient. He watched them stare at the improvised vaults, now thrown open, which appeared to contain all the currencies of the world, neatly stacked from floor to ceiling.

"You may count them," he said. "I think you'll find everything is correct. I kept records."

Bade did enjoy a reputation for that. He kept records. He excelled in record-keeping, all the way from his student days in Manchester. Others sought his help in designing spreadsheets for their clubs and activities. His student union made him its treasurer. Figures were meat and drink to him. As the evacuating team, dressed in overalls without pockets, began their task, he turned abruptly and left them alone to carry out their task, ignoring the request that he remain and witness their proceeding—and the counting.

It was that same walk that he now retraced from time to time, whenever something clicked in his mind, usually with his wife, only his wife, as audience. But uttering not a word. On that day of the initial visitation, he had indeed walked past her on the stair landing, on their way to the children's room, his feet dragging as if he were already transported to another country and another age, when felons had iron balls tied to their ankles. After calling out from the kitchen without receiving a response, she had come up to summon him for breakfast. So she was on the landing as her husband led them past to the first storage space. Maybe he saw her, maybe not, but he walked right past, not saying a word.

Was it all coming to an end at long last, the wife now allowed herself to hope, the eight months of absence, his incarceration, that had ended only to be replaced by another spell of absence, this time of the mind? Had the voice of an old friend triggered off something in his mind? Whatever had provoked the reenactment of that first walk that had ushered in the day of disaster appeared to have spent its force. Badetona simply relapsed into his former state. He sank back into his chair, his teary head held in his arms, elbows dug into the arms of the chair.

She spoke softly. "I was home when they came. It was—oh yes, two days after we had a class reunion dinner with Bisoye. He went out with Duyole—little did I know it was the last time I would see him as his old self. He woke up unusually early, I remember. Had his bath, dressed himself, and then sat, as if waiting for some guests. It was odd. I watched from the landing along the corridor. They actually walked past me, five of them. Two were in dark suits, another in a polo shirt. One was in a tracksuit. I recognized him immediately. I had seen him before, a number of times in fact, jogging past."

Trapped on that landing as they walked past her, Mrs. Badetona had indeed recognized a face, and she let out a gasp. It was only at that moment that she realized her husband and she had been under surveillance for weeks, even months, that the regular athlete was no jogger at all but an agent detailed to keep the house under surveillance until they were ready to make their move. The picture unfolded before her. Heaven alone knew how often that jogger—or even other innocent-seeming passersby—had watched the delivery unit arrive and hand over their packages. The supply came in all sizes, sometimes in cartons that had once held bottled water, beer, or fruit juices—only these contents were juicier. The watchers had probably taken thousands of photographs. Yes, even she must be there in their album, their rogues' gallery, although they never once invited her for questioning, not even after her husband's arrest. There was hardly any need—the evidence literally littered the house. Littered? Well, in a sense, but it was all neat, its meticulous rows left largely undisturbed except when they were pushed deeper into the cupboards and other recesses to make room for new arrivals. Generally they came when Badetona was home, obviously by arrangement, so he took care of the storage. But sometimes while he was at work there were also deliveries. Whenever that happened, she opened the door, gestured to the space behind the door or along the walls of the passage, especially for the larger boxes. When the husband returned—from office or audit tours—he took charge. Practiced and efficient charge. He carried the boxes to the improvised office on the mezzanine and entered the delivery in his spreadsheet, using a specially devised system. It was a system that served both physical deliveries and virtual transfers under myriad businesses and accounts that were scattered all over the globe. They did not derive from a single source. The physical deposits were, however, entirely his, and the earnings had spread over two decades, beginning with his being spotted as a natural, a near-genius in the art of creative accounting. The expression *money laundering* was considered an abomination in the vocabulary of the seasoned civil servant and his elect business circle.

Bade was frugal, discreet, unobtrusive. Anything but flashy or ostentatious. He hardly ever threw parties. When he did, he did not close up the streets and set up marquees to accommodate the city throng and advertise his splashing power. All activities stayed within the walls of the compound. These were qualities that marked him out for advancement and recruitment. His most extravagant indulgence was the annual cruise for the family. Even those adjustments to the home interior to make up for usurpation by boxes that accumulated steadily were modest. Impeccable taste but restrained in style. He deplored his colleagues who flaunted their wealth. He did not vacation in Dubai or Paris but stuck to one of the Queen liners that shifted itineraries between the South American mainland and the Caribbean, he and his wife always keeping to themselves, even on the boat. Once they flew to Adelaide in the antipodes, then took a cruise around the South Pacific islands. When asked by curious neighbours about their absence, they would answer, "We needed a break, so we went to visit our people in the village."

There was a question Menka knew he had to ask. "All these years, you said nothing to him?"

"At the beginning, yes, I did. The deliveries were irregular. Sometimes for months nothing came. Then there might be a flurry. One thing was consistent—the packages grew bigger and bigger. At first I protested—I can't pretend that I didn't know. Of course I did, and I knew it meant trouble. He said he had no choice. If he didn't take it, he said, they would grow suspicious of him and then . . . even get rid of him in some way. Others had died sudden deaths—always in mysterious circumstances, unsolved till today. Perhaps forever. Improbable motor accidents. In the end, the money simply grew and grew, spilled into other rooms. It began with his study, then the wardrobes, then any spare cupboards—he even built new ones—then the bedroom itself. At that point I moved out into one of the smaller guest rooms. I couldn't live with the sight of that thing growing and growing and growing. Then he began to use spaces downstairs. I tried to persuade him to take them to his village, but he wouldn't budge. Said the least he owed his ancestors was not to contaminate the family home."

"And since he returned from their, er, place, he's never moved beyond what I've seen?"

"You are the first to share that walk, you know, that second part. Somehow, you being here, I did hope he would go beyond . . . he's never gone past what you just heard. If only he would!" Her mood changed with an abruptness that frightened her visitor; her face contorted with a rage that he had never witnessed in the woman he had known and interacted with as the wife of a friend. Her chest heaving as if she would have a fit, she screamed, "What is it? What do they do to them in there? What goes on in that devil's hole they call the Strong Room?"

Menka instinctively shrank back, then recovering immediately, took a stride towards her, placed his hands on her shoulders, and shook her gently. Badetona appeared to have heard the scream, since he turned towards them, looked somewhat baffled, then continued to stare, as one who was seeing them for the first time.

"It's me, Scoffer. Kighare Menka. Gong of Four-o. Four for one . . ."

He had tried that several times already. It made no difference. Badetona simply stared. Menka returned to the wife.

"What they do to them? On the surface of it, nothing bad. I know some people who have been through it. It's deliberate. Psychological torture. They treat them well, good food, even drinks. Outside of that, a set time for stretching their legs for some minutes, and that's it. No books, no reading. The rest of the time they impose on them that sole occupation—count the money. Over and over again. That's all they do. Make them count the money, all the various currencies—euro, dollar, yen, ruble, naira, whatever it was they found in the home, wherever, even from the soakaway pits. They transfer it all to the Strong Room, and that is where the ordeal begins. They make them count and record the cash. Over and over again. They pretend there had been an error, if not in the accounting, then in the currency numbers. Only the Devil could have dreamt up such torture. If it was not Sir Goddie himself, then it was his clone from hell."

For a while longer they watched Badetona, but he had returned to full immobility. Menka knew that nothing else would come from his visit. He stood up and prepared to take his leave. There was nothing left to say.

"I am glad you came." Her voice turned bitter. "It's over three months since his release, but there hasn't been anyone else. Apart from Duyole, of course. All the ones he called friends, those he helped and advanced in every way, made them rich, some of them worth nothing to begin with, now multimillionaires. Do they remember him? Do they care? No, they've all abandoned him. They treated this place like their clubhouse—you know we didn't enjoy going out much, so they came here most of the time, to socialize. They ate here, drank here, cracked stupid jokes and made themselves at home. None of them has stepped across that doorstep since his release—not one of them! Except the psychiatrist. And you should see his charges!"

"What did he have to say?"

"Patience. Just give him time, he'll come round. What else did he think I've being doing? Stupid advice for the fortune he's been charging! I told him not to bother himself anymore."

Menka winced, feeling himself a hypocrite. His visit had not been completely altruistic, though he had kept his purpose to himself. "I'll be back," he promised. "Now that I've relocated to Lagos, I shall look in from time to time."

Her "thank you" emerged from the depths of the heart, which only made Menka squirm even more guiltily. Her eagerness made him wish he had never knocked on that door. Unwittingly, she drove the needle even deeper. He wondered why Duyole had not remotely hinted about what to expect.

"I know that seeing people, more people with past links to him—it doesn't matter how slight—will help. Eventually it will bring him out. Something from his past, perhaps. Sooner or later someone will say something that will bring him out of this darkness. I just know it. Even the one time that Papa Davina visited, I detected a change. Slight, but it was there. Some kind of response showed in his eyes. I don't fully trust the man, but—"

Menka stopped. "Who did you say?"

"Papa Davina. I'm sure you know of him. Everyone does."

Menka nodded. "Yes, of course. So they were acquainted?"

She hesitated. "I . . . don't really know," she admitted. "But when this trouble started, everyone, you know, advice from everyone—relations, his office colleagues, people I had never heard of before then, they all descended on us offering advice. That was when news of his arrest began to spread, then they started to keep their distance. But that was the one name on everyone's lips. For prayer intercession—

you know. So when he was in the custody of those people, I moved close to the ministry. I was desperate."

Menka nodded thoughtfully. "He does have a reputation, I know. He has a branch in Jos."

"Everyone advised I should join, so I did. I kept up tithes, for both of us. I took part in all-night vigils. Then of course when he was released, in this . . . as you see him now, this condition, I redoubled my attendance. The prophet has quite a reputation. Who knows, but for him, maybe the whole story would be even worse. At least Bade was never brought to trial. He would not have survived the public finger-pointing. I sought help everywhere, but . . . well, it was on Papa D. that I eventually landed."

"Bade went to his, er, whatever it is—what's it called now?"

"Prophesite. The holy site of prophecy."

"Ah yes, prophesite. What I'm trying to say is, in this condition? I mean, he's ventured out like this?"

She hesitated, then began to speak in halting spurts, as if she were busy retrieving a report from someone else, not her own predicament. Menka felt uneasy. "Once. Only once. And that was before this . . . this ordeal. When we became certain they would come for him. He went alone that one and only time. After that, I've tried to persuade him to accompany me, but . . . it was as if the name Davina meant nothing to him. He won't budge. You know how obstinate he can be! So I went on my own, on his behalf. Davina seemed to understand, and after that he came here himself. Just once. I understand that happens rarely. And he came in some kind of religious costume—he changes them all the time. It's as if he doesn't even want people to see his full face. There are rumours that he once had an accident and is disfigured. Some say a woman attacked him with a broken bottle and left scars. Even at the base venue, he keeps away from strong light. People go to Davina, he doesn't go to people, even if you're dying. He just sends his prescriptions—things to do or avoid. Holy oil for self-anointing, and prayer scrolls. He made an exception for Bade. Sometimes he phones to check if there has been any change in his condition."

She noticed that Menka seemed distracted. "Have you met him yourself? In Jos?"

"No." Menka shook his head. "It's just that his name came up, in fact has been coming up my way quite recently." He gestured towards Bade. "I am simply astonished that Bade actually agreed to visit. I hand it to you. You know what we used to call him in school?"

She smiled a little. "The Scoffer. I gave him that name myself. Yes, it did take some persuading."

"I can imagine. So now you are a full member of Father Davina's temple, or whatever?"

"Well, I suppose you could say that. I've attended his services quite a few times, but I don't really call myself a follower. But you know, when trouble really hits, one turns no matter where, anywhere, everywhere, for help. And Davina does have a reputation."

"So did Bade. Seeing him like this . . . it hurts. It really hurts. In school, his reputation was second to none. Brilliant. Even the staff lived in terror of him when it came to mathematics. No one could touch him."

"I know, I know."

"He was well ahead of any textbooks. And especially when it came to trigonometry. That was his favourite. He could reel off all the formulas straight from sleep. Bade? Gave the best of our teachers an inferiority complex, slaughtered challengers right and left. Did he ever tell you the other nickname he earned—his *nom de guerre,* if you like, battle name? We used to have these interschool mathematics contests."

She shook her head.

"You should have heard the shouts when the teams took their places on the stage to begin the competition. *Trigo-happy killer! Trigo-happy killer—go get them!* And did he revel in it! Need I tell you, he went ahead and mowed them down!"

There was a sudden, startled movement from Badetona. They both turned, and there was Bade rising, this time as if in a mildly speeded-up trance. Menka quickly put a finger across his lips. The wife nodded agreement, both hands superfluously cupped against her lips. They watched him move slowly but purposefully towards a stack of books on the coffee table. Badetona stood staring uncertainly for a few seconds, then bent down, as if to select one. His lips moved soundlessly, but both watchers could read exactly what they said, and it was, "Trigo-happy," his eyes squeezed together as if in a hurtful or querulous effort at recollection. So Jaiyesola jerked her head towards the door—should she leave? Menka's hesitation was of the briefest. He responded with a vigorous nod. The wife tiptoed out, shut the door. She resumed her listening post behind the door.

Behind the kitchen door left slightly ajar, positioned so as not to miss one utterance that would spell hope, Jaiyeola in her thoughts traversed the years as she waited with an intensity she had not been given cause to exercise since Bade's return, his mind far slipped into this vaporous state. On the one hand, the positive—it had led to his early release, the scared detective team not knowing what to do with him anymore. After all, he had more than "co-operated." The funds in his possession were mostly intact, and he was of no use to them even as a witness for the prosecution of others, the tough ones who held out, determined to win their acquittal through the technical wiles of their seasoned defence counsel and/or with secret channels to the judiciary. Even a change in government might result in a general amnesty, with or without restitution. It was all a question of holding out, brazening it out by showing up at public functions as if to assert a clear conscience. Even throwing increasingly lavish parties to mark the acquisition of yet another chieftaincy title or honorary doctorate—there were more than enough mushroom institutions ready to oblige for a modest contribution.

On the other hand—well, what kind of relief was there in receiving this damaged article, his razor-sharp mind scrambling in a void for a hold on reality? As had become predictable, almost instinctive since his release, those thoughts moved to explore possible gaps or errors in the no-holds-barred supplication regimen that preceded—and surely enabled—her husband's phenomenal rise in public service. So where was the source of this drastic reversal? Enemy action? Possibly, but easily dismissed. Jaiyesola prided herself on veteran spiritual credentials; these were more than sufficient to rout the most diabolical conspiracies against her man. After all, had those not failed in the first place? Where were their powers when, out of the blue, Badetona was handed, even without applying, one of the most envied and contested positions to which any civil servant could aspire—and at that age when he was already lined up for the mothball treatment? Just where were their vaunted powers?

Could it have been his early phase of refusal to acknowledge the prophet's powers of intercession? Indeed, Bade's dismissal of such aid had been nothing short of terminal, a disgusted rejection of the very notion—could that have resulted in a psychic penalty, now being manifested in his mental deterioration? Such a fatal flaw—a lack of faith would undermine the efficacy of any spiritual protection. To make matters worse, the supplication had been transmitted through a third party, even though that surrogate was his own wife. Perhaps it had taken too long to persuade him to undertake that climb up the hill of Oke Konran to consult, be blessed, and be fortified. Was this the punitive exaction for his earlier scornfulness? Just how much more were they doomed to expend? Till the last gasp of their possessions? Everything had been taken away. They had sold and mortgaged all to retain lawyers, all on the prestigious grade of senior advocates of the nation, the glamorous, elite club of registered lawyers. Now all they had left was faith, and that, alas, was patchy, partial. She lamented that she was left alone to generate, then stand guard over their promise of salvation. Badetona was too set in his cynical ways—wasn't that the trait that had attracted her to him in the first place? He himself never failed to acknowledge the contrast throughout their courtship, evoking it in favour of a union—*Like poles repel, unlike poles attract, so you might as well marry me and stop fighting your better judgment!* And the marriage had indeed remained as close to bliss as one could find in the average household, she a born-again Christian believer, he the master of deflation who compulsively found the weak patch in the most tightly sealed religious refuge. The home had been filled with laughter, the children raised in a balance of the hilarious and the solemn spaces of mutual toleration. Now there was only silence. The children were grown, dispersed. There remained only the silence they had left behind. Now it had gone beyond a silence of absent children, of an emptied home. There was the heavy pall of guilt, perhaps even of blame-passing, unvoiced. There was also the silence of hope, as if once the disaster was denied voice, confined within the walls of home and mind, the miasma would dissolve and the oppressive pall lift from the roof.

Were there gaps? Weak spots in her mission of intercession? Requirements unfulfilled? She shook her head—no! There had been none, not even through him, no dereliction whatsoever. That was the other trait in the character of the man she married. It might take days, weeks, even months, but once she succeeded in breaking through his stubborn defence ramparts, compelling him to assent to her schemes, however outlandish, he carried his part of the bargain to the letter! She paused, reconsidered. Was that perhaps the problem—*to the letter?* When it came to matters of the spirit, the letter was simply not enough. Spirit called to spirit, and spirit must be truthful. There was nothing she could do about that. One could only make do with what one possessed, and she never fooled herself that she possessed her husband's spirit. What she did with their lives was to double hers, thus reinforcing his. And she made sure there was no confusion—when she prayed, for instance, or tithed, she ensured that the watching powers understood that there was a separation of attribution: *And this for my husband, this for my beloved Bade, whom I know you will bring under your divine benefice of understanding and belief in your own good time, Lord Jesus in heaven be praised. Amen.*

In any case—and her face contorted in a frown—who was anyone to judge her? Why had none of them rallied to his side? It was always the same—each man for himself and God only for the righteous. Righteous? Yes, righteous! She dared to say righteous. Her Bade was a righteous man, no worse than the others. To hustle for one's share of public largesse was mere common sense. It was also avoidance of the sin of pride, of which no sin rated higher in the sight of God. To feel superior to others, that was the real sin—the holier-than-thou pretensions! Her life revolved around her husband, and the bond was consecrated in prayer. First pray for his advancement. Didn't she know what others did to gain their promotion? Some indulged in evil rituals. Even infant sacrifice. They made pacts with the Devil, sold their souls and signed in blood. She, on the contrary, only sought help from Apostle Davina. The success that followed was hers, she the lightning rod that overcame her husband's lack of faith and brought down manna from the skies. She compelled her Saviour to forgive the man who was his own worst enemy, the most reticent in his own cause. She would do it all over again, a million times if necessary. Who said God was an advocate of failure!

She heard footsteps and gingerly opened the door. Menka approached. She saw her husband beyond him, standing still, staring at the book in his hand. Menka shook his head sadly.

"There was nothing further," he said.

15.

Badagry

Several weeks had passed since his departure from the yet simmering city of Jos, that city of tin mines, forested hill contours still very much on his mind. His belongings had finally arrived by road haulage, having survived the elephant-trap potholes, unchecked expressway market takeovers, military-assisted police extortion checkpoints, siren-heralded in-your-face motorcades, cattle occupation, and kamikaze drivers drugged to the gills on all brands of affordable hallucinogens, local, smuggled, or traded in. He had traveled ahead and landed gratefully, having opted for the equally unpredictable domestic airline. From pottering among the contents of the advance truck, trying to impose a semblance of order on the contents of a madhouse of ripped boxes, last-minute gift packages, mini-cabinets, and document holders, the eminent surgeon Dr. Kighare Menka silently diagnosed himself weary body and soul, drained beyond bone tissue and marrow, a candidate perhaps for brain surgery at his own hands. Heaving a sigh of regret that such a prospect seemed unlikely—he was not a neurologist, in any case, just muscles, tissues, and organs—he picked his way to the beckoning drinks cabinet, sensibly prescribed and dispensed himself a restorative. His visit to Badetona was perhaps the last straw. He had placed so much hope on that alliance, but the mind of the man he knew was nowhere near accessible. Duyole Pitan-Payne was in the last throes of a looming departure. He felt isolated, alone with the burden of a discovery that, alas, did not permit of a simple surgical act of excision. Administering kicks along the way to stubborn obstacles that refused to yield ground at his approach, the surgeon meandered along a path into a deep-cushioned, enveloping armchair of his temporary lodging, one sole question preying on his mind: How long is temporary? Duyole Pitan-Payne had plucked him from the Jos inferno, replanted him in the sumptuous guest annex, and he knew he was welcome to stay there forever if he chose. He required no mind-reader to warn him, even as he let himself surrender his aches to the velvety comfort, that Pitan-Payne and his wife, Bisoye, were busy confecting every extravagant inducement to throw his way, with the single-minded intent of making him agree to do just that—accept this as his new home *sine die*. Forget Jos. Forget its parent state, Plateau. Forget the Middle Belt. Forget even Gumchi, his natal village. Or at least relegate them to a marginal, mostly preparatory bearing on his life and new career. Just relocate!

The campaign was anything but hidden, beginning when Duyole's driver had met him at the airport and driven him straight to the dinner table, no thought of permitting him a fresh-up stop at the guest annex, at which his checked-in baggage would be offloaded. As for dinner, even by Pitan-Payne's standards it was easily the most lavish impromptu spread Menka had ever survived, and survival was the most fervent prayer any guest silently muttered even for—indeed, especially for—such a modest snack.

The effort, he ruefully admitted, was unnecessary—it was mostly preaching to the converted. After all, he had himself initiated the rescue, albeit on a strictly respite basis, just a pause to recover some equilibrium. Aiding and abetting was the patriarch himself, the wisecracking, guileful, agilely ageless Otunba Pitan-Payne, and his silent consort, the buxom Mamma Kressy. She had accompanied him to dinner one evening, without notice, after years of bachelorhood since the passing of his wife, and without even the slightest intimation of her antecedents, to one of Duyole's famous "impromptu" dinners. That was Otunba Pitan-Payne's specialty—surprises, then mystery. She became a permanent family fixture, nearly inseparable from the *Otunba,* whose toenails appeared to have become her primary zone of devotion—the family swore that no matter what time of day they called at the *Otunba*'s home, her sole ministry as mistress was the trimming of the *Otunba*'s toenails, or simply massaging the gnarled ginger-root digits that bore that crowning glory. She had even learnt to crackle those toes, a most unusual feat that she would sometimes perform at dinner, the *Otunba*'s foot on her knees under the table. It took the first set of crackles for the family to understand why he always insisted that she sit across from rather than beside him. It was also the only audible contribution Mamma Kressy was ever heard to make to any discussion, however animated.

Then there was Brother Teahole, thus named for his lackluster golf-course performance and his preference for a genteel British cuppa tea at tee-end and final off-course hole—known as Hole 19—rather than the variety of more potent tipple favoured by others. Teahole exhibited either a sinus affectation or an affliction—it was impossible to decide which—the consequence of which was a tendency to punctuate even the most ordinary statements with a sniffle, most especially when he was engaged in circulating a dubious claim, which was most of the time. This made conversation with Teahole rather disjointed. *Ah, there you are, Gumchi-man himself.* Sniffle sniffle. *Only yesterday Pop-of-Ages*—sniffle sniffle—*was saying how he wished*—sniffle sniffle—*the country had a few more*—sniffle sniffle—*talented people from your part of the world.* Sniffle sniffle. Sniffle. He claimed to be a general salesman but appeared to be better known as procurer of this and that for the powerfully positioned. He was in standard embarrassing form with his weak phallus jokes.

Equally on display was Kikanmi, the "Brain of Badagry," eldest of the brood and authentic real estate agent, moderately successful. That profession had once earned him a stint as state commissioner for lands and housing under a military regime, an appointment that no other commissioner before then or after was permitted to forget, since his tenure became the touchstone for all commissioners in all state governments, living or dead, serving or retired. *You see, these people simply failed to appreciate what we did when we were in government.* In his estimation, the real estate mogul hoarded between his two ears all the Pitan-Payne family endowment of human intelligence, and it was of a very special kind. This, he felt, was universally recognized. It encouraged in him a habit of taking ten to fifteen minutes to digest a

trite passing comment, then persist in interjecting ponderous exposi-
tions on a discussion point that no one still recollected. Menka could
not resist the feeling that he considered his junior brother Duyole little
more than a roadside mechanic who happened to have merged spare-
part replacements with a flair for business. How he viewed him, Dr.
Menka, was a riddle that the surgeon never attempted to resolve.

Spluttering behind her fingers but clucking, chortling, and pout-
ing encouragement on the family assignment was Duyole's kid sister,
Selina, rushed in as reinforcement from her boutique *cum* hairdress-
ing salon in Yaba, with a reputation for being a discreet nymphet—
anything but raving. There was general agreement that she had begun
to mellow somewhat since she had met her current partner, a reformed
stud who discovered too late that he had finally met his match.

Yelping in from the compound as if to egg on the combined emotional assault, the Alsatian, Jiro, constituted all on his own a formidable family ally. Jiro, right from his whelping among a litter of
eight, had taken to Kighare on his first boyhood incursion into the
Pitan-Payne home—Duyole had simply dragged home the orphan for
vacation at school closure, and thereafter he remained an on-and-off
vacation fixture. Casual visitors assumed he was one of the family
along some line or the other—that is, until they saw the faint trident
tribal marks emerging from the corners of his mouth. The Alsatian
would later earn the alias Disloyal Hound from its habit of leaping
into the spare seat or luggage space in Menka's vehicle whenever
it sensed a move towards his departure, and had to be physically
dragged out by his master, assisted by domestic staff, led by Godsown,
the chief steward, who mostly saw to his feeding and thus earned a
little respect. If master and friend had cause to call him at the same
time, he invariably trotted towards Kighare, as if—the domestics
railed in disgust—it was the stranger who stuffed his slavering jaws.
From Menka's reappearance after more than a year's absence, he had
patrolled the dining room precincts, sending out periodic canine blasts
to let the neighbourhood know that his buddy was in town. All were
present and convivial at the first—he dreaded, yet relished—of many
more welcoming dinners to come.

The freshly celebrated, now somewhat rootless surgeon tried to
cushion his dislodgement by reassuring himself that he was embarked

only on a mere transformative project—same idea and content, different location, simply an adjustment of format. He had not lightly earned a reputation as the Gumchi Stubborn-Head. Gumchi Rehabilitation Centre—yes, he could live with that. Even if the location was Lagos, yes, that fell within the pledge of *Gumchi First*. He cast his eyes lightly over the boxes, trying to remember which one held the long-suffering mantra, last seen in its porcelain ashtray embossment. It succeeded in moving with him everywhere, once framed and hung over his bed in boarding school, neatly capitalized on the loose leaf of his textbooks, etc. It was a response to the sudden, cruel end that had thrust him among the ranks of the orphaned. It appeared to have matured him overnight. He carried the placard with him over the North Atlantic after his plight—and aptitude for learning—had come to state notice and produced the consolation of a scholarship that took him step by steady step up the occupational ladder, catapulting him into national prominence. The Gumchi Kid never forgot. He clung to the mantra as if his entire seizure of life were lodged in the placard, progressively miniaturized, then launched into virtual space by insertion in the signature box of his electronic mail account. Even when the four friends rallied round and adopted his Gumchi project as their joint venture of "giving back," there was no yielding, no watering down. Such contributed to his notorious "coconut head," at which even the smooth talker Farodion the marketing guru tilted, only to retreat with a broken lance.

The surgeon's rising cheerfulness, reinforced by these reminiscences, lingered only until his gaze again rested on the boxes. With the offloading of the first bulk luggage from Jos virtually crowding him out of resting space, the finality of his repatriation began to press home. He looked round the debris, stopped as he saw his rumpled, lightly scarified face—three lines like a trident on either cheek, radiating from the two corners of the mouth—reflected from the inside mirror of the drink *cum* book cabinet door. He hissed, glared at the reflection, then proceeded to subject it to a terse harangue: "Gumcheeky!"—the name had stuck to him through boarding school, college, and even into a professional career of over two decades. "You and your big Gumchi mouth! You've really done it this time!"

Annoyed even more by the stolid silence from his reflection, he slammed down his glass, tucked his index fingers in both mouth corners, and pulled at the soft inside flesh, stretching the cheeks and distorting his face until the tridents disappeared into bunched skin and his jaw actually began to ache. It was a self-mortification routine he had retained since childhood, when it served the adults—the schoolteachers especially—as a labour-saving device for administering punishment to the erring child: *Stand in the corner facing the class and pull your cheeks!* Snorting, Menka let his mind linger on the notion of upbringing—such treatment, he reflected, would be considered child abuse in the present. The routine turned his face all the more grotesque from his efforts to issue parental/teacher admonitions through the same maltreated orifice, the emerging sounds warped and meaningless to a nonexistent audience:

"Yes, go on, open it wider. Open it as wide as you can. Now try and put your foot in it. I know you can. You do it all the time. Go on, no one is stopping you. You never learn, do you? I said, open it wider. Wider still, mug!"

The reunion dinner resurfaced with its mixture of assurances and anxieties—warmth, exasperations: family. The couple were right to discern signs of disorientation almost as soon as they set eyes on him. They continued to observe him keenly throughout dinner, began to nod satisfaction to each other as he progressively relaxed into the company and slid into the persona of the Menka they had known. He himself began to feel fully at ease, his psyche retuned to old times, recovering a lost solidarity, almost as if the missing pair of the gang were also present. He could almost feel pieces of his scattered self floating back into accustomed places.

Badetona had been a severe setback. No sooner did he return from that somber visit than Menka tackled the engineer.

"Why didn't you tell me? Not even a hint!"

"No, it was best you found out yourself. What could I tell you? That he fumbled, lost his way and then his mind? I've visited scores of times, but he remains . . . well, as you saw him. Ever since his release. We try to do what we can with Jaiyesola, but she's also set in her ways."

"Are they planning to put him on trial?"

"That was the idea. And then they put him through something, and that's what came out at the end of it. It would be stupid, and doubly cruel, even pointless, to place him in the dock. I think they know that, so they leave him alone. Pop-of-Ages also keeps an eye on that aspect—he's close to Sir Goddie."

"Oh, I didn't know that."

"They're both members of one of these secret societies— Rosicrucians."

"What are those?"

Duyole laughed. "No idea, but that is what gives the old man his vigour. I'm going to sign up. You saw him in action at dinner."

The patriarch had been at his most irrepressible, shamelessly flirtatious on the verge of eighty. One easily recognized the source of Duyole's gregarious, irreverent streak, though the rest of that engineer's attributes appeared to be of his own secret formula. The *Otunba* had eagerly accepted to join the reunion dinner—it was his chance to broach the delicate mission imposed on him by his fellow lodge member. An earlier attempt, which had also failed to enroll Bisoye as ally, had met a brick wall, but the persistent streak appeared to run in the family. If the *Otunba* hoped to find an ally in Menka in that campaign, however, it was proving an uphill task. Menka refused to be drawn.

"So, doctor, who's your candidaate?"

At first Dr. Menka was puzzled, his mind anywhere but on election matters. "Candidate for what, sir?"

"The elections."

Bisoye interjected, "Pop, don't bother him. You know there are no elections. Everything is decided in advance."

"And to start with," Duyole added, "which elections? The political or the festival? Let him understand what you're asking. You like mixing things up, Pop."

The old man waved him away. "Let the good doctor answer. You are just an anti-Goddie fanatic, so no one is asking you."

"You did ask, though. More than merely ask, I seem to recollect."

"Not anymore. You won't even be here for the elections. No one needs your vote."

Duyole turned to Menka. "He's been badgering us to sponsor his friend for the YoY Award. Told him nothing doing. Can you imagine? Gong of Four and POMP!"

"This has nothing to do with the party. POMP and YoY are two different things. YoY is given to individuals. And institutions. Not political parties."

"Try separating Goddie from POMP and what do you get?"

Bisoye sighed. "Here we go again. I thought that was all settled."

Not for the sister, it seemed. "I still think it would have made a good merger. Like it or not, Sir Goddie is the national brand. I can just see the headlines: Brand of the Land sponsors Brand of the Nation. Doctor, what do you think?"

Menka shook his head and concentrated on his plate.

Bisoye nodded approval. "That's right, Kighare. Don't let them drag you into this."

"Doc, your young friends do not understand how things get done. You know if you team up with Sir Goddie, he'll modernize that village of yours in no time. Before you know it, another skyscraper will hit the sky. What's the present count? I forget."

Bisoye Pitan-Payne knew where her father-in-law was headed. Once the *Otunba* sensed opposition, or failure, his teases tended towards the waspish. She tried to head him off. "Pop, you know there are no skyscrapers in Gumchi."

The old man squeezed his face in agony. "No? Are you quite sure? When I last visited . . ."

Even though he knew it was a waste of time, the son joined in the attempt to stop him in his tracks. "You have never visited, Pop. You don't even know where Gumchi is."

"I don't have to visit. You can see those skyscrapers from looong distances."

"When last did you travel up north, Pop?" Selina queried.

"That doesn't matter. Gumchi skyscrapers? If you're looking for the orginal, that's where to find it. Long before the first one appeared in Lagos. Trust our people, they wasted no time pinning a name on it—*Ilé gogoro*, followed it up with the song *On'ilé gogoro*. Yes, long before all that song and dance, Gumchi could already boast at least two or three high-risers. Perhaps even before America's Empire State Building. The Americans copied from Gumchi—as usual, no acknowledgement."

His listeners shrugged. Until he had run the course, there would be no holding him. The old man chuckled. "Well, what do you call those rocks sitting on top of one another? The top ones don't just scrape, they push through to the other side of heaven. Ask your friend, he's one of the cave dwellers. They live inside those rocks, just as in blocks of flats."

Selina's ever-ready hysterical laughter filled the dining room, but the rest of the company permitted only embarrassed smiles. Bisoye and her husband exchanged looks, regretting now that they had invited the old man. Nervously, they hoped that it was just the *Otunba*'s misplaced primitivist jokes, not the signal for an evening of peevishness. The *Otunba* was fond of the family extra, they all admitted—as Kighare also was of him—but they continued to underrate the *Otunba*'s tendency to indulge in near-the-bone banter, mostly derived from notions of a sophistication of Lagosian-colonial aristocracy, superior to "natives" from the interior. There had been moments in the past that they preferred to forget, hoping that the guest victims had forgiven, or generously dismissed as the effects of old age and occasional dissociation from reality.

Menka, however, moved swiftly to douse any flickers of unease, his voice genuinely warm. "Sir, I have a penthouse reserved there for you anytime you choose to visit."

The awkward moment disappeared. The *Otunba* screamed, "Without a proper lift? You want me to climb up and down? At my age? Duyole, your friend wants to kill me."

"All right, Pop, that's my next engineering assignment. A private lift, just for you."

"Ah, that's more like it. Mamma Kressy!" She looked up from her toenail assignation with a broad smile but would not be drawn. "That's where we're going for our next Easter holiday. Spending Good Friday right next to God. We'll witness the Resurrection from a ringside seat."

The *Otunba* was rewarded with the accustomed mix of shock and laughter. The evening approached midnight, all conviviality. It was a success. By unspoken accord they would make the long-absent son feel fully at home. The seeming outsider was the other prodigal son, Damien, lately returned to the bosom of the family. His withdrawn presence generally passed without notice, certainly did not inhibit the overall upbeat mood. He alone appeared somewhat ill-at-ease, never joining in the conversation but solicitous of everyone in his quiet way, ensuring that glasses were filled, dishes assisted in the direction of emptied plates or exploring gazes. He ate sparingly, nursed the same glass without any noticeable change in its level. Bisoye ensured the relay of dishes. Finally, movements under the table indicated that Mamma Kressy had begun to refasten the buckles on the *Otunba*'s sandals. She gently lifted the leg off her knee, reverently assisted its descent to the carpeted floor. It was her signal to the *Otunba* that it was time to head home.

AFTER THEY HAD all dispersed, Kighare, seated in the cosy safety of an intimate lounge, designed as if for just such confidentialities, looked his friend over and nodded appreciatively. Nothing about Pitan-Payne surprised him anymore. The engineer had started work on a permanent solution from the word go, wasted no time on temporary measures. That was now obvious. Kighare tackled him quite bluntly. Duyole merely shrugged his shoulders.

"After that first phone call, the one you made from the club, it became impossible to concentrate on anything else."

"You're a born worrier. America's Homeland Security would grade that yellow. Still far from red alert. I thought I made that clear?"

"You think I can still recall details of that shifty code? When last did any of us have cause to resort to it?"

"Well, you should. It was mostly your handiwork. Let's see now. Farodion—that's right, he was the last to evoke it. And that was some twenty years ago."

"Oh yes, the cannabis problem at Customs. Stupid. Anyway, listening to you was enough, no matter how casual you tried to sound. Listen, Gumchi, I know you inside out—don't argue! Knew we had to get you out of there. And permanently. Not just for a short break. Even if it meant myself coming over to set fire to the damned place and smoke you out. Bisoye fully agreed."

Menka smiled. "She would! You've ruined her sense of judgment."

"Well, were we wrong?"

Glasses steadily replenished from Duyole's favourite malt whisky,

Menka felt warmed even further by the glow of a renewed friendship, and gratitude. He quickly warned himself to guard against even the slightest exhibition of the latter by word, gesture, body language, or whatever around the couple—especially the sharp-eyed Bisoye.

They did not hear the door open, just a solicitous voice asking, "Is there anything you need, Papa?"

It was Damien. "Oh, thanks, Damien. Didn't know you were still downstairs."

"I thought I would check before turning in."

"Thanks, but . . ." He looked around. "We've got everything, I think. See you in the morning."

"Goodnight, Papa. Goodnight, Uncle."

"Goodnight, young man. Your dad and I are in for a long night."

"I bet, Uncle. Goodnight, sir."

Duyole burst out laughing. "Look at him, just take a look at him. He takes after me, loves *fabu* like nobody's business. Don't worry, I'll pass on what you are dying to hear over the next few days. Let me first extract it all from him."

Damien looked mildly embarrassed and protested, "Ah, Papa. I was just trying to make sure you had everything you needed."

Again Duyole let loose one of his uproarious gusts of laughter. "Liar! Just make sure the open malt reserve doesn't disappear with you. I earned every one of those bottles the hard way, but that's a family secret. Pour yourself a glass and then leave us ancient fogeys to our conspiracies."

Damien smiled at that, threw up his hands. "You see what I get from him, Uncle."

"I get worse, Damien. Ignore him."

Damien left, shutting the door behind him.

"Where does one begin?" sighed Menka.

"Anywhere. Anywhere. All right, go from the beginning. Leave nothing out. I want to hear everything."

Menka nodded in the direction of the departed figure. "How is he doing?"

For the first time that evening, Duyole's face clouded in uncertainty. "Hm-hmm. Gradually finding his feet. One thing for sure—he is determined to settle down. Keen, very keen. I've brought him into the firm, so he's now fully absorbed into the family business. But he must work his way up. Others helped build the firm, not him. They are senior to him."

Menka nodded. "Gong o' Four to the core. I expected no less. And he?"

Duyole's face receded into deep thought. "I'm not sure. But he has no choice in the matter. Matter of principle." He broke off abruptly. "Wait a minute." And he raised his voice. "Damien!"

"Coming, Papa."

"I nearly forgot. I have something for you," Duyole said to Menka. "Someone came and left you a parcel. They said you left them only this address."

"I did?"

"From Hilltop Club. They said it's from one Baba Baftau."

Menka's face lit up. "Old Man Desert! He's one of the real genuine hearts in that place. I remember now, he did say he was going to send me some *kilishi*."

"You eat that stuff?"

"It stops the stomach gnawing when you can't stop for lunch. But there is a special story regarding this one. Not to worry, it's part of the overall saga."

Damien entered.

"If I may trouble you, Damien," Duyole said, "please look in the office corner of my studio. You'll find a brown paper package, on the flattish side. It's tied with a ribbon, somewhere on my workbench. You'll see it as soon as you enter."

"I'll bring it right away. See? I was right after all." And Damien turned to his errand.

"He always keeps his word, that old man," Menka explained. "Promised he would send me *kilishi* every month, if only to make sure I don't forget them. As if I could ever!"

"Or me either. From the moment I turned on the TV and watched that inferno . . ."

"That's exactly what it was, an inferno. Never thought that ancient building could catch fire so thoroughly. Think it was truly arson?"

"What else could it have been?"

"Either you were trying to smoke out someone or someone had

decided to smoke you out. More likely the latter. What the pyromaniac didn't know was that it was the surest way to make you dig in even deeper. He should have taken lessons from those who know anything of the Gumchi Stubborn-Head!"

"You know, Duyo, only just now, what you just said—yes—only now has it occurred to me that maybe you're right. Maybe it was I who set fire to the place. In a sense, one could say that. Some kind of chain reaction, not yet certain how that was set off, but yes, could be. Could be."

Pitan threw up his arms. "All right, I'll let you tell it your own way. Just as long as you know—to go back to what I was saying earlier—the only problem I saw was the usual one, how to get you to act in your own interest. Bisoye and I put our heads together, and bingo! She came up with the answer—what about the Gumchi idea? It was so long ago that it took seconds for it to click. Brilliant girl, eh? Then of course she had to rub it in. You should have heard her sniff—*You men! You're so different. We don't forget such things. You told me about it when we were courting, a day before you finally proposed.* I did, too. Seems it was the very day after I returned from your graduation. She said I went on and on about joining you in your remote mountain village to construct a clinic on sheer rock surface—exaggeration, of course, I could never have suggested building anything so impossible. She made that up."

Menka laughed. "Are you sure? You're talking about the morning after . . ."

"Come on. Are you saying I hadn't sobered up even after a long train journey back across the English Channel? You're just a sore loser, taking her side because I drank the entire competition under the trestle, including all three of you."

"All right, I'm a sore loser. That doesn't mean you didn't boast you would do it."

"Listen to this quack surgeon. I asked her why I would say such a thing—you know what she said? She said she thought I was trying to impress her. That's a woman for you."

Their laughter was interrupted by a soft knock on the door, and Damien reentered. "Nothing in there, Papa. No package, thin or flat. Or brown."

Duyole frowned. "You're sure? It's impossible to miss it."

The young man reassured him. "Absolutely nothing like a package. I looked everywhere."

Duyole chewed his lips. "That's strange. I could have sworn I left it there. Right on that desk. I saw it there early this evening." He waved his hand in dismissal. "I know. The usual. Picked it up and placed it where I was certain not to forget. All right, thanks. I'll find it later. Never mind, Menka. It will be delivered to you in the morning."

"More likely afternoon. I know I'm going to sleep like a log when we're done."

"I'll simply sleep forever. All right, thanks, Damien. I won't bother you anymore."

Damien protested in his high-pitched voice, "No problem, Papa. Wake me up if you remember anything else."

He left. Duyole scratched his head. "I don't recall seeing it or setting it down anywhere else."

"Forget it. *Kilishi* doesn't go bad."

Duyole shrugged. "I know. I've been browsing around the house all day looking for loose items you might need at the annex. I may have left it in a cupboard or whatever. I'll find it. Unless you're dying for a quick taste . . ."

"After Bisoye's goat meat *asun*? No way. Later for that."

"In that case, dish out the full course. What really went over in Jos? Let's have the full gist. In lurid details. With onions, trimmings, and peppers. Don't stint. Leave nothing out."

Kighare took a sip of his drink, set down the glass with exaggerated care, and leant back in his armchair. "Tumultuous hardly describes it, Duyo. Tumultuous. And weird. Somehow I lost my cool. No other day to touch it since I lost both parents that same day."

Pitan avoided his eyes. "I can believe that. Catching you on the phone just when the whole world was banging on your door and screaming for you to get you out—that was the next worst thing to being in a ringside seat. All right, we have all night. Tell!"

16.

The Codex Seraphinianus

Jos did not let the surgeon from Gumchi go quietly—at least, not that newfound suburb that was called Boriga. It followed him into Lagos. Indeed preceded him, if only he had made an effort at recollection of his early days of remote sensing. A flurry of brief forays into Lagos had, however, lulled him into a false sense of security—Boriga had done the rest. Even if the Devil had not actually relocated in Boriga, some of his disciples had. On his own admission, Menka's mind never did totally abandon Jos—Boriga was unfinished business, and for the proud seasoned professional, unfinished business equaled forgetting a pair of forceps in a patient's guts, then sewing him up for home discharge. Honours were even. It was the Yoruba saying all over again: the child who swears its mother will not sleep, let it brace itself for sleepless nights. Once settled—within the elastic adaptation of that condition—he would muster forces and cauterize the ulcerous affront to his profession. Ethics could wait. His newly acquired prominence would undergo its first value test—certainly it should provide access to the very highest levels for massive intervention.

Adjusting to a new culture was his main concern, but not an insurmountable culture shock. Badagry, after all, albeit closely intertwined with Lagos, was still Badagry. Pitan-Payne was on hand, though keeping a frenetic pace to wind up his affairs and proceed to his UN assignment on schedule. The engineer seemed to thrive on interlocking calendars, and in any case, he now had Menka to pick up the loose ends for him in his absence. The timing could not have been more thoughtfully ordained. Indeed—and he leant over to whisper confidentially to the surgeon during one of their meals together—"I did have my suspicions, but now I have solid proof. It was I who set fire to Hilltop Mansion, just to get you down in Badagry." The unexpected and the planned seemed to dovetail neatly, like the finely adjusted sprockets on his mechanical prototypes. And while Lagos/Badagry lacked the excitement of receiving sudden cartloads of human debris from Boko Haram's latest efforts to out-Allah Allah in their own image, one could count on the gratuitous equivalent from multiple directions. Such as the near-daily explosion of a petroleum tanker on the expressway or in the city centre. Or a roofless lorry bulging with cattle and humans tipping over on a bridge and dropping several feet onto an obliging rock outcrop in the midst of the river. Sometimes, more parsimoniously, a victim of military amour-propre—in uniform or mufti, it made no difference. That class seemed to believe in safety in numbers, and all it took was for even a low-ranking sergeant to take offence at another motorist, who perhaps refused to give way to his car, a mere "bloody civilian," never mind that the latter had the right of way. An on-the-spot educational measure was mandated. Guns bristling, his accompanying detail, trained to obey even the command of a mere twitch of the lip, leapt from their escort vehicle, dragged out the hapless driver, unbuckled their studded belts, whipped him senseless, threw him in the car boot or on the floor of the escort van, and took him to their barracks for further instruction. However, the wretch sometimes created a problem by suffocating en route, which left society to develop structures for neutralizing such inconvenience.

The contradicting, ironic sequence occurred to Menka only for the first time. Yes, come to think of it, the military hardly ever recorded a fatality—once or twice, maybe even three times in a month. Yes, the accident of excess did happen, but mostly such terminal disposal was left to the police, whose favourite execution site was a roadblock, legal or moonlighting. Perhaps a recalcitrant commuter or passenger-bus driver had refused to collaborate in providing a bribe on demand or insulted the rank of the demanding officer with a derisive sum. And it did not have to be the original offender but some *too-know* grammar-spouting public defender who had intervened on behalf of the potential source of extortion. The outcome was predictable—victim or Good Samaritan advocate instantly joined the statistics of the fallen from "accidental discharge." The expression was still current, but often it was anything but. Accidents had become infrequent and unfashionable. Oftener to be expected was that the frustrated, froth-lipped police pointed the gun, calmly, deliberately, at the head of the unbelieving statistic and pulled the trigger. Again, the inconvenience of body disposal.

But then the community of victims themselves—what a fascinating breed of humanity! The roles, it constantly appeared, had become gleefully, compulsively interchangeable. Allowing him only a few days to "catch your breath and get your bearings," Pitan-Payne lost no time in taking him to inspect the land designated for the Gumchi Rehabilitation Centre, for victims of Boko Haram, ISWAP, and other redeemers—nothing like striking while the iron was hot! On their way, the familiar sight of crowd agitation—how would the day justify itself without some kind of street eruption somewhere, wherever? Trapped in the chug-stop-chug of traffic, the favourite commuter distraction was to attempt to guess what was the cause, and even place bets on propositions. That morning, Menka's first in nearly a year down south, did not disappoint. But for the milling blockage by intervening viewers, they could have claimed the privilege of ringside seats. Compensating for that obstructed viewing, however, was the sight of men and women trotting gaily, anticipation all over their faces, towards the surrounded spot of attraction. From every direction they came, some vaulting over car bonnets, squishing their legs against the fenders, squeezing through earlier-arrived bodies, or simply scrabbling for discovered viewing points. They climbed on parked vehicles and the raised concrete median. Commuter buses slowed down and stopped, *keke napeps* pulled aside, drivers and passengers alike rubbernecking on both sides of or in the direction of a wide gutter that sank into a culvert. The lights changed to green and Pitan-Payne drove on, their last shared image a pair of muscular arms raised above the bobbing heads, clutching an outsized stone and slamming that object downwards into the gutter. Very likely a snake, Pitan suggested. With the rainy season, quite a few sneaked through the marshes into culverts and slithered their way into parking lots and even offices.

A police van came racing down the road against the traffic, strobes flashing and sirens blaring, so Menka looked back, saw the crowd drawing back and drifting reluctantly away from the uniformed spoilsports. This opened an avenue just in time for Menka to obtain the briefest glimpse of an object slumped over the rim of the gutter, once human, but not any longer. Indeed, the only human identity left him was his iodine-red tunic and black trousers, still recognizable as the uniform of a LASTMA officer, an unarmed unit whose function was simply to unplug traffic, stopped as readily by truculent drivers as by the roadside markets, vendors of all the world commodities who had taken over the streets, haggled, negotiated, delivered change and goods at their own pace. If the activities delayed movement over half a dozen changes from red to green and back again, it did not concern them in the least.

Later that evening, television narrated the full story. After futile spurts of preventive measures, Authority had commenced arrests of vendors and seizures of their wares. The LASTMA team, their van parked in a side street, had pursued several such malfeasants. In a desperate attempt to escape capture, one ran straight into the snout of a speeding vehicle, was tossed up, landed with an ominous thud on the sidewalk, and remained there, unmoving. In a trice, a mob had gathered. They set the parked LASTMA vehicle on fire and worked up further appetite for vengeance. The unarmed officers had already fled. A hunt party pursued and eventually brought down a scapegoat, quite some distance from the actual scene of the crime. They proceeded to the ritual battering of their catch. He broke free, ran into the gutter, tried crawling into the culvert for safety. They dragged him out by his feet, trunk and head smeared and reeking from the accumulated sludge of the blocked tunnel. Passersby, totally ignorant of the beginning or midact of the mayhem, refused to be left out. They grabbed the nearest assault weapon to hand and joined in the gratification of the thrill for the day, a new-breed citizen phenomenon. The massive stone, raised above a throng of heads, quivered lightly against a Lagosian skyline of ultramodern skyscrapers before its descent onto bone and brain. It took on an iconic dimension that stuck instantly to Menka's surgical album of retentions, a rampant insignia of the transfiguration of a collective psyche.

"I envy you," Menka remarked the following morning as they confronted the printed media coverage, their scalding coffee no match for the nausea aroused by the photograph sensationally smeared across the front page. "You are going away for a while. You'll be spared such sights."

"I feel guilty," confessed Duyole. "Guilty, but yes, that is one spectacle I shall not miss."

"Careful!" Menka quickly cautioned. "They have their equivalents over there. Ask the black population."

"No. Not like this. Occasionally, yes, there does erupt a Rodney King scenario. Or a fascistic spree of 'I can't breathe.' America is a product of slave culture, prosperity as the reward for racist cruelty. This is different. This, let me confess, reaches into . . . a word I would rather avoid but can't—soul. It challenges the collective notion of soul. Something is broken. Beyond race. Outside colour or history. Something has cracked. Can't be put back together." And then Pitan-Payne gasped, paused, folded over the pages, and passed the newspaper to Menka. "Take a look at this. Not that it changes anything, but . . . here, read it yourself."

There was a chastening coda. It altered nothing. The fleeing vendor, whom no one had even thought to help, was very much alive. He had picked himself up, salvaged most of his scattered goods, and found his way home despite a sprained ankle and some bruises. Most of the spectators had retreated to a safe distance. They continued what they had been doing earlier—filming the action with their phone cameras. The police did, however, capture the Goliath with the terminating stone, who had administered the coup de grâce. He remained on the spot, to all appearances admiring the evidence of his work.

He vehemently protested the injustice of his arrest: "I thought he was an armed robber."

IT WAS BABA BAFTAU who brought Jos to Menka in his own person, accompanied by Costello. No notice beyond a phone call to let him know they were in Lagos and would like to stop by and say hallo. Touched and delighted, Menka gave them the address. He received them in the jumble of his apartment, feeling overwhelmed most especially by the Old Man of the Desert. At his age, traveling all the way from Jos. And by road!

Baftau waved off the engineer's protestations. "It was nothing. Costello's firm ordered him to Lagos, so I asked him for a ride."

"You know I work for a construction firm, Doctor," Costello elaborated. "Had to inspect some of our projects en route. So I have no choice in the matter. It's always the road."

"And I am jobless," Baftau reminded Menka. "Not merely jobless but clubless. No more Hilltop Mansion. Since I have nothing more to do with my time, I inflict myself on our friend Costello."

"But that road is dangerous . . . oh, of course." Menka had suddenly remembered his position within government hierarchy, albeit retired.

Baftau's face grew combative. "I admit to being old and pensionable, not foolish or ready to be disposed of. If you look outside, you'll see what accompanied us from Jos. Let any kidnapper try his nonsense."

"You wouldn't know it, Doctor, but Baftau is on our board. And he enjoys going round the sites."

"After fifty years just sitting behind the desk, should that surprise anyone?"

"Not in the least," Menka admitted. "No wonder you remain so agile. I thought all you did was sit in Hilltop Mansion and reminisce over the good old days."

"And escape my wives," the Old Man roared. "Ask Costello. He visits sometimes. At my age, you'd think they'd have learnt to leave me in peace. Not they. They still want me to settle their quarrels. But now, see, our sanctuary is gone. And you know, as a good Muslim, I must not be seen in bars. So what am I supposed to do?"

Costello winked. "Pay no attention to him. He's kept himself busy. Very busy. That's what brought him."

"Us!" the Old Man corrected. "Yes, Doctor, we have been busy. You left us a very big challenge. You embarrassed me, Doctor, me especially. Inside my own native corner. You deprived me of sleep. So after the fire I called Costello—we are old friends. I said, let's go and find this place."

Menka sat up. "You found the place? Boriga?"

"Where else? Yes, in Boriga."

"And still operating?"

Costello said, "We found it, but then again we did not."

Menka did not ask for elaboration. Instead his mind flew instantly to the final encounter the night before the fire. It was more to himself that he said, "That character knew what he was talking about."

The callers looked at each other, their faces expressing the same question. Menka took a deep breath and carefully recounted his encounter with the stalking figure, the one who had assured him of the closure of the meat mall. So who was he? A floating club member? Or maybe even a ghost?

That was a mystery neither of them could solve. Old Man Desert threw up his hands. "It was you he haunted. I never even noticed any stranger all that night."

Costello mused, his face increasingly creased, "I believe I saw the figure you're talking about. He caught my attention very briefly—yes, in the billiards room. I was on my way to the toilet. But I soon forgot all about him. I was there to celebrate, nothing else. Until you launched your bombshell."

Menka looked slightly embarrassed. "So virtually overnight that elaborate establishment disappeared? Or was it burnt down like Hilltop? By the way, any clues? Any known arsonist been named?"

"One at a time, Doctor, one at a time. Now, the fire. I happen to believe it was a distraction. It was to keep us busy while the supermarket was evacuated. It was a well-rehearsed operation. Costello feels the same way."

"Very elaborate." Costello nodded. "So elaborate that in my view it was all planned. That is, they had a fall-back plan. At the first signal of danger, they would evacuate. They would transfer into a prepared warehouse, or another sales emporium. Set up, equipped in advance. Ready for occupation at a moment's notice."

The Old Man nodded sagely. "I am inclined to that view. I believe they merely moved somewhere else."

"Within Jos?"

Costello shook his head. "No, I don't think so. You see, Dr. Menka, they are crafty in this business, but you know, they cannot totally cover their tracks. They were in a rush. I am a builder, as you know. I go round the buildings. Incomplete, abandoned, occupied, prefabricated—every kind. Even sites still under demarcation. It becomes second nature. So I am pottering around. And I find something of great interest."

Costello reached for his briefcase, opened it, and extracted a partly burnt notebook. He handed it over to Menka. "Do you know anyone who knows cryptography? Look at it. It is very much in code."

Old Man Desert giggled. "Me, I can't make head nor tail of it. But Allah is great. Imagine if I had not gone with Costello."

Costello nodded. "I am Italian. And what they do here is to adopt something that was invented by an Italian—it is called the Codex Seraphinianus. So I could pick up a word here and there. Not many. But I read names of human parts of the body, and then there are brief comments. I could make sense of what this is all about. Just small-small. And these sheets belong to a larger documentation. Is like notes going into bigger work. When people move, they burn. If you like to poke nose and look place where people just leaving, you will find burning spot, not merely of paper. When people move, they burn. So, Dr. Menka, let me tell you straight. We are not dealing with one shop only. There is a network. Boriga is just one section. They are here in Lagos. There are addresses here, but I cannot read. We need a specialist to help us, someone who knows how to break into this special language. This notebook give many clues. Boriga is just one place. When I look at this diagram, I think it is telling what cities. One thing I read—here, I show you—they are developing software to make operation smooth. Very smooth. And foolproof. If you look closely, you will see that some pages look draft for ledger sheets. Another one is like order forms. It's there, in plain Italian. So I link some facts, some images and diagrams, and it all bring us close to full picture. But we must find a professional."

Menka took the semi-charred notebook, turned it over in his hands, scrutinized the scribblings, the drawings, and suddenly his face lit up.

"I know who! Even if Duyole himself can't, he's on his way to the

UN. I can't think of anyone better placed to do this for us right now."
He grew visibly excited as he reached for his phone. "I'll call him right
away," only to have Costello place a restraining hand on his arm.

"One moment, Doctor. Is this someone you can trust? We have to
keep this very close to ourselves."

Menka smiled. "This is someone I'll trust with my life."

"Who is he?" Old Man Desert queried.

"Name is Pitan-Payne. He's an electronic engineer. I don't know if
cryptography is among his talents, but we'll soon find out. We've been
friends since childhood. He's my host. He owns this apartment."

"*Alhamdulillah.*" The Old Man grinned. "If you say you trust him
with your life, that's good enough for me."

"Definitely with me, too."

Menka dialed. The exchange left the two visitors staring.

"Mission station?" Menka asked.

"Pistons cooling."

"Jos spillover. Here in flesh."

"Oh." There was a pause. "Can do can do?"

"Twosome labials."

There was relief, even delight in Pitan's voice. "Gung-ho gung?"

"Collaterals."

"Gung-ho gung."

"One-five check-in?"

"Gung-ho gung."

Switching off the phone, Menka nodded at the duo and said, "He's
home. Told him we'll be with him in fifteen minutes. He's expecting
us for lunch."

Costello couldn't resist blurting out, "What language was that?"

"Pitan-Paynese," Menka said. "Well, we all did contribute, but
it's mainly his. It's a habit, then he inflicts it on the rest of his gang. I
know he'll like to tackle this. If he can't, he'll find us someone who
can. Shall we go?"

Damien was waiting at the door to receive and usher them into
the living room, Dr. Menga introducing him as the "overseas" Pitan-
Payne who had decided quite recently to return home. Baba Baftau
offered him his card and an open invitation to visit him anytime in Jos.
Their host shortly emerged in a kitchen apron, wiping his hands, full

of apologies for his wife's absence. She was busy at the factory, winding down towards their departure, and he did not want to interrupt.

"Ignore that," Menka said. "It's his chance to get in the kitchen and prove he's a better cook than his wife."

Baba Baftau remained scandalized. He continued to stare, disbelieving.

"Good old Godsown is on duty—that's the steward. Damien will lend a hand, so why should I bother her? Damien, look after them while I conclude business in the powerhouse." And with that he was off, a somewhat regretful figure of deprivation because he could not put up in the short time a sumptuous feast for Dr. Menka's very first visitors since he had relocated. And they all the way from Jos! No matter, they would meet for a full "working dinner" before their return to Jos and his own U.S.-bound departure. In the meantime he was working something out with the housemaid, so could they relax for a few minutes? If only Menka could learn to give decent notice . . .

Menka threw up his hands. "Listen to him. They only called me up this morning."

But Duyole was already off. They heard him issuing instructions on his way back to the kitchen. Baba Baftau appeared to wake up from a trance.

"Your friend is cooking?"

Costello laughed. "But I've told you, I cook. Most Italians can cook. We enjoy messing around in the kitchen."

"Even if he doesn't cook," Baftau insisted, "*wallahi,* this friend of yours, *ko,* is he always like that? Are there many like him in Lagos?"

Menka shrugged his shoulders in resignation. "You wait. You've only known him for two minutes."

Pitan-Payne rejoined them within twenty. At the table he placed the charred notebook beside his plate and turned it over page by page. Finally he released a sigh and firmly shook his head in defeat. Too deep. Yes, he had fooled around with the war codes of the Axis powers—all part of their electronic curriculum. This was, however, different from improvising a magpie language for a cabalistically inclined foursome of youth, of which perhaps only two full-time members still retained any recollection. He would copy a page and send it to some contacts from his university days. They are great encrypters over there, he assured his guests, even though the British did succeed in cracking one famous code in World War II. That crippled Hitler's plans for invading the island.

By the end of a protracted lunch that lasted into early evening, all were agreed that Costello was right—there was more than sufficient matter to engage the mind, such as a sturdy network of the specialized body parts trade. Boriga was not an isolated case.

Allah willed it; Baftau rendered praise. Costello had indeed stumbled on a long-discarded notebook of rudimentary beginnings, a phase that had long been surpassed, had burgeoned into a sophisticated commercial life within life as an accomplished fact. An underground language was already in progress, not vastly different from SMS texting shorthand but integrated into images, the new language of a wired generation, the harbingers of space-age minds gone haywire, thriving in a world of virtually charged emoticons. Ingenious refinements. continued steadily. A glossary of terms was already in limited circulation, tailored to the needs of both veterans and novitiates, with heavily coded symbols for the more problematic ways of extracting the needed body parts and introducing new variations in the art of meat carvery that accorded the special commodity just as much aesthetic reverence as beef, mutton, venison, horse, and other herbivores, including ostrich meat, which had lately become fashionable among the cholesterol-conscious elite.

The success of the new enterprise and the rapidity of its growth were a surprise only to those who failed to give credit to specialist marketers who were masters of the profession, had done their feasibility studies across vastly different strata of society, including even the new science of consumerist simulation. The locals being a notoriously suspicious breed of business humanity—not without cause, as every single enterprise, before it was even off the drawing board, had already spawned a dozen or two imitations, fakes, adulterations— care was taken to ensure that no room was left for any confusion between the authentic item and even suspiciously marginal beings like Mami Wata, ologomugomu, ebora, witches iwin, monkey meat, and all other unsuspected, liminal creatures that sometimes appropriated human forms, if the testimonies of fishermen and farmers returning home at twilight were to be believed. Certifications were introduced for halal and nonhalal.

Secrecy was of course the most expensive commodity that went into production—the complete security of operations had to be guaranteed, and by whatever means necessary, given the yet undeveloped state of mind of a populace which was not quite ready to accept innovations even where such innovations were already proliferating and approaching the norm. Hence the intricate alpha-numerical Codex—what a historical cast of mind could possibly have thought that up!—augmented by new images. The inventory expanded all the time, supplementary pages being added online to a bowdlerized version of the Codex Seraphinianus, augmented by images from ancient mythologies—these were developed into an easy-to-memorize lexicon, constantly updated. The choice of the Seraphinianus was a master stroke of public entrapment, since, among other charismatic churches, the cherubim and seraphim order exerted the utmost fascination for even chronic infidels, their immaculate white robes, male and female, floating over the landscape, women's heads topped by a fluffy bonnet, bell and rosary swinging across streets and markets both in and out of devotional services, their demure comportment alternating with musical excitations during the tambourine, drum, and bell chorales at dedicated hours of worship. The mere reference to a Codex Seraphimwhatever was sufficient to imbue the Codex—and the business it served—with the air of scriptural authority that was equaled only by the more ancient catechisms of Christianity and Islam, the priesthood of both well versed in the skills of recruitment and conversion. Once the new commodity market acquired a tinge of religiosity, any lingering reservations among the weak-minded vanished. Trade blossomed under the aegis of spirituality.

It began with just a few, spread to embrace communities, but always under the tightest of controls. Expansion of this shopping community was measured, every sector carefully cultivated, meticulously consolidated. Dissidents were simply bypassed or neutralized through sustained online campaigns of attrition that left them choosing between silence and consignment to mental institutions, their accusations progressively enfeebled by being cast in such a preposterous light as to make them doubt their own faculty of observation, judgment, or sanity. In extreme cases there were disappearances—these had become commonplace anyway. No one asked questions of such sudden gaps in homes, businesses, or family gatherings anymore; the most recent pin-up photos behind the Missing Persons desks at police stations were at least ten years faded. Recruitment was fastidious. Each new client was pledged to recruit only from within a trusted circle, the longer the acquaintance, the safer. Even so, outsiders, especially politicians with diehard constituencies, once thoroughly vetted by the local board of trustees, could also win approval as targets for recruitment.

Penetration of the growing circles of patronage was thus largely groping in the dark. Nonetheless, there had been slips; a few, like Boriga, had been successfully closed down. These were, however, largely training centres whose security was not yet watertight. The wonder was that not one single arrest had been made. Somehow the police raids took place just when the school had shut down operation, or closed down "for vacation," never to resume—that is, not in the same location. What closed down in Yenogoa simply resurfaced in Potiskum. Yet reliable testimony about the training curriculum had been gathered—how to introduce the subject, gauge receptivity, probe leaning, proselytize, when to make the final, factual disclosure—the point of no return. The clean-cut, city-slick salesmen and -women learnt when to abandon early promising clientele as hopeless, what to do where a mistake had been made and the hesitant recruit turned dangerous, betrayed signs of whistle-blowing, or simply acted suspiciously. Cells were already self-reproducing. Each cell had its own supervisor, unknown to other members. But it was mostly a one-on-one process—one-on-one and that one on another ad infinitum. Delivery systems were constantly refined, storages rotated, schedules staggered, and depots changed to frustrate investigation. When a link was broken, it was left alone, unrepaired, but a new circuit was swiftly constructed around the weakened point, just like the stent in a coronary bypass.

The trail was long but meticulously laid. It led inexorably to where the errant limb was destined after excision, what they actually did with the newly designated spare part. It led in turn to that slow, agonizing discovery that in several supermarkets, items on display in the

refrigerated glass cases were only a cover—well, not quite; the innocent still went shopping for normal family consumption—but others
also for far more exotic varieties, and on the sustainable delivery list,
was on sale within the hidden warrens of the stores, of exotic varieties, than in the average shopper's imagination, far more than even
the most extravagant crop exacted by law from *kilishi* vendors and
allied goat enticers. No wonder the latter had such contempt for Boko
Haram and other pretenders to a higher calling, on homicidal duty to
the hereafter.

The head received the utmost reverential treatment, not surprisingly. When the suicide bomber struck, hardly any negotiable parts
were left without some drastic degradation, except the head. For some
reason the head always flew off, and not just Nigerian heads, befit-
tingly known as coconut heads from sheer bounce-around retriev-
able credentials—it appeared to be simply the law of Nature or, more
strictly, the law of dynamite or whatever was packed into the suicide
belt. History and art have stayed on the side of the head. All the way
from Salome and the Dance of the Seven Veils to Saddam Hussein and
his terminal *danse macabre* on the hangman's rope, when the head
separated from the body as the lever was pulled, so the drop proved to
be a rarity, a fleeting rarity of suspension, then a total drop, since the
noose simply slipped off the unanchored neck and the body slammed
downwards into the shallow void. Nigerians are avid followers of the
stellar events of their world, and perhaps these created the phenomenal appreciation of that crown of the human anatomy. Whichever
way, the head was the prime prize, remained very much in demand
even if degraded, as sometimes in the case of a suicide bomber. Even
then its value depreciation was negligible, and it did not take any self-
respecting pathologist that much time to make even a severely mangled
one the centerpiece of the display room in the innermost sanctum, into
which admission was granted only to the crème de la crème of valued
customers. It explained why the police were forever catching suspects
with human heads, sometimes in cellophane wrapping, a shopping
bag, inside a bag of beans, *garri,* or yam or cassava powder. Even once
in a student rucksack, smothered in loaves of bread and bags of mari-
juana. The weed, it turned out, was a clever device by the student cultists. If intercepted, they were certain that the police would pounce on

the weed as their share—that was more immediately marketable and did not require refrigeration. They met their match on that occasion, however, since it was a very strict, no-nonsense patrol which insisted on seizing both head and weed to let the students go free. The forlorn raiders were taking the head to a nocturnal football field to complete a quartet of goalposts—each head stuck on a pole—and they would not start the game until the fourth post was capped, otherwise the ritual was incomplete, which forced them to send a raiding team to the camp of the rival cult for the crucial number four. It was the same cult group, it turned out, that had been negotiating an alliance with Boko Haram for a regular supply of heads, but the match took place at the time of one of the military exercises, code-named *Atari-afori,* and the local commander who had placed himself at the head of Boko Haram's negotiating team was nabbed while buying weapons from one of the military field commanders.

Of course, there was always Onitsha Market—*You can find anything in Onitsha Market, even a human head*. That was supposed to be hyperbole, a permissible turn of phrase or song of praise. In the case of Onitsha Market, it was the latter. A case of gallows humour. You mine humour out of what you know was never meant to be funny. It was also selling strategy—where else do you send souvenir-hungry tourists? *Okporoko* or secondhand clothes markets, even craft villages and historic caves, soon pall. No matter, all tourists love to slum—call it the offbeat sectors where *other* tourists (package variety especially) never dared invade. Onitsha Market was it, but did it retain that reputation after Independence? Always some fire in Onitsha Market, razed to the ground again and again to rise from its ashes—it's known as the phoenix syndrome. War put an end to all that. War of secession, when reality overtook hyperbole. And that was one war that began with images of shell-shocked widows returning to Enugu with the heads of their husbands on flat trays, sitting on their laps . . . The mystique of the head had a long history, long before it became such a commodity hungered after by cultists and politicians, money launderers and kidnappers, to be stored in the refrigerated vaults of upscale supermarkets, supplied on order in advance of elections, court trials, and other heavy-investment ventures.

The infant head remained in a special category of its own, worth a

thousand *mea culpas* in its restoration of innocence invoked and conferred through the cyclic route of infanticide, the sublime irony that
mandates commission as guarantee of immunity. Otherwise, liver,
lungs, kidneys, genitals, spleen, all the vital organs—female breasts,
fingers, etc., etc.—nothing is wasted, all come under prescription, but
the head now, even a fragment of the skull, moved to join rhinoceros
horn as the guaranteed enhancer of male libido and metaphysical control of the rest of humanity, come rain, come sunshine, come reckoning on Judgment Day . . .

MORAL JUDGMENTS ARE risk-laden. Was it truly fair to call the
markets perverse? Scavengers are essential to the Nature cycle; someone had to clean up the mess, and abandoned property does not dis-
criminate. True, dead men tell no tales, but they mostly leave tell-tale
belongings behind. A brand-new pair of Nike sneakers, a gold brace-
let, even the occasional gold watch—some of the wearers just arriving
straight from Dubai and driving home. Christmastide and Ramadan
noted most especially for traffic accidents, accidental discharges, rise
in trafficking, and so on and on. One can hardly cavil at such voluntary sanitation schemes. Nature hates waste. That it had attained
the level of human devaluation was—*pause, pause,* now one thinks
of it—isn't it all only a matter of perspective? Another point of view
could be, and most legitimately, revaluation. A revaluation of *human.*
So what exactly is that? Who had the moral status to assess? Perhaps
only nonhumans, hopefully from outer space.

Hardly a day passed without an "accidental discharge" at both
official and moonlighting roadblocks. Weren't such "accidents"
always the fault of stubborn posturing by those grammar-spouting
know-alls, who claimed to be impeccably versed in their rights, their
civic dignity and legal entitlements? So? The lumpen clodpoles refused
to obey the unwritten law of tort on demand, sometimes no more than
a hundred naira, equivalent of twenty-five cents U.S. currency, hardly
any more than the price of a stick of cigarette in his village, less than
the cost of a *kilishi* wrap. Submission to such a simple law of supply
on demand would grant them leave to proceed without hindrance to
their destination. As principled porters of the burden of law, those

custodians of a people's safety did not deny that greedy ones were to be found within their ranks, rotten eggs in the basket who demanded five hundred—a full U.S. dollar and a half—and felt a counter offer of a mere two or three hundred—forty to sixty cents—a mortal insult that could be expunged only with an "accidental discharge" that split the egghead wide open and scrambled its yolk on the tarmac. The consequence remained the same—and someone must clean up afterwards. Enter the scavengers. A new statistic entered the local lore of transformative power, while the new industry raced to replenish its stock of consumer material. Menka did not even bother to include the steady carnage on the roads, the voluntary supply line that advertised its latest contribution under lurid headlines—"Ghastly Motor Accident in Kogi State: Seventy-Three Passengers Killed Instantly"; **"Luxury Bus Overturns and Catches Fire: A Hundred and Thirteen Passengers Roasted to Death"; "Why the Hasty Burial? Missing: Traders' Merchandise."** Or pipeline explosions as an existential norm in the heart of cities. They evaporated communities in one sensational flash, hurling sleeping citizens through the midnight air to shower their shreds over ponds and gutter streams of petroleum leakage until scattered communities attain one roaring consummation of fire. Union at last!

Innumerable times Menka found himself musing over the latest crop of human flares, usually with himself fresh but drained from yet another massed surgical marathon. How did it take so long for the new market venture to spring to life and catch fire? Sooner or later, however, the law of supply and demand asserts itself. The process was impeccable, human sensibilities coarsened by the very language of transmission. Being merely trapped in an overturned bus and burnt alive loses place in soup kitchens of empathy, becomes more distinctly palatable when transmitted as being "roasted beyond recognition." Rare? Medium? Char-grilled or overdone beyond caloric value? Indifference turns to active toleration, butchery turns vicarious, a form of grim but gleeful participatory theatre. How was it possible not to anticipate the logical end, the terminus of remorseless logics of a progressive dulling of sensibilities that underlay the furtive patronage of a once unthinkable commerce? Unthinkable? Just when was it last deemed unthinkable? When did abnormalities cease to be the norm? Difficult to set a date. Mail order of disposables of morbidity—yes, that much Menka had grimly predicted. Orders via the internet—it was bound to be the next stage: *I bought it on eBay! Blood and Brain Spatter as Retrieved. Certificate of Authenticity by the XYZ Police Patrol, Attestation by Selfie.* Like fast-food restaurants where you could view a menu complete with itemized descriptions rendered near-irresistible by luscious photography. Prized possessions under auction, heirlooms . . . after all, even Lost and Found has an expiry date. In the end, no claimants, up for auction. Yet even the geniuses of National Pre-eminence had yet to touch the logical destination where, propelled by technology, a market had moved business beyond fumbling beginnings into streamlined online transactions. But it had. It had.

Indeed it had. And it affected all four—inadvertently thrown together in a freakish pursuit in subtle to blatant ways. Duyole, in his immediate all-pistons-firing response, soon dubbed the improvised quartet the Worrisome Foursome, himself at the arrow head as the Guerrilla Worrier—to be distinguished from the Gong o' Four. It was apt. They worried even routine notifications from their banks, online bargain enticements, real-estate promotions and even familiar online cookies, presumably destined to be understood only by the Codex insiders. Even Zoom invitations to social and professional events. Words, normally innocent, took on suspect connotations. The innovation of drive-throughs—common with pharmacies, McDonalds, Kentucky Fried Chicken, etc. elsewhere—where purchases were made through car windows—took on conspiratorial angles—just who were those sitting behind tinted windows, making orders across special inset kiosks at the end of sectioned-off departments of shopping malls? Only shamelessly tight-fisted Nigerian Big Men went shopping on their own, or accompanying their stewards or housekeepers, yet some had taken to the despised ranks of "a go drive myself" plutocrats. Or else were driven through such sections, made orders through the driver but took immediate possession of both room temperature and refrigerated packages. Orders would have been placed in advance by numbers, by email or telephone. The driver received but passed the goodies immediately to Big Man seated in the "owner's corner," where it promptly disappeared into a briefcase, or the voluminous pockets of the *agbada*.

For Baftau, it amounted to finding a new mission in life. At the mandatory send-off meal for the Jos visitors, the old man revealed that he had abandoned the normal haunts of his infrequent visits to Lagos. Instead he had asked to be driven to the meat markets, strolled through the stalls like any shopper or anonymous inspector, unaccompanied. *I wanted to be sure the diabolism hadn't arrived at the stage of meat-swaps,* he confessed. *You never know with such people.* Costello moved among his local colleagues posing probing questions, eyeing each with unaccustomed suspicion and checking on their shopping habits. At least, he reassured himself, there was no indication yet of any Nigerian-made salami or sausages in the cold cuts sections of the gourmet delicatessens. A change in Duyole was the most observable. He seemed unable to disguise the fact that the situation irked him. He was the acknowledged problem solver, had failed to put his finger instantly on the vital key to unraveling a clearly entrenched marketing revolution, yet he was condemned to be far away from it all in a few days. Bisoye noticed the sharp drop in the normal ebullience of her irrepressible spouse. Still, she put it down to his approaching relocation to the United Nations, a move whose implications only began to sink in as he progressively organized that departure.

It's like a parasite, Menka mumbled. It enters the body, feeds on it and, in some cases, takes it over completely. Knowing that is bad enough. When it starts to proliferate, where do you begin?

The mood lightened only when Bisoye re-entered the dining room, stood behind Duyole's chair, and theatrically placed her palm on his forehead, as if to check for any signs of a feverish onset. Her guests, at first puzzled, moved to tease the couple at the show of affection. She shook her head.

"I've been worried about him over the past few days. Something is wrong. He never once interfered in my preparations for your send-off lunch—that's a record. Not once. Not even when it was downgraded from dinner so Papa Baftau could catch his flight back to Jos."

The ensuing outburst changed the somber atmosphere and brought them back to their accustomed selves. More or less. The good-byes were far more genial, upbeat. Even Menka began to feel reconciled to the implications of his hurried transplant. In any case, Lagos, he was certain, would lead the Boriga thread to its legitimate conclusion. He had known Duyole the longest, recognized his moods, and could bet his silver graduation scalpel that his friend was already up to something. He detected those familiar spells of absence, terminated by a sudden boisterous cover-up as he rejoined the company. In a way, it was almost back to student days and company.

Sated, Kighare returned to his apartment after Jos departed Lagos. He collapsed on the bed, fully clothed, in that blissful state of mind of an active interlude where one is confident that a problem has been assumed by others, no different from the adoption of a problem child. The surgeon no longer felt isolated. In any case he was too full to even make a pretence of attempting a further dent on the debris strewn around the rooms. Within seconds, he was fast asleep. He woke up hours later not knowing where he was, what time of the day it was, only with that out-of-body sensation of believing that you have woken up on a yet undiscovered planet. It was a short-lived sensation.

Suddenly Dr. Menka realized what had woken him up—the sound of an explosion. He sat up, listened intently. There were no further noises. No cries, no panicked movements, no cries for help, no disordered movements, curses, or praise of GodAllah. A veteran of Boko Haram's embattled northeastern front, he felt something familiar percolate through, even to his half-awakened senses. He got up, listening intently while he walked slowly to the window to look in the direction of the main house. No, there was no sign even of a fire, no flicker of impending flames, but he was certain that the deadly sound had emerged from the main house of the family home.

17.

A Deadly Rivalry

That vitality gone? It did not seem possible. Dissipate, drain away, just like that? Against all his professional valuation, Dr. Kighare Menka fought to persuade himself that the figure lying on the hospital bed, seemingly inert, was bursting inside with the world's collective energy, only it was under suspended animation. Any moment now the tormenting deactivation would end, his friend Duyole would erupt with new schemes now under hidden gestation, an effervescent laugh that childishly mocked, *Et tu, Brute?* Fooled you too! Such a force of life knew no restraint, accepted no disabilities. It was not for a lack of contenders in that special league of zero inhibition. All the way from boarding school, many had tried to rein in that spirit. Even he, acknowledged the closest, longest-suffering friend, would sometimes give Duyole a kick under the table. The response was guaranteed—a frontal discomfiture: *Stop mangling my ankle!* The company would take his side, leaving the restraining toe-cap buried under uproarious laughter. That now-recumbent form knew the effect he created in others. He relished it. It inspired him to exceed his last outrageous provocation on any space of tranquility, any space that was content with simply being left alone. Affronting neither man nor beast. There had been times in those early days when, feeling suddenly overwhelmed, even threatened by such overabundance of sheer zest, Menka felt that his salvation lay in attempting to rival him, to prove that he also could exude such spontaneity of the sheer joy of life, that he had it in him, only preferred to keep it in check, to draw on it for special occasions. He ended up conceding defeat. And who would be the first to rub his nose in it? None other than the gloating provocateur. *At heart, Gumchi Kid, you are just a desert hermit on temporary leave of absence.*

Duyole Pitan-Payne—and never was a double-barreled calling card rolled out by its owner with such vintage-port relish—*Aduyole Pitan-Payne speaking* . . . Yes, Menka nodded ruefully, his friend was right. For that surgeon from a little-known village called Gumchi, the most recent and definitive test had begun barely two months before, his reticent self placed dead centre of public attention and already wilting from the burst of notoriety. Even the handful of appearances he could not successfully escape felt like unseasonal heatwaves of public exposure, left him wishing he had never even heard of a national medal of honour. Or else that it had happened in a different environment where such incidents were taken in stride, nothing different from the new coat of paint that was once acquired by Gumchi's one and only neighbourhood shop—no increased clientele, no branching out, no diversifications, no media photo shoot, just a one-glance wonder and back to its business of selling cigarettes by the stick, condensed milk by the can, sugar by the cube, salt by the spoonful, mini-piles of kola nut on a tray, the neatly folded flat brown paper wraps of the famous *kilishi,* dried horsemeat, rounded up with an assortment of knick-knacks that looked more like leftovers rescued from the nearby capital, Abuja, to provide Gumchi a veneer of commercial activity. At such moments Menka missed Gumchi with protesting pangs of unfair deprivation.

He had not resisted when his colleagues denied him a place on the surgical team. He knew them all, had worked with them in the past. He was capable of banning emotions to one side, cutting up his friend, probing and sewing him up again. His hands would be steady as on any other patient, but the others firmly said no. They gave him a stool in the theatre, and he watched the tutored motions of their hands, sometimes the expressions on their masked faces. He followed the silent communication between them, born of decades of practice, and knew exactly what their hands were doing—probing, cutting, suturing. All that he had been able to bear. Indeed, without handling a pair of forceps, probing a tissue to extract one foreign body after another, he felt his hands at one with theirs and knew his friend was in reassuring hands. It all seemed unreal, he as spectator while others did the work, but he admitted it was best that way. He knew when the patient went into shock, then slipped into a coma. When it was all over, they wheeled him out together, settled him in intensive care. Now Menka was merely keeping watch. The coma was into a second, then a third day. All he could do was run reels of distractions through his mind—anything but dwell on prospects. Just keep him alive, both physically and in mind.

The impossible task was to detach himself from that patient, leaving only the friend, the same overqualified surrogate whose list of visitors was tightly controlled. And they were compelled to wear surgical masks to reduce the risk of infection. Infection? The surgeon found such a concern ironic—a precaution raised in the wrong direction. Any infection would be nothing more than fair returns. This friend had infected all and sundry with his rampaging virus of existence. It seemed unfair to others. Now was payback time when that antiseptic space, fenced off by clinical green screens, should be humming with friends, colleagues, and gate-crashers, lending him vibrations of strength, but they had all been banished. Resisting to the last, even his wife, Bisoye, had been forced out on that first day, but only into another room, assigned a bed and sedated until relations could come and take her home. She returned to a home where messages of sympathy and public outrage had replaced the stack of invitation cards then being readied for distribution. Saturday that weekend had been designated the multi-mega-magnum party by none other than the patient himself. And this was despite the event being supposedly conceded to his wife's less gregarious charge—menu, invitation list, band, décor, event souvenirs, and whatever else defined a Pitan-Payne splurge. It was, after all, her initiative in the first place—a send-off bash for her irrepressible spouse, headed for a United Nations assignment.

That was once-upon-forgotten time. Reality in progress left her with futile protests as that very object of celebration took it over, turning it into a triple-pronged affair. There was now Menka's success to celebrate, Duyole reminded wife and household, gardeners, callers, and guard dogs indiscriminately. *He thinks he's one up on me, but you wait, he has another thing coming. I intend to bury his award under this shindig.* Next the return of Damien, the prodigal son, so *get your Bible arithmetic right, darling girl—that calls for the slaughter of two fatted calves, one for Damien, one for Menka. Think I've forgotten?* Menka's crime, at least thirty years without hope of remission, remained an enduring excuse. The Gumchi Kid had chosen to defect after his return from graduation in Bristol, heading north where his home was instead of joining his "twin" down south in Lagos. Even when Menka was passing through Lagos en route to somewhere else, or stopping over on return, a mere sighting of him was a return of the prodigal son, each celebration more prodigal than the last.

Factually—and it was wise always to check on Pitan-Payne—the designation, as it happened, was more appropriate for Damien, the long-lost son, who had surfaced in the home under mysterious circumstances, already long in the tooth at thirty-six but kitted out with a wife and two children. The mystery was no such thing to Menka. He still winced every time he recalled the discreet negotiations that ultimately succeeded in reinserting the smooth rolling stone into the family hearth, overcoming fierce opposition from Duyole's sister, whose right of possession seemed even more violently embedded than anyone ever remotely discerned in his wife, Bisoye. She was, after all, mistress of the home, and thus the one who had the right of first refusal, as was muttered and bruited around in baffled accents from both interventionists and armchair commentators. Even preceding her in entitlement logic would be the two products of his early "off-shore" marriage, Katia and Debbie, from a black Canadian. They voiced no resentment of the family addition—more accurately, revelation. Selina brushed all such counters aside. *Only after these breasts have withered,* she thundered as she cupped both breasts in her hands as warning of a long wait ahead for all such optimists. *You want to feel how firm they still are? And that's no Botox!* She threatened to camp on the couple's doorstep night and day sooner than have an "imposter" pollute the Pitan-Paynes' vintage bloodline. *That bastard son and his second-generation white-trash bastards? God forbid bad thing!* Even the inevitable capitulation was of the most ungracious, bitter, and unforgiving mode. She boycotted the Pitan-Payne home for months until called to order by the family patriarch, Pop-of-Ages—name acquired from his favorite hymn, "Rock of Ages"—to whom one and all deferred, some of the time.

The pseudo-prodigal on bedside watch felt his shoulders sag as one pummeled all over again from the sheer recollection of his family meddling, albeit on passionate invitation by Duyole himself, his mediation embraced with relief by all, including Sister Selina. Menka was her face-saving *deus ex machina* parachuted directly from heaven. It elevated him instantly in her private family rating—still marginal, no more than an honorary status, but still, thenceforth entitled to be referred to as "family doctor." There already was one, his ancient portfolio routinely extended down from the patriarch himself to cover every new blood addition or tolerated attachment. However, it did not hurt to be able to indulge in the occasional throw-aside—*As I was saying to one of our family doctors, you know, the famous Dr. Menka, the celebrated surgeon . . .*

The two brothers were among the earliest callers, not long after Menka and the ambulance which he had immediately ordered had left. He declined to await the arrival of the bomb squad as ordered down the line by the police. *You do your duty when you can,* he said. *I'll do mine, and when is now,* and switched off the phone. The bomb squad, the noise and chaos, and the mad ambulance wail to the hospital had roused the entire neighbourhood, most of whom did hear the sound, thought it was yet another petroleum tanker. Or yet another building imploding on itself. These had become the companion sounds of existence. Thereafter the processions began—home, hospital, mortuary, in and out of the famous landmark, the Millennium Towers. At the hospital, only a handful of closest family were permitted anywhere near. Duyole's business partners, all junior, resented being kept at bay but were mostly understanding. There was Ekete, diminutive Ekete, dapper even in evident distress; Runjaiye, always with an air of permanent bewilderment, yet the stiffening backbone of staff productivity. The loyal caterer and family friend Sisi Sangross arrived accompanied by a maid carrying a headload of fresh catfish, *eja osan,* right into hospital, unable to understand why she had to be denied entry with her offering, only reluctantly agreeing to redirect her feet to the home instead. Learning that Bisoye had been taken back to the home, under sedation, all resentment vanished and she flew to the house to be by her side.

At the hospital the trickle became a flood of disappointed callers. It would be another three days before the two girls from Duyole's first marriage arrived, one from the United Kingdom, the other from the United States. For now it was shocked and sympathizing clients, media snoopers, club members . . . Sir Goddie sent a special delegation conveying sympathies and a promise of vengeance on the perpetrators. The emissaries specifically asked the son Damien to call on the People's Steward as soon as possible.

Estate agent Kikanmi, the Brain of Badagry, felt especially put-upon. He arrived at the house soon after the departure of the ambulance and was instantly joined by the general-purpose salesman. They met an inconsolable Godsown, their ancient steward, seated on the doorstep, both hands holding up his head. He pointed a shaking finger in the direction the ambulance had gone—*They done kill oga-o, they done bomb oga finish. Ambulance take in body go, etc., etc.* The two brothers joined forces, raced directly to the hospital mortuary, expressed irritation to be redirected to the hospital, then to the surgery theatre, where they were even more astonished at their exclusion from the operating room, being advised instead to return hours later or else wait at the postsurgery anteroom, where they might just obtain a glimpse of the patient being wheeled past. Kikanmi, his nose permanently turned skywards in umbrage at his surroundings, took his plaint straight to the presumed occupant of that space.

"What a backward country! In other places there is a window through which one can watch the operation." He returned to his rounds of duty, Teahole to his golf club.

Within hours the social media was dripping with blood: "The UN Energy Nominee Bombed, Mangled Beyond Recognition." Yet the same unrecognizable mush was being flown in one of the presidential fleet to New York for treatment, with no one lesser than the nation's chief of air staff at the controls.

And the same UFO was wheeled out on a guerney through the double doors of the operating theatre of the University Teaching Hospital situated in southern Nigeria, Dr. Menka pushing at the handbar himself. He remained somewhat dazed by the uncanny pursuit of déjà vu, this time seemingly personally directed. He found himself yet again following a familiar routine—left the hospital for his apartment some six hours after the operation, even though he had not physically participated. He went straight into the bathroom and relaxed under the shower. Afterwards, hot coffee with a double dose of milk and sugar, then headed back to the hospital. He stopped at the main house to check on the stricken wife. Godsown had been dislodged from the doorstep but was now seated on the stool normally occupied by the security unit, staring into space. His former position was occupied by a fully armed and kitted detective, who refused him entry. Godsown raced up to explain who he was. The policeman was adamant. Only the listed inmates were allowed entrance—on orders.

Menka restrained Godsown's looming outburst. "Just call me Damien."

Godsown shook his head. "But Mr. Damien dey hospital."

Menka paused. Only then did it occur to him that he had not seen Damien since he had driven off with the ambulance that morning.

A car drove up. It was Runjaiye from the office. Menka's face lit up. Seeing the hyperefficient Runjaiye reassured him yet again that there was someone who would hold the fort while the boss was incapacitated.

"I am not allowed in," he informed the junior partner. "We're trying to find Damien. Is he at the office?"

"No. Isn't he at the hospital?"

"No. I was hoping he was at the office."

"He did come to the office. I assumed he came to check that everything was all right. He was in Mr. Payne's office most of the time. Then he left, I assumed for the hospital."

Menka shook his head. "I remember now—he did say something to me, but it was all rather chaotic. Naturally all I wanted was to get Duyole in the ambulance and off. Bisoye refused to leave his side. I told the driver to take off at once."

Godsown intervened. "He go back inside house. Say he wan' go lock Master workshop where the bomb blow so nobody can tamper with anything until police come. Then afterwards he drive commot. I think say 'e follow you all go hospital."

"All right, let him know I was here. Just wanted to check on

Madam. I'll be at the hospital from now on. Be sure to call me as soon as she wakes up. We gave her some medicine to make her sleep, you understand?"

"Oh yessah. I see when nurse bring her back. They carry her go bed straightaway. The housemaid dey with her. And Sisi Sangross come stay with her."

"Good." He turned to Runjaiye and pointed at the detective. "Please get hold of this man's boss and let him know that doctors need to see their patients."

MENKA WAS STILL struggling to keep his eyes open and read past the same open page at which he appeared to have stalled since he took up position. At least here he could exercise his privilege as doctor where others had been expelled. It had been a long watch. He was resolved to be present when the slightest eye flicker or muscle twitch signaled a renewed claim on life. Each time his head lolled and jerked him back into wakefulness, he cast a quick look at the bed, hopeful that Duyole had not woken up and caught him nodding. He could already hear the patient's unswerving rebuke, the same retort whenever Menka warned against driving himself too hard—*Physician, heal thyself*. Menka felt overdue for ministration beyond rest; some serious healing was definitely on prescription.

More than keeping watch over Duyole assailed him, body and soul. If only it were all limited to *Physician, heal thyself*. Menka feared that it actually came down to *Physician, know thyself!* There was the seeming conversion of his body into a battlefield for keeping nightmares at bay, a fallout from grim discoveries that would forever dog his surgical faith. The award only made matters worse—the public exposure—just when he craved, longed for total anonymity, the best award imaginable, the gift of vanishing . . . and then, suddenly, a commotion!

Menka could not believe his ears, but . . . no indeed, he was wide awake, was not in the middle of a nightmare, and was not hallucinating. Within that clinical, healing atmosphere, nothing less than a violent wind was racing up the stairs in human accents. It approached the final flight, pursued by two, then three pairs of restraining hands and frantic pleading: "Madam, Madam, please, Madam—the patients . . ." The wind was, however, beyond recall. Menka threw himself out of the chair and raced to intercept it before it arrived at his floor and swept into Duyole's curtained-off space—he had recognized one female voice and it made him all the more angry. It was none other than the patient's younger sister, Selina.

"Broda mi, broda mi, se'wo l'araiye fe se bayi?"[*]

Oblivious to everyone within sight or hearing, she raced upstairs, a clear bottle of water in one hand, executing mysterious motions alternately around her head and outwards in sharp thrusts away from herself in the direction of unseen enemies, the other hand fending off restraint. Simultaneously she ejected a stream of Yoruba maledictions on all those whose envy had presumably organized the assault on the patient: "They will not succeed! You will defeat them all. You will go to the United Nations and you will return unharmed. You will earn greater honours. The world will know the name Pitan-Payne. Those who hate to hear the name will go deaf from the sound of that name in Jesus's name. The mean-spirited people of this world, envious of the blessed, those who never wish good on those whom they see being successful, whom they see prospering, whom they see doing good to others, showering good on others, those to whom greatness will forever remain an unknown commodity in Jesus's name since they cannot stand to see it in others, those whose sole goal in life is to cut down others in their prime, to ambush them on their way to glory, to drag others down from the heights of fulfillment, heights attained through the industry of their hands—oh, we know them, we know their dirty machinations, but they will sink down on their knees of failure, never to rise again in Jesus's name amen. They can pretend to any friendship they like, but God will expose them all. God will finish them off, God will frustrate their plots. I swear it, my brother, none of them will live to see their evil thoughts triumph in Jesus's name."

It was an electrifying performance. She seemed possessed, as if there were no other human being in that hospial, with her coming straight from some pool of psychic fortification whose energies—as per instructions—she was to discharge directly at the recumbent fig-

---

[*] "Brother, my brother, is it you that the malicious world has tried to maltreat in this manner?"

ure before their potency became dissipated through delay, through a mundane counteracting motion or spell, such as acknowledging the existence of the surgeon friend who tried to intercept her charge.

"I want to see my brother. He's been with you people for two days now. Where are you hiding him? I want to see what the enemy has done to him."

"Control yourself, Selina."

"Who are you? Don't you dare tell me what to do about my brother!"

"Selina, this is me, Kighare—"

"And so? Are you his flesh and blood? I say I must see my brother."

"You will. But you must be quiet. He's resting. Don't disturb him."

"They've killed him. I know they've killed him. You are all lying to me."

"Quietly, I said. You must be quiet or I'll throw you out myself. I'll throw you down those stairs."

That appeared to check her in stride. She looked at him in some astonishment. By now visitors to other patients were emerging to watch the commotion. Dr. Menka led her to Duyole's cubicle and pointed, pulling the curtain further to seal him off completely. Baffled, he watched Selina fall on her knees, bury her face in the mattress, and commence sobbing. It was a dry, racking sob that did not provide a tear. He let it run its course. As if to make up for the drought, she stood up and proceeded to circle the bed, bottle in hand, sprinkling its contents on the floor. That done, she again fell to her knees, this time selecting a position next to the head. Then she began to mouth prayers, exploding into voice from time to time. Dr. Menka signaled to the nurses to withdraw.

She remained in communication with unknown forces for another few minutes. When she was done, she stood up, smoothed her dress, and looked Kighare Menka over.

"I warned you not to bring that bastard into the family home. Ill luck, that's what you brought to the family."

She left. Quiet fell over the hospital ward. Dr. Menka checked his patient. There was no change in his condition. He resumed his watch. The interruption had banished all drowsiness and replaced it with a feeling of mockery, the resentment of a self-imposed inadequacy.

What was the point of all that training and reputation if he could not even remotely assess the depth of Duyole's coma? Or connect with him in some way, at some level? To be able to claim with some assurance that the engineer was *thinking* anything where he was? Surely some effort at recollection was in progress and thought neurons had a way of connecting. Anything shared from the past? Nothing profound or spectacular on demand, just something, any trivia to hang on to, something that ensured that one thread, however frayed, remained unbroken. Then transmission from his own realm of competence could commence. Contact. Gradually that thread would wind his friend back, inch by inch, to real life, across no matter how deep or wide the gulf!

The specialist surgeon, model of clinicality, set to, trawled his weighted net in a succession of reels, of which there was no shortage. The humdrum was tossed overboard. Duyole's track was littered with esoteric jaunts on which he would sometimes expend just as much time and energy as on his prized—and lucrative—mechanical inventions. One of that engineer's pastimes was to fabricate useless but eloquent gadgets, mostly conversions. Disgusted like millions of his fellow sufferers with the ritual failure of the nation's electricity agency, he once offered the national power agency, known as NEPA, his "masterpiece solution." This was a gadget which, he claimed, generated darkness outside Nature's regulation solar hours. He parceled the prototype to the minister of power, Menka providing the accompanying note: *This leaves you free to concentrate on the production of light, since Nigerians can now produce their own darkness at the flick of this switch.* Neither was willing to risk a bet that a high-placed employee would not race to the Patents Office with the monster trying to pass it off as his own invention. The Kids "R" Us robotic castoff, impressively augmented with silvered bottle tops, broken glass pieces, hundreds of the oblong seeds of the flamboyant tree, spokes from an ancient Raleigh bicycle in flaring circles, all emitting a fearsome roar when wound up, adorns the Patents vaults still today in a section marked ENERGY SOLUTIONS.

No sooner had Kighare Menka launched himself on that reverie than he found himself shutting it off with a shudder. The doctor was not superstitious—at least he tried to persuade himself he was not—

but this was no time to invoke darkness, even in jest, not while it was the crowing usurper of Duyole's consciousness. He scrambled desperately for a replacement—something no less manic, perhaps, also spelling mischief, laughter, certainly a swarming human concourse, a rain of bright pebbles that would land on Duyole's head and provoke him into wakefulness from wherever he was presently trapped. His mind wandered to shared Oktoberfests; together they had ploughed their way through the beer gardens of Bavaria. The raucous, high-decibel yodeling was soon silenced by recollection of the family feud—place of origin of the out-of-wedlock-son affair—and Menka just as quickly segued into the more neutral operatic arena, definitely a Pitan-Payne favourite roost. It was far more comfortable, but not where Menka could immerse himself for long with the mandatory concentration, since the doctor was notoriously tone-deaf and would sometimes loudly wonder why serious actors should choose to warble dialogue when they could simply talk like normal beings. He continued to rifle the warehouse—well, a halfway house perhaps? His favourite mix—the arts, yes, but business bordered, eating as the primal art, and what of healing and culture?

From this had sprung the alternative medicine phase—*A first step, of course, just the first step*—always a first step with Pitan-Payne, groundbreaking for something bigger, grander, more elaborate, more intricate. That was where his blithe spirit found sufficient roving space, in a geodesic bubble mind which, unlike the rolling stone, gathered moss of the most nutritious kind. *Look, you butcher, where there's traditional disease, there must be traditional cure. Look at Lassa fever—man can't even eat bush meat anymore. One day the hunters will rebel and I'll join them. Those oyinbo people have left us to solve it all by ourselves—why not? And that Ebola? How do we know the solution is not here? I mean, in traditional medicine. They claim it's our disease. Who cares? It's who cures it! It all boils down to a choice between the laboratory and the mortuary.*

Kighare flinched at the word but this time refused to back off, shaking his head defiantly and compelling the reel to continue. The aggravated exchange over Duyole's instinct that Gumchi held the key helped. *Now, a pristine village like Gumchi—just the place to research trado-medicine. Unspoilt. Close to Nature.* And Menka's own screaming reservations: *Can you get this into your head? I am only a surgeon. My specialization is to cut people up, after others have recommended that course of action.* Enter the aggravating pause and the practiced shock of innocence. *Oh? But doctor is doctor, once it's not a PhD. Wait, wait, not so fast. Let's backtrack. I knew it! Thought you'd got away with it, didn't you? I knew I'd heard that before—Muhammad Ali, that's who—What do I do for a living? I beat people up. You stole his line—shame on you!*

Menka, the triggering intent forgotten, remained wrapped up in a long-distance FaceTime call on Gumchi airwaves. Like a divination tablet, Duyole's jotting pad had emerged, jumped into place on his lap as they argued in his workshop, his enthusiasm blotting out everything else. The pencil began to flash all over its glossed surface. An hour later they had reached the stage of sealing the deal with his ritual prize libation, the single-malt Laphroaig, fifty years fermenting in the barrel, donated by that effusively satisfied client—remember him? That dangling project, the work-in-progress always on the mind, abandoned, retrieved, revisited, revised, rebuking, beckoning—surely that hyperactive brain would recall it all, fight to retrieve it, reinvest it where it belonged. It had to arrest his flotation in directionless space, reactivate the glint that had seemed glued to his retinas from birth, a glint also of uninhibited self-mockery. Menka continued to track that glint as it shifted purpose wildly, its owner picking up a phone in his presence to shut down the office early so as to lead his staff to a child-naming ceremony, join in a clan reunion or a retirement party of the gardener or security guard, chuckling, "You know, it's embarrassing, but I think we're getting the better part of the bargain—much too much. Did you see their faces when we turned up? Just seeing how they sparked, and I felt ready to dash to the workshop and put in another eight hours solid. It's unfair."

Pitan-Payne would interrupt a long-laid agenda to commandeer a spontaneous office party for an employee who had just become engaged. Known to Menka only was perhaps the true impulse of the one that set a record in office binges within the upscale commercial sector of Badagry. The lovelorn employee had brought the fiancé round—it seemed to be the house tradition—for general inspection. From a quick lunch-hour drinks break, the party grew and spilled over into the adjoining boardroom, then downstairs to the display room to accommodate gate-crashers from other offices closing for the day—they knew a good thing was when the lights came on after hours in the Pitan-Payne iconic landmark. In Lagos for a medical conference, Menka found himself cast as impromptu guest of honour—*For moral support, Gumchi, for moral support. I distrust the man.* So why bother? Why go to all the trouble? *Guilt,* cheerfully admitted the engineer. *Guilt. Never met the man before, never heard of him, so why should I distrust him? It's her choice, and she's one of the best. You see how everyone is pouring in? It's for her. They all love her—ask anyone up and down the street, or the markets where she does our shopping.*

You're just perverse, Menka sighed. *Admit it, you like parties. The desk bores you, unlike the workshop. I've observed it—you never come up with a party idea from your workshop, it's only when you're in the office.*

And again the sudden stop, the five-second rumination. *You think that's true?* A thought check crowned with a frown—duration five seconds maximum. Planning had already commenced for the next. *Stress will kill one with casus belli—time we let casus belly dictate the pace!* Same meticulous planning, even for the short-notice inflictions. Same attention. Same personal supervision. Same ardour. Same insane enthusiasm, once undertaken, his favourite formula of "inverse proportion" dominating the scale of extravagance as he extracted the hospitality chequebook—*The lower the ranks, the higher the thanks.*

Impossible to accept that this was the man whose life was ebbing away before his eyes.

Who else would set about so single-mindedly to dispel the regret that continued to prey on Menka's mind—the usual mix of logic and zaniness, interspersed with anecdotal distractions and hard, creative propositions to take his mind off that past? *You did what you considered your duty, now forget it. And if you can't altogether, at least you're doing something about those who won't let you forget it—the flesh exploiters and racketeers.* But the shadow did not prove that easy to dispel, wringing from Menka the sudden explosive wish that his path had never crossed that of the *kilishi* seller with goat abduction as a sideline! A mistake, when he finally confided the cause of the sudden descent of dejection, right in the midst of a gathering, reserving the gritty denouement for when they were alone. *Kilishi* seller! The perfect provocation for a compulsive raconteur and irrepressible mimic, even where he was a third- or seventh-hand recipient, not an eyewitness. Duyole needed no more than a phrase, perhaps simply overheard and detached from context, and the ready-made transmitter recast a scene and sent it tumbling on a wild ride to the uttermost limits of creative licence. *Did I hear you right? Horsemeat hawker my foot! The man is a genius. You mean he actually said, "Your Worship, I did not steal the goat, it merely followed me home"?*

Duyole's calculated pause and slowed-down motion of a skewered morsel en route to his mouth at the dinner table restored the broken smile on Menka's face to its fullest dimension. Pity, it was still certain to have failed to bring even a fractional ghost of it to the wagging goatees of the Sharia court that pronounced the verdict. The learned jurists were not amused. They were even less impressed by the defence counsel, who rephrased the vendor's version of events in convoluted legal jargon that was incomprehensible even to the court interpreter. The accused had already pleaded guilty, and the rest was "grammar." Unlawful possession was stealing—and there an end. A double pity no one had thought of inviting Duyole Pitan-Payne to testify in his capacity as *amicus curiae,* albeit never called to the bar, contributing nothing beyond repeating the defence of the accused in his own vocal register to break the humourless wall of turbans set against the redemptive prospects surely lodged in the heart of the average goat stealer! Variations would be unnecessary, just Duyole's mimic whine of the one-liner—*The goat followed me home, Your Worships.* Over dinner, Duyole needed no further provocation to embark on his routine, placing the fault squarely on the defence counsel: *They should have insisted on rephrasing the charges. Changed it from stealing to enticement. Question: Was it a he- or a she-goat? Assuming it was a he, the accused probably bleated like a she on heat, thus inducing the goat to follow him home. Hunters do that, they master the calls of the wild to entice their quarry to the kill. The counsel should have called on the accused and made him bleat like a she-goat. The goat would respond amorously and . . . case dismissed! Anyway, isn't it notorious knowledge that the verdict is always decided in advance, and by the village head? Much depends also on the party affiliation of the accused. In any case, where was the press? Not a bleat from them that anyone can recall. . . .*

"A-M-B . . ."

Stirred into consciousness, slowly, a little disorientated, but . . .

"A.M.B."

Clear, unmistakable, albeit weak, the voice of his "twin." A bass-baritone voice emerging almost spectrally enfeebled, as if it could not bear the weight of consciousness as he clambered into its peripheries. Menka was startled out of his bedside chair. He felt mildly displeased with himself. *Watch and pray*—wasn't this why he had taken up residence by Duyole's bedside? He passed the back of his hand over his eyes, blinked.

"Duyo?"

Who else could it have been? There were just the two of them in the screened-off corner of the recovery ward. And in any case, whose irreverent self ever called him Absent-Minded Butcher? Still somewhat shakily awake, Menka turned his eyes slowly in the direction of the sound that he was now certain had emerged from the propped-up head. The occupant of the bed tilted his head slightly in Menka's direction.

"Keep still." Menka heard his own voice, hoarse with emotion. His reward was a febrile smile from the patient. Menka returned it. "Where have you been, my friend?"

The retort was true Pitan-Payne. Menka stood over the bed and managed to lip-read, "No, where have *you* been? I've been watching you over an hour."

Menka grinned sheepishly, overwhelmed.

Factually it was a mere five minutes, even slightly less, since he had emerged from the coma, kept still for some seconds, rolled his eyes to obtain his bearings, registered Menka through the watery corner of one eye, and settled there, puzzled. But that was Duyole Pitan-Payne for you. It was the only indication needed by anyone who ever crossed his path that the famed jewel in the Pitan-Payne dynastic crown had indeed been restored to the extended family display room, and with undimmed sparkle. Friends, family, and business had long abandoned all presumption that such an acknowledged technical mind would leave others discomfited by a strict adherence to facts, but no, the engineer blithely dismissed such dry-as-dust entities if they got in his way, that way being a mission to "celebrate" facts so as to eliminate boredom from the world. As for a mutually intertwined scenario being guided along Gumchi neural paths by Menka's desperate watch to lure him back to his friends and family, he of course had no notion. Pitan-Payne woke up wondering what he was doing in a screened-off section of the reception room, scattering and reordering his thoughts for a prime ministerial audience. What he found strange, an instant later, was that he was not merely there but lying flat on his back, under some constraint, yet waiting to be summoned into His Presence. There was a bedside sink, with the now mandatory hand sanitizer, supposed to fend off the raging virus—that was the sole image that linked him to a slipped memory. He last recalled it as a cloud-blue porcelain sink, the moisturizer encased in a soft, padded sheath, branded with the national crest. Now the sink was a gleaming white, slightly cracked at eye level; the sanitizer bottle was plain, while a faint smell of antiseptic replaced the parfumerie of the anteroom to the reception. As his mind raced to unscramble the mystery, a name invaded his mind, an unfavourite but irresistible character from a distant fictional world to which Duyole had remained addicted all his life—the world of Charles Dickens. He made no attempt to explain it, even to himself, but that world dominated a large part of his existence, which appeared to have begun larger than life from birth. It required only the right provocation for Mr. Engineer Pitan-Payne to break into his hilarious rendition of Oliver Twist redux—"Please, sir, I want some more"—as he stood still, plate and cutlery in hand, eyes rolling in salivating admiration from end to end of a gastronomic spread on an accustomed Nigerian occasion. As for restaurants where the portion, he felt, was niggardly, he calmly desecrated decorum with his baritone rendition of the orphanage plea, voice deliberately raised to ensure that other diners heard and saw, then responded whichever way—he did not really care: discomfited, offended, conspiratorial, or openly nodding approval, sticking up their thumbs in solidarity with a long-sought champion of the fundamental rights of *casus belly*. The serious side to the overgrown Twist was hardly ever in public view, but it was at the heart of his unspoken contract with society. *Gumchi*

Kid, everywhere I go, there is someone there who desperately needs some more. What do we do?

But Duyole's mind was far away from that orphanage castaway. It was a totally different kettle of Dickensian fish that bobbed up into his consciousness. Menka was only mildly surprised when, after a silence, a near-total stillness that followed Duyole's first indication of life, his next sentence was "Why does Uriah Heep keep us waiting?"

"Who the hell is Uriah Heep?" Placing his ear close to Duyole's lips so as not to miss the sheerest sound. But it was as if Duyole's notorious "dropping off" had merged with the massive pool of the deep in every mind. There was a smile on his lips as if he enjoyed Menka's frustration, as he entered or perhaps merely reentered a world of his most insistent memories.

Duyole's mind wandered far and wide. It had arrived at that time of life when schemes sprouted from their winter headgear to supply heat to uprooted tropical sprigs like himself, poised like mushrooming clouds straining to discharge moisture on parched segments of the world. And which arid expanse needed that most? For him and his companion crusaders—Menka ever the constant figure—the answer was lodged in the common admonition "Charity begins at home." And that was where their sights were set, each in his own field. For Pitan-Payne, engineer and gadget freak, it was to set up a precision tools company, explore the reaches of alternative energy. Training, graduation, practical attachment in Munich, Salzburg, Koblenz, overwhelmed by the then-notorious North European work ethic, sometimes credited to the Swiss, other times to the Germans. Until such practical contacts, Duyole had assumed that this was a monopoly of the Pitan-Paynes and allied families of colonial aristocracy, Anglican strain, where the catechism was drilled into their childhood existence even to the extent of making them work for their pocket money on chores that were obviously contrived just to impress on them the guiding fact of life: money was the manna from heaven that grew on the tree of diligence. Discovering much later that his father, the clan patriarch, Pop-of-Ages, had indeed directed his postgraduate feet towards Europe north to immerse him even deeper in that extracurricular reputation. "History falls on us in Badagry," he exhorted his children, "and the Pitan-Paynes are the frontline of that historic call." Duyole was never fully certain which end of history filled the old man with such pride—that the family fortune was built on their lucrative role in the slave trade or that the Pitan-Paynes were among the earliest to abjure the trade when British gunboats sailed up Badagry creeks to enforce their abolition crusade. The old man continued to see Duyole's commercial success, culminating in this last international call to service, as the continuing march of the Pitan-Paynes in historic formation, from Badagry and the tragic point of departure to the United Nations! This was history rounding itself up in family triumph. Duyole frankly admitted there was some symmetry about it. Indeed, he found it quite gratifying, except, of course, for those protocol ports of call en route. There he was in filial disagreement with Pop-of-Ages. If it were possible, the old man would have accompanied him on the visit to Sir Goddie, togged up in his full uniform of the Rosicrucian Order.

Duyole Pitan-Payne imbibed more than a rigorous Germanic regimen. A scientist committed also to the ethic of a rounded education, he did not neglect the refinements of the mind. And thus, Oktoberfest, the Munich Beer Festival, for instance, registered its first conspicuous African regular in the person of one Duyole Pitan-Payne, electrical engineering student from Badagry, Lagos, Nigeria. It was a short bus ride from Salzburg, at whose university the engineer obtained his initial degree, in a nation famous for its tradition of a different kind of music—the Viennese waltz. The elder Payne had encountered in his youth that elegant diversion then known as ballroom dancing, a colonial importation whose promotion was assiduously pursued by the rival cultural interests of Britain, France, Germany, Belgium, etc. Their colonial officers conducted classes, passed the tradition down to a line of dedicated local teachers and missionaries. The waltz was Otunba's favourite whirl—no question about it. Pop-of-Ages in his youth became famous in Lagosian social circles as one of the most graceful terpsichoreans of that genre. His life ambition was fulfilled when he eventually visited the production centre of such marvelous music, Vienna, undisputed world capital of the waltz. Thereafter nothing mattered but to ensure that all his children headed for that city for the development of their minds. The pioneering son proved something of a wanderer and ended up in Pordenone, northern Italy, where he died in rather mysterious circumstances. Duyole had followed, a contrast in achievement. He did not obtain admission to Vienna itself, but Salzburg not merely came close, it pipped Vienna with its annual Salzburg Music Festival. From that fortuitous base, the young Duyole, heir to the musical gene that was passed down the family line in some erratic pattern, discovered a far more varied musical world than his father ever suspected existed. That multitalented son further expanded the family attribute in an eclectic spirit. Thanks to a fellow student, he discovered the largely harmonica-based chorales of Munich's Oktoberfest, a beery event that Duyole found much closer to his temperament and less than a two-hour bus or train ride from Salzburg's lecture halls. He made an exception for Mozart, attended the Salzburg Festival religiously whenever that composer was featured. However, Munich was a different impulsion, a different climate, one that fulfilled the primordial meaning of *festal,* as in *festivity,* in Duyole's intuitive understanding. Steadily it turned into an annual pilgrimage—the same Badehof Hotel every year, converted from its YMCA hostel origins—the same reserved room, number 121, thereafter designated by him his lucky number. Even after an elaborate interior makeover and refitting, Room 121 succeeded in retaining its penthouse position with a generous balcony, from which he could survey the Bavarian rooftops and obtain a bird's-eye view of the street parades of kettledrums, leather-kitted bandoliers, Tyrolean hats with their fluttering feathers, brass bands, and quaintly attired barmaids of the fiesta.

A rushed marriage of convenience to a buxom fraulein was no surprise, largely promoted by the imperative, Yoruba brand, of never denying a child born out of wedlock the entitlement of your name, no matter how suspect the paternity. *Did you ever? Or didn't you never?* DNA tests were yet unheard of. A court ceremony, swiftly followed by a divorce, proved a model of mutual amicable separation. Both remained friends for years afterwards. Endowed with an untrained booming voice which he had exercised in operettas since early school in Lagos, Pitan-Payne played Mario Lanza's rendition of the title role of *The Student Prince* until the needle pierced through the groove of the Bakelite long-playing disk. He was the most astonished amateur musician ever to discover, years into mature life and expanded tastes, that Mario Lanza was not considered even a serious voice of the operatic stage, much less the best tenor voice that had ever lived.

The world of micro-engineering—electric specialization—was what set his fingertips, in his own words, "a-tingaling!" And that, most specifically, was the microworld he swore to implant in that hometown depot of former slaving, Badagry. Brand it with a product uniqueness whose seal would be globally recognized—and maximally valued—as a specialty that became synonymous with its soil of origin. Silicon Valley? Why not Badagry Vale, once the Vale of Tears? It would form his contribution to the "Master Dream Collective," the parenting vision to which he was pledged, with the other three in their projection of "sweat after swot"—Duyole's rendition of life after graduation. It all seemed to fit into the historic cycle of transformations, but that was just the romantic fillip, a marginal bonus. The trademark, marketed globally as Brand of the Land, was a gong from Benin—yet another and even more brutal slave depot. The linkages were unending. The story of the whimsical appropriation of that gong reached all the way back to student days, a mordant tale kept mostly secret "except among friends" and cigar-end ashes of all-nighters, when roaring reminiscences shattered the peace of the night. Twenty years had passed; the gong had indeed attained a status enjoyed by the equivalent of a hallmark seal on the gold block or the Green certificate of a Google site. And there was the landmark Millennium Towers to flaunt it before the entire city, and even nation! To say it had caught fire was to be unduly expansive. Certainly the flames had flickered into the precincts of the United Nations, and this had happened most fortuitously, through its cultural arm, UNESCO. Now what desperate fortune-teller would have dared predict such an unlikely trajectory?

A fellow scientist, the Greek permanent representative in UNESCO, sought to track down the bronze original of the trademark—it had affinities with a long-vanished four-headed deity in the Greek pantheon, a double Janus, he asserted. Dogs, griffons, horses, dragons, serpents, and other mythical monsters—these all had extant representations, the multiple heads usually lunging forth from the shoulder on equally convulsing, auto-driven necks, not a static, fused four-in-one human head as in the Benin bronze, each head nearly fully executed. No, the diplomat learnt, there was no four-headed beast or deity in any African mythology, just the modest endowment of two, the most notable being that irrepressible lord of the crossroads, Esu. The man's curiosity appeared insatiable. The search led him logically to Duyole's Badagry factory. Could he at least see the original piece from which the logo was derived? And perhaps meet the sculptor, if living? Pitan could not guarantee the latter but drove with him to Benin City and the bronze casters' sector. Travel by road was the caller's choice—a wish to "drink in the environment." He did, staggering drunk—to all appearances—from the vehicle at each rest stop all the way to Benin. Still, the ride through kilometres of a succession of moon craters was largely relieved by engrossing exchanges on human inventions even before Archimedes and into the solar panel. In Benin he was thrilled by the kingship rituals and the historic defence moat that encircled the "City of Blood." The sculptor could not be identified, but at least the starved mythologist could commission a replica, which duly landed on his desk in Paris a few months afterwards. The return journey to Badagry was much smoother, despite the air turbulence that bedevils flights during the rainy season—he had drunk his fill of potholes! Finally he departed with an enhanced understanding of the origins of his own Grecian mythology, especially that of the disordered mass from which all phenomena are supposed to emanate—Chaos.

Thus commenced a fortuitous journey that now landed him in the parent body, the United Nations. Out of the blue, some eighteen months later, came the enquiry, then a formal offer to join the Energy Commission, all thanks to the sculptural clout of a four-headed gong—not really a startlingly unique composition, in his view. Or beauty, for that matter. Indeed, squat, graceless, nearly ugly. But it was a four-in-one. And perhaps the sculptor had had in mind the four elements—earth, water, air, fire, all composites of matter, the matrix of the engineering occupation? And then, much later, Duyole argued, it captured the serene essence of Yoruba royalty, never mind that it was unambiguously of Benin fabrication; even schoolchildren knew of the intertwined histories and cultures of Edo (Benin) and Yoruba, so who was arguing? The four-headed serenity, the engineer argued, came from embracing the world in one single spiritual compass. All that came later, rationalizing an already settled choice, which actually began with an adapted Viking drinking ritual—with beer as the ritual libation, not even the tourist-addicted Greek retsina or Spanish sangria—far from the land of palm wine, sorghum mead, and fiery *ogogoro*.

18.

A Vigil Too Far

Damien had awaited the police and bomb squad in the home after the departure of the ambulance. He remained with them while they pottered about the workshop, dusted their way through debris, took samples, and asked questions. He followed them back to their station as he was anxious to share with them, in confidence, some of his observations. He did not wish to do this in the house—fear of eavesdroppers—and he insisted on speaking to no one below a commissioner's rank. When he joined Dr. Menka by the sickbed, the surgeon was relieved to see him valorously trying to play the man, to let everyone know that he was someone the rest could lean upon in a crisis, even though he was bleary-eyed and looking distinctly sleep-deprived. That was one potential patient less, and Menka was more than grateful. Running a brief clinic on the situation, he prescribed that he could begin to concentrate on his number-three patient—Dr. Kighare Menka!

"I almost feel I'm back in Jos," he declared. "So I may as well go with the routine. I'll head home, try my best to enjoy dinner, stop by the house to check on Bisoye, and then back on duty. They'll make me a bed somewhere near."

Just then the patient stirred, showing signs of life for perhaps the third time that day. His gaze took in Damien's presence and that appeared to stir something in him. His lips moved, and Menka brought his ear close to his lips. He was rewarded with some decipherable words.

"My briefcase . . . office . . . briefcase . . . tell Damien I . . . want it."

Menka shook his head, half in irritation, half in despair. His voice was terse. "I'll tell him nothing of the sort! Will you kindly forget all about work for now? To hell with your briefcase! How are you going to recover if you keep worrying about your business! Leave Runjaiye and the rest to do their work." He turned to Damien. "This father of yours is incorrigible. Can you imagine him worrying about a briefcase? At such a time!"

Damien threw up his arms. "Uncle, he's your friend. You know him. Now you see what we have to cope with. He thinks nothing can work without him. Anyway, you be on your way. Take your time, I'll stay with him."

Menka noticed that Duyole had become even more agitated. This time, however, his restlessness did not appear to stem from physical discomfort but from a state of mind. Menka could make out the words formed by his lips even without the sound, and became exasperated—the lip-reading still spelt *briefcase*. Then he thought, well, who could tell what he was working on anyway? There he lay in bed, physically immobile, unable to articulate every need, but who knew where his mind was functioning, and at what? He decided to dispatch Damien, if only to put his friend's mind at rest.

"Get the briefcase, Damien. I'll defer my break till you get back."

The briefcase was Pitan-Payne's mobile office—documents, diary, aide-mémoire, cigarettes and lighter, and other minor human crutches. He kept his most secretive papers in it, including his "special dossier"—scribbles on business ventures and deals that, put simply, required close examination through his special, protection-needy contacts. It had proved crucial during his consultative stint with the power ministry. Most of the scribbles were in a special code that was at least two or three levels more specific than the Gong o' Four–improvised lingo, which was more reliable in gesture, tone, and context than meaning-specific. The briefcase itself was protected by a seven-key combination lock—a chance of one in over five million, he boasted, in favour of any safe-breaker. The engineer was separated from that mini-vault only when the driver or a messenger carried it to or from the car ahead of him, both constantly kept in view. Well, maybe just seeing the briefcase on his hospital locker, under his own custody, would make him relax.

Menka nodded again to Damien. The young man left.

It was painful to watch his friend clearly agitated by something he could not express. His eyes indicated something pressing on his mind, something he desperately struggled to confide or request, but all efforts merely wearied him, and he soon subsided. It was a relief to see him drifting off to sleep. The periods of apparent relief grew longer and longer, and finally his body went limp altogether and he began to snore softly.

Perhaps it was the background sibilance of Duyole's snores against the silence, but something slid a discordant note into Menka's mind. A small thing, perhaps, he considered, but it left him unsettled. Several times his mind had returned to the morning of the explosion, reliving every second from that first ominous sound that accompanied a just-breaking dawn—the dash downstairs, a run to the main house, and the sight of Godsown struggling out of sleep, dazed and confused, the familiar smell of cordite that eliminated all doubt. Then the series of motions in speeded-up tempo. Bisoye appearing from upstairs—the struggle to keep her away, force her back into the bedroom while Duyole was evacuated. The explosion had occurred in his basement studio. Damien, it would seem, had slept through it all, emerging, he learnt later, long after the ambulance had left, with Menka accompanying the concussed engineer, hardly breathing, covered in blood. Then, after the operation, when he returned to the house to check on the wife, Damien was nowhere to be seen—he assuming that he was in the office; the office—that is, Runjaiye—assuming that he was in the hospital. Remained missing for quite a while, even while stragglers—business associates, friends, the media—still hung around for news despite being refused admission to the patient, all hungry for any scrap of news on the victim's condition. Casual exchanges afterwards would appear to have placed Damien as preoccupied with securing the workshop, once he had woken up. He had elected to remain and protect the studio while awaiting the arrival of the police. His services to the police over, he went on to Millennium Towers—to secure his father's office, he said. Not until the afternoon of the day did he come to the hospital. So the doctor transposed himself: *Now you, Kighare, place yourself in that young man's position, a father hovering between life and death—would you give a damn about securing the scene of crime? As for the office situated some five kilometres away* . . . Menka shook himself free of the disquiet, subsumed the play of priorities under one dismissive word: Lagos!

What was on the patient's mind shortly became clarified by the arrival of the next visitors—his mother-in-law, with Bisoye's brother, Denrele, in tow. They needed a document in Pitan-Payne's custody, and it was urgent.

Denrele explained, "You see, Doctor, by a coincidence, we came in from Kwara this afternoon—we hadn't even heard of the morning attack. Mr. Pitan himself gave us the date. It's not the time we should start bothering you or him with such matters, but . . . well, you see how awkward it all is. The document is crucial for a court sitting the day after tomorrow."

Menka was relieved, and then suddenly worried. If Duyole kept anything important, a document in action, so to speak, it would be in his briefcase. Who on earth would know the lock combination? Certainly not Bisoye, nor any of his children, nor his business partners. Duyole, a believer in the need-to-know principle, kept secrets in that briefcase. When Menka turned to look at the patient, as if hoping to find a solution there, he encountered a twinkle in his eye, followed by a perceptible nod and the ghost of a grin. Menka grinned back and completed the gung-ho gesture which he knew he badly wanted to add. If that was indeed what had made him restless, then his mind was fairly back to normal functioning. Again, it was with a sense of marvel mixed with excitement that the surgeon realized that Duyole's mind had retained the appointment. He felt an overwhelming urge to celebrate.

Soon after, Mr. Damien himself came huffing up the stairs, a folder in hand, but not the briefcase. He saw the visitors. "Ah, you're here already," and he waved the affidavits triumphantly.

"You found them?"

"Yes, I guessed that's why Papa wanted his briefcase. I was present when he gave you the appointment."

"Oh, you knew the combination."

"It was unlocked. He had it open in his studio. Must have been working with it when . . . well, when it happened. I noticed it at once on his work-desk. Open."

Overwhelmed, the woman embraced Kighare. Embraced Damien. Leant over and planted a kiss on Duyole's forehead.

"I'll see you off myself," Dr. Menka said, ushering them out. "Then I'll take a break. I must confess I am getting weak around the knees. Hands a bit trembly. I feel hunger."

"And sleep," insisted Damien. "Uncle Kighare, please go to sleep—in your own bed. I'll take this shift. The hospital has a doctor on night duty. I promise to wake you up when I sign off. I'll knock you up, I swear."

Again the engineer's agitation appeared to resurface. Something he needed to say, struggled to say, but the effort only weakened him. He rolled his eyes between Damien and Menka as if to link them together in some way, but the ability to speak appeared to have been exhausted by the few words he had uttered. And then the enquiry about a Uriah Heep who kept them waiting. Where? Finally the patient appeared to resign himself to the helplessness of it all, shut his eyes, and fell asleep.

Menka resigned himself to the needed break. Four hours later he was back in the hospital ward. Damien occupied his vacated chair, fast asleep. Menka sent him home, commending his luck on inheriting his father's gift for dropping off. Before settling down, he checked the notes on the bedside card, then gave the patient a routine examination.

Dr. Menka turned instantly, raced down the corridor, and sought out the night nurse. The doctor on duty was already on his way up the stairs. Thereafter the world appeared to whirl in demonic tempo.

"Dr. Menka?"

"Yes."

"Sorry, but the news is not good. You saw my notes."

"Yes."

"I checked on him about half an hour ago. The critical drug is not in our pharmacy."

"Are you serious?"

"I was on my way from the store. We do not have even one ampule."

"We'll find it. Let's start checking other hospitals."

Before full dawn there was a conference of doctors, plus private consultants who could be roused. Aneurism! Thrown down its bloody gauntlet. One drug was on the tongue of everyone, but the hospital had none. Phone calls to sister institutions—the university hospitals all over the nation, always beginning with the closest. It all ended in absence. Damien had hardly settled into bed when he was roused, conscripted, and put in charge of coordinating all efforts. Private hospitals, again fanning outwards in concentric circles—they actually opened up their Google maps. Next the tantalizing wait for opening hours, giving silent thanks that it was not a weekend, followed by the agonizing wait for the doors of pharmacies to open. Where the pharmacists were known—Lagos and Badagry, Abeokuta, Ibadan, Benin—they found their breakfasts interrupted by frantic calls. Millennium Towers ordered all its cars and dispatch motorbikes fueled, drivers and riders ready to take off in whatever direction. The drug was nowhere to be found, neither in Badagry nor in Lagos. Pitan-Payne's condition worsened. It appeared to have been complicated by a stroke.

The consensus was total. "It is time for the drastic move." Menka sighed, distressed by the irony—Duyole, of all people, obliged to join the so-called medical tourist trail!

"Even for an airlift, we must first stabilize. The drug is essential."

"I know," Menka snapped.

It was the irony that provoked his unaccustomed irritation. A state-of-the-art diagnostic clinic was among the blueprints of Duyole's Millennium Towers projects; indeed, it reached far back into three decades, the umbrella theme of a collective commitment of which Duyole was pivotal. Now they could not even find a basic drug. But at least they could begin to hunt for an air ambulance.

Menka continued in a more even tone. "We can't wait until we find the drug. Whichever comes first waits for the other—no, well, strictly the drug first. Air ambulances can't be kept hanging around for too long. A patient of mine in Jos has links with an oil company which of course has an air ambulance. I can rouse them immediately. If needed, we'll even appeal to the prime minister."

Damien quickly interjected, "I hope it won't get to that. Papa wouldn't like to be obliged to—"

"The devil? Right now, Damien, your father's views don't count. Apart from anything else, he is international property. And a national responsibility. Even honour—if there is any left in Villa Potencia!"

They began to work contacts, fanning outwards—east and north. Menka called his former hospital in Jos. The result, zero. The staff of Millennium Towers joined in the search, contacting mission hospitals and hole-in-the-wall patent medicine stores in their towns and villages—one never knew what might be hidden far from the regular circuit. Even if the drug had expired, they might just try out an ampule or two. Those expiry dates preferred to err on the side of safety, so there was always a gambler's margin. Bisoye, once her sedatives had worn off, turned to steel. Calmly but sternly, she called up her class— *Dial up all your medical contacts, but find me this drug!* Brand of the Land activated its dozen or more branches all over the nation. Nothing surfaced. It seemed unbelievable, but the drug was nowhere to be found.

Finally, it was indeed a hole-in-the-wall, a modestly stocked pharmacy owned by an eighty-year-old retiree in an obscure village near Ogbomosho, that produced the miracle. The state governor was contacted; he agreed to provide an escort to rush the drug to Badagry.

THE COUNCIL OF EXPERTS dispersed, the rustled-up logistical team took up the reins, divided the tasks for Pitan-Payne's evacuation among themselves, reinforced by family, firm, and friends. The brother Kikanmi dismissed Menka's offer to procure an air ambulance through his professional links—the family, he assured him, had its own spheres of contacts and would take care of that item. The linkage extended all the way back to Duyole's student days, when the old man had joined him in Salzburg for the first time, on his graduation. On his list of sites of interest was a branch of the famous Lindtz chocolate factory situated just outside Salzburg. The *Otunba* had promptly negotiated representation of the company within Nigeria, a partnership that became a two-way affair as the shrewd businessman also took to serving as agent for cocoa exporters from within the country. His attempt to extend this interest to Ghana was not so successful. The Lindtz people were willing and contracts were signed, but nationalist sentiment from that veteran cocoa source proved intimidating, and the *Otunba* wisely sold his Ghanaian partnership to a local company, concentrating on the quite sizeable Nigerian market and its increased export market. The Lindtz are our people, announced Brother Kikanmi; we can rely on them for the ambulance. Only later did Menka learn, and with great satisfaction, that the service had indeed been called upon before. A family member had sustained hideous injuries from a motor crash and the Lindtz firm had come to the rescue. The new assignment was handed over to Teahole. He would contact the Austrian embassy and undertake all chores relating to documentation—landing permit, emergency visas for crew, their lodging, exemptions, etc., etc. He brushed off all offers of assistance. He knew *everyone;* his clout with aviation on the ministerial level was comprehensive. He would see the crew through immigration protocols on arrival and obtain clearance for departure.

Menka was only too relieved to have the family throw itself into the fray, especially for the acquisition of the most crucial requirement—an air ambulance! It released him to take on chores of nearly equal criticality, such as organizing his admission at the teaching hospital of Duyole's former Salzburg university, linking Badagry and Salzburg together. There was a brief hiccup, soon cured, as the siblings launched a flirtation with Dubai, then the raging choice of medical destination. Against the patriarch's chocolate link and his passion for the Viennese waltz, however, it was no contest. Now they could prepare the patient for evacuation on the land sector. Menka organized a Highway Patrol escort from Badagry to Ikeja airport. His clinics had involved constant interaction with the traffic police—the guaranteed crop of road casualties requiring stitching up and worse—he knew just who to call all the way up the hierarchy. Damien would pick up loose ends and act as general factotum. Menka made it understood how critical it was that once the land ambulance arrived at the airport, it should obtain a direct passage to the tarmac to avoid any loss of time or delays that would prove deleterious to the patient's condition. Duyole would not be moved from Badagry until the plane was virtually ready to take off—all documentation taken care of, the crew in position, the plane fueled and cleared for departure.

Menka did not hesitate to exploit his new status, often astonished—and frankly delighted—to find how much clout it commanded within the nation's establishment, even recesses normally considered inaccessible. He swore never again to complain over the negative impositions of the recognition if Duyole came through this in solid shape. In the meantime, he would exploit it to the hilt. He let the highway commandant understand that this was the patrols' chance to exercise all their frustrated sadistic instincts in clearing any traffic clog along the way, bring to bear their skills of stealth, bullying, and kamikaze drill to ensure that the patient arrived at Murtala Muhammed Airport in Ikeja at a pace that would be restrained only on the authority of the accompanying doctor charged with the patient's well-being. *If he says crawl, then drop on your bellies. If he says fly, turn the ambulance into an attack helicopter!* Then he began to work the phones, running last-minute checks on every detail of departure. He did his best to pull back from time to time, make his colleagues feel that Duyole was their patient and he just a spare tyre, but intent lagged far behind conduct. In a nation like his, over matters of life and death, the logistics of such a departure carried the most slithery burden of execution. It was no longer a case of professional competence, where he could confidently leave his friend in other hands. The reality was that he would rather conduct a full day's sequence of delicate operations than an hour negotiating bureaucratic obstacles and other lunacies of officialdom. He called. Harangued. Intervened. Aggravated. Teahole's boastful confidence, presumptions on club tie bonhomie, salesmen networks, and guaranteed delivery in a crisis bothered him. As delicately as he could, he asked the senior Kikanmi to keep a supervising eye on his junior's assignments. As politely as, presumably, he also could, Kikanmi reminded him that this was primarily a family undertaking. Menka absorbed the snub, retracted his antennae.

The surgeon was the first to admit it—he was a creature of intuitions. If everything had gone right, followed careful plans and designations, he would have insisted on a place on that plane as an emergency patient in need of mental attention. Kikanmi triumphantly reported the arrival of the ambulance plane, but he went there to see for himself, first booking himself into an airport hotel for the night. At the airport, the parked plane was pointed out to him. Only part satisfied, he still checked to ensure that the plane's documents matched the plane—make, lettering, colours, and description. Everything tallied. The circumstances notwithstanding, Menka declared the sight the most beautiful object he had seen since the Jos mountains. He treated himself to a sumptuous solo dinner at the hotel's Mediterranean restaurant, slept soundly. In the morning he drove to the terminal to await the land ambulance. The all-clear had been given and the motorcade departed from Badagry. Menka crowed with delight, eased himself out of his car and walked into the airport building, reported his presence to the clearance desk.

All was in order. They were expected, the route cleared for their passage directly onto the tarmac. The officer in direct charge of the plane's departure joined the accompanying motor attendant on his walkie-talkie, monitoring progress. Dr. Menka listened in, fished out his mobile, and spoke to the doctor to enquire how the patient was faring. His condition was stable, nothing changed. The crew had also received the all-clear. Shortly after, their minibus drew up at the specially designated departure gate—only then, seeing the shuttle, did Menka realize that he had in fact stayed in the same hotel with them. Lucky crew, they little knew they had been saved a maniac's ingrained pessimism. He watched them walk confidently into the airport building and felt that it was he taking off to nowhere. Involuntarily he began to intone a long-forgotten school victory chant. All was well with the school team!

Then came the frowns, the desperate voices and wild gestures at the desk. Mr. Fixer, it seemed, was nowhere to be seen. Missing also were the flight permits and accompanying documents, a part of which he, Menka, had checked, then celebrated the previous night. Fixer Teahole was last seen haring off in the direction of the domestic terminal, then lost to sight.

That was when the Gumchi man finally welcomed the long-expected ants crawling up his intestines. It brought a sense of relief—at least it had finally happened, and in the fashion it always did in the land of happy people. Last-minute. Irrationally. Near irreparably. At least there was now something in relation to which some form of counteraction was possible. That read progress! He introduced himself to the crew. Until their arrival at the airport, they had remained blissfully unaware of any glitch. Arrival in Lagos the day before had been flight-perfect. Now, together, they learnt that there had indeed been a problem in that most essential department—documentation! Virtually at the last moment before takeoff from the Austrian airspace, based on the very last receipt of x-rays transmitted to Salzburg from Badagry, it was decided that a neurosurgeon should accompany the patient from Nigeria—an emergency operation on the flight was unlikely, but it was deemed a possibility. The plane was already equipped for just such an emergency. It meant, however, that Salzburg would supply an anaesthetician who would arrive with the plane. All that was agreed before takeoff. Immigration was alerted and the reception team primed for the changes.

Arrival was indeed flawless. The crew, plus the sudden extra, were cleared by Immigration. Now that they were ready to take off, however, to take their leave of the land of happiness, some airport official, military brand, had pre-empted them, rejected the explanation for an increase of one in the crew's complement. In vain the protocol officer for Brand of the Land pointed out to him that the extra member had been cleared to enter Nigeria the previous afternoon. No! Permission, he insisted, had been sought and given only for a team of four—why then should there be five who had arrived the previous day and were now attempting to leave the happy land? That extra was an illegal immigrant. He seized even the passports they had all surrendered as guarantee of their morning departure on schedule. Explanations that had been accepted as rational on arrival were now treated as proofs of some sinister plot—against whom, and in what cause, no one could tell. All available papers seized, the adamant guardian of the realm departed, no one knew into which office. There would be no clearance to leave the country.

It was not a time to take umbrage, but Menka did worse. Not for the first time, he had pitied Duyole for his unfortunate sibling acquisition, forced at times to wonder if the most valued return he could make for their friendship could not reasonably take the form of his quiet elimination of one of them, Teahole especially. Menka felt betrayed. His mobile had run a high temperature the entire evening—it became hot to the touch—mostly due to calls connected with Teahole's assignments. And it was not the surgeon who initiated all the calls—others called him, the nation's medical laureate, to check if he was indeed involved in demands being made by the salesman, some of which had nothing to do with a patient's emergency evacuation. Teahole was not the kind to miss opportunities.

Over and over again the surgeon went through the checklist. The plane had arrived—item ticked. Crew passed Immigration? Ticked. Checked into hotel?—ticked. Ambulance—ticked. Escort—ticked. He demanded to know from others if anything had been overlooked, if there were any last-minute problems or simply uncertainties where he, or anyone else, might need to intervene. If there was any need for him to summon help from any direction, no matter at what level, please, Menka implored, please call on me. I remain available round the clock—I promise you, I can do without sleep for days. I am accustomed to being woken up in emergencies. Just let me know. However, it was not sufficient for the all-capable Teahole to even say a simple no, thanks. He had a desperate need to put everyone on notice that he had virtually taken over all the services in the nation, even for the purpose of gaining entrance into the airport toilets.

And now the Fixer was missing, and no one seemed to know where he was. Caught in the notorious Lagos traffic? Ensconced in the control tower, scanning air traffic and weather conditions for the best moment of departure? Ticking off the head of state for stalling his brother's departure for overseas surgery? All that had filtered through—thanks to some sympathetic zones of airport officialdom—was the nature of the problem and perhaps, just maybe, how it could be resolved.

The ambulance maintained its progress from Badagry, arriving within minutes of the projected time. It drove straight onto the tarmac to a screech of sirens, escorted by the local SWAT equivalent. Instead of the projected instant transfer, however, land and air ambulances now stood staring at each other across perhaps twenty metres, unable to transfer the critical charge from land stretcher into the plane. Menka opened the doors of the vehicle, where Pitan-Payne lay strapped to the stretcher, and exclaimed. He should have known! There was Bisoye with the patient. No, there was more. Her much-traveled suitcase—he recognized it immediately—was beside her, all ready to accompany her man to Austria. He slapped his head in annoyance with himself. He should have warned her. He assumed that her brother-in-law, who knew, and indeed had assented to the plane's capacity, had taken on board the emergency addition, would have warned her. He had himself considered flying out with the patient, and only realized it was a nonstarter when he had seen the plane the previous night—all enquiry into the plane's actual passenger allowance had met with stonewalling. Menka found it extremely baffling, almost as if this were a state secret. There was room for the medical staff that came in it from Austria and for one more person only—the neurosurgeon.

"Come down, Bisoye," he told her as gently as he could, and helped her down, first reaching for her suitcase. "You'll join him later. Look at me. I'm a surgeon, but not a neurosurgeon. There is only one spare seat, and it belongs to our Lagos specialist. You are not even a nurse. Right?" She shook her head submissively. He could see she had not slept all night. All the earlier energy appeared to have evaporated. Bisoye seemed to be in a daze, as if the enormity of Duyole's departure, and the uncertainty of the mission itself, had only recently dawned on her. The stiffening in her spine had thawed completely, perhaps from the termination of the chores she had undertaken towards his departure and the absence of any new challenges. Menka sensed that she must have passed the night in that condition, completely depleted, capable only of following Duyole wherever he was bound.

Menka led her into the airport, found her a seat. "You should go home and rest. I'll find you a taxi. I'll arrange your flights even before I leave the airport."

She perked up immediately. "Today? I could still fly out tonight."

"Bisoye, you need to get your strength back. Surgery will not be for another week—that is our confident projection. Unless, of course, there is an unforeseen change in his condition. Otherwise, nothing less than a week. After the flight he must be restabilized. You have a lot to do for him right here, before you leave. Go home, rest. Put the home front in order. Check things in the office, so you can take him news. That's what Duyole would wish—you know that. He feeds on the latest. Am I right?"

She smiled weakly, nodded agreement.

Just then Teahole emerged, even more depleted. The flight papers had been taken to the airport commandant, who had his offices at the other end—the domestic end—of the airport. Teahole had chased the papers there, and now he was back, looking harassed, bewildered, left a sizzling rump steak and returned a congealed leftover. He stammered out his ordeal—virtually flung out of the office by the commandant, with a tongue-lashing for disturbing his peace of mind over papers that were clearly irregular. He had no intention of releasing a plane that had treated the nation's immigration rules with deliberate contempt, and now, as had become apparent, with the connivance of "unpatriotic Nigerians!" What did those foreigners take us for? A banana republic? It was the script of "bloody civilian" collaborators with foreign enemies all over again.

"What do we do now?" wailed Teahole.

"First things first. Bisoye needs to get back to Badagry—she came in the ambulance. Let's get her a taxi."

With astonishing eagerness, Teahole offered his car. "My driver is here. He can take her home. I'll find my way back, no problem at all."

Menka could not believe his ears—Teahole so readily self-sacrificial? Something truly unprecedented must have hit him in the commandant's office. Or perhaps simply from watching all the well-laid plans collapse around his presumptions. But the surgeon only nodded approval, registered the relief with which Teahole picked up Bisoye's suitcase and escorted her to where his car was parked.

"I'll be by the ambulance," the doctor shouted after him. "Let's meet there and do some brainstorming."

It was, fortunately, one of those early mornings of freshness and coolness around the airport, so Menka told the nurses to take down the stretcher and place Duyole out in the open. The police escort had peeled off; the ambulance itself was working to a timetable, and departure time was only a half hour or so away. There was no point retaining a vehicle the hospital might need for other cases. Most absolutely Duyole was not returning to Badagry—that much Menka had resolved. Whatever it took, the plane would leave and his friend within it, under professional care. The Gumchi jaws were set as he watched the nurses extricate the stretcher and place it carefully on the tarmac. Perhaps it was this action that provoked the next eruption.

An open jeep came roaring towards the group, veering off at the last moment to stop parallel to the stretcher. A uniformed soldier leapt out—armed, impossible to tell his rank. Whatever fulmination was in rehearsal en route, however, froze on his lips. Instead he straightened up and saluted.

Menka saved him the trouble of questions by pointing to the stretcher. "My friend needs fresh air. I don't like him being cooped in that vehicle, especially as we don't know how long it will be before the plane can take off."

"Oh, does this matter involve you, sir?"

"Very much so."

His eyes widened. "The plane is in trouble, sir. Big trouble."

"So I gather. Tell me frankly, what does your commandant want? We are at an impasse. The papers he wants do not exist. They cannot be produced. There is nothing, absolutely nothing we can do. The Austrian embassy has been contacted, they're working from their end, but every moment's delay jeopardizes the life of the man lying here."

The soldier moved confidentially close. "Sir, that man, the one in charge of this operation, messed up. The one with the moustache. Instead of handling the situation gently, he began to make threats. So the commandant scooped up the papers and took off."

"I was not present, but I think I can imagine what happened. Question is, what do you recommend? You know your commandant, I don't."

The man moved even closer. "Thank God you're here, sir. If our *oga* sees you, he will release the papers immediately. I know that for sure."

"All right. I came here to see off my friend, not watch him die on the tarmac. I'll do whatever you say. Where's his office?"

"In the domestic section, sir. You have to go out again—"

Menka stopped him. "Go out, enter the traffic, go through the toll gates, enter yet another traffic stretch. In the meantime . . . ?" And he pointed to the stretcher.

"No other way, sir."

"What do you mean, no other way?" Menka gestured in the general direction of the domestic terminal. "It's the same airfield. The tarmacs open into one another—look, that's a service vehicle coming in from the domestic. It's regular traffic. So where's the problem?"

The soldier's eyes opened even wider. "You mean . . . ?"

"I mean." He patted the jeep. "This is one of the patrol vehicles, right? You go up and down, round and round. Even we bloody civilians can see that while seated in the plane. You have your dedicated lanes, and you are actually on duty. That includes emergencies." He pointed to the stretcher. "Now, that is an emergency! A matter of life and death."

The soldier's mouth opened and shut. He took one more look at the stretcher and the burden it carried.

"Jump in, sir."

They raced along the peripheric lanes, cut across tarmacs, and were beside an operational sector of the domestic in no time. As he pulled up outside the commandant's office, the officer pleaded, "But don't say I told you he's here or that he has the papers. He's been denying they are with him."

Menka winked. "What do you take me for? Your commandant will be glad that he performed this good deed, I promise. And if you get into trouble, don't worry, I'll leave you all my contacts."

"I'll park behind this building so he doesn't see me when he sees you off."

"If you'd rather not wait, I'll find my way back," Menka offered. "He can give his instructions ahead while I fight my way back through regular traffic."

The soldier grinned and saluted. "I'll wait right there, Doctor."

Dr. Menka entered to the sound of bantering, laughing, flirtatious registers—all the accustomed happiness noises not normally associated with the office of a commandant of any national security outfit. An alert corporal manned the reception desk, looked up. Recognition, then disbelief all over his face. He leapt out of his seat, courteous and solicitous. Menka felt himself begin to fill a role, progressively, that was being instinctively accorded him. In as offhanded but businesslike a voice as he could muster, he told the corporal to inform his boss that he, Dr. Menka, was there on a matter of absolute urgency, a matter of life and death, to be understood literally! The corporal leapt into action. At the door he hesitated briefly, then knocked.

A voice from within bellowed with rage: "Who the bloody hell is that again? I thought I told you I was not to be disturbed!"

The corporal turned to Menka with a helpless gesture. The surgeon pushed past him into the office. The commandant stared, ready to explode. The next moment, recognition also leapt to his face. His chair was scraped backwards and he rose in a salute.

"Doctor, very sorry, Doctor, no one told me you were waiting for me."

"I've come about the detained ambulance plane," Menka announced.

"What plane? Oh ... the ... that plane. Sit down, Doctor, sit down, please." He turned to his guests, two women and a male. "Er ... excuse me, will you? Come back later, when I've finished with the doctor."

He ushered out his guests, screamed for his assistant, and resumed profuse apologies. "I didn't know you were involved at all. Nobody informed me ..."

"It doesn't matter. Please, whatever red tape you need to cut, I count on you to do it. My friend's life is ebbing away, right on the tarmac. We've lost nights of sleep over this, over a full week planning, and finally ... we end up trying to kill him on your tarmac."

The commandant blubbered. "They should have told me. No one told me. Hey, you, bring me the file on the detained plane!"

"Sah?"

"The Austrian plane, are you deaf? Which other plane did you detain?"

In another ten minutes Dr. Menka was back on the tarmac, international side, with the clearance papers. Teahole was waiting by the plane with Bisoye. Quickly she explained, "Uncle T. told me about the delay, so I begged to be allowed to remain until it was sorted out. At least I would wave him good-bye. Sorry I looked so washed out earlier, but I'm okay now."

Menka laughed. "Oh yes, I forgot. You're the original problem freak. When there's a problem, then you summon the reserves. Sure. We'll all see him off together. Everything is now in order. We have clearance. The commandant is issuing necessary instructions."

He handed Teahole the tied-up papers and the salesman broke into a song and dance of praise, the obverse of his sister's earlier rain of curses on her brother's tormentors, all interspersed with his accustomed sniffles.

"Enh, aah, Gumchi-man"—*sniffle sniffle*—"it was God who made sure you were here today." *Sniffle sniffle.* "Only you could have done it." *Sniffle sniffle.* "They're all bastards, those soldiers. Do you know, he even threatened to shoot me. Then threatened to impound the plane! As if we don't know that all he wanted was a bribe. *Awon oloshi.*"

Now it was only a matter of getting the crew out of their informal confinement, getting the engines started so that Duyole could be lifted into an air-conditioned plane, then sending him off into the stratosphere. Dr. Menka gave last-minute instructions and moved away some distance from the stretcher so that the couple could spend a few moments alone together. Also, he felt a need to savour, all by himself, what he had just achieved for a friend—far more delectable than bumping off one of Duyole's more expendable siblings—before he lost the taste of its immediacy, even while cautioning himself not to get too used to the convenient status.

LATER MENKA RETURNED gloomily to his apartment. Desultorily, he attempted yet again to place some order on his junk from Jos, gave up. Instead he simply repacked his travel bag, ready for the summons from Austria, where his friend would undergo his make-or-break surgery. The timing at least was kind, he reflected. He was jobless. His time was his own, and some of that time had to be dedicated to some deep thinking.

It was a habit he could not help, totally involuntary, but then, he did not consider it abnormal, and even if it was, then it was abnormality calling to the abnormal. Once the day had been marked by any event outside the norm, what else could be expected? And so, as he sank wearily into an armchair, he found yet another tiny occurrence, one that he had forcefully dismissed, rising once again to the surface the moment his mind began to review the day's offerings.

Why would a son refuse to perform such a simple chore? Your father wants his briefcase—well, bring the briefcase over! Even if one

item of total insignificance created the need for that suitcase, he—
we—asked for the briefcase, not any item inside it. Why go searching
for a document within the suitcase instead of just bringing the damned
briefcase? Why assume that the man would not ask for something
else tomorrow, today, even before your return with this isolated item?
Why?

Part II

19.

The Discreet Funeral of the Bourgeoisie

And then, just as it always does, it was all over—hopes, questions, uncertainties. Duyole Pitan-Payne made it to Salzburg, but not past the third day in that city of song.

Suddenly, virtually overnight, the Pitan-Paynes underwent a puzzling transformation. A death in the family, and especially of one who has come to represent the living force of that family—living, that is, not feeding on the past, real or mythical, but alive and breathing, re-creating and socially reinforcing whatever legacy there was or was merely imagined—such a death can prove a most traumatizing event in the self-regard of that family. It went beyond being perhaps even the breadwinner of the extended clan. Like the proverb of the elephant, the event is not only "something that just flashed past—*fiiri!*" but a sinkhole opened up in the midst of a crowded intersection; the family finds itself teetering on the unstable verge, poised to tip over or regain its balance. How else, Menka asked of his apartment walls—how else understand it? He was only a surgeon, a spare-parts manipulator where the parts did not involve the brain. And so the Gumchi man felt lost, wished—not for the first time, and from different causes—that he had selected a different specialization. When he tried to formulate the change, he found that the handiest formula was simply to accept that the Pitan-Paynes had chosen to catapult their members from being just a family, even a notable one with a recognized pedigree, to being The

Family. Capital letters. Or Dynasty. With perhaps a capitalized first letter as encountered in ancient illuminated manuscripts.

No matter, whatever it was before, the clan appeared to have finally found itself, dusted up its unacknowledged pedigree and destiny. Normal humanity might undergo the indignity of being buried in natal earth; not so The Family—capital letters. Difficult to deny that once breath is gone, the rest is sentiment. Nonetheless, the entire community around this one individual—business associates, friends, cronies, debtors, beneficiaries—appeared united in the belief that a Brand of the Land, even without recognition in other lands, was simply not donated to other lands in perpetuity even if its purveyor died completely insolvent or had become so ostracized that friends and associates could not bear to pass the hat round to bring him home. Unless, of course, the circumstances of his or her departing were so unspeakable that it made the return to his own earth an abomination. The Family thought differently. When the tally was made in all objectivity, and as amply manifested in the unraveling of events, The Family appeared to consist of just a quartet—the patriarch and the siblings—so Menka took to referring to them as the Otunba Quartet. And it appeared to perform on discordant strings. It did not seem possible, but the quartet was resolved that the life and soul of the family, of Badagry and beyond—Duyole Pitan-Payne, embodiment of an original reading of the spirit of the happiest people in the world— should be buried in a far-off land, simply because that was the place where he happened to draw his last breath. But it was not "simply because." It was much more, as his bosom friend from the craggy hills of the Plateau was about to discover.

Protestations were predictably instant and pithy, covering every nook of association and even casual encounters. Duyole's juniors in the firm, Runjaiye and Ekete, led a delegation from Millennium Towers to the *Otunba* home. They found him unusually minus Mamma Kressy, his toes at peace inside his bedroom slippers. They had protested earlier to Timi, his sense of omnipotence restored. He heard them out, in between sniffles, then delivered a curt message, straight to the point. Mr. Timi instructed the emissary that even the closest colleagues were still outsiders. They had no business in the arrangements for Duyole's burial. *Yes*—sniffle sniffle—*you are indeed Duy-*

ole's business colleagues—sniffle sniffle—*but that relationship ends at Millennium Towers. You are not part of The Family, to whom the ultimate decision belongs. We have taken that decision—interment will be in Austria.* Ekete, his voice pitched high in disbelief, gathered the staff together and narrated the one-sided exchange, his already slight frame alarmingly shrunk thinner by the rebuff. The following day he requested a day off.

It was now Menka's turn, and the doctor posed only one question to the brother: "What does the widow, Bisoye, want?" She had flown out the following night to be with her husband—it proved impossible to restrain her any further—and was at the hospital, but not at his bedside, when he breathed his last. Was it conceivable that she was part of such a decision?

It was difficult to believe, but The Family did not consider the wishes of the young widow of any importance. The Family, it became apparent, did not extend to his widow; neither did it, at that stage, include even the children. The children were apparently conceded a special category of their own, to be courted piecemeal, calculating that the spoils of death would break their ranks and forge new alliances. The Gumchi surgeon found himself in strange waters, floundering. He had of course encountered variations of the same "family culture," even of more horrifying nature, still in practice. Menka knew of societies where the widow underwent hideous ordeals to prove that she had had no hand in the death of her spouse. In some communities, after bathing the dead man, the woman underwent the medieval torture of trial by ordeal. She was forced to drink the residual slop from the ritual washing of the corpse. If she vomited, then she was a murderess. If she retained the sludge in her stomach, well, too bad. She had to find a way of recovering from the nausea, and even poisoning. By then, of course, her head was already shaved clean, her body subjected to whipping. She was kept locked up in a dark, dingy room in which she ate, urinated, and defecated. She was brought out periodically and subjected to a collective inquisition by the women of the family—what had she cooked for her man that had sent him to join the ancestors? Such sessions were indeed welcomed by the widow, since that was when she enjoyed the luxury of light and fresh air, except of course that such questioning was done at the height of the sun at midday to burn the guilt out of her soul. And so she sat on hot sands in the sun while her interrogators flung questions and accusations at her from the comfort of a shaded verandah. After which, back to her cell and iron rations, a hard baked mud or cement floor, without even a straw mat. But wasn't this supposed to be Badagry, and a full century at least since the cessation of the slave transportations? Kighare Menka began to wonder which was worse, among the Badagry aristocracy or back in Jos, where at least human remains were treated to commercial respect.

Thus commenced an emotionally bruising saga, a plunge into family intrigues that made him seriously consider seeking delivery at the hands of Papa Davina, or indeed any handy divine. He could no longer resist a strong suspicion that either The Family was possessed by demons or he was. For the moment, however, he contented himself with consulting a medical colleague, checking his blood pressure. As he had begun to suspect, all the symptoms for stress were superabundant. Duyole's constant caution reached out to him from the void: *Physician, heal thyself.* It compelled him to douse all rousing emotions, return to basics. Calmly he asked himself, just what did the code of the Gong o' Four demand of him in such a pass? The answer was straightforward: Bring Duyole home. Take him to Gumchi, if that was what it meant, and bury him there. It emerged as a quiet, fussless resolution, taken in the conviction of what Duyole himself would have done if he, Menka, had been the object of a morbid tug-of-war. *You don't want him? Very well, I'll keep him.*

Menka drove the thirty miles of gutted road into Lagos, indifferent to the jolts of new pits that had not been on that route even twenty-four hours earlier. He found Teahole at his desk, his confidence restored with his apparent designation as principal facilitator and family spokesman. Mr. Timi was expansive. Death was a robe that was several sizes too large for the general procurer, but he strove valiantly to fill it. He was on the phone to Austria, dictating funeral arrangements to the Austrian undertaker. If Teahole felt any grief, none was in evidence—but then, Menka admitted, neither were his own emotions on display. It was not the time, and there was no immediate cause to yield some space to grief. It was sparring time, and the outsider was ready to take on the entire clan of Pitan-Payne impostors, one by one or all together.

"Timi, you know why I'm here. Just let me have a straightforward answer. Whose decision was it to have Duyole buried abroad?"

Teahole exuded pure, undiluted confidence. It was the decision of Pop-of-Ages, but one with which The Family fully agreed.

"I know you have your reasons. May one share, so we can all be on the same wavelength?"

Teahole settled fully back in his chair. "Ah, Gumchi-man"—*sniff, sniff*—"you know our people, they like noise. They love ostentation. All they want is an opportunity to make a show. They'll come from far and wide, everyone wants to put in an appearance, but"—*sniff, sniff*—"eh, a-Gumchi-man, which of them are really grieving? How many in that crowd have merely come there to be seen? To show off? Vulgarity, that's the problem with our people—not so? You know that, don't you, eh, Gumchi-man? People like you will understand. You are a surgeon. You lock yourself away upcountry, attending to victims of Boko Haram. Until this recent award, did anyone know you? Did you care? No. That's your style. You detest ostentation, that's why you are different. Most of these people, all they're interested in is the 'see me here' part of it. How many of them really care for Duyole?"

Menka listened, disbelieving. He failed to grasp the relevance. In any case, he could only marvel—could this man have failed to recognize himself, his values, in the very social type he was denouncing? Not that it inserted any rational validity, but could he really fail to recollect that he, Mr. Teahole Procurer for high society, was the prop of the emptiness, the vapidity, the falsity of values and exhibitionism of the soufflé society he was decrying? His gorge rose. Duyole had been a crowd man. Selective, yes, but he loved company. He loved people, just loved to be with people. Was this impertinent hustler criticizing his friend? Did he dare? Menka's fingers itched. He breathed in and out. It would be healthier to change the direction of the exchange, and he prepared to leave.

"I take it, then, that the decision is final."

"Definitely. It is the decision of The Family. And it's not as if Austria is strange to The Family—in fact, we consider Salzburg almost a Family extension."

"Because Duyole studied there? Because he graduated there?"

"More than, Gumchi, more than. Pop-of-Ages—you may not

know this—he has long had business connections with them over in Austria. We've made friends. The Lindtz people know us. We know them. They've visited here, you know. I've taken them round Nigeria. They know their way around here, maybe even more than you do."

"What does that prove, Timi? What is all that to the widow, for instance? To the children?"

"The Family is in full agreement."

"Does that include the wife, Bisoye?"

"I spoke to her yesterday. She's most amenable, yes, amenable to the idea, yes, quite in agreement."

That was unexpected, and a setback. Had bereavement also warped Bisoye's thinking? Bisoye? No, surely, that couldn't be! For a moment Menka wondered if he was the one whose sensibilities had gone askew, then recalled that Runjaiye and company had been before him on that very protest mission. "You're sure about this, Timi?"

"Oh yes, I told her that this was what The Family wanted . . ."

"You keep saying *The Family, The Family*. I am referring to Duyole's family."

For the first time the procurer looked defensive. He shifted uncomfortably. "Well, I am including the children. They are in agreement."

"The children! Oh, of course, yes, that I can readily believe. I warned Duyo to bring them home more often. Not let them grow up thinking Europe and America were the entire world."

"At first they too were thinking like Ekete and the others, but Damien assures me they've all come round."

Oh, Damien? Damien was a special case. And who had brought home Damien? He, Menka. *Serves me right,* he thought. So how did one describe what the children had become, how they regarded themselves? As part of the Nigerian, the Yoruba family? It was a question that Duyole often put to himself. But then again, his widow? The same Bisoye, a princess in her own right, being a daughter of one of the ruling houses of Ondo. The house was that close to the throne, the "asking ceremony" took place in the palace of the Osemawe, the paramount king of them all. They had all rallied round, accompanied Duyole to the asking event, bearing the traditional gifts of yam, palm oil, bales of *aso oke*, kola nuts, and what else? There they had undergone the solemn rites of asking for her hand, receiving her formally on Duyole's behalf, and celebrating their betrothal. No, something was screwy. Menka could not see Bisoye consenting to have Duyole abandoned on foreign soil, any more than he could imagine that Duyole, if he could exercise his will at that moment, would fail to denounce—even disown—his family for what they were about to do. Mixed up though he was in some aspects of his choice of a lifestyle, there were far too frequent, profound, and consistent statements of the dead man's mode of existence that did not permit of any such travesty. Menka had to dispute Teahole's claim.

"If Bisoye said you should bury her husband in Austria, she was not herself. She was overcome by grief—you should know that. In her state of mind, she would probably agree to anything, not even knowing the implications of what is being said to her. It is easy for me to imagine her condition. I wouldn't take her consent as conclusive if I were you."

"We-e-ell, a-Gumchi-man, you know the tradition. Duyole belongs to The Family, and the widow's wishes are really dependent on what The Family says."

"Don't talk guff, Timi. You know you won't be permitted any rest. No one will applaud this decision."

"I know, I know. I've already been bombarded by protests, but see? That's typical of our people." And it was as if he knew where Menka's mind had been in the preceding moments. "They know how to forget tradition when it's convenient for them, but they're always the first to call on tradition, tradition. Eh? That's consistency for you. You are a traditional person, not so, a-Gumchi-man? You know that tradition forbids the father to attend the funeral of his child."

Menka wondered why a united bolt from all the divine custodians of tradition did not smash through those office walls and blast Teahole off his seat, scorching him en route for submitting his hearing so patiently to such non sequiturs of a damned illiterate. This surpassed the uttermost limits of distortion that he had yet endured. His hardened eyes asked Teahole if he was raving. Perhaps Brother Timi saw that and decided not to await its voicing.

"Bringing him back to where Pop-of-Ages is—it comes to the same thing, if you look at it properly."

"Wait, wait, Teahole, just hold on a moment. What kind of cockeyed reasoning are you trying to fob off on me? I'm not a Yoruba, but don't think you can pull a fast one on this deep-dyed Gumchi-village-born. Your old man doesn't have to be within a hundred miles of the funeral. What are you talking about, for heaven's sake! Duyole could have died here, he could very easily have died at the Badagry hospital. Or right on the tarmac, where you and the airport commandant kept him for hours when he should have taken off. He was already dying on the tarmac, within this same Lagos where you were all raised by the old man. What then? Would you have ordered the ambulance plane to continue with his body to Austria to ensure that his father was not present at his funeral? Teahole, please, spare me. I badly miss my friend and maybe I am not being coherent. But I am clear-headed. So let's allow some logic into this!"

"Ah, a-Gumchi-man, you don't understand, you see. You have to think of Pop-of-Ages, the *Otunba* himself. Let me tell you what he said, eh? Then you'll understand the true nature of the man. I asked him, what do you want us to do about bringing back his body? You know what he said, eh, a-Gumchi-man, you know what he said? He said, 'Is this idea of bringing him back so you can put him on the table and serve him for my dinner?' See? That's the kind of man he is. He wanted to know what was the purpose of our bringing him back. What was the point? So it comes to the same thing. He was reminding us of tradition."

Menka wanted to hear it again, but this was the reaction also of many. It seemed to have become a habit. Some pronouncement from Teahole, and the listener asked to hear it all over again, just to ensure that his or her hearing had not got twisted under the famous Teahole sniffling impact. The salesman obliged, his eyes shining with a strange, near-fanatic pride.

"He's tough, the *Otunba is,* real tough. What was the point of bringing him back, that's the point he was making—you get it? 'Is this idea of bringing him back so you can serve him out at table for my dinner?'" And Teahole shook his head in sheer wonder at the profundity of the patriarch's declaration. "There are not many like Pop-of-Ages, I tell you. The man is deep. Really de-e-e-eep. Sometimes too deep even for us, his children. He is one of a kind."

Teahole walked on air for the rest of that day, and even for some days before the funeral. At one of the planning sessions of The Family, he narrated how he had floored the surgeon with an unanswerable riposte. "I tell you, that finished him. The Gumchi man simply got up slowly. He was so dazed he didn't even know he was walking backwards."

The general salesman was quite truthful. Kighari Menka did get up slowly, backed off nearly all the way to the door, staring at Teahole with the eyes of a madman. In his churning mind there was only the alarming question, could Otunba Pitan-Payne be on the clientele list of Codex Seraphinianus?

EVEN LESS COMFORT awaited Kighare Menka in Austria. He arrived braced for the dreaded moment. That was it. Nothing more to be said, only evolve a strategy for minimal contact, bid his friend good-bye, go somewhere to lick his wounds, then return and occupy his time with the Codex affair. He was grateful for that. It was something to engage his mind, take it away from living nightmares. It had proved a hectic day, repacking all his junk from Jos so soon after beginning to unpack and settle into a new abode, but the omens were clear. The Gong of Four had struck its last peal; it was finally back to Gumchi. Bring Gumchi to Lagos? What a dream! The new order called for him to find a small cottage in Abuja, perhaps Bida—yes, why not Bida, the home of pottery? From there he would commute to Gumchi, slowly, gradually build the Rehabilitation Centre, continue the work he had embarked upon. Gumchi First? No, Gumchi Now. He had been right from that very beginning when he had resisted all Duyole's blandishments to settle down south so they could fulfill the dreams of youth—Lagos was simply no place for the Gumchi dream factory. Leave Lagos to the Pitan-Paynes, now deservedly emptied of its one sustaining soul. That was one soul which truly understood the worth of happiness. He permitted himself a wry smile of gratitude—he had been saved making himself at home only to pull up roots again. As for the pangs of bereavement, all that would come later. For now, grief was relegated into a mere knot of insensibility. He felt nothing. He had to confront the young widow—just what form of consoling words could he possibly utter?

She was in her room, kept company by Selina. At least she now had a woman's shoulder to cry upon. He tried to imagine what it had been like for her in the few days before Selina's arrival. It must have been a double cruelty. The bereavement, yes, but that Duyole should die so far away from home, which left her deprived of the consolation of the women of the house. They would have taken turns to be with her, never leaving her for one moment, sleeping in her room and watching over her until the funeral, and even remaining with her for days, weeks afterwards—that was the other cruelty. Kikanmi, who had arrived before anyone else had attempted to fulfill that role, aided by Duyole's two daughters—he was none too sure how much empathy could be expected of them, considering their long-simmering, quite understandable resentment towards "the new woman."

The surgeon was prepared for the effect of his appearance but had underestimated the intensity. Also, he had not been aware that he had arrived on a battlefront. He was instantly overwhelmed by the emotional outpour. Even Selina brushed off a furtive tear. Perhaps this was the product of sudden memories of times shared, times now forever over, and a genuine love for the absent begetter of those times. Her mind also remained on her duty—to prevent the widow from injuring herself through excessive grieving. Bisoye went into successive waves of sobbing, becoming inconsolable, and Selina took charge with an efficacious mixture of compassion, gruffness, and mock anger at her ward: *All right now, that's enough. Yes, yes, it hurts, I know it hurts. It's unfair. Life is unfair. Yes, sometimes we wonder why God deals one such a heavy hand, but . . . Yes, yes, by all means, grieve. It can't be helped. But enough now, enough. That will do. You have to look after your health, you know. I say, that will do! Do you want me to go away? All right, I'm off. If you think all I have to think of is mopping up the floor after, you'd better think again. Do we have to go through all this each time a friend or associate of Duyole's turns up? There, there, come on now, come on. Compose yourself . . . Oh, never mind me, look at me trying to keep up the pretence. But excess is wrong, you know that, excess is quite wrong, it becomes self-indulgence. There, there, there, take heart. Auntie Selina is here, we'll see it through together. . . .*

Menka had witnessed such scenes numerous times, an intuitive gauging of the degree and phases of distress, the deft rebandaging of a wound as it is opened and reopened. Selina came truly into her own, displayed totally unexpected expertise and affectionate concern. Menka was genuinely relieved, and resolved to relate to her with greater empathy from then on. Misjudged her completely, he decided. The Damien affair was just an aberration.

The storm subsided at last, and Menka broached the subject on the mind of everyone. "I suppose, Selina, there has been no change of mind from The Family? We are not here to accompany Duyole's body home?"

The transformation was instant. One moment Menka was listening to the purr of consolation, the next it was the hectoring voice of The Family.

"Uncle Kighare, it was the best decision we could have taken. There was no other choice. In fact, we're lucky in a way that he died here, it's an act of God. They are professionals over here, I mean the funeral parlour, not like all the noisy and messy people we would have had to cope with at home. Those who are able to attend will come, those who cannot will remember him in their own ways. But they will learn that we gave him a royal sendoff."

The surgeon turned to the widow. "You agree with this?"

She wrung her hands. "I suppose so, Doc. I really don't know what to do."

"Timi told me that you are in full agreement."

Selina jumped in instantly. "Oh yes, we've been discussing nothing else. Sentiment apart, Doctor, is there any other choice? You know, we are so lucky he studied here, so many people knew him. We went to look at the facilities, checked everything. It's all so classy, you'll see for yourself. And the music! There was a funeral going on at the time— the undertakers arranged for us to peep in and also walk around. You won't find that level of taste and decency when it comes to our own people."

Menka rose. "Ah well. There was no harm in hoping. It appears all settled. So be it, then."

In his mind, however, the surgeon had resolved that this was anything but the end. Bisoye was clearly under some emotional control and Selina was the agent of transmission. In any case, Menka had finally had his fill. It left him feeling sick and angry. Bisoye saw him to the door and asked what room he was in. Menka told her, adding that he was going first to the bar for a badly needed drink. And then something in her expression—it was an unambiguous plea from a prisoner seeking release. Menka had not earned the title Dr. Bedside Manners for nothing, but anyone with even the most calloused antenna in the world would have picked up that mute plea. She had her back to Selina, so it was nothing especially subtle. It read, quite distinctly, unambiguously, *Please, get me out of here!*

"Come to think of it," the doctor drawled, "why don't you come with me? I've a feeling all you do is stay cooped up in your room all day—am I right, Selina?"

"She can't be made to budge, Doctor. I've tried."

"Well, this time she will." Menka took her by the shoulder and propelled her towards the corridor.

"But, Uncle K. . . ."

"I'll bring her back in thirty minutes, Selina. She's going to have a drink with this doctor, even if he has to force it down her throat."

He propelled her out, walked at a fast pace, half expecting Selina to come barreling out of the room with the unarguable proposition that she also needed a drink. The door remained shut, however, while the sluice-gates of Bisoye's emotions burst open all over again. The resulting downpour continued all the way to the bar, arrested only when Menka asked her, "Where do you *really* want Duyole buried?"

"Where else, Doc? Where else but in Nigeria? In Badagry. I *know* he would want to be buried right there, where he chose to settle. Not even Lagos. In Badagry, where he left his mark. Where he launched that infamous street party on escaping from the government cage. I know he wants to rest where he raised Millennium Towers, the first of its kind in Badagry. What deep ties has he ever claimed with Salzburg? He studied here—so what? Everyone studies somewhere."

"Let me ask you once again, do you want Duyole's body brought home?"

"Could I possibly want anything different? Is it possible for anyone to think of any other place? I don't understand what they're all doing. Auntie Selina dictates to me and speaks on my behalf. I am not allowed to say anything. All I hear about is the family this and the family that. They have taken over everything to do with Duyole. They don't permit me a say."

"You mean you never expressed a wish for him to be buried here, in Austria? At any time?"

"Uncle Kighare, during the first two days, did I know where I was? What I said? What I was doing? What clothes I was wearing? What do you think I understood about what anyone was saying? I could have said yes. Maybe I did. I probably did. But was that what I wanted? Did anyone ask me what I truly wanted? When Auntie Selina came, all she kept hammering into my head was the need for him to be buried here. What need? Whose need? No one explained. Everything had been decided, everything. I was merely being informed. No one bothered to ask what I wanted. I was being told only of family decisions. Until Debbie arrived, and Katia, and they both began to protest, I didn't even know who had really decided what or how. I kept asking for you—*Where's Doc? Where's Doc? Why isn't Dr. Menka here yet? When is he coming?* I called your number, left recorded messages."

The doctor shook his head. "I picked up nothing. Nothing at all. Did you do your own dialing?"

"No. Auntie Selina always volunteered. I don't even know where my phone is."

"Yes. It figures."

"I had no one, just these people telling me what to do, what was being done. No one consulted me about the funeral arrangements. They settled on which funeral parlour, which cemetery, they picked the burial plot, spoke to the undertaker. I no longer know if this is a Lindtz event or the funeral of Duyole Pitan-Payne. It's a strange family, Doc. They are all strange in that family. I think that's why Duyole moved out. He was different. There is something weird about the rest of them. No one acts the way they've been doing since the attack. And in the one week since his death . . ."

The bar was largely deserted. As she grew calmer, it became possible for Menka to nudge her gently into sharing with him something he had tried to capture all by himself—Duyole's final moments. He was not sure if it was the right time, but from whom else, apart from the doctors, could he learn of such a defining, particularized moment? He could anticipate the bathetic rendition of the Brain of Badagry, probably punctuated by some coarse comment that he would take to be an expression of manliness. As for Damien, Menka preferred not to even think of him.

Menka would have been wiser to have thought of that son, for what little there was merely succeeded in inserting yet more kinks in the template of morbidity, even for a veteran like Menka. The confident schedule underwent an unexpected setback. A sudden seizure, and the brain virtually ceased to function, its electrical pulses getting weaker and weaker by the minute. He was placed on life support, his brain pulses becoming fainter. Phone calls were made to the patriarch four thousand miles away. Damien had arrived and was collating and transmitting views as he thought fit. The doctors made their recommendation. The burden of decision was beyond his stricken wife—how could she ever consent to take Duyole off his life support? She was able to rise to direct, practical challenges—how was she supposed to assess this one?

Who finally pulled the plug? That was Damien. He had remained by the father's side—a departure from the Badagry scenario—most of the crucial day. Who took the final decision? Bisoye did not know, only that Damien and his uncle Kikanmi in Salzburg, and the other uncle at the Lagos end of the telephone line, had been involved in brief exchanges. Finally the doctors affirmed that even the feeble pulses had ceased. Turning off the system had become purely academic. By that time Bisoye had become too distraught to recollect the sequence of events. One detail of the son's narration of her husband's end, however, remained stuck in her ravaged mind. When she arrived at that point, her demeanour changed. It froze her tears, and a hard, near-incandescent glint of disgust came into her eyes, and it took a while for her to regain her voice.

The Family—including its latest addition, Damien—appeared to be endowed with an unusual capacity for the freakish sentiment, almost as if its members held a secret contest to find out who could make statements of the most bizarre nature, uttered in a manner that was considered by them but no one else to have touched the very silt bed of ocean profundity. Such was the patriarch's *Do you wish to bring him back to serve him up for my dinner?* which seemed to have set tingling a long-rusted sector of Teahole's cerebral pulsations, since he made it a duty to repeat the mantra at every opportunity. Or perhaps it was simply the nature of personal loss, or prospective loss, that promoted the ascendancy of the grotesque in this family affliction of phrase-mongering wisdom. What was beyond question, however, was the compulsive attribution of uniqueness, the garb of revelatory import draped around an eerie utterance that contested the last such in the stakes for the oddest taste in the mouth.

After the decision had been taken and duly transmitted to Damien, to whom that task had apparently been assigned by The Family, or which he had simply appropriated like his father's briefcase, Damien sat by the bedside as his father's life ebbed away. His intimations of mortality or continuity were bequeathed to the world in words that he thenceforth paraded before all manner of audiences, beginning with the widow, directly after the event:

"I held his hand, and I felt his strength flow into me as he died. I could feel his strength pouring into me."

Incapable of absorbing this confident annunciation of a mystic inheritance, and in a phrasing that was probably acquired from some pulp fiction, the masochist in Menka would not rest until he heard it from Damien's own lips. He seized the first chance that evening to encourage Damien to make him a part of his sublime experience, one which, in all his professional years, he had never yet encountered. Damien required no encouragement, employing nearly the same words as he had used in sharing his acquisition with the widow, and with all who crossed his path in Salzburg and for some time afterwards:

"Yes, Uncle, I could feel his strength flowing into me, it was flowing all the way into my body, passing through his hand into me."

MENKA WAS TRAPPED within the dense circle of grief, quite close to the centre, but to all appearances he remained immune to its crippling emanations. He felt grateful for that, and his salvation was made possible by the fact that there were also touching or intersecting circles of demand and dependency that taxed his strength. Most of those who came to Salzburg knew Menka, knew of his closeness to the dead one, and so they behaved as if the doctor was the centre of each of these circles, that he held the key to the mystery that overwhelmed all those who now found themselves together, some for the first time, the scattered humanity that had revolved, often independently, around the deceased. One after the other they made a beeline to his room or trapped him at the bar or along the corridors. Uppermost in their concerns was, invariably, the means to find a key to the decision to bury Duyole in Austria, and next, what the reasons for it were. And, to begin with, was he a part of that decision?

From Nigeria they came, from Lebanon, the United Kingdom, France, from the United States, from Italy and Cannes—it was summer, and both affluent and barely solvent Nigerians were already dispersed over the surface of the globe. There was a haste about the funeral, as if the proponents of its irreverent doctrine were ill at ease with their own decision and sought to limit the number of witnesses to a moment of betrayal. It was a warning the surgeon should have taken to heart. Still, it was a most impressive number that made the journey, all who could, despite the extremely inadequate notice, some arriving even after the funeral was over. Such was the comportment of many— sullen to simmering—that they left Menka wondering whether they had come for the funeral itself or simply to voice a protest, to register their discontent, or just to demand an explanation for an abnormality. It was one thing to be faced with a sudden emptied space in one's life, quite another to be denied ritual accommodation with it, negotiate a peace with that sudden void in the physical surrounds of a shared space of vitality. Perhaps their journey served also as a therapy, since it took their minds away from the domination of what would otherwise count as a vicarious bereavement. An inconsolable hurt and resentment had usurped the province of loss.

Why, why, why? But why? Why are they doing this? Surely, Doctor, you must know.

I cannot believe that the family would take such a decision on their own. There is something behind it, some kind of pressure somewhere. Surely they must have consulted you.

No, they did not.

Such was the desperation for an answer, some minds turned to politics. *Is it the government? Did Duyole or the family clash with the prime minister? Or the president? But Duyole stayed off all those politics. Have they forbidden the return of his body to Nigeria?*

No, it is not the government, Menka assured them. In fact, we know that the old man is a buddy of the prime minister. You have to ask The Family for explanations.

Perhaps the closest of Duyole's business associates was the shipping magnate Rimode Isame, from Yenagoa but based in London. It was the funeral arrangements that catapulted him into Menka's room, like the others, once he had deposited his luggage in his own room.

"What do you know of this, Kighare? Why have they chosen to bury our friend in this place?"

Kighare expelled his twentieth sigh of the day. "You'll have to ask his siblings."

"Is it too late? I mean, what can we do? Have you spoken to their father? Maybe we should phone him together. We can't let this happen. How are we going to explain this at home? What will people think of us? Is Timi here? Is Kikanmi part of this?"

"Solidly. As for the old man, he is the chief promoter. They say it's a family affair, and The Family—capital letters—has spoken."

Isame let out a prolonged wail. "This is not a light matter, you realize—it's far more serious than we think. This is Duyole Pitan-Payne of Millennium Towers! If he wanted to be buried outside Nigeria, he would have built his towers overseas! People will imagine all sorts of things. You'll see. They'll even insinuate . . . oh, I can just begin to picture it. Media rumours. Gossip. They will say he died some kind of embarrassing death, anything, you can't put it past our people to invent all sorts of stories. What are we going to do to stop it?"

"It's too late," Menka said. "All we can do now is start planning his exhumation."

"Eh? What did you say?"

"They're a stiff-necked lot with false values. They'll come to their senses—maybe. Whether they do or not, it doesn't matter. You think Duyole's friends at home will let them rest? His *real* family? There is a family one is born with, I know that. But I am just learning, pushing sixty, that there is also a family you acquire, one you build around yourself. I've just met several members of that family. Obviously there are hundreds more. So you're right. There's going to be an almighty squall over this."

"But we still have to go through with this funeral?"

"Unless you know how to convince the family patriarch that he won't be force-fed on his son's remains, I'm afraid so."

Isame was naturally baffled, and Menka proceeded to bring him into the full picture.

A knock on the door. Menka answered it, and this time it was the children. The two girls clung to Menka, drenched his shirt with their tears and flung themselves on his bed. Then they saw Isame and tried to show some self-restraint.

The shipping magnate rose. "Never mind me." He smiled. "Kighare, let me go and settle in. We'll speak some more."

Damien had followed them in, dragging his feet. Despite Menka's anxiety for them, he found himself studying them individually, intently. He was touched to hear Damien express concern—and he sounded genuine enough—about how his Uncle Kighare was bearing up. Beneath his solicitousness, however, Menka thought he detected some element of sheepishness. The cause soon became clear.

The effervescent Katia opened up without any preliminaries. "Uncle Kighare, why is our father being buried here?"

The elder, Debbie, instantly added, "We don't understand it at all. Why isn't he going home? He wouldn't want to be left here, we all know that. The whole world knows it."

Menka slowly lowered himself into a chair, aghast. He had obviously done them an injustice. "But I was made to understand that this was what you all wanted."

"No way!" The girls' screams emerged in unison. "Badagry is where he belongs. That's his city. As for business, only Grandpa has connections with Salzburg. Dad came here mainly for his annual medicals, and that was a carryover from his student days. Even that annoyed him—it embarrassed him."

"Mind you," Katia adjusted, "he did look forward to the music festival."

"Yes, yes, and popped over to Munich for the Oktoberfest. It was his annual break. Beyond that, tell me what attachments he had to Salzburg!"

"But your uncle Timi—he told me clearly, distinctly, that this was also your wish."

"Don't mind him, Uncle. That's all Damien's fault. He's weak. He went along with what Uncle Timi told him. All that was before we got here. We've since straightened him out and he's with us. We don't want our father left here."

Damien hemmed and hawed, looked even more sheepish. Preceded by what must have been a severe scolding by his sisters, he cut the image of a naughty schoolboy caught in a petty infraction.

"Well, Uncle, I also assumed that he would be taken home, but when I phoned Uncle Timi, he said this was what had been decided by The Family. Uncle Kikanmi confirmed it."

"Damien is a pushover in their hands," Debbie chided. "He let them twist him round their fingers. He phoned me while I was still in the U.S. and I told him that it didn't make sense. And he certainly had no business speaking for us."

"No, I didn't," Damien protested, and never had Kighare heard him sound so meek. It was as if someone had knocked all the stuffing out of him. Menka had the feeling that because he was the man of the family, he had forgotten that he had an elder sister, and realized belatedly that he had overreached himself, taking decisions on behalf of others. Did this include the turning off of the life support? No, that was not his decision, but he continued to carry himself as if it was. Later Kighare learnt that he had indeed become a fervent convert to The Family position and had tried to bring his two sisters over to the idea. He gave up only after they had shrieked him into submission across the telephone wires.

Menka took a deep breath. The room became even more crowded with the arrival of their mother, Duyole's first wife. She knocked, was also admitted. Menka's room was fast becoming the gathering point for the family—small letters—and other dissidents. Even as they embraced, the soft-spoken divorcée was pleading through her tears, "Kighare, why are they doing this? You are his friend. Don't let them get away with it. Why should they abandon Duyole here? Is this what he deserves—to be left among total strangers?"

Menka calmed her down. "I spoke earlier to Bisoye. All I can tell you is that you all seem to have been grossly misrepresented. Once Bisoye escaped Selina's clutches, she could hardly wait to launch into the same lament and protestations."

"Selina is a mind-control bitch. I know her," Katia said.

Menka permitted himself a smile. "All right. Would I be correct in saying that you all seem agreed? You all want Duyole back home, am I right?"

It drew a passionate babble of pent-up frustration, anger, and pain.

Menka hushed them. He felt very calm and confident as he made his pledge to this other family, though it was more a vow of solace to himself: "I shall bring your father home."

No one asked him how he proposed to do this, and he had no idea of his own. While speaking to Bisoye, his mind had begun to explore several scenarios for what was already a silent commitment, no less. He had begun to envisage a lawsuit in the Nigerian courts, in the Austrian courts, a public campaign, involvement even of the church, a diplomatic offensive, an appeal to the nationalist sense, pride, media campaign, whatever else was the boast of those professionals of emotional trafficking. He saw possibilities of even creating incidents after the initial interment was over, incidents that they could then play up in the Nigerian media until calls for the repatriation of Duyole's body to Badagry overwhelmed The Family conspiracy—if conspiracy it was. All he *knew* was that Duyole was coming home, and sooner than The Family envisaged. Never was he more certain of that homecoming.

"Very well. Since I am a doctor, the very first thing that occurs to me is embalming. You have to ensure that he is properly embalmed." He turned to Damien. "Damien, do you think you can make that your special preoccupation—you seem to be reasonably close to your uncles, so pile on the pressure. I shall look into it myself, but try to remember—and that goes for all of you—I am not blood family. I am not even your family doctor. I've already been reminded of that fact, and not all that subtly."

"I'll do that, Uncle. I know he's seeing the mortician tomorrow."

So here we go again, Menka thought. *And déjà vu shall follow me all the days of my life* . . . The same scenario as in Badagry, when they all divided up the labour for getting Duyole into Austria, now the reverse saga. He held up both hands. "Let me be blunt with you children. I am glad your uncle Timi is not part of it this time, which means I assume I won't be looking over anyone's shoulder. I'm going to assume that when you commit, you perform. It's a family affair, so you just have to help and monitor one another. Don't let your uncles and Auntie Selina rest. Pile on the pressure. Who knows, it may not be too late to put a stop to this—the actual interment. If the pressure is sufficient, even now they may find themselves forced to reconsider. The *Otunba* may yet change his mind."

THE *OTUNBA* DID NOT. There was a stage when a HOLD did appear on the horizon. Even the Brain of Badagry poised his negotiations for a casket. The clusters of guests became more animated yet relaxed. The compromise was simple: a memorial, the usual "celebration of life," in Salzburg, then the funeral at home. Kikanmi ensured that the news spread quickly, and he walked around with a jauntiness that remained absent while he endured the brunt of popular opprobrium. Teahole arrived from Badagry, and it appeared that it was he who had brought the good news. When he moved among the crowd that same evening, he exuded the air of a beneficiary of a celestial amnesty, dispensing the atmosphere of concordance with the rest of the world. Even his sniffles emerged more like a statement of relief than of a cultivated affliction. The bar rebounded with the exuberance that underlay all notions of a celebration of life.

By morning the patriarch had reverted to form and the luscious display of the Austrian breakfast buffet lay in ruins. The news came through as strange, very strange. Indeed, incomprehensible. All had considered the bedtime assurance the most rational resolution, a welcome, albeit belated, conversion to the humanity of a man's or woman's life partner, decided by either in full maturity and sanity. Over and above the wishes of the widow came the fiat—interment in Salzburg! The gathered guests made no effort to conceal their displeasure, and the three elders of The Family in Salzburg found themselves isolated. They were grumpy, defensive, and aggressive, conciliatory and defiant—it did not seem humanly possible, but it was indeed the pattern—all within the single gesture and pronouncement. It made no difference. The most humiliating rebuke came from the expatriate friends, whom they expected to applaud the decision of Europe as Duyole's terminal home.

The *oyinbo* proved the most implacably hostile. Seated in the bar the following afternoon, Menka pricked up his ears when he heard

Kikanmi, increasingly chastened under the general onslaught, concede, "After all, anything can happen in the future, when everything has quietened down. We may then find it appropriate to exhume him and bring his body home."

The common, voiced response: "So why bury him here in the first place?"

An Englishman, whose demeanour had remained undisguisedly disdainful in that mild English manner cultivated over centuries, spun on the padded barstool and joined in the conversation for the first time. "When *what* has quietened down, Brother Payne? I spoke to my colleagues in Lagos, and the point in fact is the total lack of noise. There is nothing brewing to quieten down. Nobody even seems to know that Duyole is no longer in Nigeria. No one even imagines that such a thing was possible. And anyway, why bury him here at all if you're only going to exhume him later on?"

Teahole snapped, "Well, it's too late for a change of plans. All the arrangements have been completed."

"What is too late?" the Brit persisted. "What is too late about this? We could hold a service tomorrow as planned, yes, but what compels us to follow it up with a burial? I've checked. The undertakers don't mind. In fact, they love it. They get paid twice. We'll contribute. Why are his own people being deprived of paying their last respects to him? Of course it's not too late—I don't want to hear that. It's anything but too late."

And he turned his back on the rest of the lounge, only to spin round again. "And let me tell you this, in case anyone attempts to tell you different. Duyole is still very much admired in the university community. They remember him, and they've followed his career, yet they assumed you were here to take him home, and they deplore your decision to bury him here." And he spun round again, tossed down what looked like a snifter of aquavit, and left.

"You will seek the advice of the undertaker, won't you?" It struck Menka as the perfect opportunity to interject his main concern. "Since you admit the possibility does exist of taking him back home at some time in the future, you will make sure he is properly embalmed, right?"

Seven to eight listeners in that bar turned eagerly towards the Brain of Badagry for his response. "Oh yes," he promised. "I'll make sure of that. As I said, all this can change overnight. There is no need for us to keep flogging the issue."

A BUS WAS WAITING to take the mourners from the hotel to the morgue. They all knew when the bus had entered the final stretch into the place of liturgical farewells. As it drew close to the chapel, the driveway grew increasingly floral, the demarcation borders impeccably manicured. Even the air took on a regulated ascendancy of scents, as if the very wheels of the minibus triggered hidden valves that released measured puffs of floral scents into the air. Everything was indeed precise, ordered, predictable.

There had been a delay at the hotel. Yet another friend had flown in that very morning, and they waited while he had extricated himself from registration formalities. While the bus waited, the one element that seemed natural in that unnatural situation took control—an awareness of the closeness of that moment of truth where terminal good-byes are said. No more recriminations, no more resentment. Only an encroaching consolidation of grief. The burden of a permanent absence had begun to weigh on each one individually. No more subterfuge. No more disbelief. The silence could be quantified.

Quietly Menka said to Damien, "Did you carry out your assignment?"

"Yes, Uncle."

The straggler arrived, flustered and apologetic. The bus took off, and they all submitted themselves to a renewed seizure of looming absence. Then Menka heard the sound of someone sucking in a long breath and exhaling it in spontaneous eulogies.

"Just look at the beautiful Austrian flowers, just look at them. At home they would have been left to the mercy of goats, who would make a meal of them." It was Selina, her voice oozing with contempt. "Our people simply have no sense of beauty."

The silence resumed, but of a changed texture, which the woman perhaps misread. It only encouraged the restlessness of her tongue. Menka threw a quick glance at the young widow, Bisoye, saw her eyes widen in shock and disbelief.

"At home," the bereaved sister raced on, "it's a waste of time to leave wreaths in the graveyard—the same goats go in there and chew them up." Then a sad, disgusted shake of the head as she spat her disgust through pursed lips. "Our people have no use for things made for beauty. For them it's a waste of time. Anything they cannot eat they don't value."

The ensuing silence was no longer the onset of grief. Embarrassment pervaded the bus interior with its assortment of nationalities—Lebanese, Austrians, British, Germans, an American, and others. Covertly Menka cast glances around in search of reactions. He encountered only bewilderment and averted faces. Then he thought, is this not the sister of that same realtor who used his influence to have a governor tear up playgrounds, uproot an ancient graveyard, destroy a green space shaded by cashew and almond trees, in order to congest the city of Lagos with a squat, ugly office and business complex? The same who ploughed through the already diminishing green belts of Lagos—the token park of Onikan and the famous Marina lagoon promenade bequeathed by the colonial masters, among others? All in order to satisfy the developers' lust for suffocating high-rise buildings? And now, in "cultured" Salzburg, a concerted sibling gush in praise of the preservation of green spaces?

Selina waxed more ecstatic, and more correspondingly disparaging of her own. Her normally brittle voice had become a piece of grit scratching on the windows of the bus that turned all others into a captive, resentful audience. The mourning sister embarked on a mission of enlightenment, the bus her schoolroom for retarded pupils. She treated all to a running commentary on the European love of their countryside, their gardens, and the unmatchable sensibilities of professionals to the demands of grief and funerals. "What do our people really understand about funerals?" she demanded of the passing Salzburg hedgerows. "Oh yes, getting drunk and bursting at the belly with free food, and the hire of as many bands as possible to sing praises of the departed and make *miliki* all night long—you can trust us there, oh yeah, we know how to milk the funeral. We have never learnt how to honour our dead, except with noise, excess, and ostentatious consumption. Just look at this, look at the scenic surroundings. Christ! What a contrast!"

MUSIC WAS ALREADY being piped through the chapel as they disembarked from the bus, nearly uniformly grateful that the torrent of eulogies to Austrian horticulture was, at least for the moment, stemmed. The morgue was separated from the chapel by a fair-sized verandah through which friends and relations filed to pay their last respects.

That day, cremation earned Menka's approval. There is nothing that can be done to a once-expressive face from which vitality has fled. Only a death mask remains to mimic what one has known. Such forms were supposed to be his meat and drink—he shuddered; "meat and drink" was no longer a neutral, innocent expression—but this was usurpation of a vitality that had become inseparable from his total self-awareness. There was nothing, no resemblance whatsoever between the inert form and a companion with whom one has wined and dined, laughed and quarreled. The occupant of that lined casket, dressed to imitate life, had been accorded the technicality of details—the pocket handkerchief in a double-breasted jacket, a carnation—but it remained a deception. Still, this was his friend, and now his double, since he already saw himself in his place. He had substituted himself and now lay still, eternally unconscious of faces, if any, staring into his, admitting to themselves the same feeling of having been cheated of reality, since this was nothing but a plasticized mimicry of the face they had once known.

They followed the path of music into the chapel, a Handel, streamed seamlessly in muffled acoustics. It seemed to provide the just measure of solemnity and sedateness, a soothing neutrality that made it all things to all listeners. Already a few eyes had begun to glisten with teardrops, the sniffs came louder and more frequently, and the surgeon wondered how long it would be before he himself succumbed, his eyes joining the faucets springing up all over the pews. He held out, perhaps thanks to the aggravation of that morning's bus ride. Also, an interlude of tributes, beginning with those present, who rose, spoke their hearts, returned to their seats. They were not all maudlin; some were even cheerful reminiscences, spiced with home wit and rough affection. *Viva voce* was followed by the transmitted, barely arrived by fax, and read by none other than Teahole. Among them, one came from the prime minister, Sir Goddie. That was more than sufficient to stem any furtive trespass from the tear duct. Indeed, Menka was stopped—he exaggerated—from desecrating the solemn rites with a derisive guffaw only by the terminating passage. The message praised the "painful but courageous decision, a shining display of patriotism," to inter the people's hero exactly where he had fallen. That drew gasps and exchanges of puzzled looks around the chapel. What was Sir Goddie's interest in this openly resented event?

The eulogy that finally took his breath away, however, following immediately after Sir Goddie's, thoroughly savaging Menka's already frayed mask of self-composure, came from the founder of the one and only world prophesite, Papa Davina! Davina? What on earth did Davina know of Duyole Pitan-Payne, that he should join in sending him off with a tribute and moralizing cant? To rub salt and pepper in the injury, Mr. Teribogo proceeded to echo Sir Goddie's sentiment, this time lauding the "pious and humble submission" of the family in their decision to bury their son in faraway Austria, where God, in his infinite wisdom, had chosen to call him home. The doctor felt himself personally affronted, this time truly close to leaping out of his pew to snatch the sheet of paper from Teahole and rip it to bits. Then, just as suddenly, it all subsided. He prescribed for himself instant calm. Oblivion. The dead are a free-for-all for the world to feast on; so be it. *Aren't we well and truly about to inter our own in their alien place, accompanied by ceremonials of their own spiritual world? Of our own choice? Of our own free will?* His anger took its silent war to the officiating priest—*Yes, you, sir, to begin with—just who the hell are you, Mr. Clergyman! What are we to you? Or to any one of these alien faces? What relationship or understanding do you bear towards the earth by which we live and die, to the pendulous goats that would eat up hedgerows and flowers and wreaths left in our graveyards? Most aggravating of all, just what do you know of Duyole Pitan-Payne, founder of the Gong o' Four? What do you know of his whims, his foibles, his generosity, the betrayals he has endured even from those closest to him? What can you feel of this very latest betrayal? Just who are you to pronounce words and order hymns to accompany this son of Badagry across his point of no return?*

The service felt mercifully brief. A change in music accompanied the mourners as they filed past the now-closed coffin and into the lane where the hearse waited to bear Duyole to the burial ground. Their bus preceded the hearse; it rolled inexorably towards his final resting place. Kighare Menka already knew how far he would accompany him or, more accurately, up to what moment he would not accompany his friend, but he had no idea where exactly he would take his leave. Every moment grew longer. Sprung from different corners of the world, a common loss had herded so many together, and the tussle had actually succeeded in creating a sense of community, one that could even boast outcasts, ironically the formal hub of that community, shamefaced, barely tolerated, and dreadfully conscious of their ambiguous presence. Menka felt he owed solidarity to that community, continued to delay the moment of expressive revolt. He was resolved to turn back but found it difficult to take the step that would diminish that stricken family. The exit from the chapel would have been ideal, but he sensed that this would have been too soon, too abrupt. When he walked past the coffin, he should simply have continued walking, walked out of the chapel, out of the entire complex of death and away from the desecration of Duyole's existence. He had missed that moment, and now he felt trapped.

It was the cemetery itself that came to the rescue. This was an enclosed, not an open, burial ground. An elbow-high stone wall surrounded this terminal destination, leaving an opening for the hearse and its accompanying procession. He now understood why the bus preceded—to enable the mourners to descend and walk to the graveside ahead of the hearse. No one could gainsay the immaculate condition of the interior of this enclave—a glimpse through the open gates revealed a resting place for those whose antecedents could perhaps be traced backwards to pre-Hapsburg settlements, the relics of centuries of wars, uprootings, resettlements, and clan consolidations. The lawns, the marble headstones embossed with names of family dynasties, the carefully regulated pathways between graves, all testimonies to cultivated fastidiousness. This, then, was the chosen resting place for Aduyole Pitan-Payne of Badagry, once the point of no return for slaves that were herded across the Atlantic.

And so, at that entry where the bus stopped and the mourners began to disembark, so did Menka, only he stood to one side and waited while the procession filed past, then the hearse, its burden covered in flower wreaths, and bade his friend a silent *Au revoir*. It had now moved beyond a mere pledge or conviction, it had hardened into a duty. Menka accepted that he had declared war on this charade, and for the first time since he had arrived in Salzburg, he experienced utter tranquility. He walked back to the bus as if all was now resolved and there was nothing left to aggravate the soul.

The graveside party returned half an hour later, tear-streaked and eyes reddened. At the definitive moment when the ultimate abomination was committed and the casket was lowered into the grave, there had arisen a sudden outburst of wailing, the like of which had never been heard in that discreet graveyard, a detonation so startling that the officiating priest stopped dead in his liturgy, frightened, not knowing whether it was a protestation at something he had said or done, some cultural offence he had given at what he had always known as moments of silent grieving. Isame, the shipping magnate, was the first to break, and it was like the starting signal for a contagion that spread instantly. A deluge, a cacophony of shrieks followed. The ancient Teutonic stones reverberated with the howls of primordial anguish from the heartland of a distant continent and the priest stopped, puzzled, unable to continue. He could only watch helplessly, disconcerted at this spectacle for which his training had not prepared him. Culture shock—yes, that was it, in full manifestation.

Finally, however, the uproar subsided. The priest hurried through the rest of the service, dreading, no doubt, another unseemly outburst, but no, the cascade had been stanched, leaving only the occasional sniff. The mourners left Duyole among his newly acquired family and clan and retreated to rejoin the living.

The weeping bout appeared to have brought catharsis; certainly it acted to dispel the cloud of silence that would have accompanied them on the journey back to the hotel. Now it was all banter and friendly blame allocation. They argued over whose singular shriek had terrified the poor priest and nearly made him drop his prayerbook. On the actual initiator of the epidemic there was no argument—all agreed that this was Isame, and now they proceeded to identify the next tear duct to catch and spread the affliction. Rimade interrupted that line of debate and delivered a nod of mockery in Menka's direction. He, Isame, was at least more courageous than some, such as the supposed rock-hardened Gumchi product, a medical doctor to boot. No, worse, a surgeon, used to cutting people up without batting an eyelid. Yet it all collapsed at that moment of final leavetaking; Menka could not even bear to pass through the gates to the graveyard. The Gumchi outsider was, however, in no charitable mood; he refused to concede a misreading towards this loosening of tensions. Unsmiling, and in a flat register, he responded that he came from a culture that could not bear to witness abominations, such as interring one's own flesh and blood in foreign soil, except on compulsion.

Runjaiye, the junior partner, nodded agreement. He had taken a seat near Menka and now spoke in his halting Yoruba. "I could not help myself. I howled with all the rest—in fact, I caught it early. But it happened to me only when I suddenly thought, *Is this real? Are we really abandoning Duyole on this spot?* That was when I felt something rupture inside me. I could no longer control anything."

Menka turned and faced Kikanmi squarely. "I hope you can get the Austrian army to set a twenty-four-hour watch on that graveyard. Because—let me tell you straight—I am coming back to take Duyole home."

IT WOULD APPEAR that it was not merely stentorian grieving that proved contagious among that motley assemblage of the bereft. Perhaps there was a virus of anthropophagy in the air, imported all the way from Badagry. Also, tossed between fathers who conceived of having their sons for dinner—even via the denial route—and sons who played mystic vampire and piped the life force from their fathers into their own bloodstream, Kighare Menka, temporarily relieved from a network of human consumption, found himself craving a vicarious share before leaving Salzburg. Or perhaps simply as a cauterizing strategy, to take the other kind of man-eaters out of his psyche? No matter, his affliction took the mild form of sharing a meal with the departed in absentia, perhaps with an empty chair set for that absentee in time-honoured ritual. It could have stemmed from a feeling of incompletion of the earlier farewell rites, since he had stopped short of the graveyard and resolutely rejected any further participation in the interment. Above all was a desperate need to escape from it all on his last night in Salzburg, having resolved to flee the following morning early. He wished to be nowhere accessible to The Family's representatives, not even if they had begun to rethink and commence plans for Duyole's exhumation. They would all dine, he knew, at the hotel. He would arrange that one meal—his first of the day, which brought it even closer to communion—by himself; that is, alone, but not quite. There was nowhere that Duyole had stopped for a meal, even a sandwich, in all of Salzburg that he had not left a permanent record of exceptional gusto. All Menka had to do was find one such place. He would order exactly what Duyole had had for his last meal in that restaurant. If they did not remember it precisely, he would simply ask for any meal that they recalled serving him anytime before. That would be more than sufficient. He and Duyole had never been together in Salzburg—Paris, Frankfurt, Rome, Milan, Cannes, London, etc., but never Salzburg. The need came over him suddenly to partake vicariously in one of the missed spaces of his rich existence. The more he thought of it, the more it approached a spiritual, cleansing need.

Just as suddenly—how on earth could he have forgotten!—Menka recalled that Duyole often spoke of a restaurant just on the outskirts, not far from the Lindtz chocolate factory, one of the many discoveries where he had left his mark. He knew also just who to ask—from the moment of his arrival, one of Duyole's college acquisitions had called and offered any assistance Menka might need to tide him over what he sensed would be a painful stay. He had heard much about the surgeon, member of the Gong of Four, from Duyole, referred to as his glorified butcher friend of Gumchi, whose population was not even one-tenth of Salzburg's. After the burial, perhaps anticipating some psychological wounds that Menka might be tending, he preoccupied himself with the visitor's plans for the rest of his stay, and especially in the immediate, for the evening after the burial. Heaven alone knew what he must have been thinking, but the man had clearly made up his mind that Menka was not to be left to his own devices. He had been most persistent, feeling that this was something that he owed Duyole, to look after his friend the surgeon. He left him his card.

Menka now fished for the card, found it, and called him. Did he know at which restaurant Duyole might have expanded his stock of eating notoriety? The man laughed out loud—of course! Could he direct him there? He would like a meal there, Menka said, and if the waiters remembered Duyole's last visit, he would like to have exactly what he had had for lunch, dinner, or whatever.

It proved a cruel night, a night of unforgettable crassness. As he started out, thinking to slip away before others began assembling for dinner, he saw them! They were together with his volunteer host, awaiting him. The friendly, solicitous man thought it was such a befitting idea that he had decided to invite the entire family of the deceased. Everyone. The Family, the family, the extended family, the consenting family, and the dissenting family. Silently Menka upbraided the friend he had planned to celebrate for his choice of local friends. How could the man fail to have sensed that he desperately needed to be alone? Alone, alone, alone, alone! And if that proved impractical, then just the children and the widow. But certainly not The Family.

Escape was impossible. Briefly he thought of retreating to his room and ordering whatever, but the shipping magnate was also there, looking foward to being with him. Menka felt trapped. He blamed himself. If only his mind had been less cluttered by the day's events and its looming demands, all the travesties that passed for a solemn farewell, he would have anticipated the expansive nature of his volunteer host. He gritted his teeth, submitted to an evening of penance. They piled into the provided minibus, the same that had served as his Purgatory earlier in the day.

The maître d'hotel made his recommendations and took orders. Yes, he recalled most distinctly what Duyole had ordered, and he would treat the doctor to that very pasta and venison. The extraneous garnishing—not from the kitchen—was anticipated but not in such heavy dosage. Even he had underestimated The Family's capacity for plumbing down to base sediment in pursuit of the banal.

If only they would keep quiet!

Were they genuinely enamoured of the day's proceedings? Surely they must know that they were isolated by the choice they had inflicted on everyone else! Or did they feel so resentful of the evident disapprobation around them that they felt compelled to justify their action through a continuing glorification of the assets of strangers? It was doubtful if they knew the answer themselves, only that they felt driven to talk and talk, endow their taste with enforced appropriateness. As for dinner itself, they wolfed down their orders with undiminished relish while others grew increasingly embarrassed and upset, squirmed, threw covert glances at one another, and perhaps upbraided Duyole silently for his one unforgivable error of emerging from such an incongruous nest.

That cemetery, do you know how many generations of Austrians have been buried there? Getting a plot in that place was not easy, you know. If we hadn't had connections, I mean, they know the Pitan-Payne family here . . . You know the Austrians, they're very strict. The cemetery can take only so many—the limit is all decided in advance.

You bet! After a certain number, that's it. Doesn't matter who you are. And of course they are most selective—not like it is at home, where t'aja-t'eran* can find room anytime . . .

And those flowers . . . beautiful, so beautiful.

The music—didn't you love the music? I told them my brother loved Mozart, and that's what they chose. These undertakers really do honour to their profession. They know how to put people in the right frame of mind.

The overall atmosphere . . .

Oh no, don't even talk of the atmosphere . . . overwhelming. Simply superior. How could they keep a cemetery so neat, just like a garden?

As I said, the goats would have eaten all the flowers. Pigs would be let loose to root as they please. No, just tell me, where in all of Nigeria could one find a garden—I mean cemetery—so well kept? Our people have such a long way to go. Oh yes, a lot of catching up to do.

Do they know it, though? Are they aware of the huge gap?

Well, they travel, don't they? They see these things. I mean, it's not as if they haven't got eyes in their heads.

But it makes no impression on them, none at all.

It's sad. Eating and drinking, that's all we understand. Their idea of a funeral is to bring in the band and carouse all night. People you've

---

* Dogs and cattle.

never known will show up. They'll even sew aso ebi* *and parade themselves in it. God, what a contrast! Everything so sedate here, so decent
and tasteful. Dignified . . .*

Oh yes, dignified. It's what I call respectable and dignified.

Bisoye stood up quietly, excused herself, and went to the toilet.
Half the table followed her anxiously with their eyes, but the trio did
not miss a beat. A waiter escorted her in the direction of the toilet and
pointed the way. Then the maître d' reappeared in his white overall,
and his voice was a mixture of surprise and displeasure.

"Your food is getting cold, Herr Doktor. I make it special, the way
your friend liked it. You haven't touched it."

"Oh, I am so sorry." And Menka quickly stuck his fork in the
pasta and tried to wrap a few strands around its prongs.

"Or perhaps you don't like it? You can order something else."

"No, no, please. It is delicious." He was not lying, and he quickly
rammed a forkful into his mouth. The maître d'hotel hovered around
him for a few moments, then went on an inspection tour of the rest
of the table. The siblings had no cause to fear his disapproval. Menka
was beginning to twirl the next forkful when the voices of provocation
resumed once more. It was Kikanmi in full flight yet again, and the
surgeon knew that the rest of his pasta was doomed to stay down in
the plate and slowly congeal.

"Mind you, quite apart from everything else, it's fated, you know.
There is a bond between our family and Austria. We lost a brother
here, you know. He died and was buried here."

"Your brother died in Austria?" asked the Englishman whose
voice Menka had last heard in the bar.

"Oh yes." Selina added, "He was something of, ah, you know, a
wanderer. How he got himself here, heaven knows, but it was after
Pop-of-Ages first visited Vienna. I think he heard about the city so
he decided to try it. It was all between him and the *Otunba*. But we
received news one day that he had died. The Family sent word that he
should be buried in Vienna. Who would have known at the time that
we'd have all this close connection with the Lindtz people?"

* Group outfit for a social occasion.

"Yes, that's right," Kikanmi agreed. "The Family seems drawn to Austria. Our destinies are linked in a strange way. Maybe from a previous life. I'll probably end up being buried here myself."

Menka found his voice. "You really would like to be buried here? If you had a choice, you would?"

"Of course. Wherever I drop dead, just dig a hole there and bury me. One thing you learn from dealing with land is that all land is the same everywhere."

That provoked instant howls around the table. His fellow diners, both citizen and transient, began to shout out competitive experiences—what they had had to shell out informally, then undergo formally, to secure the specific patch of real estate they badly sought for specified business—forget even as basic domicile. Other voices screamed last-minute deprivation of allocated land—certificate of occupation issued, stamped over government seal, only to have excuses and offers of alternative acreage, most notoriously lagoonside land reclaimed with public funds but shared only among the anointed. Testimonies flew like flaming arrows over being offered substitutes of such value sameness that they turned down the offer sight unseen. Such was the torrent of passion generated that the Brain of Badagry could, if he wished, fairly claim that it was only thanks to him that conversation finally overcame the somber evening, became spirited and unforced.

About twenty to twenty-five minutes after his profound pronouncement, Kikanmi finally appeared to catch up with his thoughts, emerging with yet another family revelation. "Mind you, The Family has a soldiering tradition. We have an uncle—he's still alive—who actually fought in Burma. He was in the West African Frontier Force, commissioned in Ghana. He used to say, when you sign up, your body belongs to the Queen. So one patch of land is just the same as any other."

That ended Dr. Menka's prolonged reticence. "Cultures differ," he remarked. He had sworn himself to silence, praying that Kikanmi would take the same Trappist vow in deference to the occasion. It would, in any case, merely conform to his spasmodic bouts of presumably deep reflection. Now Menka felt personally assaulted. "No! Speak for yourself or your, er, Family. But don't you dare suggest it's a universal military code. The Israelis sometimes risk losing more soldiers just to bring their dead home. And the United States is still looking for the bodies of her soldiers from the Vietnam War. So don't tell me it's a military thing."

"Quite right." It was the Englishman again. "I was about to make the same point. There are armies where it is considered a matter of honour to bring home their dead if at all possible."

"At the time your brother died in Austria," Menka continued, "it was a far more complicated business to bring home a corpse. Cumbersome and expensive. It happened quite a while ago, didn't it? The journey would have been by boat."

Timi rose to the defence of family honour. "The Family never had a problem looking after its own, no matter what it took. It was simply a decision it made."

"Ah well," Menka sighed, "when you finally get your wish to be buried in Austria, in an exclusive, dynastic cemetery, just recall that a character called Adolf Hitler was an Austrian. Then pray that one of his heirs does not take over your newly acquired borough as mayor or burgomaster or whatever. He might just decide that your presence desecrates his ancestor's memory, that a big black buck nigger was once buried on his Aryan soil and that it was time to restore the graveyard's racial purity. You try and tell him then that the Salzburg destiny is intertwined with that of the Pitan-Payne family."

It was at this point, wishing he could evaporate and resurface on Plateau soil, that Menka looked around and noticed that Bisoye had been gone nearly half an hour. Alarmed, he commented on the prolonged disappearance, pushed back his chair, and went looking for her. Selina made a halfhearted effort to rise, but the doctor forged ahead anyway, muttering, "I'll just make a quick check." He found her in the joint vestibule, weeping out her soul. Now he regretted not waiting for Selina. He tried to console her, persuade her to rejoin the company, but stood no chance. "It's not simply grief," she succeeded in blurting out. "It's all that horrible talk issuing from the mouths of his brothers and sister. I couldn't bear to listen to them anymore."

Selina arrived moments later. Menka left the widow in her loving care and walked slowly back to the table. The maître d's voice was caustic as he offered to reheat Menka's plate or make a fresh dish. The chastened client winced, begged him not to bother, apologized, and hoped he would understand.

"I came here for a sort of Last Supper," Menka improvised. "But I think I only betrayed your Christ all over again."

Of course he only left the maître d' confused. That proud professional sniffed, but stuck to his guns. "I've kept for you our famous apple strudel—would you like it cold or slightly warmed up? Your friend never missed it to round out his meal."

"I believe that. But no afters please, I lack his sweet tooth. Hardly ever touch dessert."

The man was scandalized. He looked ready to throw him out. "The Austrian apple strudel is not a dessert, Herr Doktor. It is tradition."

"I know, thanks. You should hear our friend sing its praises. But believe me, I'll just restrict myself to the main course."

Gingerly Menka resumed his seat, pulled his plate close, muttering to himself, "Penance time, Gumcheeky—*one for two, gung-ho*—eat!" Becoming slowly aware of it only moments after his commencing motions, he became increasingly deliberate with every gesture, especially when he broke off some bread, sipped from his long-neglected glass of wine, and resumed eating. He forced himself to swallow forkfuls of congealed pasta and venison, rare, indeed still oozing red blood, albeit thin, stuffing his mouth, masticating with a slow, reverential awareness. The maître d' remained by his shoulder, implacable, unforgiving.

20.

Homecoming

Kighare Menka did not, could not mourn. Certainly not yet. The churning of his mind left no room for grief. True, there was the constant companionship of loss, but it was without any sense of dejection. With so much ferocity within, there was simply no room left to mourn, and what little room was left was occupied by a sense of urgency.

You want to bring his body home—why? To serve him up for my dinner?

Yes, Sir Patriarch Pitan-Payne the Otunba, *dearly respected Pop-of-Ages, if that is indeed what that means to you, you had better start setting that table, bring out your best silverware, and spruce up for dinner in your lodge outfit. For that is exactly what I plan to do!*

To begin with, was there a daytime flight to Lagos?

There was. Going via Frankfurt. That meant the Lufthansa airline. Refusing to consider that he was now virtually locked within a blind zone of pure obsession, Dr. Menka rose early—he had barely slept—before the rest of the hotel began to stir. This time he was prepared to encounter any of The Family, if there were any somnambulists among them. He would walk straight past, out of the hotel, exchanging not a word. If he was unlucky enough to find himself in the same shuttle, heading for the same airport, he would refuse to acknowledge their existence. The sole exception would be Damien, and that was only because he had a question for him. Menka had personally entrusted him with a mission that stood to affect his plans, and he needed to obtain the result. At dinner he had asked the question of the one who was primarily in charge of that task, big brother Kikanmi. As they all began to play musical chairs around the large table—actually several put together—trying to decide who should sit next to, opposite to, close by, etc., Menka walked up to Kikanmi and put the question, but the answer that came back was vague, shifty, and even near dismissive. It was delivered with such offhandedness that it was with great difficulty that Menka stopped himself from repeating it aloud for the benefit of any listener, just to put Kikanmi on the spot and extract a straight answer that his intuition already proclaimed. Now he had only Damien left to provide him with a truthful response. Come to think of it . . . and Menka picked up the phone. He paused, glanced at his watch, hesitated, shrugged off all sense of guilt, and dialed Damien's room anyway.

The voice was heavy with interrupted sleep. "Who is this? Wait a minute . . . what time is it?"

"Never mind the time, Damien. Can you hear me clearly?"

"Yes, Uncle K. Is something the matter?"

"No. I'm leaving, and I want to know if you passed my message to your uncle."

"Message. What message? Ah—oh yes, I did. I was with him."

"And did he embalm?"

"I'm sure he did. I delivered the message with the undertaker present. I left them together—I had to go to the florist . . ."

"All right. See you in Nigeria."

"Are you leaving?"

"I'm off. Sorry I interrupted your rest. Go back to sleep."

Some four hours later, all checked in at Frankfurt and awaiting his flight home, he called his nation's ambassador in Vienna. That diplomat had attended the funeral on behalf of the government and departed as bewildered as everyone else. He had planned to be present anyway, but revealed in confidence to the family that the prime minister himself had phoned and ordered him to be there, representing the government. The message that was read followed soon after. Also—this in strict confidence—the minister of foreign affairs on his own had instructed him to find out discreetly why the famous engineer and United Nations consultant was being buried in Austria. The diplomat had returned from Salzburg to his base a frustrated being—"a stiff-necked lot," he grumbled aloud all the way back to Vienna. Over the phone, it was as if he had been waiting to let off steam.

"Dr. Menka, I didn't know what to make of those people. I pleaded with them. I warned them. I said, 'Listen, you people, you know this is part of our duties. When one of our nationals dies, we get involved.' So we have the experience. Some people make this decision in a state of confusion—they just want to get things over with. A funeral. Just any funeral. And then, of course, they think of it as a most natural way to go about it if they happen to be living abroad at the time. But in the end they change their minds. They want to take the body home, so they come to us for help. They don't consider that it then becomes more complicated. You have to exhume. So why the rush? I advised them to leave the body in the morgue and give themselves another week or so to think about it. And this is someone we happen to know about. I knew him personally. He's not the kind of person you leave on foreign soil."

Menka felt lighter in mind. "Thank you, Mr. Ambassador. You'll be hearing from me."

"Anything I can do, just let me know. You'll see. The family will change its mind. They usually do. But these ones would not even give it a thought. In fact, they barely stopped from telling us to mind our business. As if that is not why we're here. It is part of our business. So I left them with our standard advice, the senior brother especially—embalm. Make sure you embalm, and get a strong casket. That's always been our advice from the embassy."

It was as if the ambassador knew of the persistent thread running in Menka's head. "You did that? You gave him that advice?"

"Of course. What else could we do? We've been involved since Pitan-Payne was flown in for surgery. And when it happened, we moved into our routine for assisting the body to go home. So you can imagine my surprise when they said they would inter him here. I met them, together with the parish priest. We both preached and preached, but it had no effect, so all I could do was give them the usual advice—embalm, and get the strongest casket you can afford!"

The surgeon thanked him.

And still he had no idea how he would fulfill his—no, Duyole's desire. He did not need to be told—that was what Duyole would have wished, nothing else! And so, institute a lawsuit in Austria maybe, on behalf of his widow and children? No, perhaps best done in Nigeria. Or else embark on a covert operation to disinter the body and take it home? He did not consider that in the least outlandish—Menka was confident, could swear that the Salzburg authorities, the burgomaster or whatever, would cooperate in full. What was the Nigerian engineer to them? Why should they want his body in the graveyard consecrated to their families and ancestors? If worse came to worst, Salzburg would accept the authority of the wife over that of his weird siblings. Or parent. Menka made his calculations: wife plus ex-wife plus two and a half children (Damien making up the half, as a dubious factor) versus father and three siblings. Even wife alone should trump the rest—any sensible judge would find for her. A trial was not even needed. All that was required was a court order, from any court, as long as they moved before the enemy uncovered the plot and moved to obtain an injunction or counter order—so yes, a straightforward court order would be best. He was prepared to do anything, *anything*, to obtain one. What mattered was to present a document to the embassy to obtain its formal cooperation. If it had to be forged, he, Menka, would personally forge one.

He spent his waking hours on the flight home on nothing else but the plan, beginning with a short list of colleagues who had trained in Austria. Or indeed any German-speaking university. Useful, but not crucial, since English was virtually the second language of Austria. One such jumped almost instantly to his scouting mind, and providentially close to hand—he was engaged by the Lagos State University Hospital. That young doctor had graduated, he recalled, from Frankfurt University. Menka wasted no time—it was straight from the airport to the teaching hospital. The young yet unsuspecting body snatcher was on ward rounds. Menka sat down to wait. Wryly, his mind flashed to the visitors from the business combine whom he had met waiting on his doorstep, another haunting sensation of a persistent déjà vu! When the young doctor returned, he was visibly overwhelmed by the sight of the famous senior, ushered him into his office with apologies for having to wait. Dr. Menka countered with his own for intruding without an appointment, and there ended all preliminaries.

"How soon can you leave for your former base, not exactly Germany, but next door—Austria?" Menka enquired.

The young doctor blinked. He had not yet recovered from the presence of this elderly star of the medical firmament, one who had so recently honoured the profession by his work on Boko Haram victims, culminating in the National Pre-eminence Award. In a few sentences, Menka outlined the mission.

"But my duties here, sir—"

"You can leave that to me. I'm coming straight from the airport, and you are my first port of call. Once you've agreed, I shall speak to the provost. I have consulted here before—I'm even considering a resumption of that association. Take it from me, they can spare you for a week. If needed, I'll even volunteer to cover your schedule, but it won't come to that."

Ekundare stuttered his readiness to oblige.

"Good. First thing tomorrow I'll arrange the tickets, get you some money for hotel and feeding . . . Wait. You still have a valid visa, I take it?"

"Oh yes, my wife is even still in Germany, in fact."

"Ah, that's good. You'll be able to stop over and see her once you've carried out your assignment. I'll work on this all day tomorrow so you can take off on tomorrow's night flight."

"That soon, sir?"

"How soon do you think? You're a doctor, so I don't have to tell you what happens to a corpse underground. What you and I know is happening right now!"

Menka made no attempt to avoid the image of the decomposing body, stage by stage. Deep in his marrow, he knew that Kikanmi had not embalmed his friend's body. Even without the evasiveness of his answer at the dinner, he had read the answer on his face. He and The Family had resolved to make the repatriation a *fait non accompli* even before the effort, to place every possible obstacle in the way of anyone bringing their brother back home. It was a strange tussle, since he had also discerned nuances, even in their most stubborn iteration of a finality, a done deed—lurking behind it all was a graceless acceptance that repatriation might prove inevitable. It was there, perhaps the effect of their complete isolation. The odds, they secretly acknowledged, were against them, and they felt ostracized. A part of them even objectively assessed that they could not stand against the combined rights of the widow, the children, and their mother, together with the moral weight of Nigerians and the obsession of one busybody named Kighare Menka. Spoilers, however, they could make it prove extremely untidy. But why, why, why? This was something Menka found frustrating.

Next Menka was confronted with a practical matter. He was a guest at the home of Duyole, and his host was dead. His next mission was on his own behalf—to find a new place to rest his head, store his worldly goods, and plan his offensive before The Family threw him out. Gumchi ultimately, but right now a consultancy with the teaching hospital. They would find him a temporary apartment. If not, one of their lodgings for extended supervision cases. If necessary he would find a small hotel until there was a vacancy. The thought suddenly sobered him—he seemed sentenced to become an eternal wanderer. His jaw tightened—that made two of them. One would also find his peace when the other was finally laid to rest.

Then, quite distinctly, Duyole spoke from beyond the grave. A week after his Austrian funeral, the family was summoned to the home of the deceased by the executors for the ritual reading of the last will and testament. On reflection, Dr. Menka suspected that the executor, Cardoso, an ancient business associate of Duyole, had deliberately brought the reading forward. He knew the contents of the will: Duyole had decreed that he be buried in his birthplace, Badagry, and specifically in the cemetery of the university's Chapel of the Apostles.

Dr. Menka already felt fulfilled, just by that one intervening voice by itself. The news was gleefully conveyed to him by a junior in the executor's chambers—he could not wait to describe the rapid tics on the face of Teahole, especially as that item was broached. Debbie's call followed almost immediately, effervescent with excitement—she had of course diverged home for a while before resuming her sojourn in the United States. All who could, and were entitled, had ensured their presence at the reading—The Family in full complement, minus the patriarch. Menka felt reenergized, embarked on a renewed burst of frenetic activities. If he could have, he would have joined the solitary advance team to Salzburg to commence digging his friend out of foreign soil, if necessary with his bare hands. To leave arrangements for exhumation in the hands of The Family was certain to ensure delays. Deliberate delays. It was logical, and he could read them, one after the other. The covert acts that accused some of the members of a perfidy, the refusal to embalm their brother yet lie that it had been done. Naturally they all would wish to postpone the day of reckoning until it no longer mattered. Move only after the heat of bereavement had fizzled out and the rest was mere depersonalized ritual. The advance team had to be reinforced.

Ruefully Menka checked his resources—yes, he could afford one more flight ticket. Even two. If needed, he would borrow. Bisoye was obviously out of it—she was to be left alone with her grief, and the cultural demands on her status as freshly widowed. Menka spoke to her and she was only too grateful to leave everything to him—*Please do what you have to do, whatever you want, just bring him back*. Debbie was next. As the eldest daughter, she would represent family authority, and she had been battle-ready even without the backing of the will. With the formal validation from Duyole's will, the surgeon felt ready to take on ten Families! Yet even in his now galvanized rush, Menka succeeded in forcing on himself a sense of propriety, always conscious of the fact that he was strictly an outsider, a member of neither The Family nor the family. *For Duyole's sake, Gumcheeky, right? Four for one and one for four-o. Dig into that conciliatory reserve and blow up only when it's all over. Gung-ho, gung-ho, take a deep breath!*

Working up a conciliatory spirit with every trick earned from professional practice, Dr. Menka braced himself and moved on The Family. He called on Kikanmi with the conscripted doctor in tow and introduced him as his personal contribution to The Family's efforts to fulfill Duyole's last wishes, which, he knew, had become paramount in their minds. He explained that the doctor was merely an advance team, sent to facilitate what was now a binding commitment. He, Menka, planned to follow him immediately, once he had put a number of logistical offerings in place for the return home. He knew that The Family must be feeling the pressure of time—as a family friend, he was there to take off some of that pressure. As a matter of fact, he ought to travel with the young doctor, but there were a few things that needed organizing locally. Quickly running a fast spot check over his pronouncement, Menka felt certain that Duyole would have applauded his placatory delivery. He intended to maintain the grade.

Kikanmi finally appeared to recognize that the stalling was over. However, the objections were not. And so Big Brother reminded Menka that in Salzburg he had himself openly declared that the affair was not thereby concluded, that the remains might yet be brought home once the fuss over Duyole's death was over. He could not understand how a trained surgeon could subject himself to such rush—why didn't he just go at a pace that commonsense and practicalities dictated? *We can safely leave it all in the hands of Lindtz.* The Lindtz machine was in any case far more efficient than anything even Gumchi-man, with all due respect to the laureate of National Pre-eminence, could set in motion, whatever connections he had. Lindtz might even arrange to fly Duyole's body back in the same plane that had taken him out, which would simplify the course of action no end. After all, they had not let the side down over the first repatriation. And The Family could send one of the children to accompany the body home—Debbie, for instance. *Whichever way, Dr. Menka, the Lindtzes are on the spot, they know the terrain, have the necessary contacts and influence, experience, and so on.*

Kighare Menka listened attentively, acknowledged that everything The Family proposed made sense, and was indeed thoughtful. All he was doing was augmenting their obvious efforts to repatriate their brother. He had merely recruited expertise for a time-sensitive operation, nothing more. And it was time-sensitive. Moving a live body was less complicated than exhuming, then repatriating, a corpse. *We have a situation on our hands where the time factor dictates*—didn't he agree? The sooner the better, and this doctor would appreciably hasten the process. Menka looked Kikanmi straight in the eye and addressed him quietly, emphasizing every word.

"Even with the best embalming, before being moved from its present resting place, the body will require some final cosmetic attention, do you agree? If you do, then obviously the sooner disinterment takes place, the better. Dr. Ekundare will work with the undertaker. His findings will affect arrangements over here—for instance, will it still be possible for Duyole to lie in state for his very final honours? Or will it be a straightforward journey from grave to grave? So you see, we are not speaking of an identical objective. Now that the wishes of Duyole have been spelt out unambiguously, every moment is vital. Ekundare is a godsend, virtually a native. He knows his way around Austria, speaks German. It turns out he also knows Salzburg itself. His advance visit will facilitate all necessary action that would naturally flow from Badagry—or indeed from Lindtz."

Finally the real estate mogul attempted to regain control and unveiled a firm Family position. The Family had to protect its honour. Therefore it would not take kindly to others spending their own money on its behalf. There was no need for it, since the Lindtz people were more than ready to oblige. They were virtually members of the family, so why didn't Kighare simply wait another day or two so the company could arrange the young doctor's flight? Even his, Menka's—the company would pay for everything, just give it another day or two. Things should be done in an orderly fashion—he found the doctor's proceeding too rushed and untidy.

Menka signaled full accord with The Family's position. He had no intention of assailing the Family honour. If it was reinforced by having their foreign business partner, Lindtz, pay for his ticket or refund the cost or whatever, it was all to the good of his bank balance, and he had not the least objection. However, he happened to be a doctor by profession, and he knew that his role was to return at once and assist. He could not, however, so this young man would go ahead and act for him. And yes, what a great idea that was—Debbie should indeed accompany him! He was certain she would be ready to leave any moment! So, nothing wrong with a relay—Dr. Ekundare this very night; he, Menka, the following day; Debbie to follow at her own pace. Impossible to fault such an arrangement. "The widow has expressed a wish that we proceed along that initiative. So what do you say to that? It takes nothing away from anyone." Kikanmi gazed into space, expelling non-committal sounds.

Seeing Dr. Ekundare on his way, Menka found himself stopped by the young man. "Doctor Menka, I feel honoured to be entrusted with this assignment, but may I ask you a question?"

"Sure. Go ahead."

Ekundare hesitated. "Anyone could read the tension—it made me very uneasy. You, a stranger, wanting the body back—that man, the brother, he was like a man being dragged to the gallows. Why? Unless, of course, it's a matter of medical confidentiality?"

"Not in the least. I just want to count the body parts, make sure nothing is missing."

Ekundare looked startled. "Are you serious, Doctor?"

Menka shook his head. "No, of course not. I'll answer your curiosity, but later. It's a long story. Right now, *bon voyage*. Keep me posted at every stage."

Almost simultaneously, in his home the patriarch, Pop-of-Ages, was fully exercised with the same puzzle, albeit from an opposing stance. He had of course been instantly briefed on the content of the will and on Menka's reckless haste, even the man's impudent attempt to take over what was so clearly a Family responsibility. He snatched his foot from Mamma Kressy's soothing fingers, stood up distractedly, and bristled. "But what is the business of that primitive—wherever bush he's coming from? Why does he meddle in a family affair? I just hope these boys know they must move to protect the family honour!"

Perhaps it was this famous sense of "the family honour" that now began to propel things forward. It was an immediate, extraordinary reversal, one that should not have been surprising, however, since the great Otunba Pitan-Payne's family set great store on public image. The Family dropped all further objections, let it be known to a restricted public circle that it was happily involved in the repatriation of its son, and that the eldest daughter would accompany a doctor on behalf of The Family on a preliminary mission for that very purpose.

The advance mission traveled as planned. Dr. Ekundare appeared to hit the ground running. Straight from landing after a night flight and reinforced by senior embassy staff, he took the train to Salzburg and met the undertaker, who had been alerted and had indeed carried out the first stage, once he had received authorization via the embassy: exhumation. Ekundare called Dr. Menka to let him know that there was no need for him to rush to Salzburg just yet; there was absolutely nothing for him to do until the mortician had completed his work. Indeed, he advised him not to travel until some restoration had been done to the remains. Ekundare would stay only one more day, stop over in Frankfurt to see his family, then return almost immediately to resume duty in Lagos. He would bring back a detailed report, with photographs. Over the phone he conveyed the summary to Menka—nothing approaching revelation, simply that the body had not been embalmed.

The undertaker, Ekundare reported, turned out to be a very disturbed man. Everyone involved in the passing of the engineer appeared to end up only too anxious to unburden. In this case, the undertaker was relieved to talk to someone from the same part of the world as the deceased, and for a change to someone who fortunately spoke the undertaker's language, understood his culture, and was a colleague—well, in the sense that they both worked on the same material: the human body.

Yes, indeed, he had advised—and strongly—that the body should be embalmed, and had warned the elder brother from experience that funerals that took such a contested course hardly ever ended in permanence on foreign soil. It was not unusual for the family to change its mind later on. The undertaker had interacted with the Lindtz people. All voiced deep concern. No one in the entire Lindtz outfit, he declared, showed support for Duyole's burial in Austria. Indeed, their Nigeria-based staff were shocked and disappointed; they had begun preparations to play a conspicuous role in the plans—they assumed—to receive and accompany the Pitan-Payne scion to his final resting place. Leaving cynicism aside, the undertaker said, it was good public relations for the firm. It had operated in Nigeria for decades, even before their formal Nigerian franchise was granted to Pitan-Payne the elder. Their managers had become absorbed into the culture, since they often visited the cocoa farms to establish quality control and had been involved in the termination of the black pod disease in West Africa, sending out experts to train cocoa farmers in preventive measures. They considered themselves part of the nation's economic development, long before the oil discovery. They had looked forward to celebrating with their adopted compatriots the passage of this individual through their lives.

His certitude on this very outcome, the undertaker recounted, had made him offer further advice to Kikanmi on the choice of a coffin. He had taken pains to go into technical details with the real estate dealer:

the soil was heavy, he informed him, so it was advisable to choose a sturdy casket that would not be crushed under the weight of earth. The brother, however, had shrugged off all advice. He preferred a coffin made of cheap, low-density wood—his very expression—but with an impressive layer of varnish. As for embalming, he settled for simple facial cosmetics, nothing more elaborate.

The mortician was merely another ring in the circles of the instructed, but Kighare's instruction was of a different kind. Despite all efforts to ward off the undesired image, Kighare had followed his friend down into that darkness and had witnessed the slow deterioration of his body. He could actually see his face, watch it disintegrate slowly. He felt he could touch his skin. His final brief—phoned to Ekundare at the departure lounge—had been unsparing: *First, get the body out of the earth as fast as you can. Immediately. We've lost valuable time as it is, but let the mortician see what can be done with the face. Once we get him back, the casket will remain sealed during his lying in state. A tinted window over his face, even frosted, as dark as can be, so there can be some physical outline, a shape that is visible through tinted glass, of the Duyole Pitan-Payne we all knew. That's the best we can hope for.*

Ekundare returned with photographs. The face had indeed begun to collapse. The undertaker promised to do his best but advised that close family should be kept away even from the tinted-glass viewer. Only those with a strong constitution should attempt to look, and even they should be warned to steel themselves in advance. Ekundare assured him that every detail was in competent, even enthusiastic hands—the mortician, undertakers, the parish, the partnering firm, the embassy, everyone was on board. Debbie was on the ground, right in the heart of activities. Menka could finally concentrate on arrangements for receiving the body on home ground, ensuring that Duyole at last received the sendoff he deserved, a sendoff equally craved by those who had stumbled, even by accident and however marginally, into his orbit. Gratefully, he canceled his planned sector of the relay. The embassy would play that role, see the body onto the plane. He would remain on home ground to receive.

Then he received the news from Debbie: her office in the U.S. had ordered her back. She had already overstayed her leave of absence, and her boss refused any further extension. When she had left for Austria, it was to travel onwards to the U.S. after she had seen her father off in Frankfurt. So much for the earlier relief, when Menka had been assured that the embassy would cover his self-assigned role. Now, once again, in an underestimation of his own infection by the bug of possession, he succumbed to a deep distrust inserted into his marrow. Any ensuing internal debate was short-lived—to remain and receive or to travel and accompany? Menka decided to travel to Austria and personally bring the body home. On the one hand, he felt—yes—it promised a therapeutic bonus. But then also—he attempted to appraise himself—was this not an onset of paranoia? He admitted that it could be. It would help if only he could remotely guess at, much less fathom, what it was that motivated The Family. But then, neither could anyone he had encountered within the compass of that death. No option, then, but to project their likely acts as broadly and irrationally inconceivable. At that stage, his grim projections refused to shy away from the possibility of The Family's obtaining the corpse of some illegal immigrant and bringing it home for a Nigerian burial. It could end up garnished with the famous wiener schnitzel to be served up for a father's ghoulish dinner.

It seemed the better option to losing more nights of sleep. Menka revalidated his ticket, readied himself for departure. And so once again the unremitting cycle!—a division of labour—with The Family's grudging, even pointedly graceless acquiescence. Indeed, not unexpectedly, the capitulation of The Family proved to be no more than a posture of public relations. The quartet had retreated only to regroup, recoup, and launch a rearguard action, based on tactics of attrition. Menka realized that he had underestimated the tenacious hold of some kind of mental conditioning in them that was akin to a religious zealotry, involving perhaps an exorcist ritual that had to be conducted from a distance? Had he, perhaps, truncated a family ritual? His mind swept to Selina's boast of another brother buried abroad. Accident? Or design? Whichever, that made two of them. It was up to The Family to accept that he also suffered from the same affliction, only his operated from the opposite end of the demonic axis. He permitted a grimace, recollecting one of his early rudimentary inductions into the scientific field, a proven fallacy on all grounds but still applicable as a guiding principle: Action and reaction are equal and opposite.

Listing the responsibilities for Duyole's homecoming, everything that needed to be done while Dr. Interloper was away, The Family affected a retreat into a junior partnership position of a joint undertaking, seemingly content—not without what could only be described as a mix of scorn and sulking—to let others work themselves to death while they looked on. On appearance, this not merely suited Menka, it served as a palliative for the neglected areas of his existence. It took his mind off the root cause of his displacement from Jos, even though he did make the occasional call to Costello and Baftau—did they need any input from him? They did not. It left him utterly grateful. A reporter from the veteran newspaper *The Vanguard* had done an extensive interview with him over his work on the casualties from Boko Haram's bombing spree, and subsequently on his award; he contacted him, linked him up with Damien. Together they would work on the modest amount of publicity that needed to precede Duyole's arrival, enabling his friends to come and take their final leave of him. The journalist was so thankful to be involved, he offered Damien a desk in his own office so that he had all facilities to hand. Anything at all, just ask, he promised.

As Menka sensibly feared, the capitulation of The Family was only between partial and scheming. Others could work, they would undermine. Every step of the way, the formula had become transparent. Even as Menka's hastily assembled team moved to implement the agreed arrangements, the implacable, inexplicable, but active hostility from The Family began to dispense with the last vestiges of subtlety. Orders were issued bluntly, largely from the desk of the same Big Brother—Duyole's homecoming was to be kept as secret as possible. It was back to the Salzburg theology. Deploying every known tactic, The Family resisted all attempts to let Duyole's people, his acquired family, know that their man was coming home. Damien, appointed Mr. Publicity Co-ordinator, was simply co-opted as arrowhead of deception and manipulation. Bypassing Bisoye, as had now become routine, and against all comers, The Family insisted on a workday, not a weekend, for reinterment. But why? What was it to them? Why a weekday?

With Debbie gone and the widow incapacitated, there was only so far that Menka could move. And his main charge, he had decided, was to bring the body home. Even if the weekday chosen was one on which human motion became impossible, leaving no one to accompany the coffin to the graveyard, what mattered was that Duyole should rest eventually within the soil of Badagry. Menka shrugged off a weekday burial, confident that sufficient numbers would sacrifice even a month's salary to pay homage to their colleague, as long as they knew of the event in advance. The Family caviled over the simple wording of a press release, dismissed, refused, agreed, indeed insisted, on taking on other chores, other functions, for the sole purpose of ensuring that they were never discharged, sabotaged others with brazen declarations that those duties were already fulfilled. Menka shrugged, insisted on only one thing—he would personally ensure that that body entered the plane's cargo, he would ride on that same plane. He would accompany Duyole home. And he would personally inter his body in his chosen final abode!

It was not altogether adequate but Menka placed a shadow behind every chore that had been appropriated by The Family, including the most basic, mundane, and unskilled roles, which were suddenly transformed into "Family responsibilities," too sacred to be left to outsiders. Fortunately, crucial input, such as security, proved their scope of appropriation. There, at least, Menka succeeded in asserting full control, a firm, unscripted KEEP OFF sign on display. All the doctor had to do was deliver a stern, angry reminder of how the outward mission had nearly ended in a fiasco, thanks to Teahole's vaunted control over the entire nation's security agencies. "I intend to take care of that myself," Menka warned quietly, and proceeded to outline methodically a step-by-step schedule of movements. On his way out, he would personally visit his newly acquired friend, the airport commandant. It needed no psychiatrist or soothsayer to predict that a mixture of guilt from two directions—one, his earlier obstructive conduct, and two, news of the eventual death of the patient at the centre of it all—would put even the hardiest gladiator in a compassionate, compensatory frame of mind. Menka resolved to exploit that to the fullest, quite shamelessly. He would insist that a detail of his airmen, together with the Highway Patrol escort from the outward journey, meet the plane on the tarmac, offload its sombre cargo, then accompany the cortege straight from the airport to the family home in Badagry. A motorcade of no more than a dozen vehicles, Menka reassured the shrinking violet of the funeral coven. A vigil would be held in Duyole's living room, with the coffin lying in state. His widow, her relations, and Duyole's children would take over for that phase. The following morning, he would personally inter his body in his chosen final abode.

Everyone declared he had grasped his or her part—what to do when Duyole finally arrived home. Almost with a light heart, Menka finally flew to Frankurt, then Salzburg. The mystery of Family attitude remained a nagging point, but not one that he permitted to disturb his newly obtained tranquility of mind. Tranquil, yes, and yet neither the plane nor the train could move fast enough to deposit him in Salzburg. His first stop, even before checking into the hotel, was the funeral parlour. He met the mortician. The exhumation had been carried out without a hitch, he again assured his visitor. He only lamented that it was not how he would have wished the body to leave his clinic. Menka questioned him about his exchanges with members of The Family, what advice he had given over embalming and the choice of a casket. The undertaker confirmed every detail of Dr. Ekundare's report. It was an unrelenting chorus—he had yet to encounter such a perverse attitude in his entire career. Well, he gestured, he had done what he could. Would Menka like to see the body? The surgeon told him that he had already seen the body. The man looked startled. "Surely you remember me? I was the one who refused to enter the cemetery on the day of the burial." Yes, now the man recalled. "Well," Menka continued, "I have never left my friend since that moment, and I know how he is now. I know exactly how he looks. I'm a doctor, a surgeon. I also viewed him when he was laid out in your chapel before the burial, but I have already decided on our parting image and see no reason to efface that image. You want to know what that is?" The mortician nodded. "A foaming beer tankard at Oktoberfest."

Kighare received a check in his headlong careering, something about the laws of other lands. No, he could not travel to Frankfurt from Salzburg across the Austro-German border with Duyole's casket as his luggage; the laws of both nations appeared to frown on such quirks. The transfer of custody to the airline commenced at the mortician's and would be relinquished only in Lagos. Sealed and delivered, Duyole became the airline's responsibility. So the doctor took an earlier train to Frankfurt airport to await his friend, tracking his move every inch of the way until he arrived at the Customs warehouse. *So, my friend Duyole, you are now designated freight? That would have tickled you no end.* Knowing that this was how, more or less, everyone ended up anyway did not make it any easier. Duyole as *freight*! But the surgeon had become far too immersed in procedure to permit himself to dwell too long on such travesties. He operated as an automaton. His task was to ensure that the freight did not get left behind for any reason. Menka followed every bureaucratic demand and advice. He obtained a copy of the freight's waybill and, from his base at the Sheraton Airport Hotel in Frankfurt, continued to monitor every movement of the freight, ensuring that the coffin was actually loaded into the cargo hold. From freight to waybill, his bosom friend, Duyole? He was not even permitted into the warehouse to check—just the alphanumeric identity substituted for Duyole Pitan-Payne. The documentation now reassured him that Duyole was not being jettisoned for some more urgent freight, perhaps furniture for a newly completed mansion for a politician or businessman. Calmly settled into his flight seat, he felt he should have realized, perhaps, that there was actually no cause for concern. This was not the kind of freight that airlines liked to have on their hands one moment longer than necessary, and in any case the much-touted Germanic efficiency had taken over.

IT WAS EARLY EVENING and already dark when the plane landed in Lagos. All were on the alert, the airport commandant in his element. He met Kighare right at the plane doors, in the company of the head of the luggage handlers and the most senior Customs officer on duty. Nothing was permitted to go wrong on this return of the son of the soil, the people's unaccredited ambassador to the United Nations, accompanied by no less than the winner of the National Preeminence Award. Together they descended the side gantry down to the tarmac, to take charge of the freight as it was offloaded. The hearse this time, not an ambulance, waited on the tarmac. It drove up to the hold of the plane to receive its august occupant, pulled up close to the offloading bay. It felt only mildly déjà vu in reverse rewind. All proceeded smoothly. The Customs officer had already taken possession of the waybill. All that was left was to fit the number to the package. His men, alerted to the nature of the freight, kept turning over labels, comparing, moving from one to the next likely shaped object below the belly of the plane. Impatient now, Dr. Menka joined them, the commandant assisting. As Menka straightened up once to look around, he saw an unscheduled observer at the proceedings—the Brain of Badagry, Kikanmi standing aloof, arms folded, his lips curled in the familiar lofty detachment, even disdain, his posture ostentatiously disclaiming any connection with the obscene activity around him. Menka felt like lunging at him. Why the presence? he asked himself. His chores did not involve his presence at the airport—indeed, he had made it clear that he would rather not take part in receiving his brother's corpse. So why had he put in an appearance, if all he planned to do was stand and survey the scene with such obvious, condescending composure? Was this some macabre game of which non-Family were kept in ignorance?

Minutes passed. The luggage hold was emptied. Then came the moment of panic. The casket was nowhere among the pieces strewn all around the bay.

Menka waded through various packages of likely sizes, all taken out of the hold under his own eyes. But of the casket there was no sign. He withdrew a little, tried to cast his gaze around and attempt to buttonhole any Lufthansa ground official. It was then that he heard a voice, laced with the deepest scorn, behind him: "Yes, what else can one expect? Too many cooks."

He turned round. He had not realized that the brother had shifted position. The estate agent was not turned in his direction, but he had no difficulty in scanning the indescribable sneer on his face as he turned away to contemplate more elevating activities around the tarmac.

With difficulty, Menka turned his concerns to their original intent—finding the official handler for Lufthansa. He saw the Customs man coming towards him, the waybill flashing in his hand.

"I think there has been a mix-up, sir. There is a case over there with the right number, but it's not what we are looking for."

Dr. Menka looked in the indicated direction, and then suddenly it struck home. Of course! There it was, sitting conspicuously on the tarmac! He had got them all looking for a casket, they had all been looking for a casket shape, but since he had last glimpsed it on arrival from Salzburg and driven into the airline warehouse, it had been repackaged in a plain cardboard container, disguised to look like any other outsize freight. Passengers, he recalled, do not like to travel on a plane containing a corpse; maybe even flight crews balk at it, for all he knew. Hence this final camouflage work on a plain casket. As Menka pointed with relief at the correct freight, a movement caught his eye, and he turned just in time to see Big Brother turn his back and walk away, illumined by the spotlight that was played on the patch of activity. He got into his car and left the scene.

THE CRUCIAL VEHICLES—Hearse, pilot car, security—were lined up, but where was the rest of the reception line? During the frantic two days of planning, the number of friends who had announced their intention to come to the airport to receive Duyole numbered over forty. Duyole's return had been planned as a triumphant reentry, triumphant but not carnivalesque—the motorcade was reduced to a maximum of twelve. Now Menka saw only three or four cars of private ownership. The smell of sabotage rose rampant. However, he did feel a twinge of pity for The Family saboteurs—insistence on a dozen as the minimum had come from others, the children especially. For once he found himself sympathetic to The Family side. No matter in whatever direction from the airport, traffic remained a nightmare, and fewer cars meant less disruption by the already problematic convoy. Even so, it was clear that something was amiss. These were friends who, if they had known that Duyole would actually be buried in Austria, would have flown there on their own—most could afford it. Some could not but would have traveled anyway. They simply had not imagined such a possibility, and the deed was over before they could improvise. The moment they learnt of the final homecoming, however, they made arrangements to come to the airport, swearing to remain not too distant until his final interment. So where were they?

The convoy set off for Badagry. Dr. Ekundare had joined the firm's house doctor, and a pathologist from the Teaching Hospital had been summoned. They were waiting in a room set aside in the basement of Millennium Towers, Duyole's iconic addition to the Badagry landscape. Kighare hoped, longed to voice a hope, that the patriarch had been duly warned and had locked himself indoors somewhere remote. He, Menka, would refuse to accept responsibility for any accidental encounter with the casket, which might compel Pop-of-Ages to dine on its contents. It was agreed that the three doctors would inspect the body; the undertaker had warned that the flight and other motions were certain to have undone some of the patchwork he had performed. Menka did not accompany them to the makeshift morgue.

After their inspection, they advised that even the tinted glass should be covered with the wooden slide provided for that eventuality. Damien was eagerly in attendance—usefully, Menka considered. He would testify to his siblings and absent family that it was indeed their father's corpse, not a substitute. Then again, as the privileged recipient of life's secret essence from a dying father, he would be at hand to receive any residual emanation that was still trapped in the coffin, perhaps? Whatever went on in the mind of the young lord, the medical trio did their duty and warned him that it was not advisable to view the body. It was his choice, however, and he was allowed into the basement. Perhaps six pairs of eyes viewed the body in that state—the three physicians, Ekete, a board member of Brand of the Land, and of course Damien—a sufficient number to certify that this was indeed a close approximation of the Duyole Pitan-Payne they had all known. Only then did they take him to his home some fifteen kilometres away. They rested him on an improvised catafalque made up of two tables covered in the famous *aso oke,* the traditional weave of the Yoruba.

Menka could not wait to take Damien into a corner. *Where are your father's friends? Where are all his friends and colleagues who have been screaming their heads off in frustration? Where are they? Did you notify them?* No, Damien had not. *The list—what happened to the list, the absolute minimalist list of acquaintances conceded by The Family to lesser humanity? Show me. Who has it? Those who, even the crassest sensibility admitted, must be notified, no matter what—do they know that tonight is his lying-in-state?* Damien's shifty gaze took over and he scuffed the carpet with his feet. It was the uncles again. The uncles had put a stop to everything. *Everything?* Everything! *Does that include the notices in the newspapers, which—again in concession to the delicate sensibilities of The Family—would not be inserted until the day before his arrival so as to minimize the crush, to keep out the prying eyes, the busybodies, the nobodies, the wreath-eating goats, the vulgar horde, the unwashed masses and gossips who would desecrate The Family's decorum—where were the few, the very select few good enough to scrape their dirt on The Family's doorstep? Did anything appear in the papers of that morning, as agreed? The announcement that was winnowed down to the very barest essentials, namely, that Duyole was coming home, that notification of the details of his funeral outing and the memorial service would follow, that there would be no more than one day between the appearance of that notice and the day of interment—in other words, tomorrow, this very next day after, the gregarious engineer would be interred in the cemetery of the Chapel of the Apostles? And that other memorial events would take place sometime afterwards, when the gates of Purgatory would be thrown open to the inmates to emerge and belt out songs of remembrance, belch from overeating and drinking, and banalize the rarified image of The Family? Just what happened to this absolute* reductio ad absurdum *concession?*

Bisoye was in her room throughout, attended by an aunt who had traveled from her hometown to be with her. She had been dispatched from the palace—all part of the family support system. Royalty or peon, the tradition was sacrosanct, and a most efficacious one for the grieving. Bisoye remained oblivious to all that went on around her, however. She had no idea that all notices had been withdrawn, as Damien now mumbled, looking around him like a trapped animal. It was a thoroughgoing blitz. No sooner had Dr. Menka been airborne than the dismantling had begun. The parish priest, invited to conduct a brief service over the casket, was contacted by The Family and told to take his offices of the dead elsewhere. Even those on the shortest of short lists ever drawn up for an oral notification of the burial of a pauper in a nation notorious for joy and celebration of both living and dead had been deactivated. At most, some ten or twelve people, mostly from Millennium Towers, dropped by Duyole's home that night. It was then discovered, purely by chance, that Ekete's wife was actually a deacon in their church. She was drafted to conduct a brief service of worship over his coffin. Menka felt increasingly baffled. This went beyond mystery. He felt he had been landed in the middle of a fierce battle whose causes he could not remotely guess at. And now, additionally, his limbs were trembling. He knew that the cause was not from the emotion of rage but physical—hunger. It had been a tense day, largely sustained on caffeine and throat-searing spirits. During flight he had declined even the prelunch snacks. By lunchtime he was fast asleep, waking up just before landing—the night flight of the previous day, during which he had hardly shut his eyes, had taken its toll. His stomach had signaled deprivation, but now it was clamorous. That came in useful. He needed to get away from the house to think, so he went out of that place of abandonment late that evening to look for food. All he had to do was summon the steward, Godsown, but he did not wish to eat within those walls, and there was nothing, he recalled, to eat in his apartment—he had abstained from further provisioning, meaning to remove the last traces of his brief occupation the day after the second funeral. He knew just one place where, at that hour, he would find something for his stomach before retiring—a Lebanese restaurant not too distant, where he was certain to be remembered as an eating foil to Duyole's gourmandizing. He drove there, praying the kitchen was yet open. It was. He gulped down a meal while the proprietors sang praises, thrilled to learn that Duyole was back in Badagry.

It was not yet eleven when he returned. As he drove past the main house, he slowed down. It seemed dark inside, with scattered pools of dim light. Everything looked very still, peaceful, and silent. That was strange. A vigil, known as a service of songs, was supposed to be taking place, and it normally would not end till about two in the morning. Tributes, reminiscences, banters, soloists, poetry readings, hymnings, lyric recitals of ancestral history, sedate drinking, even the occasional boisterous outburst. . . . Menka reversed the car, parked, and went into the house. The entire crowd had disappeared; the small swarm of outsiders had retired to their homes. Even The Family was missing. He stepped into the lounge where Duyole lay in state, invisible in his casket. As he entered, he saw a solitary figure bent over a book, seated beside the coffin. There was nobody else, not a soul. No one from Millennium Towers. Neither the small family, staying of course in the Pitan home, nor the relations. No acquaintances. Just the widow. He had been away for under an hour, and it was not even close to midnight. He had expected to find them grouped around, seated in neat rows or haphazardly spaced, indulging in ceremonies of the wake which, Duyole loved to contest, had been purloined from Africa by the Irish.

Pointless the question, but he nonetheless asked, "Where is everyone?"

"They've gone home."

"And Katia? Damien?"

"They've gone up to their rooms. I think they are all exhausted."

"But the vigil—the programme says a service of songs?"

She stared. Then resumed reading her missal—at least he assumed that was the book in her hands.

"You mean you've been sitting here all by yourself?"

"My aunt from home is upstairs. I made her go up when others left—she hasn't been enjoying much sleep. But Mrs. Ekete will be back soon. She came straight from work, so she went home to change when Brother K. sent everyone home. She's coming back."

The silence was eerie. Such vigils went sometimes into the early hours, and even, for the more extreme, into morning, when breakfast might be offered. This was a home whose hospitality was notorious, where permanent enmities were made between friends because one had obtained an invitation to Duyole's shindig and the other had not. The home of a man who sometimes took over the joys and sorrows of others and made them his own. Duyole had crossed half the world in a casket, only to lie abandoned in a world where wake-keeping was a way of life and of death. Where on earth was this land of happiness, even in death?

Menka was not enamoured of these rituals, but this struck him like an accusation. He had brought Duyole home to Badagry, the sole night remaining to his burial, specifically timed toward a wake, one of the therapies that society had devised for dealing with loss. The irony was not lost on him—he was indifferent, even hostile, to funeral wakes. If Gumchi were not so distant, he would have been content to take the body with him all the way to Gumchi, sleep soundly while

Duyole lay at peace in his living room till the following morning, then brought him back to his home for his interment. He felt tricked. He had delivered his friend to those to whom such things mattered, only to have him abandoned? Everything had been timed for this, including the decision on a day flight, to enable arrival just a few hours before the commencement of the wake. He had not bargained on leaving him alone in his own home, abandoned in hate on one hand and unwittingly by those whom hate had kept away.

He heard footsteps. It was Deacon Ekete returning, as good as her word. Menka pulled up a chair for her, and all three sat by the bier. The two women took turns reading from the Bible, then broke into prayers. He sat with them, then observed the strain, the utter weariness on the widow's face. Suddenly she was racked with fresh sobs. Both urged her to go to bed, but she resisted—*Sorry, sorry, I'll be all right, I'll be all right.* It went beyond grief; the aberrations that surrounded this death had begun to sap her morale. Finally Menka persuaded the deacon to escort her to bed, then go home herself. There was a brief tussle, then Bisoye agreed to go upstairs when Mrs. Ekete took her leave. No one else came, not even the junior sister, Selina, who had crashed onto the sickbed of her brother, sprinkling holy water and heaping imprecations on whoever might have been responsible for assaulting him. Menka couldn't help feeling that a sprinkling of holy water was truly required in that household, a full-service exorcism dedicated to getting rid of the demons that plagued it.

They heard a car draw up. "That would be my husband," Deacon Ekete said. "He was to come for me after two hours." There was no further resistance from Bisoye. Menka watched them go upstairs, then heard someone meet them on the first landing—it was the aunt, and she took over. The deacon descended a few moments later and went out the front door. Menka stood for a long while, staring into space. Then he walked slowly towards the bier, placed his hand on the casket. "This," he announced, "is my second vigil by you, Duyole. But this time I don't have to worry about falling asleep on the job, and I have no intention of falling off the chair. So if you have no objection . . ." He picked up a cushion from a chair, adjusted it on the carpet for a pillow, and stretched himself beside the bier, a big yawn already emerging. He sank nearly instantly into his deepest sleep in days. He was awakened by sunlight pouring into the lounge, its beams across his face and splashing across the bier. Duyole and he were still the sole occupiers of the living room. There was no movement in the home.

Rubbing sleep from his eyes, Menka went into the bathroom to splash water on his face. He then moved to the French windows and pulled aside the curtains to let in a little more of the sunlight. There was a movement outside, and then Menka realized that he had not after all kept Duyole company alone. Seated on the grass, his back against the glass door on the outside, was the figure of Godsown. It was clear that he had also kept vigil all night. Menka was moved. As his eyes swept across the empty lawn with its swimming pool and well-trimmed croton bushes and yellow-red clusters of bougainvillea, devoid of any other sign of life, he was struck with sudden apprehension.

Could it be that a similar scenario of desertion had been set up for Duyole's physical reinterment? Had The Family worked to deprive Duyole of company even at his actual burial? It seemed not merely possible but extremely likely. Maybe they would see it as some kind of personal triumph that they needed, to ensure that even though Duyole had returned home to rest, it must prove a nonevent, a hollow victory. No one would know about it, so they could deny that he was ever brought home. What did they want, or, perhaps more accurately, what was it that they dreaded from a farewell tribute that involved the presence of his body? Indeed, from any final tribute? A memorial service afterwards—oh yes, that was also agreed on the programme, but it committed them to nothing. The nation knew that Duyole had already been buried in Austria, and the majority could be made to endorse that as a permanent fact.

Menka went upstairs, knocked up Damien from his sleep. How far had it gone, he demanded, this blackout on the news of Duyole's return? Where else was censorship in rampant operation? Damien seemed fated to stand surrogate for his uncle, and Menka wrung the truth out of him. Yes indeed, Uncle Kikanmi had called him at his assigned desk in the office of *The Vanguard*, where he was carrying out his duties. That call was to check on neither the wording of notices nor any changes or details in the programme. It was to stop all further activities in the media. Other arrangements," the journalist and his squatter were informed, were being made to get the news across to those who needed to be present. The arrangement with the newspaper was no longer required.

Now the picture was clear beyond all further subterfuge. Menka rushed to the telephone and called up the homes of the editors of a local Badagry newspaper, then two others in Lagos and Ibadan. Their reaction was, predictably, one of disbelief. Duyole Pitan-Payne, the murdered engineer, Mr. Brand of the Land, had been brought back to Nigeria? So where was he? They had heard nothing. No one had contacted them. And he would be buried that morning, that same morning? Yes, Menka assured them. *I am calling from his home, and we plan to go through his gates in one hour from now. We shall proceed in a convoy to the burial grounds of the university chapel, according to his wishes.* After a church service? No, no church service, Menka informed them, only prayers and a few hymns by the graveside. It was not an hour when reporters were to be found in their offices, but both editors promised to track down their journalists and dispatch them to the Payne home or else to the graveside. *I want photographers,* Menka said—*be sure to send photographers!*

The battle of restriction was now ripening, it appeared, and all masks were progressively ripped off. There were no more greys, just black and white, starkly delineated. Duyole's staff at Millennium Towers had been assured by The Family that the remains of their leader would be brought to the house that Duyole had built, the Miracle of Badagry, Brand of the Land, that the coffin would remain there for fifteen minutes, maybe half an hour, while they paid their last respects. They had come to work in suitably sombre attire, and sat in their offices waiting to be summoned. It had taken hours of stiff negotiation for Runjaiye and Ekete to wring that concession out of The Family, but finally Kikanmi had given solemn assurance of this last homage. When Runjaiye came to the house of bereavement, however, simply to ascertain when the cortege would take off from the house, he was confronted with a denial. Kikanmi, now apparently master of ceremonies, funeral conductor, and chief mourner, had arrived early. He informed Runjaiye that the cortege would attract too much attention. They would proceed straight to the burial ground.

The poor staff representative did not believe he had heard right. Attract too much attention? In his view, their friend and boss was attracting far too little. What, he demanded, could his staff offer their late employer in return for so much but to pay him just those final minutes of homage? No, it was not the homage of the staff that worried Big Brother, it was the noisy, vulgar homage of the crowd, all those busybodies around Millennium Towers who had never learned to mind their own business. There was no escaping them, he moaned.

Menka had returned to the living room when he overheard the exchanges. He listened for a while, wondering all over again if he had not strayed into yet another nightmare whose outer-space denizens had taken over the bodies of a strange clan that called itself The Family. It was all right to sneak the corpse of Duyole into an improvised morgue close to midnight, in the basement of the house that he had built, but it had become unseemly to have his coffin pass through that building in broad daylight while his colleagues, his staff, yes, even his lovers, walked past and bade him adieu? Into what kind of a warp, he asked himself, had he drifted all the way from Salzburg with Duyole's corpse, himself as insubstantial an entity as a ghost? Trapped? Well, perhaps, but also possessed of the practical means of pulling the plug on the mad torrent and imposing some semblance of reality on the present. He felt the rise of his Gumchi blood. It all grew weirder by the second. Something was missing, something which, if only he could reveal it, would let the participants in the surreal proceedings know that the world that was being projected onto Duyole's casket was unreal, its actors deranged. Let them know that it would take only a word from him, a gesture, a look, or a touch, to make them realize that they were victims of some forces beyond their control and that their salvation lay with attuning themselves with the reality that belonged to the world of Duyole Pitan-Payne. Looking for a swift code, a snap code of inducting them into that world, an instant magic key, he went a little berserk.

It was quite fortuitous, but lucky perhaps for one and all, that the newly recruited doctor, Ekundare, drove onto the family premises at that moment. His duty had ended the previous night, but he had put on formal attire and returned to take his place behind the cortege for the procession to the burial ground. It was the voice of the young doctor that brought Menka back from the edge of insanity, cutting through his own voice, which was now stridently slashing and lacerating the air of the staid neighbourhood. Menka heard young Ekundare saying to him, "No, you're quite right, Dr. Menka. It is those who are opposing this who have something to hide. It's they who have something to be ashamed of."

Only then did Menka become aware of what he had been screaming, and he could hear it echoing in his head all over again, demented chimes bouncing off the walls of his skull, the walls, the iron gates, the gravel paths that crisscrossed the frontage of Duyole's home, and all it declaimed was that he had had enough of The Family obstructionists.

Do you all hate him this much? Is there something I don't know? Is there an awful family secret I don't know about? Did my friend commit an abomination, some unspeakable act that would make the earth of Badagry spew him out if we tried to lay him in its bosom? Are the people of Badagry going to retch and spit on the coffin if they know he is being buried here? Is there some unpardonable crime he has committed that his funeral procession will not pass peacefully through the streets of Badagry, past the ancient slave barracoons, past the shacks and colonial houses? How can Duyole's remains not pass through the house that he built, pass through the symbol of his achievement—how could all the people I have known who revered him, railed at him, and laughed with him, even those who envied his success, who applauded his achievements, who swore by his generosity, who were thrilled by his company, were tolerant or driven to distraction by his eccentricities and excesses, who sought to emulate him or distance themselves from his quirks, all those who knew all the foibles that made him human, yet greater than all of you—how have these suddenly become "busybodies" who must be excluded from the final rites of passage of their . . . yes, friend, mentor, and benefactor through their streets? If you Pitan-Paynes have a sinister secret in the family, lay it out in the open so we can all go home and you can then take his corpse and throw it in the evil bush, or dine on it if you prefer. Until that moment, however, until you reveal what bothers you, I am in charge of his remains. We have encountered nothing but obstruction, hostility, manipulations! Every inch of the way, sabotage! To what end? In fidelity to what custom, what usage, what tradition? Just what gods do you serve, if any? What crime has Duyole committed, I want to know now! What is the unspeakable secret? No matter, the

body within this casket is mine. I brought him home and I have taken
charge of him. Duyole is going through Millennium Towers, and no
one is getting in the way!

Damien had come out of the house, roused by Menka's raving. He
stood, looking a little frightened, beside a bewildered Cardoso, the
executor of Duyole's last will and testament. Menka did not know
in fact that they had been parleying with Kikanmi, Cardoso largely
playing broker between those who sought this homage for Duyole
and those who were resolved to deny it. After Ekundare, Menka heard
Damien saying, in a soothing voice of which he was also sometimes
capable, "It's all right, Uncle, it's all right. Uncle Kikanmi has agreed.
It's all right."

Menka had, however, moved beyond appeasement. The real target
of his rage was not the naysayers but himself. He felt he had somehow
betrayed his friend by getting into a situation where anyone felt that
they could bargain with his body. He held all the cards. The security detail was his, and they would take orders from him and no one
else. He was inflicting on himself an avoidable wound called compromise, and it was festering. He turned his ferocity on Damien, and on
a bewildered Ekundare.

"Agreed or not, Duyole goes through Millennium Towers. The
contents of that casket belong to me. Those who left their property in
Salzburg should go there and look for it. But the body in that casket is
mine. It goes where I direct it, and by what route I choose. I concede
the casket. Anyone who thinks that the casket is his, feel free to open it,
empty it, and take it away this minute. But that body stays with me!"

Damien again reassured Menka that Runjaiye, Ekete, and others
were now working out the finer details but that the passage through
Millennium Towers was already conceded. That, at least, was settled.
All that was left was to decide what route the cortege would take to
the burial site. Menka laughed out loud, an incongruous sound that
made the thin crowd flinch. It seemed to him that he had forgotten
how to laugh, and now a funeral was teaching him how to be human
once again. What had been settled? he asked again. Settled by whom?
No one had any choice, he repeated, and the drivers of the pilot car
and hearse would stick to his instructions. Nothing was left to decide.

Once again capitulation was partial, it appeared, and the conceding side was constantly scrabbling for more concessions or nibbling at the edges of consent. Faced with the inevitable, even at that moment, Big Brother still balked at a graceful withdrawal. There seemed to be suddenly two worlds—Lagos and Badagry—and, not for the first time, Menka accepted a difference, or at least that the two defined two conflicting compositions even within one family. The Family might have their roots in Badagry, he realized, even an ancient family home, but they lived in Lagos, had been raised in Lagos. They ate, drank, and breathed Lagos. The patriarch himself was a Lagosian at heart, his confectionery store was in Lagos, his social orbit within Lagos, his affectations all Lagos-saturated, even his perception of the world outside it. He had created the quartet but failed to expand it to embrace the most human, most gifted, and most successful of his brood. Well, Menka resolved, he would make all understand at least that that day, in Badagry, Duyole was now the death of his colleagues, the death of his Badagry family, not of the Lagos Family, from whom, it became glaringly evident, he had had good reason to flee, albeit not sufficiently far. But he had distanced himself, from choice. He could have built Millennium Towers in Lagos, established the Brand of the Land in Lagos, but he had chosen Badagry. Badagry was his Gumchi. Duyole was simply not one of them. He ceased to be one of them from the moment he took his decision to move to Badagry, seek his personal identity, and plot his future on his own.

After negotiations with the Head of the Millennium Towers staff in front of the house, while Menka paced restlessly in the living room, a compromise was finally reached. Duyole would not lie in state in Millennium Towers. On orders from Lagos? Or from his own, Kikanmi's, reductionist allergy? Duyole's cortege would now enter through the rear gates, built on a lower level, then make its way through the driveway that linked rear and front gates on the upper street level. The staff would line the driveway all the way up and bid him good-bye as he departed slowly through the frontage into and along the busy street. This took them straight into, and through the heart of the city of Badagry at an hour when workers and traders were moving into place, resuming work, and setting up stalls. Menka could only wonder what the Brain of Badagry felt he had gained for the quartet in the shortfall, the excision of the fifteen minutes when Duyole would have remained at an improvised desk in the conference room of Millennium Towers, honoured by his staff.

Even so, it was with enormous difficulty that Menka restrained himself from screaming an astringent veto to the agreement. It would have posed no problem. The escorts were under his control. He had taken the precaution of ensuring that even the hearse had been donated by the non-family. And of course every person in the procession apart from members of The Family was an ally. Finally, the people of Badagry, the entire environs of Millennium Towers, constituted the renegades of the non-family. A word at no more than a minute's notice and they would block any deviation as determined, take charge of the streets, and ensure that Duyole remained within their territory for as long as it suited them.

There were, however, others waiting for them at the graveyard, friends who had been successfully contacted, circumventing The Family's barricades. Next consideration was the sense of desecration that was already real and would only be compounded by a tussle over Duyole's body. It would teach The Family a lesson, but in the end? In any case, he had now calmed down considerably. He was grateful to the young doctor, who virtually took charge of him—he smiled—at his age! Ekundare's calmness doused the furnace that was lit up in his head. Its contents had relapsed and settled back to functioning in a semi-detached phase, calling out orders to an automated form. They would all be diminished by any fracas, but most of all, it was his friend, already deprived of lawful rest through this unseemly succession of alienated burial, exhumation, the treacherous refusal to embalm him, his enclosure in a collapsible coffin, an orphaned reception at the airport . . . The list of aggravations was endless. He could not add to it. This was his friend, over whom one brother had uttered words on the tarmac, words that Menka had futilely tried to expunge from his mind—"Look at him, lying there helpless, where is all his *gra-gra* now?"—while the other had cast his disdainful eye on the moment of Duyole's return to his own land. Yes, any further delay in laying him to rest was a further act of desecration, one that he did not deserve and that would diminish them all, without exception.

Still, it hurt. Deep within him, Menka had to admit that it hurt. And he longed to lunge out like a vengeful wraith and let loose Selina's goats on their straw masks of pretentiousness, hypocrisy, and fakery in a way that would make their patriarch long for his rightful space, now usurped by the son. The surgeon yearned to instruct them that he knew their son better than they could dream, that it was that son who had turned an Edo gong into a world brand with his illimitable slap-dash, even freakish humour—to instruct the infidels that Duyole's cortege was passing, as if by his own choice, past his beginnings, where he had first erected a temporary shack that had led to his more sophisticated constructions. For the first time Menka sought to assuage his bereavement with their humiliation, but he silently intoned the gong mantra. He could not turn Duyole's return to the earth of his choice into a melodrama; there had been more than sufficient bathos already.

DUYOLE HAD HAD little time for religion, though he tended to waver between belief and skepticism. Certainly he was no churchgoer. Unlike Badetona, however, he was no Scoffer. He simply preferred to let religion be, insisting in turn that religion let him be. There was never any question of a Christian funeral for him. The nonadherence to a religion proved the perfect excuse for The Family, as if the absence of Christian funeral offices meant that any such being should be buried like a pauper—no, worse, like a vagrant without an identity, or else like a cast-off branch of a suspect family tree. Still, a Christian priest had been engaged by The Family to conduct a truncated Christian office of the dead by the graveside, backed by a small choir. Menka had ensured the presence of two groups, a traditional chorus and a dance troupe. He had sent them ahead to perform by the graveside before the arrival of the cortege. Brother Kikanmi had also driven ahead of the cortege, presumably to ensure that all had been prepared and that goats had not eaten nearby flowers. Not for him a place in the procession—that contradicted his patrician abstemiousness.

Menka's traditional chanters were already assembled at the graveside, the Zangbeto chanters of Badagry. The Family had not anticipated any such addition. On arrival, Kikanmi failed to recognize the singers as artistes as they were not in costume, unlike the dancers, who were conspicuous in their decorated costumes and were thus easily identified. So the realtor shooed them off long before the arrival of the cortege. The singers opened up voices on sighting the cortege, and Kikanmi went into a controlled frenzy of exasperation. Menka watched him, still at a distance, continuing to urge himself—*Calm, calm, Gong o' Four—calm down, it's nearly over.* He watched the brother haranguing the leader of the group, who wisely stepped to one side, away from the singers. Kighare was none too exercised; his mission was virtually fulfilled, Duyole close to his final destination. Their leader, however, came up to him to complain that there was a man who kept urging them to disperse and forget the chanting—he promised that he would see that they were paid just the same. Kighare told him, "Take his money and then stop. When I give the signal, resume. Did he come at you with his fingers at your singers' throats?" No, the leader admitted. "Well then, this being a university campus, we do things our own way here—he doesn't know that. He's a real estate agent, and he thinks he owns the earth. Begin with the solemn chants—I'm not Yoruba, but I am sure you have some chants which it would be sacrilege for anyone to interrupt. Am I right?" The man grinned and nodded. "Good, you start with one such, and when he comes at you, simply wave a deterrent signal with one finger, like this. He'll retreat, I promise. From the ritual songs, move on to incantations, belt out the *ewi, ijala*—those are the only two names I know. You know how you honour your own kind, don't you?" The leader nodded, rejoined his choir.

The university went about its normal business, unaware that a few metres from the lecture rooms to the staff club, where Duyole had delighted audiences with his impromptu baritone voice, their colleague and friend was being buried. Students who had participated in Duyole's infamous madcap street party admitted later that they had actually walked past, little suspecting that their agent provocateur was being buried there. So did a band leader who had played with religious regularity at Duyole Pitan-Payne's famous New Year's Eve parties. When he learnt of the burial, he broke down and bawled like a child. The first musical instruments that he had ever owned were bought for him by Duyole Pitan-Payne—the instruments that had enabled him to create his own band, which became famous as The Benders. He could not believe that this thing had been done to him, that he was within yards of Duyole's open grave, preoccupied with nothing but his daily chores, when his friend and benefactor was being buried. Others were simply stunned, speechless, and confused. A number cursed. And not a few tried hard to puzzle it out and, failing, clung to a conviction that it was not Duyole whose body had been repatriated but a substitute, or nothing. An empty coffin. The rumour spread, took hold, and could not be dislodged that there was a disease hitherto unheard of, a disease so wasting that it had left no fragment of Duyole left to consign to earth. It had all been an elaborate, expensive charade in which his best friend, the National Award winner, out of loyalty, had collaborated.

The priest intoned his last offices. The small but resentful group paid brief tributes, laid wreaths, and threw clods of earth onto the lowered coffin. Menka's eyes sought out the dance troupe, which, he learnt, had been shooed off by The Family's agents just before the arrival of the cortege, confused by the frenzied counter-activities of the graveyard prefect, supposedly a mourner and brother of the deceased. Menka gave a slight nod to them and they commenced their motley gyrations. Again the surgeon experienced bewilderment at the brother, as a hitherto unremarked animation took over his resentful limbs, a complete contrast from the sneering lethargy with which he had been suffused at the airport while the "too many cooks" searched for the box that contained his brother's remains. He rushed to the dancers and tried to shoo them off again. They resisted, having seen the choral groups, both Christian and Zangbeto, deliver their wares. The mourners showed their disapproval, and the Brain of Badagry retreated. The troupe opened their limbs into another dance, a slow, sinuous routine that narrated the dirge of finality and set a seal on Duyole's departure.

The brief ceremony was over. For Kikanmi, the waiting gravediggers could not move fast enough to begin sealing the grave in concrete. That was a customary precaution, to thwart grave robbers in their nocturnal activities. In Menka's accusing frame of mind, however, this eagerness read only as a continuation of an impatience to seal his brother off from sight, to place slabs of nullity over his existence. Still, even Menka agreed that this was no task to be left till later, and he knew that Damien, to whom the duty of supervision had been entrusted, would close up the smallest chink that permitted any sliver of light into the grave. For once the contentment was mutual, only, as he watched the concrete slabs cemented down impermeably, his came from knowing that this time Duyole would be finally at rest, would sleep deep beyond intrigues and pettiness. He stayed long enough to watch the trowel make the first incisions into the slurry, slap down the first concrete mush and flatten it. Then he turned around and left.

ONCE AGAIN HE WAS back among his bits and pieces, scattered as haphazardly as they had been since offloaded mere weeks before. It seemed strange to feel that he need not have arrived so early for a funeral, since it now struck him that this was all he had come to do in Badagry—bury his friend. He should have felt relief, he thought. He had finally discharged a burden that would have weighed him down for the rest of his life. This definitive burial should have constituted the release papers that would enable him to take back his life. True, he had failed to ensure the heart's survival, but at least its casing was where it belonged, where he wished it to remain and turn to dust. This should have been the beginning of a withdrawal, of closure, and perhaps even the commencement of mourning. It proved to be none of these. He had yet to experience grief as a dimension of Duyole's absence, and the cause was unmistakably the intrusive demands placed on a bond by the unnatural conduct that followed Duyole's passing. He was in fact left in limbo, rather like the restless spirits of legend whose deaths remain unappeased.

Menka's return to the cluttered apartment should have been the commencement of reconciliation with loss, but no, that was not yet to be. There were already signs that could not be ignored. Indeed, the conduct of The Family over Duyole's second burial had warned of a ferocious, vengeful storm to come. Graceful capitulation, even to the dying wishes of a free spirit, was not in the vocabulary of The Family. They would feel, not relieved, but humiliated. *You want to bring him back? To serve him up to me for dinner?* And then an outsider had done just that, brought back a dinner that was indigestible. He anticipated a storm that would finally bring relief, since it would drown what was left of the sham courtesies between The Family and the family, those "presumptuous upstarts." It would nearly succeed in drowning the peace of all who had partaken of Duyole's friendship and responded with loyalty, but it would not.

It would be a purifying storm—of that he was certain. It would cleanse Duyole's earth of the foulness that had accompanied his passage home. At the end of it all, he, Kighare Menka, would know peace, and be made whole again.

21.

Ziggurat or Death

The funeral storm, to all appearances, had abated. Mamma Kressy opened the *Otunba*'s confectionery shop as usual and took her accustomed position behind the cash register. This was the *Otunba*'s retail outlet, his place of modestly gainful repose in the ancient Oni-kan section of Lagos Island. Once exclusively residential, it was now pocked with supermarkets, offices, keep-fit gyms, and even a multi-floor parking facility. The shop itself, an architectural contrast to the rest of the building, was a modernist frontage to an interior room of genteel mustiness, with faded, heavy framed photos around the walls and poised on narrow stands and a central round table, an imported escritoire with twin inkwells, black and red, both long dried up from disuse, the steel-nib pens still stuck through their covers, a leather pad of blotting paper. The antimacassars spoke of a bygone age, and thick wall-to-wall carpeting still retained its full absorbent efficacy. In this room the *Otunba* received friends and fellow socialites and occasion-ally conducted business meetings. Mostly, insulated from the rest of the world, he and his visitors dissected the day's news, mulled over the latest gossip, compared quotations on the stock exchange, and tried to outwit the pundits on nominations for the YoY Awards. The main attraction, the shop itself, was an ultramodern study in contrast to the interior parlour—by which designation the *Otunba* and his household still addressed the living room. The display cases were a combination of chrome and glass, every bit as seductive as their contents—designer sweets, chocolates of every nation, extravagant themed gift boxes, variously shaped jars, toffees and cubes of exotic Turkish delight in glossy, ornate wrappings. There was a section for cigars and accessories. The entire outfitting was a gift from his late son, who had designed, built, and occasionally restocked it. The final touch was a concessionary, filial variation on his own quality mark, a placard that swung on a golden cord across the velvety curtain of the entrance to the inner sanctuary: BRAND OF THE GRANDEE.

The patriarch was seated on a high stool that he sometimes occupied, quite close to the inward entrance that enabled him to escape unwanted customers. He clutched a legal folder and turned the pages one after the other, squinting and scrutinizing their contents through steel-rimmed spectacles. Occasionally he frowned, placed the folder on the counter, and jotted down notes in the margin with a pencil. The document in his hand was the last will and testament of the son, now late.

Mamma Kressy sat behind the cash desk, her glances at her partner increasingly uneasy. In a seismic break from the norm of her four-year insertion into the Pitan-Payne extended family, Kressy quietly ruptured the morning silence, raised her voice, and said, "Papa"—it was the only way she ever addressed the *Otunba*—"is that not your son's will?"

"Eh-hen?"

"I think it's unlucky."

There followed a genuine pause of mystification. "What is unlucky?"

"To read the will of one's own *pickin*. It's unlucky."

The patriarch looked at her with mild curiosity. The break in routine had yet to sink in. "Where did you pick up that superstitious nonsense?"

"In our part of the country, we think it is unlucky."

Otunba hissed, "You think it's unlucky to try to find out who killed my son?"

The woman digested that for a while. "Papa, you think the will can tell you who kill your *pickin*?"

"I know who killed him. I just want to confirm what I know. This will may contain the answer."

"Papa," she said, in the same level monotone, "why do you think his friend killed him?"

The folder nearly dropped from the patriarch's hands. Even then the disruption of the norm, embedded in the identity of the inquisitor, had yet to fully penetrate. "What is the woman talking about?"

"You think his friend killed him. The doctor."

Finally it hit the patriarch. Far more destabilizing than what she actually said was that Mamma Kressy was speaking at all. Beyond the exigencies of dialogue that bedevil all who keep shop and thus must speak with clients—a chore that she mostly assigned to an assistant, expected to resume duty within the hour—and beyond routine enquiry over Papa's daily fancy for lunch or dinner—when, and would there be company, etc.—Mamma Kressy hardly ever joined in conversation, much less initiated one. Her entire world of apprehension was wrapped up in the faculty of listening, and without any suggestion of being even remotely engaged in such a taxing occupation.

Otunba was now riveted. "Since when did you become involved in affairs of the family?"

She shrugged. "I am not, Papa. But people say things in my hearing. I can't help it if I hear things."

"Well, among the things you hear, did you ever hear me say anyone killed my son?"

"No. But you think he killed him, Papa."

"What is going on in your mind, woman? Good God. Are you trying to make yourself a witch in my household?"

"Each time the doctor's name is mentioned," she continued, "something happens to you, Papa. I notice it, especially if I happen to be massaging your toes. Some tingling pass through your feet. That tingling, I feel it like electric shock."

"Well, maybe you should be working for NEPA. That way we can be sure of getting electricity instead of darkness. We only have to connect you to all electrical appliances. The man you're talking about brought Duyole back. Against The Family's wishes. That's enough for me to discharge any amount of electricity when I hear his name. Whether it's electric shock or madness in your head, that is your business. He went against Family wishes."

"Yes." Mamma Kressy nodded, somewhat sadly. "That is how I know you believe he killed him. Because he brought the body back."

Otunba slammed both sides of his head with open palms. "God help me with this woman! Does two and two make five in your part of the world? All right, I'm listening. Explain to me how one thing follows another in that cooking pot you use for a mind."

"You told me a story once, about Badagry. You know, not long after our church introduce the two of us and we begin to meet. Do you remember? About the time when our people were catching one another and selling slaves to the white people. Something about when the captured ones were being marched to the coast and they were made to drink from a well."

It was called the Well of Attenuation, implanted in the ground perhaps three kilometres from the embarkation point. It was a routine stop for rest, and the slaves were made to quench their thirst from its waters. All drank without hesitation; they did not need to be persuaded—that went for any stop during the long trek from the interior. There was talk that its water was laced with some herbal hallucinogen, since those who drank from the well lost their memory—at least, such was the intention. They forgot home, land, captors, even killers of their kith and kin. Their memories vanished totally. No will for revenge accompanied them into the ships, no spur to rebellion. And when they died on the plantations across the ocean, their ghosts retained the same mental blank. They never felt an urge to return and haunt those who had wrenched them violently from their homeland. Their restless spirits remained where they had drawn their last breath, among their foreign masters.

The *Otunba* looked puzzled. He recalled regaling her with stories of his family ventures in the trade; that was one of them. He threw a scornful look at the woman. "Is that the story now bugging you? How has that story scrambled your brain? Are you still capable of using your head? The doctor brought back the body. If I thought he killed Duyole, why should I oppose his victim being brought back? Would I not want his murderer to be haunted for the rest of his life? I would bury him myself in his Gumchi village, next to his family home!"

"So, Papa, you are saying you don't believe the doctor killed him?"

"I am saying nothing about my son to you, you stupid woman. Since when have I taken to discussing my sons with you? Who invited you to poke your nose in my family affairs?"

"You, Papa."

"Me? Otunba Pitan-Payne? Woman, have you been drinking again? It's too early in the day for this nonsense." The *Otunba*'s voice had risen to a scream. "You are back to your secret drinking. Where is it? Where do you hide your *ogogoro*?" He leapt from his stool, his eyes scanning likely hiding places in the shop.

"Papa, that is what I hear you say. You were phoning somebody. You said Doctor Menka put something in Uncle Duyole's body during the operation here. You say he has to take it out again after he died, because it's exactly like those slaves, only the other way round. The doctor thought he would die here. First he tried to kill him with the bomb. Then he put that thing in his body during the operation, but the son died overseas. That is why he had to bring the body back. Something he has to take out and use again here. I did not mean to listen, but I was there with you, and you were speaking loudly. You said that is the reason why you don't want the body to come back, why you said the body should remain overseas. Am I lying?"

Otunba was sputtering madly, nearly incoherent. "Of all the dangerous witches I've ever encountered! You mean I cannot discuss with my son what I hear people saying?"

Kressy nodded slowly. "I thought so. So it was your son to whom you were talking."

"Yes, my son, you dirty eavesdropper! This is what comes from trying to put some knowledge in an empty head. You've gone and mixed fact and history together. Mamma Kressy, I hope you've never opened your mouth to talk this garbage with anyone. In all my eighty years, I have never heard such rubbish coming out of a woman's mouth! Go and wash it. Go and wash that mouth of yours. It is dirty. Go and wash it with strong detergent. Now!"

She got up calmly. As she walked round the counter, however, she stooped and picked up a mildly heavy object. As she came round to the front, Otunba saw what it was—a suitcase.

He gasped. "What—is—that? Where do you think you're going with that?"

"This is all I came with, Papa. I was just waiting for you before taking my leave."

"Leave for where, you drunkard? I picked you up from the gutter, cleaned you up, and brought you into a respectable home. Do you know where you are at all? You want to go back to your slum?"

"I'm afraid to remain here. All this business of saying the doctor bring back your son for dinner and other this and that. Is making me afraid. I never hear that kin' talk in all my life. Maybe for my area, we take too much *ogogoro,* but we don't eat our *pickin.* Let me just carry myself go."

Disbelieving, Otunba Pitan-Payne watched the figure of Mamma Kressy step through the door, walk with the voluptuous steps that had seduced him on his first encounter and led to his requesting her priest to bring about an introduction. He watched her calmly receding down the road, dragging her suitcase, her all-purpose pouch of a handbag slung over a shoulder. She turned at the end of that stretch, paused, looked back at him, and waved to the patriarch in the most amicable manner, then turned the corner and vanished from sight.

Otunba remained rooted to the spot. He only returned to the present with the sound of a timid voice that had repeated, "Good morning, sir," for perhaps the sixth time. It was the shop assistant reporting for morning duty.

IN THE EVENING of that same day, across Lagos Island, in a new but already run-down expansion called Lekki Gardens Phase 4, where one room was sometimes shared by a family of seven or eight, with a toilet that served an entire block of six or seven such rooms, a tens-of-thousands-strong chorus of yells and curses, moans of long-suffering, resignation, frustration, and rage suddenly ripped across the sky over the tenements. Godsown was barely halfway through a narrative before the descent of the huge gloved hand silenced him and blotted out the neighbourhood. Huge, coal black, it snuffed out all things visible from one end of the earth to the other. Another blackout! It was always like that, Godsown reflected; one could almost feel the imprint of the diabolical palm on the forehead. Or celestial? It all depended on whose—he hesitated—yes, perspective, was involved.

The thought brought a smile to his face. Even if nothing else, his preacher's "perspective" theology had definitely rubbed off on him, and he was profoundly impressed that he, on his own, should invoke it almost without thinking. Just like the preacher would gently massage the believer's forehead before smacking it with the heel of his palm, and with a force that jerked the proffered head backward and sent its owner into a paroxysm of possession, self-repudiation, recantation, and/or testifying, this invisible hand caressed its earthly victims, whose moans were, however, not of spiritual surrender but of angry impotence. No one ever received warning of its approach, but suddenly there it was, forcing one and all instinctively to commence the blind man's shuffle and grope and make allied motions of adjustment to the imposition of a universal pall.

For those caught outdoors—as Godsown was, together with his caller, Dr. Kighare Menka—a thin streak of residual light lingered over a distant rim of rooftops, treetops, and hilltops, the last being sometimes camouflaged mounds of multi-textured garbage jutting out between the glove's widespread fingers and unseen ooze. The space permitted to its affected populace was circumscribed by that impenetrable shroud pressed down to frustrate recognition of familiar, domestic, companion landmarks of human transactions. As for sounds, the high-decibel medley of *fuji* rap, *juju* survivals, Afro-reggae, revivalist harangues, relics of international Top Twenty and latest presumed new-generation musical breakthroughs, crossover beat and exotic genres—all were abruptly silenced. The silence was not prolonged, though. It was replaced by the progressive orchestration of generator spurts, gearing up for extended runs. They drowned out the agonized and resentful shrieks that presumably reassured frustrated citizenry of signs of life under the sudden eclipse. In some way this leadenness equated with what Menka felt within him as Godsown poured out his long-pent-up message in a nearly uninterrupted flow—at least, until the blackout. The recorder, tethered to a light-bulb power source through the window of Godsown's recently hired room in the *face-me-I-face-you* multiple occupation building, hiccupped, then slowly slithered to a stop.

Menka sighed, bemoaning the loss of the fluidity that had built up in Godsown's revelatory soul as he warmed up in his narrative. He looked round, eyes squinting to make out features of his surround, while mulling over what he had heard so far. Godsown was equally frustrated, eager to continue and conclude. After all, it had taken a while to track Dr. Menka down in his new, temporary abode, and he had been most pleasantly surprised and appreciative when the doctor offered to meet him in Lekki, thus saving him the trouble of traveling across Lagos Island and all the way to Badagry.

"Get one small stall next street," Godsown offered. "I sure say the woman get batteries inside all her *wosi-wosi.*"

Menka nodded, dug into his pocket for money, and handed it over. Godsown waddled off on his uncoordinated legs, one of which, Duyole had cruelly remarked—but only out of his steward's earshot—pointed to Maiduguri, the other to Sokoto. That was one of the few traits Menka had found uncomfortable in his "twin"—Duyole's teases were often too close to the bone, especially in commenting on any anatomical landscape. He remained incorrigible, could never resist a comparison of retreating bottoms or advancing "headlamps." Menka grinned—he could do with a real headlamp at that moment, or simply its power source.

The chorus of neigbourhood protests continued, surged and criss-crossed in ragtag imprecations against the accustomed violation, then petered out. It was all too familiar. Menka decided to switch the Walk-man to the batteries, glad that he had earlier tested the equipment. No one used those things anymore, but his ease with gadgetry had stopped at the fax machine and Walkman. He had relied on Duyole, in addition to his multipurpose factory staff, for any technical aid, except of course in his own field—medicine. The recorder spun, the battery light at pale yellow indicating that there was still some life to it but not much. He kicked himself. He had meant to stop and buy extra batteries on the way, but . . . Not for nothing had Duyole nicknamed him AMB—Absent-Minded Butcher—swearing he would never trust himself to Menka's surgical blade as Menka would be certain to har-vest the wrong body parts or leave his forceps in his guts. Strange turn of events when such banter took on dimensions of real life and death, and now accusations of deliberate homicide! Could either ever have imagined flippant moments twisted into intimations of sinister intent?

And then the pact—that pact, that uncanny, or should he call it pre-scient, pact—between them, at least seven years old!

With a recall of the pact came a renewed chill in his bones as he awaited Godsown in that unrelenting darkness, found himself assailed by a wave of vertigo. It was as if the world was dissolving around him, a near-identical sensation to one he had once had in Duyole's workshop. Then Menka had had more time on his hands—Boko Haram was yet unheard of—and he would visit Badagry on a whim and watch Duyole at work, curious to see what latest contraption was under his ministrations. That day something happened and he felt lightheaded, perhaps from inhaling too many fumes. He sat on a bench to avoid fainting in the converted garage, littered with clogged motor engines, singed gaskets, coils and tubes, normal discards which became a personal challenge to Duyole's restless mechanical fingers. A floating scrim now emerged from total darkness, superimposing Duyole all bloodied on the operating table, with a steel array on a surgical tray, gloved arms probing his body for foreign metallic pieces that threatened to put a stop to the smooth functioning of a damaged engine. Perched on a narrow space of the workbench among tools and spare parts, Menka began to feel somewhat dizzy. He shook his head and moved nearer a vent lodged high up in the wall. Duyole saw the change of position and accurately assessed why. Menka heard that voice all over again, his irrepressible chortle—*Serve you right, you knock out your patients with that anaesthetic stuff, now you can't stand a little whiff of my own garage equivalent.* And then Duyole stopped abruptly. He stopped speaking for so long that Menka felt compelled to ask him what suddenly was eating him.

"I've just thought of something. I saw a documentary yesterday, and I didn't like it one bit."

"Well?"

"Not one bit. So here comes another pact."

Kighare sighed. "All right, spell it out."

They had several pacts, mostly ridiculous, sprung from negotiating the final drops from a wine bottle. A number were, however, far from trivial, such as those that involved business or family, dependents, both close and in extension. Nothing was ever written down, but no sooner agreed than they took to reminding each other of details from time to time, whenever the theme accidentally surfaced or individuals involved crossed their sight lines, however tangentially. Menka shuddered. Suppose he had been in Salzburg! Duyole's voice returned to haunt him:

"No. Didn't fancy it one bit. I mean, to end like that man, dragging it out for so long . . . What's the point?"

Menka waited patiently. "Let me know when you're ready."

"Sorry, nothing complicated. Let's do it this way. If ever it comes to a situation where someone has to pull the plug, it must be you. Right? You'll take the decision, no one else."

"No big deal," Menka agreed. "We encourage that in our trade. It frees our hand and we can concentrate on what matters."

"I suppose this is one I'd better put down in writing, get it notarized. Give you a copy. That documentary, I didn't like the way it went. It was an eye-opener. The family tussle? Never seen anything remotely like it."

Menka nodded. "Any way you decide. And of course you'll do the same for me if I go first."

Duyole's rejection was vehement. "Me? You must be joking. It doesn't cut both ways—not in this instance. You are a doctor, not just a buddy. You are used to it, I am not."

"Stop trying to cheat," Menka admonished.

"No. I'm not trying to cheat. This is one instance when there cannot be reciprocity. It's elementary."

Menka shook off the fog of apparition and gulped down a lungful of the night air, now perfumed by the fumes from a hundred generators.

He attuned his thoughts to practical decisions. Godsown's resurfacing had startled him, and yet, what else could he have expected? The phone calls, beginning so soon after the burial; the persistence, even desperation. He could virtually see him, his moustache bristling, the ever-faithful steward in a seamless sensibility of loyalty, seeking him out after leaving the stricken household without notice. He had simply packed his bags and quit, first ensuring that the *megadi*—watchman—at the gate clawed through the shiny, indeed polished, suitcase that held all his belongings. And he made sure that the rest of the house staff were present—cook, gardener, resident laundry man, and even the next-door security staff, switching as usual to their common fragmented delivery of the white man's language.

"My resign notice is dey for dere dining table," he announced grandly. He had waited until the home was virtually empty, regretful only that he had to do this to the widow, quitting in her absence and when she was most vulnerable. "I done get new job, but I no want any trouble. I just wan' commot peaceable. Make nobody come follow harass me for anything wey miss. Before God and man, as I come, so I go. Wetin I take come, na in I take go." And he offered to pay the gardener's taxi fare back to the house if he would agree to follow him to his new employer's home and verify his new job and possessions.

Menka wondered whether, despite his protestations, Godsown had actually left his old employer without even one item, at least a memento to which he had become perhaps no more than sentimentally attached. It was an unfair thought, and he rebuked himself, slanting it to mean whether or not Godsown would miss the cut-glass bell that he, Menka, had found so embarrassing. It had been one of the minor irritations he tried hard to manage in that second home. An attractive bell with a penetrating tinkle, guaranteed to be the trigger for routine ideological umbrage, with minor variations, all depending on the state of their lubrication. It always struck Menka as incongruous between Duyole's quite fleshy fingers, but that was how he chose to summon the kitchen staff to the table, Godsown most frequently, since he did most of the waiting. That glass bell, to tell the truth, was quite musical to the ear—Duyole had picked it up in Salzburg in one of the souvenir shops. It was, however, one item to which Menka never adjusted, and he found it feudal that anyone should use a bell to summon another being. "Why don't you just call him?" he once snapped. "Use your blasted baritone bellow!" Duyole's riposte was instant—"I prefer sopranos, Comrade Gentry"—guaranteed to plunge the evening into the same contumacious waters—crystal bell equaled the bourgeoisie, the human bellow was a leveler, still, both were unable to escape master-servant relationships, to which Menka had yet to find a solution. And the only ponderous question left to them to solve was which advocate would be first to be thrown into the revolutionary furnace when it was eventually lit and stoked. Or it could be the opera—did they admit guilt for that pastime of the middle class and affluent, a mark of decadence? What undiluted full-blooded product of Senghorian negritude would go and hear an opera? They both did, even the tone-impaired Menka. So, might as well be damned through and through, one growled, while the other nodded agreement—*Pass the malt, capitalist ogre. Shame on you, proletariat butcher, you should drink only* ogogoro, *ideally spiked with motor battery acid.* Duyole pushed the crystal decanter towards him . . . and so it went. Now Menka interrogated the darkness: Was this the friend he was supposed to have murdered or assisted in murdering? Damien did casually mention to his uncles that his father had sent him one late night to fetch a package that had been brought by Dr. Menka. He did not find one, but his father was sure it had been left on his work desk. Damien no longer recalled all the details, but it did become a central ingredient at the lunch that followed the reading of the will. The police had yet to reveal the exact point and means of detonation, but the package provided solemn exchanges of looks—among other dire significances.

At first Menka thought he would simply listen to Godsown, make a summary, and have him sign it. At the last moment, just before leaving his new residence, he recalled seeing the ancient Walkman among his junk. Tested it, and it was still running—and of course he meant to buy new packs of batteries on the way to Lekki, where they had agreed to meet at a petrol station, then proceed to Godsown's new home. Instinctively his finger went to the rewind button. It whirred, so he pushed Play to listen to the recording so far. There seemed to be a fair amount of juice left. His voice was first to emerge.

"Well, Godsown, we have to do this properly. First you will introduce yourself. A brief background, you know—the police will want to know all about you, your previous place of work before you joined the Pitan-Payne household, present employment. Then we'll get down to the real thing, Godsown. What made you leave the Pitan-Paynes and so on. In your own words, so I wouldn't appear to be prompting you or anything like that. Just in your own words, why you decided to find me and ask for this meeting. You understand why all that is important?"

Godsown was eager to go. "*Oga*, everything is between me and my conscience. It is ziggurat or death."

"Sorry, what did you say?"

"Ah, don't worry, sir, you will know what that is when I tell you my life story. First let me finish with this lunch when they discuss the matter."

"All right, do it your way. It's all yours. The recorder is already running."

"My name is Godsown Porkari. I am now forty-six years old and I used to work for the engineer Mr. Duyole Pitan-Payne of blessed memory who built Millennium Towers. I want to say what I know of these people in the family of the engineer and what they say about who killed my master. I have no children yet, but it is not for nothing that my parents called me Godsown, because God does not forget his own and we all know that God's time is the best.

"Before, I was in the north, in Kabba. How I ended up in the north does not matter, but that was how I met my wife, the daughter of a kola nut trader. May I just say that she was like the blending of the kola nuts in the tray she balanced on her head. I mean, Mr. Menka, sir, the way she walk, balancing that pretty tray on her head, and that head balance on her delicate neck. I look that skin, and is like God take the red kola and mix it a little with the yellow-white kola nut, and you get a complexion for which even an angel will sell one of his wings, I swear. My pastor once warn me that it was the Devil that had get inside my mouth to talk such blasphemy, but I can't help it. Anyway, that was nothing to the curse that shoot out of his mouth when I tell him that this blended walking kola nut breast, the one on which I want to lay my head, was a Muslim! He curse me, so I leave his church and marry her in her own village, where they admit me as son. I move to Kabba with my then master, whom they transfer from Yenagoa to become the railway station master. I never go north before, but I know say it is Destiny that take me there, to meet Zainab, who hawk her father's kola nut at the railway station. So much for my family. She still stay with her father, come to visit me from time to time at Master Pitan-Payne place, but I now bringing her to Lagos with this new job.

"Now, to this matter of my master and his friend, the doctor. It happen at lunch which the family had after the reading of Mr. Pitan's will. That was in the sitting room of my master's house. I am the one serving all the people who come for the reading, then later waiting on them at table. The two brothers and the sister are there, and some relatives. After they finish reading the will, they say a small prayer. Many of the family people leave, but two brothers and the sister stay. In fact, the two brothers have been more or less living in the house since the funeral. I am the one still serving them. The son also, Damien, and one of the daughters, Katia, and I think three other people. I know one of the others because he is the lawyer to the two brothers and he has been coming to the house now even more than before. But he is not my *oga*'s lawyer. My *oga*'s lawyer is Cardoso, and he leave immediately after they read the will. So, on that day, as they were talking, the young brother even bring out a newspaper which he showed the others. It was an old newspaper, not the whole of the paper but just two pages which he had been keeping, and it carried a story of my master and the doctor, Dr. Menka. I see the headline while serving them, and it read RIVALRY OF THE INSEPARABLES. It was a special story. It had their photos, and I know it was writing about how they have been rivals from schooldays, even overseas, and then they come back here and begin to win medals. I remember very well because the paper even call them *korikosun*—which means, if they don't see each other, then they can't sleep. And now those people, they begin to laugh. They say all the time Dr. Menka was a false friend because he jealous his friend too much. They say he know about the bomb. And when that doesn't work, he put something inside him when they perform operation on him at university hospital in Badagry.

"I have to say that this pain me too much. The people were laughing and talking very bad things, and I know is all because the friend bring his brother back to Badagry, and the matter annoy the father very much. In fact, while they were eating, the father call them. I don't hear what the old man say, but of course it was about this putting of something inside Master's body because I can tell from how the brother Kikanmi is answering and saying things to the others at the table. He even give the phone to the younger brother, Timi, and the same thing happen all over again. It all make me feel very bad, all this only a week after they have buried the engineer. As if this was a crime, when it was what everyone has been wanting since he died overseas. One thing which I remember very well is that after Mr. Timi finish speaking to the *Otunba,* he turn to the others and say something like, *You see, I am always telling you, Pop-of-Ages is deep, just deep. He sees farther than the rest of us.* Something like that.

"Thank God, since the day my master die, I decide I must leave that home, so I begin looking for a new job. I get offers from Mr. Pitan's friends. I tell them the truth, why I want to leave, and after that lunch I think I reach the breaking point. I know say, I have to choose. In fact that is not really a matter of choice. It is a terrible feeling, sir, that moment when a man looks right and left, up and down, inside and outside, and knows you have only one way to go. But that is the same as saying you have no choice at all, because if you have only one choice, then what are you choosing? I mean, what from what? If you have not been through it, you can never understand it. My master's people can talk all the grammar they want—their mission in life seems to be to argue over everything, after which everything is exactly as before—but I don't think they have ever come face-to-face with that moment when they find they must choose, really choose. Or perhaps they do that after all the argument, then tell no one about it. I am talking about that moment which I can only compare with sitting on an anthill during a flood. I won't say I am talking about myself, but let us just say as it happened in the village near Kabba when the smaller river which flow into the Niger overflowed during the night and there was nothing dry left to sit upon. Even the few baobab and neem trees disappeared, leaving only the top branches, which cannot support the weight of a newly hatched chicken. Everyone had fled their huts. The ladders of the silos had been washed away, so there was no way to climb up to the top for safety. The only place left until the waters dried was on top of the anthills, hoping that those mud hills themselves would not dissolve in the rising waters and suck you under. But then all the ants—soldier ants, workers, foragers, all of which had remained in hiding for all these years, making one think they had long abandoned their upstairs if you like also began to desert their underground bedrooms and climb higher as the waters flooded their secret tunnels. The waters did not cool their appetite for giving you terrible bites and stings, so one had to make a choice—endure their stings or take the risk of wading through water that is now rising above the shoulders, hoping to find something higher and more friendly before you were swept away. Your mind turned to a church tower or a mosque or minarets, ziggurats, or whatever—we had one of each in the next village, which is much older than ours. For once they could do what they were built for—saving souls. But of course you had to get there first. Now that is what I call a bad matter of choice—you can abandon the fiery ants and go and look for safety on the rooftop of church or mosque, or share their home with them and be stung to death, So there I was my mind is on one of my favourite ziggurats—no one called it that in the village, of course, neither did I at the time. But when I started work in the Pitan-Payne family and relax with the heavy picture books in his sitting room, I see the name and I say, *Ah, so that one is a ziggurat.* And whenever I came to a moment of danger or any problem where I must choose, I would say to myself, *Godsown, it's ziggurat or death.* So that is what I was saying when I first begin, the matter of ziggurat.

"You see, you are sitting on top of this mud hill, and they are swarming all over you, crawling, rushing, racing with one another, columns and columns of them, getting more and more disturbed. When you disturb them, they begin to sting. You climb higher and higher, and finally there is nowhere else to go. And could they sting! The soldier ants, and the ones we call fire ants, who not only sting and bite but leave a painful red blister behind—yes, they begin their work. All that so-called man courage is gone. The fire ants, you didn't know, they had already traveled up your trouser legs . . .

"So what choice you get? Nuttin' at all. First you take off your trousers, but it is already too late. The soldier ants are already entangled with the hairs of your *blockos*! You simply must take off your trousers, then the underpants. This is not in one corner-corner place where you can hide yourself, it is in public of other people, men and women, even children. But you must take off those trousers and all these people are looking at you from their own place in the flood, some on treetop, so you begin to pick out those fire ants already lodged inside that bush you hide from the neighbour. So much for the neighbour you once slap for poking her nose in your family affairs! She's looking at your real family affair and there is nothing you can do about it. Unless you jump inside water and swim to the next tree or anthill or church tower wey still dey above water. Or ziggurat.

"So, sir, is like that. To remain in that house one day longer, it was simply not a matter of choice. Those people be like fire ants. They enter your nostril and mouth, sting your *blockos*. If you no dey for dere side, you done become enemy. A friend find me this place quick-time, because I tell him is urgent. I cannot stay for dat house one more day . . ."

The steady whirr turned to a nerveless whine, and finally only a dismal moan emerged. End of battery. Godsown's return was a feat of perfect timing, but it did not really matter. What Menka had heard so far was more than sufficient. A decision already taken, and his mind fastened only on trivial proceedings. Once he had recorded the entirety, posed some questions, his first duty—not that he remotely considered it a duty, but simply as the first course of action, if only as a preliminary step—was a visit to the police station. The notion felt odd; then again, quite logical. No one would claim that his predicament was unheard of. Even so, it was not every day that a doctor, a much-sought-after surgeon, found himself associated with a crime. The victim of that crime none other than his friend, a pre-eminent profile poised to enter the rarefied zones of global influence. Duyole was already basking in the prospect of shedding the burden of vested interests, ascending—he ceaselessly quipped—from a private scientist to a scientific statesman. "From now on," he boasted, "I no longer need a passport. I have joined the ranks of the stateless."

How true. Duyole had indeed made good his timeless prediction, joined the ranks of the stateless. Permanently. Again the riotous images—the only man he knew who, even encased in a constrictive three-piece suit, would break the robotic mould and perform feats unmatched by any trencherman of history, effortlessly celebrating each new culinary encounter with a mini-paean, just like Muhammad Ali. Strangers became his pupils and would repeat after him any of his favourite refrains—*tongs and tonsils, tongue and tonsils, time for tongue and tonsils*—as he rolled his eyes as if each dish were a newly discovered planetary body under exploration, tuning up a discriminating yet accommodating palate that provoked total strangers to futile emulation. It was unique, that one should make an art of that common pursuit of humanity known as feeding, create around himself a zone of reverential isolation—an invisible card that read *Do Not Disturb*—yet at the same time exude a bearing that preached, *Communion time, enter, come and do thou likewise*. It was a mystery, but one that produced a rich album of recollected images, the ever-intruding succession of festive slides that fused both work and play. Menka had watched Duyole take a complex machine, obsolete or simply discarded, to pieces. Once it was a turbine rescued from the storehouse of a wastrel governor. It could be an "izophone"—something he invented and patented but never explained even to Menka, growling that he did not give seminars while communing with affairs of *tongs and torque*. The growl became pronounced if he was using his basement studio and the aroma of cooking wafted through from the kitchen. That was the only time his hands moved a little faster—grease, detach, file, oil, refit, unscrew, reassemble. Yet these gestures never failed to receive equal dedication, and those who saw him at work swore he handled the machine parts with the same solicitude that he brought to bear when cleaning and preparing a haunch of venison—macerate, simmer, a gentle pressure and a turnover and slide into the oven, only to be released in due time, resurrected and transformed in hues, textures, and functions.

Decimation was no different an aesthetic. The thoughtful mastication, each morsel rolled round and round the secret nodes in a unified working of hands and light metallic accomplices that transferred choice bits to his mouth for a prolonged interior interplay of flavours, as if he had a secret periscope through which he viewed the internal seepage of condiments into flesh and bloodstream. Was it someone else, or could it truly be this compulsive performer about whom Godsown now continued to speak, Menka's adopted twin, as designated by families, friends, and acquaintances? Yet Godsown's tale, interrupted by the Fist of Dark, was that he, Kighare Menka, stood accused of enabling, even aiding the attempt on the life of his twin, Duyole, then finished off the unfinished business under cover of professional ministrations.

He shuddered all over again. As if implacably committed to complicating his existence, Duyole's will had made him his main beneficiary, after his widow and children—and not merely substantially but in dedication to the Gumchi pledge! No wonder Cardoso had gone to such lengths to make him attend the reading. That effort was one non-starter of a lifetime—he had no wish to set eyes even on the most innocent of the surviving Pitan-Paynes. But that Duyole should remember and keep faith with a pledge of youth, alive or dead—he found it extremely moving, wafted him into a state of high elation that, on his part, he had brought his friend's body home in fulfillment of a nonexistent pledge. *For once I trumped you there, my friend, admit it!* There was just the unnerving thought, suppose he had been by his bedside in Salzburg? What if the doctors, even without knowledge of the pact between them, had insisted that he, in the dual role of professional colleague and friend of the patient, should make the decision on when to pull the plug? He refused to contemplate the outcome.

One for four and four for one, gung-ho? Anticipating the certainty of forces already mobilizing to thwart the dream of Gumchi, he permitted himself a twinge of pity for the dead man's Family.

22.

The Board of Happiness

I t would appear that the late engineer's interventions in joyless existence were by no means over. If anything, he continued to dominate the environment, though not quite in the manner that he would have chosen during his earlier mode of existence. His will had taken on a life of its own, thus conspiring to make the feast of life perpetual. If the proceedings of the Prime Ministerial Task Force, in association with the Oromotaya National Inquest organization, were anything to go by, the Festival of the People's Choice, which was now redesignated the **Branding the Land Festival,** in honour of the slain engineer, it would be no surprise to discover that it proved in the end indeed one for the record books, unlikely to be matched, much less surpassed, in this century or the next. And yet it very nearly did not happen. And as usual, the behind-the-scenes buildup made for far greater instruction—and indeed excitation—than the grandiloquent event itself.

The pre-festival meeting of the National Board of Happiness, summoned by the major shareholder, Sir Godfrey Danfere, consisted of a highly eclectic bag of representation, a crisscrossing grid that sought to cater for every group interest, taste, and social adhesion—trade union, the learned bench, domestic services, academia, etc., etc., not forgetting . . . religion! Papa Davina was present in magnificent form, while the State of Zamfara boasted a selection that had been made nearly exclusively from the dynamic and progressive Islamic sect known as the Yantulai al-Yarimeh. It was this group that launched the most potent threat to what was intended to be a harmonious bonding for a nation of remarkable diversity. Even before the start of deliberations, the Yantulai mobilized to stage a walkout. When reminded that the meeting had not begun and thus there was nothing out of which to walk, they reasonably resolved to go into a prayer jihad until the meeting formally began, take their seats, remain seated during the national anthem, chant their way through any opening prayers, await the commencement of the welcome overture by the prime minister, then stage a protest walkout into the waiting arms of the villa press corps.

Their leaders had leafed through the lushly printed draft programme handed to each participant on arrival in the anteroom. Their sharp eyes instantly detected one repulsive item that had obviously been entered to give offence to their religious sensibilities. That item was *beauty contest*! Nothing, they declared, could persuade them to participate in a festival that contained such an exercise, which promoted female prostitution. This was worse than even serving alcohol at the festival, or roasting a pig on a spit, as, they had earlier learnt, had actually been contemplated by Chief Orotomaya and his religious bigots, namely Papa Davina. The chief leapt up as if stung by a school of scorpions, denied it strenuously, and demanded a withdrawal. Teribogo was ensconced amidst a small group of devotees in a different part of the anteroom, oblivious to the brewing storm only a few yards away from him. They had it on good authority, the Yantulai insisted. They were aware that wiser counsel had prevailed, that the piggy offensive had been eliminated. However, there were strong indications that alcohol was being smuggled in via a most devious route—and by none other than one who called himself a man of God and advocate of religious pluralism. Let him deny that he had tried to insinuate an alcohol-saturated event into the festival in the name of ecumenical values. Fortunately they had done their homework thoroughly and knew what they were talking about. They would have the world know that they represented the new breed of believers, not to be confused with mere fanatic agitators. They were scientific in their approach, and could not be easily manipulated by Christian and other closet Islamophobes.

Eyes swiveled curiously to the spot where Papa Davina was standing, exchanging urbane wisdoms with his circle of adoring delegates. Other delegates converged on the accused, curious but also anxious to preserve the peace.

Teribogo was somewhat taken aback, as the matter had surfaced at the most elementary stage of planning. This consisted of the usual nationwide call for event propositions, to which artistes in every genre, cineastes, colleges, war veteran associations, social clubs, market women, and every conceivable institution and contract hunter responded with ideas, supply offers, and even demonstration videos. It had all been amicably resolved. Was this a renewed offensive by an aggressive offshoot of one of the Boko Haramic schools of religious persuasion? He beckoned to Chief Oromotaya to join them and corroborate his rendition of events, the initial glitch to which, he revealed, had been triggered by a different school of protesters. That was none other than the nation's increasingly powerful Green movement, avid protectors of the world's ecosystem. Approaching the spirit of the people's fiesta through his globally recognized ecumenical perspective, Papa Davina explained, he had indeed felt moved to offer a unique religious contribution—a Zoroastrian Fire Temple to be erected on the festival site. "According to computations within our Ekumenika ministry," Teribogo further detailed, "the festival season falls on the cusp of Zoroaster's birthday. It thus struck us as a divinely ordained opportunity to kill two birds with one stone—introduce Zoroastrian presence into the ecumenical family while blessing the festival with a fire temple. The only question was where? There are no mountains in Lagos. We looked around, and our sights were divinely guided to none other than the nation's capital, which boasts our famous landmark, the Zuma Rock. However, there are other, lesser-known rockhills in that area, notably the Gumchi rockhills, close to the very centre of the nation and the highest elevation in the Abuja region—higher, many are unaware of this, than even Zuma Rock." This prompted the Green movement to raise an alarm. They feared that there might be air pollution—which of course was proven quite scientifically baseless.

Oromotaya took up the story. His imagination, he admitted, had indeed been fired on receipt of Teribogo's fiery concept. It was an opportunity to raise the festival literally to new dramatic heights.

Gumchi had sprung back in the news since the assassination of the nation's famous export to the United Nations. The completely anonymous rockhill village had first come into public notice when her surgeon son, a Dr. Kighare Menka, had won the prestigious National Pre-eminence Award. Then, before it could fade back completely into its accustomed obscurity, along came the tragic assassination of his lifelong friend, the famous engineer Duyole Pitan-Payne. The will of the deceased was read, and lo and behold, he had bequeathed to that same son of the soil a large chunk of his wealth for building a state-of-the-art rehabilitation clinic in the same Gumchi. It was all in fulfillment of a pledge made in their schooldays. The media could not get its fill of yet another episode in the long-running saga of the rivalries of the inseparable pair.

Merutali had joined him, injecting the political boost. The prime minister, a most sensitive politician, had instantly committed his government to match the bequest, act as a full partner—staffing and operation, equipping, etc.—to ensure it became a medical mecca for both nationals and the world's stream of medical tourists. It would be named after the late engineer himself. Breaking of the first soil had been inserted into the festival programme. The nation could look forward to a unique, multidisciplinary edition. What else could be expected? The world was witnessing the triumph of the creative partnership of government and the private sector. Demonstration once again of the commitment of POMP to citizen partnership, which had been the cornerstone of POMP policies from the inception of the government, certain to expand as a solemn commitment once it was returned to power.

The baton was again picked up by Oromotaya. He reminded one and all that the festival had always been a moving feast. Bringing it to Abuja would further cement the sense of unity and belonging that had formed the cornerstone of government policies since the capital of the nation was moved from the coastal, marginal Lagos to the nation's geographical centre. The year's fiesta was now designed to explode within and around the ultramodern national stadium, not the decrepit National Theatre, which was sinking by inches in the swamps of Iganmu, a decaying suburb of Lagos.

It would now devolve on the members of the task force to spread the word and expand the deed, each in his or her own zone of influence and operations. The passing of a great man would bring people closer to people, enhancing the popularity of the tested party of vision. It had already inspired the introduction of new variations in Teribogo's weekly homilies at Ekumenika, enabling him to evoke the universal message in an ancient fire that was different from the fires of Purgatory, cleansing as opposed to burning, the vision of an ancient seer called Zoroaster. Oromotaya was even more vibrant and innovative, very much in his element. A sudden flash of the Olympic Torch descending from the skies propelled him in the direction of the embassy of Switzerland. Could the embassy recommend a company of professional abseilers? Yes, it could, veterans of the Alps whose experience extended beyond Mount Everest to Kilimanjaro. The deal was sealed. Papa D. obtained the franchise to build his Temple of Fire on the ledge of Mount Gumchi, shielded by ancient boulders. The Festival Torch would be lit from the Zoroastrian temple. The abseilers—the entire spectacle captured and transmitted nationwide by drone cameras—would ignite the torch from Mount Gumchi, first descending and ascending in a torch play, passing the torch from one to the other until the final bearer set foot at the mountain base. Runners would then continue on flat ground all the way to the National Stadium, where they would ignite the Eternal Flame, which would remain illumined throughout a festival now named **Branding the Land.** The concept made Oromotaya reel with an ecstasy that was equaled only by Teribogo's anticipation of securing a sorely craved foothold in Gumchi. The rockery of that time-bypassed village remained in blissful ignorance of its future service as a nation's futurist historic site.

It all seemed spectacularly inspired, until the objections began. The eco-warriors instantly registered strident opposition, demanded that an ozone quality check be conducted around Mount Gumchi to ensure that no damage was done by a fire lit so close to the skies, a rockhill that was notorious for vanishing for weeks at a time, completely shrouded by clouds. Negotiations followed. The conclusion was favourable to the project—a bit of firewood splashed with some paraffin for instantaneous combustion at the dramatic moment would constitute no harm to the ozone layers. And of course there was no risk of a forest fire on the barren rocks. The Greenies' intervention had, however, provided a lively debate that consumed days and reams of newsprint. Festival preparations became virtually the monopolizing content of national discourse. Firewood, matchstick, and paraffin appeared to have resolved the issue, and media attention was taken up with more mundane festival aspects, when it was revived from a most unexpected quarter.

Provocation had merely transferred ownership, providing the very first grounds of the Yantulai al-Yarimeh conscientious objectors. Let it be understood, they thundered, that the nation was no longer dealing with any kind of untutored *almajiri*. They represented the new wave of Muslims, every bit as educated as any other part of the nation. They had aerospace engineers among them; among their ranks were authors of numerous books on every earthly phonemenon. They had done their research and knew that paraffin was alcohol-based and thus unacceptable as inflammatory fluid. They began to mobilize for a massive boycott. Hurriedly Sir Goddie got his minister of science and technology to issue rebuttals and assure the nation that paraffin was extracted from wood resin and contained no alcohol. Chief Benzy and Papa Davina weighed in, issued both separate and joint public assurances that, irrespective of scientific debunking, they had no need of paraffin and would studiously avoid its use throughout the festival, if only in deference to religious sensibilities. They would settle for kerosene or even petroleum, which would also demonstrate a commitment to the use of indigenous material, since the nation would have to import paraffin, while petroleum was in sufficient local abundance to douse the entire Gumchi rockhills and leave them perpetually aflame if the festival so required. It was this last reminder that came to the rescue. Reluctant to be denounced as unpatriotic in a preference for imported material over the local, the Muslims softened their stance somewhat. The boycott was suspended, but they reserved the right to revisit the subject.

Bunched together in a corner, with the draft festival programme flapping and bristling versus the rest, the Yantulai al-Yarimeh now declared that they had suddenly realized that the entire alcohol debate had been nothing but a hoax. A ruse. The paraffin debate was a smokescreen. It was a grand conspiracy by all three—the Temple of Ekumenika, Oromotaya's *The Inquest,* and the Greenies, with Sir

Goddie's POMP possibly pulling the strings in the background—all joining hands to create a diversion from the real destination. While they, the Yantulai, were busy denouncing that outrage, the real business was being organized, readied for the presumed rubber stamping by the Prime Ministerial Task Force to become a fait accompli—a Beauty Contest! The Yantulai al-Yarimeh delegation moved into their now-patented stonewalling strategy—they declared a prayer jihad, drew a virtual laager against all comers in the anteroom, and invested it. It could not be breached. From within its sanctuary they demanded nothing less than a removal of that event from the programme— otherwise the suspended boycott would be reactivated. Together with sympathizing states, they would withdraw from all further participation. And they hoped the prime minister knew what that meant for his coveted votes from those constituencies. Villa Potencia was flooded with the cadence of prayers that rose and fell from long practice, passing from one cantor to another, a brand-new resistance weapon that had become the hallmark of the Yantulai and was spreading quite appreciably to a number of states in the northern region.

Shekere Garuba came panting up the stairs to the residential section of Villa Potencia, found Sir Goddie at breakfast. He explained the situation. Goddie thought for a moment.

"What state did you say it was?"

"Zamfara. It's the Yantulai al-Yarimeh sect. I know them quite well."

"All right. Let me just finish this *akamu* while it's warm. I'll speak to the governor—no—better still, to Papa Davina. In the meantime, get yourself back to the conference room. Keep them locked in. They are not to leave the villa."

"Nothing to worry about on that score, PS," the adviser assured him. "Once they declare a prayer jihad, they will not budge from the spot until a counterfatwa is recited. That takes at least half an hour from start to finish. Just like the original prayer jihad—it runs in half-hour cycles and must not be broken. So we have at least another half hour in which to take action."

"Good. I can finish my breakfast in peace. Wait outside while I think." The People's Steward continued his breakfast, grumbling,

"Inauspicious beginning to the day, damn it. What else is in store? I wonder."

A soft, empathizing belch, followed by a thoughtful caress of his stomach, signaled the end of breakfast. Sir Goddie picked up his mobile phone and stabbed at the buttons. The voice at the other end cooed: "Peace of Ahura Mazda, Lumen ascendant, Druj in flight, this is Father Davina of Ekumenika Ministry."

Sir Goddie snapped. "Cut that out. I hear you're standing right in the middle of a crisis—is this a time for the prayer mat?"

"There is a time for everything, Sir Goddie. Let me counsel you with the biblical chapter and verse. . . ."

"No, thank you. Teribogo, let's stick to business chapter and verse. And the last you cited to me was that you'd brought the Yantulai into full partnership."

"Indeed we have. Two of their members are on the board of governors."

"And—payments. Are those regular?"

"Up front. Human Resources guard their track record jealously—no one knows that better than you, Your Excellency."

"So, why are they making trouble?"

"Greed, what else? The human failing called—avarice. I've ignored them so far. I recommend that you do the same."

"That's easy for you to say. You are not the one standing elections."

"They'll come round. It's all about bargaining. Holding out for more."

"In that case, what about increasing their shares. . . ."

Papa Davina's tone was firm and dismissive. "Not the way to go, Sir Goddie. Which Peter do we rob to pay Paul? You? Or me? We can't run a business on extortion. It's unethical."

Sir Goddie snapped shut the mobile, snarling: "Hypocrite!"

For a while he sat still, staring ahead. He blotted his lips neatly with a napkin, began to pick his teeth. With that ritual went some of Sir Goddie's most inspired bouts of thinking. Suddenly he stopped, carefully laid down the toothpick, and raised his voice.

"You, there. Come back in!" Shekere returned. "Explain to the delegation that the maximum age of participants will be thirteen. So this event that is upsetting them will consist only of beauties between three and thirteen years old. Nothing above. And there will be opportunity for takeaway. Now get going."

Shekere moved, then stopped. He turned round slowly.

"What did you forget?" Sir Goddie snarled. "Didn't you hear my orders?"

Shekere stammered badly. "I just wanted to be sure, PS, sir. Did you say thirty? Or thirteen?"

"The fool is also deaf! Thirteen! Thirteen! Now get going!"

"Yes, People's Steward, sir. How soon do we expect you, sir?"

"What time did we set?"

"Ten o'clock, PS."

Goddie glanced at his watch. "Well, it's nearly time. Go and make the announcement and get them into their places. And I don't want to hear any more objections to anything. Always act with cultural sensitivity and there will be no problem."

Sir Goddie was right. The Festival of the People of Happiness could now move forward. When a breathless Garuba returned to the conference chamber, banged on a table for attention, and made his announcement, the relay chanting of the Yantulai al-Yarimeh stopped abruptly. The pause lasted just a few seconds, then resumed. Even the crassest tone-deaf *kafri* could assess a distinct change of tonality that exuded pure, undiluted spiritual ecstasy.

Shekere breathed a sigh of relief, allowed them a few more minutes' rapture, sensed the approach of the end of the current round of the counterrecital, and began to herd in the guests. "Honoured delegates, kindly take your seats. All is resolved. The People's Steward will be with you shortly and the inaugural ceremony will begin."

The nominees, old and new faces, found their seats from the small placards placed on the long semi-bifurcated oval desk in the Villa Potencia Cabinet Room. It was where the Executive Council normally held its monthly meeting. New members to the board were already sworn in. Only then did His Excellency the People's Steward Sir Godfrey enter the chamber. All rose. As soon as the chair of the People's Steward was pushed back and he inserted himself into the created space, the national anthem resounded—just the first verse. He remained standing, as did the others.

His eyes took in Papa Davina immediately and turned to him. "Father Davina, perhaps you will assist us with prayers for successful deliberations?"

Papa Davina, robed as could not be faulted in any postmodernist concept of Zoroaster in person, bowed. With his arms from shoulder to elbow liturgically pinned to his sides, elbow to hands angled upwards, both palms upturned, Papa Davina pronounced his divine attestation, specially prepared for the occasion and placed in advance before every seat of the participants.

To you the Almighty GodAllah, known in other climes as Ahura Mazda, Begetter of the Universe and Benevolent Master of Wisdom, Dispenser of Happiness, we give praise and thanks and seek blessings. Preside over our gathering in these chambers. Grant us the creative strength that focuses the mind and imagination, enabling us to deliver to our people their heart's desire at this forthcoming festival. Let Asha the Good prevail over Druj, the Slave of Evil. Let goodness and harmony prevail among us. Amen. Oooom. Allah Akhbar. Shanti. A-a-se. So be it as you will.

Sir Goddie took his seat, followed by the others. A folder was already in place before him. The Steward of the People opened it and proceeded to the business of the day—the inauguration of the Board of Happiness, tenth edition.

"Once again, ladies and gentlemen, it is time to commence preparations for the great day. As some of you will undoubtedly have noticed, we have quite a few new faces among us. As we proceed, you will get to know one another. Right now, I wish to bid them welcome. We are a nation of great diversity, and therein lies our strength. Thus we continue to endeavor to cater to that richness of diversity and ensure that every sector of the nation, every group interest, every professional sector, has a voice in the onerous task of ensuring for this nation a sustainable state of happiness. This is what underpins the commitment of this government to the annual Fiesta of the People's Choice. For those who do not know it, this very chamber is the room of power. It is the very room where the Executive Council holds its monthly meeting. What does this signify? I shall tell you. It means that for the next three weeks to a month, that is, the countdown towards the People's Fiesta, you are the government. Your word is law!"

416 Chronicles from the Land of the Happiest People on Earth

The records at this point read, *"Spontaneous applause."*

"I do not wish to paint a dismal picture, but I must be frank. This has been a particularly problematic year. Crisis after crisis. Terrorism. Arson. Murders. The pride of our nation, of our very race, a global icon, was blown up under our noses. I shall address that tragic event in greater detail before the end of our sessions. In the meantime, let me give an especial, heartfelt welcome to the sister of that martyr, Selina Pitan-Payne. The widow of our murdered citizen, unfortunately, could not join us, as she is still in mourning, and our culture does not permit her participation. The lady you see here, the bereaved sister, volunteered to take her place, and her presence here, co-opted as a member of the Board of Happiness is, as you have surely guessed by now, not unconnected to that tragic event and a nation's statement of solidarity.

"Let me state here again, without fear of contradiction—everything imaginable, indeed sometimes beyond imagination, has worked against the peaceful and joyful celebration of the People's Fiesta. Indeed, at certain moments my government debated whether or not we should proceed with the festival. Some voices clamoured that it would be more appropriate to substitute a national week of mourning. Fortunately, that raised the issue of copyright, as there is already in existence a movement known as *The Nation Mourns,* which goes into sackcloth and ashes for a full week annually. It is always safest to be original in these matters, to avoid treading the beaten spoor. And so in the end common sense and national pride triumphed over pessimism. The fiesta has become a tradition. I don't have to remind you that we have already applied for its placement on the UNESCO annual calendar, thus making it a destination for global tourism. To miss even one edition is to tell the world that we are not a serious people. So all proceeds as scheduled. If it takes nothing less than a miracle to pull it through, then we must produce a miracle. After all, we have among us that man of God Papa Davina—he just led us forth with an ecumenical invocation—not that he needs any introduction." *Mild applause.* "However, it is also said that heaven helps only those who help themselves, and we do have seasoned, public-spirited hands like Chief Modu Oromotaya—there he is over there." *Mild applause.* "Our unstoppable governor, Chief Akpanga, has also joined the board. That is one man guaranteed to add spice and colour to any occasion. As you see, we continue to inject new blood, and that means new energy, new ideas—"

The People's Steward stopped abruptly, his head swiveling to the right. Irritably he spat, "Yes?"

The side door that led directly to the Steward's offices had opened furtively, and a head recognizable as belonging to the presidential adviser on energy, Shekere Garuba, was inserted into the opening. It was now followed by the rest of the body, apologetic.

"Yes, what is it?"

Shekere entered fully, trotted the few steps on padded feet to Sir Goddie's chair, and slipped a note face-up on the desk. Sir Goddie read, and his countenance was seen to change. It read: *"Mayday! Mayday! Abort, sir, abort! Abandon speech, sir."*

He waved off the adviser and turned to his audience. "You will have to excuse me. What did I just complain of? A season of crises. No sooner do we resolve one than another develops." He turned towards his image-maker-in-chief. "Dr. Merutali, please take over. This may take a while. Dr. Merutali, I suggest you simply proceed with general brainstorming and exchange of ideas. Chief Oromotaya can brief everyone on how he has designed things, the state of play, etc., etc. It's his baby, after all."

He rose, stopping the assemblage in their respectful midrise. "No, no, no more disruption. Merutali, all yours." A flustered Goddie sped from the room, followed by his dutiful aide, who carried his papers behind him.

His chief of staff was waiting in his office, apologetic. "I thought it wise to interrupt, Your Stewardship, knowing of some crucial items in the draft speech I had prepared. The situation was desperate."

Sir Goddie waved the note in the face of his chief of staff. "'Mayday! Mayday!' Are you a pilot? Whose plane is crashing?"

"Sir, I merely quoted the man. He was frantic—so was I, Your Stewardship. It has to do with the very meeting of the board. And I recalled, you did say he was to have priority access on his return."

"Who? Me? Who is he?"

"The man who went to Zamfara, Your Stewardship."

"Zamfara? What's my business with Zamfara? You mean you didn't ask him what it was about?"

"First thing I did, sir, but I think you'd better listen to him in person, Your Stewardship. I did recall that your instructions were—"

"All right, all right. Bring him in."

"Very good, sir."

"Hold on. Ah yes. Just want to make sure we're talking of the same man—is it the Indian? The geologist? Back so soon?"

"The very one, Your Stewardship."

"Better bring me today's papers."

"Right before you, PS. Plus this. Please read it, sir. That's what got him racing to the villa."

Sir Goddie looked down on his desk and found that, yes indeed, the day's clippings were right before him, pinned down by his bowl of kola nuts and company, just so he would not miss it. Fiercely his eyes ran over the relevant news. He exhaled.

"Only speculation in here, thank goodness. The fakir seems sure of his facts."

"I think it is wise to assume so, PS."

"All right. Send him in. If this is a dud, he's on the next plane back to his curry and chapati!"

Sir Goddie settled behind his desk, composed himself. A few moments later the cause of interruption was led in by the chief of staff, who promptly took his leave. The People's Steward was alone with his guest, the geologist Dr. Mukarjee. Sir Goddie blinked.

"Your news must be really desperate."

The caller looked down, saw the clippings. "I see you have the matter before you. That was why you had to be stopped."

"Oh yes, I recall. You came to see me just before your departure."

"The very one who fled from Zamfara with his tail between his legs. Today, however, is a very different meeting, Your Excellency. Very, very different. The last time was very stressful. But you instructed your chief of staff to ensure instant access on my return. It was most prescient. I don't know what faith you follow, but it must have been divine intimations."

"Do take a seat. I wasn't expecting you back so soon, and in person. We get so many of these false alarms. Lucky you had my CoS on your side. He has been a most consistent advocate for your ventures."

"Ah yes, Your Excellency. I returned from Delhi just two nights ago. I had not imagined that I was in a situation of emergency. Then, this morning, in the papers, I saw the news. The inauguration of the board, and then, Sir Goddie, I nearly choked on my breakfast. News about dedicating a clinic in Gumchi village in respect of the departed son of the nation as part of a coming festival. Sir, when I recovered, that was when I called up your chief of staff. You will forgive me, but I told him it was a matter of life and death—and I invoked you as being mortally endangered. I hope you will forgive me. It was crucial that you should mention nothing of the will in public."

"I already have," said Sir Goddie.

"But was it an official statement, sir? In the newspapers, it did not come directly from you."

"Whether it did or not, Mr. . . ."

"Mukarjee, Your Excellency. Mukarjee."

"Yes, whether it did or not, a will is sacrosanct. Unless of course pronounced invalid by the courts."

"If I may make a pun, sir. There is will and there is will. There is the matter of a people's will."

Sir Goddie leant back, a broad smile fanning out on his face turning into a chuckle. "You know, Dr. Murkajee, you won't believe this, but I have always preached that we have a lot to learn from India beside your lessons in small cottage industries. Yes indeed, a will—such as testamentary—is one thing, and the will—the state will—is another. Here, the latter is known as Doctrine of Necessity. We are no strangers to that recourse, even in recent history, I assure you!" Sir Goddie sat back, locked his fingers together across the desk.

"Now, I take it you are dying to enlighten me about why we may find ourselves invoking that doctrine, right?"

"I was not mistaken," Dr. Mukarjee responded, relief all over his face. "But I wanted to avoid unnecessary hassle. I am from India, and I think you know our politics are very much alike. Very much so, I felt at home here from my first arrival fifteen years ago. So please understand why I panicked."

Sir Goddie moved to put him at his ease. "Relax, my good Indian compatriot. I hadn't even got to the board's formal inauguration, so fortunately there is no public commitment. I hadn't even finished my welcome address. You know the media, they love to speculate. That's their job, trying to scoop competition. Yes, we did mention that the engineer's last will would be on their agenda, its provisions integrated into the Festival of the People's Choice. There are other posthumous awards proposed, but nothing announced as yet. Speculations are normal. In any case, a government is free to reverse itself."

The Indian smiled and nodded. "True, true. You must forgive my nervousness. But I have noticed, among your people, they tend to take government pronouncements at face value. Then the media jump in."

Goddie chuckled. "The public is the same everywhere. Just like humanity. So? Welcome back. Now let's get to the good news my CoS says you brought with you."

Dr. Mukarjee did relax and grew expansive. "Tradition, Your Excellency, is a mighty force. I give praise to the family tradition in which I was raised. Yes, Sir Goddie, as I carefully hinted in my message, you are sitting on gold."

Goddie melodramatically adjusted his sitting posture. "You can see me adjusting my seat."

"I was already sure, but of course, as again I hinted to you, I wanted to return home and make further tests."

"Frankly, I thought you were crazy. You went to Zamfara and were lucky to return with your skin, and still you were talking gold."

"That governor put me through hell. My team and my humble self. When he invited us to prospect, he did not say that the religious banditry had anything to do with it. We went in with our eyes closed."

"You came out alive, thank goodness. Some others did not."

"And came straight to you to complain, Sir Goddie. To lay a formal complaint before talking to our government. Looking seriously for foreign partners, that's not the way to treat them. People should always lay their cards on the table, then there is trust. Business depends on trust." The People's Steward showed signs of losing patience. Dr. Mukarjee made matters worse by pointing to the crystal bowl. "That includes you, Your Excellency."

Now Sir Goddie's risen hackles admitted no disguise. "Explain yourself."

But the geologist's complacent smile only kept broadening. "Before departing, I sent a message. Your chief of staff assured me it was delivered. But we received no reply."

"What kind of a reply did you expect? You were granted an audience. You left me still shivering from the Zamfara experience. That was the last I expected to hear from you. Then, some days later, you apply for a prospecting licence from a place you admit you have never been. Never set foot on its soil. The question was, what had you suddenly discovered all the way from India?"

It seemed impossible, but Mukarjee's smile grew broader still. "What a mystery the world holds for us, Your Excellency, what a mystery. What surprises. Here I was, still grateful for my life. I had responded to a call from one of your governors. That visit ends in nothing but loss and lamentation. I leave Zamfara and head home to lick my wounds. Luckily our Nigerian partners urge me to stop at the villa and lay a formal complaint. I do so. You are a busy man, Sir Goddie, but you managed to spare me a minute or two. You apologize, then send me on my way."

Sir Goddie tried to mollify the geologist, evidently still suffering from effects of the trauma. "You know, as a businessman, one hits duds from time to time."

Mukarjee shook his head vigorously in disagreement. "No, Sir Goddie, this proved to be nothing like a dud. Let me explain, Your Excellency. You see, there are great goldsmith families, sublime craftsmen in their own right, all over India. In my part, however, which is near Kerala, a small town called Kochi, there are a few families who are not just goldsmiths but are trained tasters. You know, like tea. Or coffee. Even wine or alcohol and liquors. Please note—taste, I said, not test. I am speaking of places where the tradition is to beat gold so thin that it requires great sensitivity of the fingers to pick up a leaf of it. You need tweezers. And you have to choose the right gold for it. Not just any gold you pick up. The kind of gold you can beat thin. Very, very thin. Thinner than sheer gossamer. Think of the powdery wings of a butterfly, not even the wing itself but the powder on it, then imagine that powder as a single sheet. That is what we do. We beat the gold so thin you cannot hold it. Are you with me, Sir Goddie?"

"I'm all attention."

"I had to give you the background. Take weddings. What you normally see are gold bangles and earrings and bracelets and necklaces, etc., etc. But when a girl marries, it forms part of her wedding feast.

Those nearly intangible gold wafers are placed over her food. The significance of that garnishing is that no matter what else happens to her in life, she has tasted gold. Riches. Wealth has become part of her body and spirit, and no one can take it away from her. She eats that gold on her wedding night."

Goddie's eyes popped. "Eat . . . gold? That's metallic!"

"Not when we have beaten it insubstantial. Her meal is covered in those wafers. Yes, Your Excellency. And so for us in that lineage of goldsmiths, our palates are trained from childhood to taste very tiny flakes of gold, sometimes just the dust. We pick up the tiny bits from the work surface—very special cover material—with the tips of our tongues, tiny, nearly invisible bits. That is how we grow up detecting the presence of gold in anything. Sir Goddie, the majority of the world doesn't know this, but gold has a taste, a flavor. For those of us who are especially gifted, gold even has a smell. The true gold wizards can smell gold from across a room. But mostly, for the rest of us of normal talent, we can only taste it. But that is enough for our profession."

Sir Goddie was riveted. "Yes, go on."

"My earlier visit was unfortunately short—a very busy day for you. But you were most sympathetic. Very gracious. On leaving, you offered me a kola nut from the bowl on your desk—yes, that very bowl. I see you still have some." An embarrassed giggle emerged from his throat. "I confess I did not quite share your taste in the kola nut refreshment—I think it's an acquired taste. However, on returning to my hotel room I did attempt a bite . . ."

The People's Steward's body snapped straight up. "You mean . . . ?"

"Yes—gold, Sir Goddie. Your kola nut tasted of gold."

"You don't mean it!"

"Yes, I do. I believe it's the same seam of geological formation, with breaks through some long-forgotten seismic history, from the Zamfara deposit. And here, Sir Goddie, the formation is more surface than underground. It explains that most unusual rock formation that has been remarked so often by every specialist, including television's *Discovery*. The rockhills of Gumchi are bursting with gold. I lay my family reputation on it."

The People's Steward sat back. Took a deep breath. "Saved by the bell," he said. He flipped over a page of his interrupted speech, stabbed a section of it with his finger. "Read that!"

Mukarjee read the indicated section.

When the late engineer's will was read, the family found that the late engineer had bequeathed a portion of his wealth to build a model rehabilitation centre in the village of his lifelong friend, not far from this very spot. The government of our great party, POMP, uses this occasion to associate itself with that bequest and undertake to build the clinic as its first major action once it is returned to office. It will become a world-class rehabilitation centre for the victims of Boko Haram and a diagnostic centre for other victims of trauma. At the end of this address you shall all witness my formal signing of the C of O, the Certificate of Occupation, to that friend, Dr. Kighare Menka, witnessed by the family representative, here present among us.

The geologist whistled. "Sir Goddie, this was indeed a narrow escape."

Sir Goddie nodded. "As our good preacher likes to remark, it is well and truly the hand of God. Nothing unusual in a government reversing itself. We could always substitute a piece of land nearby, even here in Abuja, but this would have been a tough call. That pestilential media would never let go. As for the beneficiary himself, the surgeon—another pain in the neck!"

Mr. Mukarjee wagged his head in satisfaction, rose. "I know it's a busy morning for you, Your Excellency. Permit me to take my leave."

"Certainly, certainly, Mr. Mukarjee. You shall of course be hearing from me. You are part and parcel of this—rest assured."

"Your Excellency, I place myself totally in your hands."

"You have given a most auspicious start to this year's festival."

The prime minister had already pressed his bell, and the Equivalent appeared on cue to see off his visitor. He sat back thoughtfully, instinctively reached out for the refreshment bowl, took out a kola nut, separated the lobes, and thrust a piece quite absentmindedly into his mouth. As he bit into it, his countenance changed and his entire body was galvanized. Moving rapidly, he pulled the crystal bowl closer with one hand, opened his desk drawer with the other. He shoved aside the toffees, sweets, and other cookies, picked out the remaining kola nuts one by one, laid them carefully in the drawer. He shut the drawer and removed the key, tucked it in the breast pocket of his *agbada*. He recomposed himself and pressed a button. Shortly after, the chief of staff appeared.

"Bring me that C of O. Give me ten minutes, then call Teribogo from the Ex Co chamber."

"Yes, Your Stewardship."

As the door shut behind him, Sir Goddie bit savagely into the kola nut still lodged behind his teeth. "That bloody engineer! He's still engineering problems for me from beyond the grave. This time, however . . . Let's wait and see."

Father Davina was ushered in a while later, his habitual collected self somewhat on the skewed side. For the inaugural occasion, he was costumed as befitted a priest of Zoroaster, the anniversary of whose day of self-revelation to humanity—pronounced by Papa Davina the Day of Illumination—had been computed for that week. Celebrations had already commenced at his prophesite, conducted by his aides-in-worship, in far-off Lagos and close by at the Lokoja confluence. He had already organized a small service of worship in—of all places—Gumchi! The divine ceremony of the purification of souls was already in place in a makeshift Temple of Fire, to be lit at the appointed hour and in the presence of none other than Chief Modu Oromotaya. That chief had been both delighted and puzzled at the invitation, but not altogether surprised. He was not a fan of Davina and his ministry, considered him a charlatan and a hypocrite. However, professionalism called to professionalism, and he could not deny a secret admiration for Davina's skills and mobilizing talent. Bestowal of one of the YoY Awards was already in the works by the astute entrepreneur—*form alliances with your competitors if you cannot beat them*. The People's Steward had been penciled in as guest of honour but had yet to formally accept. Sir Goddie was a practical man. The voters' list in Gumchi at the latest count amounted to no more than thirty-three thousand. Even under the most desperate situation, that could hardly be boosted higher than twice the authentic figure. Gumchi was not merely population-shy, it was physically circumscribed. Anyone could stand on one of those rock mounds and physically count the population if he was patient enough to remain there a few hours from dawn. Sooner or later the entire population would surface, and then all that was left was to make allowance for the bedridden and geriatrics and do the arithmetic.

Still, the innovation of the Festival of Fire? It would be the perfect prelude to the People's Choice Fiesta. Pitan-Payne Elder was not far wrong in his depiction of the village, but he was unaware of a remarkable cliff ledge just below the topmost boulder, as if a boulder had changed its mind midformation and flattened out itself instead of rounding out. It was mostly invisible to those below, since its positioning was nearly uniformly covered by clouds. Because it was set on the eastern side, the sun poured onto it with its first emergence. Gumchi was filled with legends totally disproportionate to its size and population, all kept alive among the taciturn villagers, especially as they became largely converted to Christianity. The platform was once reputed to be a place of worship that involved human sacrifice, with the victim secured to the centre of the platform—by what means, no one could actually say, since the ledge itself was polished smooth, with no evidence of any stakes driven into it, no markings of any sort, no inscriptions. The ledge was not uniformly flat, however. In the midst of it, nearly mathematically centred, was a wide bowl, nearly forty feet in diameter, smoothly symmetrical, just like a television dish, but embedded. Its deepest point at the centre would be no more than four feet.

Legend had it that the victim was placed there at dawn and had vanished by the sun's setting, sucked up, presumably, by invisible sun flues. The sacrifice of the victim was a guarantee of rains. In the equivalent of summer, there was evidence that a fire was lit within the obviously man-made bowl. At the end of the dry season, it was ritually cleansed by the priesthood to prepare it for the rains. That rainwater, gathered within the bowl, served the villagers as drinking water throughout the coming year. They made a pilgrimage up the rocks, each household reverentially gathering sufficient water for drinking—strictly for drinking. There was a stream at the base which flowed through the kola nut plantation, one whose value was about to increase astronomically and endanger the village's character. That stream served for all other purposes—cooking, washing, bathing, cleaning, etc. But the water from the elevated rock bowl of the platform was restricted to drinking—no other purpose. It was alleged to prevent or cure no matter what diseases. It was sacrilegious to use even a drop of it for any other function.

Christian conversion notwithstanding, Gumchi believed almost in totality that the platform was an abode of the deities and a meeting place of ancestors. They descended annually from the skies to observe the fortunes of their offspring, intervene in their activities and well-being. It was a place of reverence in which no strangers were ever permitted—at least, not until the arrival of the Christian missionaries. The Gumchi could gather water only on certain days of the year, when the deities were supposed to have been present. They bivouacked on the ledge on their way down to humanity, then departed. It was they, it seemed, who lit the fire in the hollow each year, feasted, descended into the rest of the world, inspected, returned, climbed, enjoyed a final banquet, then had themselves sucked back into the sky on the original transporters, long before *Star Trek*.

That legend lent itself to easy conversion as the original Jacob's ladder; thus the missionaries, to their later chagrin, encouraged its mystical hold on the people. Even before Papa Davina's numerous scouting missions in search of a permanent home for the world's first prophesite, he had heard of the legend. He had conquered the valleys, the rivers and their confluences, the ghettos and other marginal dwellings of humanity. Even while ensconced in the confluence of rivers in Lokoja, Papa Divina had set his sights on the rockhills of Gumchi and their hugging clouds as a spiritual reserve, the physical elevation of the Ekumenika march of divine colonization. Now with the approaching Festival, the exigencies of business beckoned. Gumchi Hills had acquired a multipurpose potential.

Teribogo entered Sir Goddie's presence and took his seat. He was taken aback to encounter an unsmiling People's Steward, a dramatic transformation from the avuncular being who had addressed the new board members in the executive chamber a mere half hour before. Without a word, Sir Goddie pushed the forms towards him. Across the front page of the Certificate of Occupancy were two thick diagonal lines drawn in red and the word RESCINDED.

Davina looked up at the Steward and asked, "What is this?"

"I have decided that we must abide by the terms of the will," pronounced Sir Goddie. "It is best that way. Neatest and safest. Certain complications have come up, and this is no time for controversies. The project is not safe."

Teribogo shook his Zoroastrian head in disbelief. "You are worried about safety? The Julius Berger people have constructed a first-class serial platform climb, with rest stations. Everything has been tested."

"I am not speaking about physical safety. And anyway, nothing stops your procession and your service of purification or whatever you call it. But from now on everything is limited to your Fire Temple. The festival kicks off with that event—nothing has changed. It will be like the Olympic flame—to formally launch the week of festivities. A first. You should all be proud. I think, even if I say it myself, it's a brilliant adjustment."

Teribogo was also undergoing transformation. His voice became hard. "And what becomes of the world headquarters of God's Ekumenika?"

"I have thought of that. We'll find you a new place to build your headquarters."

"With equivalent elevation? With the very clouds of the heavens nuzzling those rounded boulders? You can suggest a functional equivalent of the Gumchi—literally—skyscrapers of God's own boulders? Sir Goddie, this was a project signed and sealed in Lokoja. It is Gumchi or nothing. The view alone is nine-tenths of the spiritual capital!"

"I see you are shocked. Political exigencies do have their way of interfering with well-made plans. That is life for you. My job is to allow for and manage the unexpected. This is simply one of those occasions."

"We have printed hundreds of thousands of brochures, invested in ancillary business outlets. Sir Goddie, you and I have gone through the feasibility studies—this is a milk cow, the pinnacle of spiritual tourism. There are spinoff assets, other prospects stretching into infinity. This is one opportunity you cannot let pass."

The People's Steward shrugged. "Don't blame me. You killed an innocent man. He left a will. Again and again I've told you, I do not like your methods. I find them distasteful. Abhorrent. And dangerous. They endanger me. They threaten to undermine everything I have meticulously built. This is different from the Ikorodu thug. He would have ended up on the gallows anyway. Several times over. I agree you saved the nation a lot of headache. But this!"

"No one meant to kill him," Teribogo calmly protested. "It was an accident. The operation was simply to destroy some dangerous items in his studio."

"On account of what, Teribogo? Maybe it's time you came clean. You keep hiding things from me—I do not like surprises. From now on, no more hidden agenda!"

Teribogo took a deep breath, then looked nervously around. Sir Goddie reassured him. "This office is safe. I have it constantly swept, every morning. You'll find the irony hard to believe, but the very man at the heart of all this problem—it was his firm that set up the system."

"The Brand of the Land?"

Sir Goddie's smile was twisted. "The same. His firm consulted for us, you recall? Over the energy crisis. Well, while he was here, I had him set us up with his Austrian partners. Didn't use their local people—no way! But he facilitated the process. Their experts came and set up the blocking system. Any eavesdropping bug and it zings nastily." He pressed a button on the speakerphone on his desk. A red light came on, and a scratchy voice responded.

"Yes, People's Steward?"

"Tell Merutali they can break for lunch whenever. Get Shekere to look after that item and make them thoroughly comfortable."

"Yes, PS."

"And I do not wish to be disturbed till I signal."

"Very good, sir."

Sir Goddie rose, disrobed himself of his voluminous *agbada*, leaving just the less cumbersome long-sleeved tunic. He began to roll his neck and shoulders like a gladiator about to enter a ring, resumed his seat, and sat facing Teribogo squarely.

"All right. I'm listening."

Teribogo rose, began lifting the turbanlike headpiece, unwound the loose shawl that looped around his jaw, and arranged it all carefully on the corner of his side of the desk. His countenance changed to one of relief.

"Very good, Sir Goddie, here we go."

"Drop the *sir*. We are alone. Just assume we are at the lodge."

Teribogo shrugged. "I'll bring you into the full operation. Just remember this, we are in this together."

"But not all together. Bear that in mind."

"Those are niceties. We sink or swim together."

"At this stage, I do not need reminding," replied the People's Steward. "It's two sides of the same coin. Yours the spiritual side, mine the political. The meeting point is business. But you have the advantage of me, because mine is time-bound. Just four more years to go—assuming we win, which is no assumption or my name is not Godfrey Danfere. But yours is guaranteed to go on and on and on and on. In the meantime we are put to pasture while you regulate your alliance with the newcomer. So remember that, Teribogo. It means I am likely to be more desperate. And right now I wield the power. Is that understood?"

Teribogo nodded. "Time we both laid our cards on the table, face-up. We should not work at cross purposes—there is far too much at stake. It's not good for business."

"That is exactly the kind of sound I like to hear."

"Very well, I shall bring you up to date, beginning from the night before the explosion. A call came through to me at Ekumenika. It came on a dedicated number, known only to perhaps a dozen subscribers. It is used only in extremity—our cardinal rule, as I keep reminding you, is that we keep flesh away from the realm of the spirit. That way, each is protected against any weakness in the other. And so, receiving a call on that number, it could portend only something close to a catastrophe.

"The voice was that of a frightened young man whom I had personally recruited and trained on the job. All he said was, 'Medina has fallen.'"

23.

Clash of the Titans

Student days over, followed by inevitable dispersals, the ancient Gong o' Four mostly kept loose touch with one another—at least to begin with. Farodion was the first to vanish. He had always been the most prominent outsider—a badge that he carried with pride, often boasting that he would be an outsider even in a group of two. Except with the female sex, with which he was never short of company, yet even within those relationships he remained the outsider, and so the attachment never took root or lasted long. The closest in temperament was Badetona, but his detachment was of a different cast—it was simply that figures alone were his true friends and lovers. He had time for little else. Duyole, all acknowledged, was the gregarious hub, the mine of ideas that could be shared, not hoarded. No wonder they all gravitated around that hub, but of course his bond with Kighare was special. When the then student engineer found himself a designated father, the gang rallied round—*Four for one, one for four, gong-ho!* They shared the chores and the fallouts, mundane to the sensitive, such as who would notify Pop-of-Ages that he was again Grandpop-of-Ages, willy-nilly. He was exceedingly willy—an Austrian? An entire breathing and breeding Austrian in the family? He always knew that class called to class, pedigree to pedigree. He could hardly wait to visit his newly acquired in-laws and never understood why an invitation never arrived in the post or was conveyed by his son. He sent chocolates; they responded with the eau-de-vie called Korn. But there it ended.

There were lesser chores, such as the search for an immigrant versed in Yoruba tradition. Duyole desperately craved one for the naming ceremony, ideally one who knew where to find the sacred items— palm oil, kola nut, *orogbo,* camwood, etc.—for the newcomer's induction. In the end they improvised. A student recited liturgy from an anthropology doctoral thesis that contained the *odu* of Ifá divination. And they dug out a willing employee at the embassy in Vienna who cooked Nigerian food, so an authentic Nigerian feast ushered the newborn into the world. Each in his own way ensured that the mother felt herself part of the close family of four. They accompanied Duyole when he took the child to parks, rode donkeys with him, turned up at the home to take him out to a passing circus, or simply donated entire afternoons out on the town. Divorce came not long after. The child's mother remarried soon after. For them it merely imposed an additional charge—to ensure that the young one did not feel isolated or unwanted in the new home. They monitored him as he grew up, observed the commencement of character formation, especially his outlook on his personal situation.

Perhaps it was to be expected—young Damien soon took to blaming paternal abandonment for his indifference even to a modest achievement in studies. It alarmed them. Duyole kept in touch with the ex-wife as far as her new situation permitted. Education was primal to him; he ensured the young man's financial comfort, even to the extent of compensatory indulgence, all through school and into university, until Damien chose to graduate as a confirmed dropout. Growing up, the young scion showed signs that he expected to be kept in the style to which he felt his father was accustomed.

That father became disillusioned. He was dealing with an adult parasite, who, despite being now married and the father of two children of his own in quick succession, still expected to be subsidized for life. The engineer wrote him off. The self-styled paternal collective progressively withdrew, but not entirely. One continued to study him, check on news about him until he himself vanished from sight—that was Farodion. He studied everyone, himself included, but not with any accuracy. Like the others, he identified a weak character, easily manipulated. He kept in touch with him, even bailed him out once or twice when he received a note from him in a tight spot—a shifting zone that was also second home to the budding marketing guru and man of many parts. It was Uncle Farodion who prodded the delicate intervention by Menka that eventually led to his father's reaching out. Damien received an open invitation to try his paternal home as an alternative habitation and the chance of a steady career. And thus home came the prodigal son, his wife and children. Apart from the cloud of unremitting, barely disguised hostility from the wife's aunt-in-law, Selina, and her halting proficiency in English, it was culture shock on all fronts. She soon abandoned an inclement environment and returned to her successful career in Graz, an Italian-speaking part of Austria. Damien remained behind, visiting from time to time, bringing his family home for the Christmas and New Year's holidays.

The congenial environment of his father's firm was not, however, without a strong dose of resentment. The young scion had assumed that he was brought back to be the heir-apparent, as the eldest and indeed only son. It was difficult adjusting to Duyole's sense of a career ethic. The engineer made him begin at the bottom, like every new employee. Damien seethed at taking orders and being served formal queries by his superiors. He looked around, resolved to strike out on his own. He mixed with the expatriate community and soon felt totally at home with local life. His recruitment by talent scouts for any high-flying enterprise was limited only by his own choice—young Damien Pitan-Payne was very much in demand.

Engineer Duyole had a tenacious mind. He continued to worry the code—never mind his concession that the code was beyond his skills; nothing was further from the truth. It preyed on his mind, became a challenge. Being an electronic and micro-engineering fiend was not sufficient. One of his hobbies was crossword puzzles. As a student, he had also been a Scrabble champion in the two languages in which he operated, German and English. Even while his fingers toyed with some sensitive wiring on a modular board, his mind was engaged in acronyms and wordplay. *Brand of the Land* was his concoction; so was *Gong of Four,* not to mention minor lunch and dinner ditties such as *tongs and tonsils, tongue and tonsils,* and allied Muhammad Ali poetics. And thus for two or three nights after the visitation, a small cluster of letters he had deciphered from the charred pages continued to juggle and reform in his head, morphing into one another. Finally something coherent stuck. Quite ordinarily, he remarked on the coincidence to his wife, Bisoye—it was something he did all the time, bouncing off ideas and gestations. He continued to toss the word round his head. That word was *median*. Let it rest, Bisoye advised. You know it will all fall into place of its own accord.

At an unusually early hour the following morning, Duyole sat up in bed, eyes popping in his head. He scrambled out of bed, flew downstairs to his studio and straight to the shelves on which rested the heavy tomes of manufacturers' bibles. He extracted one and dashed to his desk. Duyole was like a man possessed. He gathered up the scraps of paper on which he had scribbled word combinations and associated images. He resumed—this time with fingers working frenetically—his arrangements of word scraps on crisscrossing grids vertical, horizontal, thematic, random. He opened his fat volume of a long-forgotten German *Medina* technical cookbook—began to rearrange letters more methodically on the magnetic board he had unearthed from his junk shelves since he had taken possession of the scorched notebook . . .

Median: borders—separation and connection. *Medina* was a German invention. Duyole lifted the heavy pages. The description summed up his recollection: "pre- and post-processor . . . element analysis . . ." The clues flew up and hit him in the face! And they frightened him. The engineer calculated the odds of any local manufacturer being in possession of a tome he had secured as a student over thirty years before, a copy of its very first print run—not on open sale—when Daimler-Benz patented the system. Again his brain attempted to calculate the odds against any other firm being in possession of that pioneer edition. As he turned over heavily laminated pages with bristling multicoloured page flags, he began to encounter underlining, annotations, circles drawn around diagrams and photos of automotive and aerospace parts. He stopped at a marginal notation—*CS* followed by a figure; it was undoubtedly a page reference. "If CS does not stand for Codex Seraphinianus, then my name," he muttered, "is not Aduyole Pitan-Payne!" Both Medina and Median—it leapt out without any effort—acronyms of one name: Damien! The two volumes acting together held the code, easy to access by cross-referencing, simply matching Codex images to the mechanical spare parts. It was ingenious, sophisticated—but also conceited.

Now, far more calmly, fully possessed of all his faculties, Duyole sat back and prodded himself into recall. He began with a number of unusual absences, strange callers on Damien, parcels arriving and vanishing through special delivery services. The young man had once requested a different office from his original allocation—and that was not long after joining Brand of the Land. As the son of the house, he was quietly accommodated—in any case, there was nothing unusual in a young expatriate requiring his own secluded space. He opted for a disused storage space with strong barred windows, supposedly suited to requirements of his specialized assignment. After all, he had been brought back home to Badagry under a highly confidential breakthrough with foreign partners, a discovery that was already a target for technological espionage by rival firms, from Western powers to North Korea—who were his colleagues to argue?

Damien's activities noticeably intensified during Duyole's prolonged stint in Abuja, where the boss was fully preoccupied with his government assignment. Damien established an aura of a hush-hush operation that brooked no interlopers. The space was off-limits to all, gradually opening out to tolerate a very select few, who in turn took on the airs of an elite, privileged cabal. The boss remained blissfully absorbed in the challenge of power production. His sole orders had been given: the new recruit was to be treated just as one of the junior executive staff. The few breaks that the engineer took to reoccupy Badagry found him in his penthouse office, taking critical decisions for Brand of the Land. The dramatic increase in parcel traffic—delivered and redirected—was beneath his radar. He did not, however, fail to remark the increased flashes of ostentatious wealth—a brand-new Mazda SUV, certainly beyond Damien's means and earnings. He explained that it was a gift on his thirty-fifth birthday from his Graz wife. The father chose not to interfere. There were nights on the town, company with the children of billionaires, cruises and weekend parties on private yachts; only the rarest social heights were acceptable to the fastidious young executive. But above all there was the ease and rapidity with which the new entrant had slipped into the cream of society. It was as if he had arrived with an advance master key that opened every door, or a socialite chaperone dedicated to just that purpose, over and above anything even the Pitan-Payne family had ever known . . . Duyole stared down on a remorseless book of indictment—Millennium Towers as the epicenter of Codex transactions! A glorified meat mall for a steadily expanding clientele.

Only five more days before his departure, and the engineer spent more and more time in his studio, feverishly transcribing. What he encountered was no less than a roll call of names, and assigns of the infamous Okija shrine in Anambra State, eastern Nigeria, a saga that had transfixed the nation on its necrophiliac exposure some ten to twenty years before. The most riveting aspect of the Okija cult was that its members were compelled, by fearsome oaths, to donate their remains to the shrine after death. It was an unbreakable commitment, it appeared, as irrevocable as the oaths administered to recruited prostitutes, most conspicuously from a sister state, Edo. Thereafter the recruits, mostly young and vulnerable, committed to serve the exotic needs of Europe and other destinations. So compelling were the oaths that young girls, once trapped in the trade, feared not only for their lives and sanity but for those of their families if they even thought of breaking their terms of service. It took the equally revered traditional ruler, the Oba of Benin, to challenge the state of enslavement. The Oba performed a mass public exorcism ritual, in which he attempted to liberate the girls from their oaths, then place their "managers" and madams under a complimentary curse.

The gruesome feature of the Okija shrine was that the corpses were never buried but condemned to lie exposed in open air, some in their coffins—the upper class, perhaps?—but still exposed until they decayed, dessicated, and then—what? In return, members asked for whatever was their innermost desire—wealth, children, fame, power, position, American lottery win, women, or whatever. The roll call, it was alleged, included a former head of state or two. This was not a mumbo-jumbo, cockatoo-feather, dried-leather-thong, cowrie-and-tortoiseshell operation but a sophisticated, bureaucratized enterprise, every bit as methodical as the *Otunba*'s Lindtz chocolate outlet service. It kept records, meticulous ledgers of payments and dues, names and addresses with signatures—and thumbprints. Its carapace of secrecy was cracked, however, when the governorship of Anambra came under contention—not before or during elections but after, with a declared winner. The successful aspirant found himself kidnapped, detained, then locked in a toilet until he fulfilled conditions imposed by Okija for taking up his governance reins.

The luckless technocrat was saved by a sympathetic police sergeant turned gaoler, who found his oath of office bombarded by the intolerable clamour of conscience. He aided the governor's escape. In the interest of his own safety, the endangered incumbent let out a squawk that was heard in the Urals, fled to the protection of a counterforce of the spiritual realm—his church—unburdened himself, and underwent purification rites. The chief of police, for whom it appeared merely a routine summons to duty—there was a clear break in the communication chain—raided the domain, scattered its sacred contents wider than King Pentheus the crow feathers and other sacred appurtenances of the shrines of Tiresias in the Bacchantes.

To his chagrin, Mr. C of P found himself called to order by authorities beyond his understanding. Too late, the marauding innocent had already revealed publicly that he had taken possession of the Okija register of membership and that the nation would be shaken by its list of subscibers. Thereafter the nation was abandoned within a cocoon of silence. The police chief, no raving innocent himself, later found himself dangling on the rope of indictment—billions had entered his personal accounts, of which there were many. The accounts, never touched by himself, were administered by ghostly signatories, serving as conduits to other mysterious accounts, which petered out like rivulets into parched outlets of insatiable irrigation fields. He was indicted, convicted, and sentenced to a derisive spell of imprisonment. For good measure, a fine was also imposed, which could barely cover the cost of a calabash of stale palm wine.

That history, long forgotten, speeded Duyole's mastery of the encryption. As he decoded name after name, place after place, sum after sum, item on item, all was laid plain; the pioneer manifest of Human Resources had merely entered the ultramodern spreadsheet age. He could read the rest blindfolded and sleepwalking.

In the Pitan-Payne home, where Damien doubled as watch over enemy action from whatever direction, it was not difficult to discover the hour when the engineer cracked the code, almost to the minute.

Barely twelve hours later, as he bent over the display of transcriptions from his triumphant labour, the ceiling appeared to lift, then descend in near-simultaneous motions. The noise deadened his eardrums and snuffed out his consciousness. The sound woke everyone except Damien. He had remained wide awake since he had telephoned the apostle of Ekumenika, Teribogo.

"HE CALLED ME late evening, the day before the explosion," Teribogo admitted. " 'Medina has fallen' was all he said."

"You? Why you?"

"Who else, Goddie? I was his minder. He was directly responsible to me. And he was most effective in that safest, most respectable of safe houses. It was as if he had found his true calling. Young Damien truly thrived on it. No one would ever suspect the prestigious Millennium Towers as the centre of the . . . Human Resources."

"I take it, then, Damien knew all about the code."

"Knew? He set it up for the company. It was his primary assignment. But vanity! Vanity upon vanity, all is vanity. The downfall of man since the creation. That was definitely one trait he did not inherit from his father. The fool used his own name as the foundation of the encryption—a three-ply construct. Once you broke through to one . . . I'll say this much for his father—he would never have done that. He would look for something far from his own person. So what was I supposed to do? The entire operation was compromised. We had to take care of that studio, if only to buy time."

"Just as in Hilltop Manor?"

Teribogo indulged in a demure smile. "We never claimed to be original, Sir Goddie. How many government buildings have gone up in flames in the midst of an audit? We merely followed tradition."

"Try not to divert attention from the present, Your Eminence."

"Not trying to. Not in the least. It is simply charitable to give credit where credit is due." He stood up, looked round. "Since it looks as if we're going to miss lunch, at least . . ."

Goddie gestured over his shoulder to the rear. "Help yourself."

"Thank you." The drinks cabinet, an ornate shimmering import, was covered by a light drape. Teribogo pulled the drape aside, pressed a button, and its doors swung smoothly open, an imprisoned children's chorus within it bursting into a "Jingle Bells" rendition. He lifted a heavy decanter, eased out a glass and poured himself a heavy shot, tossed half of it down his throat, and moved back towards the desk.

"Yes, quite right. Just as in Hilltop Mansion. With such a sensitive evacuation, there had to be a distraction. Think we would risk another Okija? Kighare Menka was a mistake. What should a surgeon care about body parts, as long as they weren't created on purpose? And there was his history—that amputation work on the *kilishi* seller. One would expect that to squash any moralistic qualms. But look at the way he reacted! He could have said a simple no. But not that village crusader. Set himself on a warpath against us. I'm sorry to say this, but sometimes even the most accomplished of humanity, cannot be trusted to behave rationally!"

Sir Goddie threw back his head and indulged himself in a prolonged roar. "I like that, Teri. Actually, you become almost human when you say things like that. There is such honesty in your disappointment—I find it refreshing. It makes me feel almost a hypocrite myself."

"Laugh all you want, Goddie, but that was a most complex operation. Evacuating, relocating all in one night—"

"Not forgetting burning down an ancient landmark—"

"It was an anachronism. Disposable trash. Who misses it except a few black *touranchi*? And it was convenient. Everyone blames infiltrators from Boko Haram."

There followed a long spell of silence. Both men appeared lost in their own thoughts. These consisted mostly of weighing up each other, yet without actual confrontation merely staring into space, into vistas of power, rewards, domination, and intrigue. Finally it was Teribogo who broke the silence.

"We must relocate from Millennium Towers."

"Do you have to?" asked Goddie. "It's still safe enough. Your Median is still there—very effective. He's in a position of influence. Why another flight? Stay put."

Back at the desk, Teribogo put down his glass, placed both hands on the surface, and stood over the People's Steward. "My good friend Goddie, have you met the family? The brother? You've now met the sister, but do you know her at all? Even our lodge-mate the *Otunba*? He sleeps with a copy of the will. He can quote its provisions verbatim!"

"Wills are tricky things. Have you thought of transferring everything to your own parish—Oke Konran? Religion is perfect camouflage for no matter what."

Teribogo held up his hand. "Please, Goddie, we've been through all that. Render unto Caesar what is Caesar's."

"Isn't it rather late for scruples?"

"Who says anything about scruples? We are talking security. You cannot deal in flesh and cater to the soul—not within the same space. The two do not mix. Call me superstitious if you like, but look at Zamfara. Gold and zealotry—it's a toxic mix. The jealous God won't stand for it. Check with our partners in Yantulah. They collect their dividends on the dot but—no, they refuse us storage space in their minarets."

"So what of Zoroaster?"

"A beautiful cover. Who's ever heard of the seer? He's to serve as the festival motif, then remain to serve as cover. How many converts do you imagine he'll rake up? Count them on one hand. But his temple—what a facility!"

"I suppose Lokoja . . ."

"Impractical. Unsafe. Like Oke Konran, it's too open. Up on the hill, it's impossible. Going up and down that rancid sector—are we going to use donkeys? By contrast, Gumchi is perfect. Every bit as secure as Millennium Towers and just as immune to suspicion. No one would ever imagine Gumchi as a depot. Contained, virtually an independent enclave. It can be policed by no more than a small detachment of the special forces. Listen, Goddie, Gumchi has been on my radar for years, and not necessarily for the ministry. Oh yes, I did think of its possibilities as a film location—villains tumbling off the heights as they screamed their way into hell. You should visit the place. I liked what I saw. One visit only and I cast down my bucket there—mentally."

Goddie was unsmiling. "Then you had better pick it up at once.

The will of the murdered man has disposed of it, thanks to none other than you, Your Zoroastrian Eminence. And your tenacious surgeon doesn't strike me as the kind who gives up his vision."

Teribogo was losing patience. "Come on, Goddie. We've handled far knottier issues than this before now. And we've made it all easy for you. He's going to be kept so busy he won't remember his pet project."

"How do you do that?"

"All sorts of ways. For a start, he's an obvious murder suspect. First-line suspect. I don't buy the *Otunba* motive—envy. Cheap. Or the sister's dark murmurings about an affair with his wife."

"What?"

"You haven't heard? You should keep your ears more to the ground. Like we do."

"Wish I'd known that. I would never have let her be close by."

"That's where we are different. She's the perfect type to represent the family at YoY. But the motive is unimportant. He had the means. Had the opportunity. It's so straightforward. Who brought in the *kilishi*?"

Sir Goddie looked lost. "*Kilishi*? What has *kilishi* got to do with this?"

It was Teribogo's turn to fake disbelief. He resumed his seat. "Haven't you seen the police report? One would imagine the head would first report to you. You don't know how the bomb was disguised?"

"No. I try to do a hands-off whenever I can. And this is high-profile, with the international community hovering around like hawks. I leave the police to do their work, then report to me. Investigation is still ongoing."

"Of course it is ongoing. But the report is ready. That's the procedure—surely you know that, Goddie. You want to call your police chief?"

Goddie sighed. "No, no, just tell me what you know. Whatever is in the report."

"It's straightforward. Kighare Menka visited in the company of two men—one a foreigner, the other a pensioner called Alhaji Baftau, known as the Old Man of the Desert. And they brought with them a package of *kilishi,* a gift for their friend, the honoured surgeon. At least, that was what it was claimed to be. The surgeon transferred it to Duyole and it was kept in the studio. At the appointed time, it was detonated—by remote control, obviously. There were two packages, in fact. The bomb squad found the earlier *kilishi* in the studio, intact. Quite harmless. But the one that was brought by Dr. Menka—that was the lethal package."

Goddie looked at his informant, marveling. He muttered, "I am supposed to be the prime minister."

"And so you are, Mr. Prime Minister, but you cannot oversee everything. We exist to make your task easier. If you stick to governing, we will take care of the rest—including your reelection. My friend, as you remarked, you are only here for . . . maximum eight years? We are here forever. That is the reality. We have more at stake than you do. When we protect you, we secure ourselves."

Sir Goddie nodded gravely. He continued to study the priest of Zoroaster—at least for the YoY Festival.

Teribogo leant forward. "Of course, there is also the alternative theory. Would you like to hear it?"

"I am curious."

"Take your mind back. Remember, I was here, around, waiting, when our late engineer paid you a courtesy call."

"Yes?"

"You saw him off. That fellow, one of your aides—the Brain of Potencia, we call him—he was supposed to see him off with a welfare package."

"Hm-hmm? I remember. The fool wasn't ready with it when it was time for Pitan to leave."

"That's right. And you ordered him to take the man's Badagry address and have the parcel delivered to him. Right?"

Goddie sat upright, looked at the speaker in disbelief, his mind instantly churning. He remained speechless.

Teribogo's lips pursed with satisfaction. "I am glad you see the possibility. Nothing has to be proved. Simply, it's election time. The YoY Festival is just round the corner. The electorate can be swayed by any trite speculation."

For a while not one eyelid of the People's Steward so much as twitched. Then, quite abruptly, his demeanour changed. He brought out the key to his desk drawer, opened it, and extracted a kola nut. He weighed it in his hand, tossed it just a few inches high, and caught it. He rolled it round in his hand, placed it on the desk. Then he stood, picked up his discarded *agbada* from its stand, thrust his head through the opening, and settled it over his shoulders, arranging the sleeves with studied care.

"Shall we join the others? We don't want them thinking we're cooking up a separate agenda. I've kept you away too long."

Teribogo did not move. "And the procession? Is that still on?"

Goddie smiled broadly. "I shall participate myself. All the party leaders will be there. Plus the cabinet. We shall all join in lighting the Zoroastrian Olympic torch. There are surprises you know nothing of. Our friend Benzy has really gone to town on this edition—it is going to be one for the record book. He'll brief you himself. Let me give you a preview—he's importing abseilers from Switzerland. One will light the torch from your Temple of Fire and a relay will pass it down the rockface. Then begins the ground-level relay all the way to the National Stadium in Abuja to light the eternal YoY flame. You shall have your day at YoY, but you know something?"

"What is that?"

"Try Lokoja. Or wherever. But not another word about relocating to Gumchi."

"You are going to stick to the terms of that will?"

"Let us just say, Teri, that the interest of the party of POMP coincides with respecting the provisions of that Pitan-Payne will." And Goddie picked up the kola nut lying on the desk. "May I remind you, Gumchi is home to the small plantation from which this kola nut is harvested."

Teribogo threw up his hands in disgust. "For heaven's sake, what is so special about this damned kola nut? I've tasted it. Are you going to sacrifice all this investment for a mere kola nut taste? Human Resources needs to relocate!"

"Yes, Teribogo. You see, you may boast of having even my chief of police under your spell, or in your pocket, or both, but even you do not know everything about this stimulant."

"What is there to know about kola?"

"Everything." He dug his nail into the fissure of the nut, separated the lobes, and pressed a piece into Teribogo's hand. "Try this piece. It comes straight from that special preserve. Here, we call it the prime ministerial pod."

A baffled Teribogo glanced up, rose slowly, his eyes boring into Sir Goddie's face. "You are keeping something back from me, aren't you?"

The prime minister shrugged. "We made no pact of mutual disclosure. And you? Are you sure you are keeping nothing from me?"

Teribogo glared. "All right. Let's go." He followed Goddie towards the door.

Goddie stopped, looked him up and down, then pointed towards his desk. "Don't forget your costume."

Teribogo struggled to regain composure. He turned back, fully possessed, re-set his turban, wound and tucked in the loop under his chin to link up aross his ear. Goddie remained by the door, his hand on the knob.

As he patted himself down, Teribogo, in his most matter-of-fact counseling register: "Oh, I hope you have no objection if the police deport young Damien."

"On what grounds? No objection, I am simply curious."

"The police will decide that. I told you there are several scripts, so—the Damien script. He could have installed and/or set off the bomb. Time, place, motives—everything fits in. Qualifies him to be a prime suspect. When he is confronted with that, he'll go quietly."

"And quite right. The young man is now a liability to everyone, himself included."

"Absolutely. His continuing presence here is a time-bomb—well, a fitting expression. The earlier the better. Maybe even tonight. He should be allowed no time to prepare—take nothing with him beyond his passport—and even that will be handed to him when he's safely on board the plane." Teribogo threw the last length of loose shawl over his shoulder, gestured his readiness. Sir Goddie opened the door, waved him forward, his voice lowered but with absolute clarity:

"After you, *Fa-ro-dion*."

The priest of Zoroaster stopped dead in his tracks, completely stymied. He stood ramrod for nearly a minute. Finally, his shoulders slackened and he grinned, a little sheepishly. "Well, you were bound to work it all out soon enough. That's more than the rest—the Gong o' Four—have done, even till now."

"Don't be too sure about that. You've left trails. In any case, Menka will, by tonight. Inside report is that he's been working things out, like the true surgeon he is, he probes. Compulsively. In any case, he's on his way. He was invited, and we got word from him this morning—he'll arrive in time for the afternoon session. Apart from some other . . . side benefits, do you realize into how many votes his project translates—potentially? This is Villa Potencia—we try to earn the label."

"So did we, so did we—as Brand of the Land—each in his own chosen field." Teribogo's expression, earlier impassive, slid into his favourite apostolic—the bland—smile for all seasons. "We made a wager—at least I read it as one—which of us four would get to be the pre-eminent brand of the nation. Did your . . . research go that far back?"

"Far enough," said Sir Goddie. "One must protect oneself."

"Of course. In your shoes, I would dig all the way back, even into the womb."

Sir Goddie rocked himself back on his heels, looked intently at Farodion. "I must admit, you are definitely outside my league. I mean, to actually recruit the son and heir of the Gong Leader into this business. And appropriate his headquarters!"

"Why not? It's business."

"That's the spirit." Goddie opened the door wider, beaming grandly: "As your friends declaim it on Broadway—*Show Time, Baby!*"

Acknowledgements

For the creative seclusion sorely needed for the emergence of these Chronicles, I owe a debt of gratitude to my young colleague Manthia Diawara of New York University, whose cottage in Yene, Senegal, permitted nothing more intrusive than the roar of ocean waves.

Past president John Agyekum Kufuor of Ghana, aided and abetted by his son Chief Addo Kufuor, raised isolation to baronial heights in the hills of Aburi, sustained by lavish hospitality.

To one and all, plus the volunteer "space explorers" Alessandra di Maio, David Awam Amkpa, and Ivor Agyeman-Duah—Thanks!

WS

A NOTE ON THE TYPE

The text of this book was set in Sabon, a typeface designed by Jan Tschichold (1902–1974), the well-known German typographer. Based loosely on the original designs by Claude Garamond (ca. 1480–1561), Sabon is unique in that it was explicitly designed for hot-metal composition on both the Monotype and Linotype machines as well as for filmsetting. Designed in 1966 in Frankfurt, Sabon was named for the famous Lyons punch cutter Jacques Sabon, who is thought to have brought some of Garamond's matrices to Frankfurt.